Alif the Unseen

'A Harry Potter-ish action-adventure romance that unfolds against the backdrop of the Arab Spring . . . Improbably charming . . . A bookload of wizardry and glee'

New York Times

'G. Willow Wilson has a deft hand with myth and with magic, and the kind of smart, honest writing mind that knits together and bridges cultures and people. You should read what she writes.'

Neil Gaiman, author of *Stardust* and *American Gods*

'An ambitious, well-told and wonderful story. *Alif the Unseen* is one of those novels that has you rushing to find what else the author has written, and eagerly anticipating what she'll do next.'

Matt Ruff, author of *Fool on the Hill* and *The Mirage*

'G. Willow Wilson is an awesome talent. She made her own genre and rules over it. Magical, cinematic, pure storytelling. It's nothing like anything. A brilliant fiction debut.'

Michael Muhammad Knight, author of *The Taqwacores*

'Driven by a hot ionic charge between higher math and Arabian myth, G. Willow Wilson conjures up a tale of literary enchantment, political change, and religious mystery.'

Gregory Maguire, author of *Wicked* and *Out of Oz*

Alif the Unseen

G. WILLOW WILSON

CORVUS BOOKS
LONDON

First published in the United States of America in 2012 by Grove Press, an imprint of Grove/Atlantic Ltd.

First published in hardback and trade paperback in Great Britain in 2012 by Corvus Books, an imprint of Atlantic Books Ltd.

10 9 8 7 6 5 4 3 2 1

A CIP catalogue record for this book is available from the British Library.

Hardback ISBN: 978 0 85789 566 0
Trade Paperback ISBN: 978 0 85789 567 7
E-book ISBN: 978 0 85789 568 4

Printed in Italy by Grafica Veneta S.p.A.

Corvus Books
An Imprint of Atlantic Books Ltd
Ormond House
26–27 Boswell Street
London
WC1N 3JZ

www.atlantic-books.co.uk

For my daughter Maryam, born in the Arab Spring

Alif the Unseen

The devotee recognizes in every divine Name the totality of Names.

—*Muhammad ibn Arabi,* Fusus al-Hikam

If the imagination of the dervish produced the incidents of these stories, his judgment brought them to the resemblance of truth, and his images are taken from things that are real.

—*François Pétis de la Croix,* Les Mille et Un Jours (The Thousand and One Days)

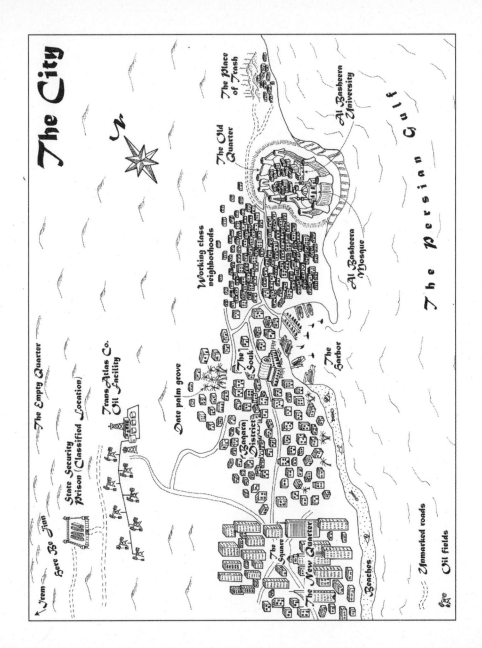

The City

The Persian Gulf

The Place of Trash

Al Basheern University

The Old Quarter

Al Basheern Mosque

Working class neighborhoods

The Harbor

The Souk

Date palm grove

Bandara District

The Square

The New Quarter

Beaches

Trans Atlas Co. Oil Facility

State Security Prison (Classified Location)

The Empty Quarter

Sare Be Sini

Irem

Unmarked roads

Oil fields

Chapter One

The Persian Gulf
Now

Alif sat on the cement ledge of his bedroom window, basking in the sun of a hot September. The light was refracted by his lashes. When he looked through them, the world became a pixilated frieze of blue and white. Staring too long in this unfocused way caused a sharp pain in his forehead, and he would look down again, watching shadows bloom behind his eyelids. Near his foot lay a thin chrome-screened smartphone—pirated, though whether it came west from China or east from America he did not know. He didn't mess with phones. Another hack had set this one up for him, bypassing the encryption installed by whatever telecom giant monopolized its patent. It displayed the fourteen text messages he had sent to Intisar over the past two weeks, at a self-disciplined rate of one per day. All went unanswered.

He gazed at the smartphone through half-closed eyes. If he fell asleep, she would call. He would wake up with a jerk as the phone rang, sending it inadvertently over the ledge into the little courtyard below, forcing him to rush downstairs and search for it among the jasmine bushes. These small misfortunes might prevent a larger one: the possibility that she might not call at all.

"The law of entropy," he said to the phone. It glinted in the sun. Below him, the black-and-orange cat that had been hunting beetles in their courtyard for as long as he could remember came nipping across the baked ground, lifting her pink-soled paws high to cool them. When he called to her she gave an irritated warble and slunk beneath a jasmine bush.

"Too hot for cat or man," said Alif. He yawned and tasted metal. The air was thick and oily, like the exhalation of some great machine. It invaded rather than relieved the lungs and, in combination with the heat, produced an instinctive panic. Intisar once told him that the City hates her inhabitants and tries to suffocate them. She—for Intisar insisted the City was female—remembers a time when purer thoughts bred purer air: the reign of Sheikh Abdel Sabbour, who tried so valiantly to stave off the encroaching Europeans; the dawn of Jamat Al Basheera, the great university; and earlier, the summer courts of Pari-Nef, Onieri, Bes. She has had kinder names than the one she bears now. Islamized by a djinn-saint, or so the story goes, she sits at a crossroads between the earthly world and the Empty Quarter, the domain of ghouls and *effrit* who can take the shapes of beasts. If not for the blessings of the djinn-saint entombed beneath the mosque at Al Basheera, who heard the message of the Prophet and wept, the City might be as overrun with hidden folk as it is with tourists and oil men.

I almost think you believe that, Alif had said to Intisar.

Of course I believe it, said Intisar. The tomb is real enough. You can visit it on Fridays. The djinn-saint's turban is sitting right on top.

Sunlight began to fail in the west, across the ribbon of desert beyond the New Quarter. Alif pocketed his phone and slid off the window ledge, back into his room. Once it was dark, perhaps, he would try again to reach her. Intisar had always preferred to meet at night. Society didn't mind if you broke the rules; it only required you to acknowledge them. Meeting after dark showed a presence of mind. It suggested that you knew what you were doing went against the prevailing custom and had taken pains to avoid being caught. Intisar, noble and troubling, with her black hair and her dove-low voice, was worthy of this much discretion.

Alif understood her desire for secrecy. He had spent so much time cloaked behind his screen name, a mere letter of the alphabet, that he no longer thought of himself as anything but an alif—a straight line, a wall. His given name fell flat in his ears now. The act of concealment had become more powerful than what it concealed. Knowing this, he had entertained Intisar's need to keep their relationship a secret long after he himself had tired of the effort. If clandestine meetings fanned her love, so be it. He could wait another hour or two.

The tart smell of *rasam* and rice drifted up through the open window. He would go down to the kitchen and eat—he had eaten nothing since breakfast. A knock on the other side of the wall, just behind his Robert Smith poster, stopped him on his way out the door. He bit his lip in frustration. Perhaps he could slip by undetected. But the knock was followed by a precise little series of taps: سطح

She had heard him get down from the window. Sighing, Alif rapped twice on Robert Smith's grainy black-and-white knee.

Dina was already on the roof when he got there. She faced the sea, or what would be the sea if it were visible through the tangle of apartment buildings to the east.

"What do you want?" Alif asked.

She turned and tilted her head, brows contracting in the slim vent of her face-veil.

"To return your book," she said. "What's wrong with you?"

"Nothing." He made an irritated gesture. "Give me the book then."

Dina reached into her robe and drew out a battered copy of *The Golden Compass*. "Aren't you going to ask me what I thought?" she demanded.

"I don't care. The English was probably too difficult for you."

"It was no such thing. I understood every word. This book"— she waved it in the air—"is full of pagan images. It's dangerous."

"Don't be ignorant. They're metaphors. I told you you wouldn't understand."

"Metaphors are dangerous. Calling something by a false name changes it, and metaphor is just a fancy way of calling something by a false name."

Alif snatched the book from her hand. There was a hiss of fabric as Dina tucked her chin, eyes disappearing beneath her lashes. Though he had not seen her face in nearly ten years, Alif knew she was pouting.

"I'm sorry," he said, pressing the book to his chest. "I'm not feeling well today."

Dina was silent. Alif looked impatiently over her shoulder: he could see a section of the Old Quarter glimmering on a rise beyond the shoddy collection of residential neighborhoods around them. Intisar was somewhere within it, like a pearl embedded in one of the ancient mollusks the *ghataseen* sought along the beaches that kissed its walls. Perhaps she was working on her senior thesis, poring over books of early Islamic literature; perhaps she was taking a swim in the sandstone pool in the courtyard of her father's villa. Perhaps she was thinking of him.

"I wasn't going to say anything," said Dina.

Alif blinked. "Say anything about what?" he asked.

"Our maid overheard the neighbors talking in the souk yesterday. They said your mother is still secretly a Hindu. They claim they saw her buying *puja* candles from that shop in Nasser Street."

Alif stared at her, muscles working in his jaw. Abruptly he turned and walked across the dusty rooftop, past their satellite dishes and potted plants, and did not stop when Dina called him by his given name.

*　　*　　*

In the kitchen, his mother stood side by side with their maid, chopping green onions. Sweat stood out where the *salwar kameez* she wore exposed the first few vertebrae of her back.

"Mama." Alif touched her shoulder.

"What is it, *makan*?" Her knife did not pause as she spoke.

"Do you need anything?"

"What a question. Have you eaten?"

Alif sat at their small kitchen table and watched as the maid wordlessly set a plate of food in front of him.

"Was that Dina you were talking to on the roof?" his mother asked, scraping the mound of onions into a bowl.

"So?"

"You shouldn't. Her parents will be wanting to marry her off soon. Good families won't like to hear she's been hanging around with a strange boy."

Alif made a face. "Who's strange? We've been living in the same stupid duplex since we were kids. She used to play in my room."

"When you were five years old! She's a woman now."

"She probably still has the same big nose."

"Don't be cruel, *makan-jan*. It's unattractive."

Alif pushed the food around on his place. "I could look like Amr Diab and it wouldn't matter," he muttered.

His mother turned to look at him, a frown distorting her round face. "Really, such a childish attitude. If you would only settle down into a real career and save some money, there are thousands of lovely Indian girls who would be honored to—"

"But not Arab girls."

The maid sucked her teeth derisively.

"What's so special about Arab girls?" his mother asked. "They give themselves airs and walk around with their eyes painted up like cabaret dancers, but they're nothing without their money. Not beautiful, not clever, and not one of them can cook—"

"I don't want a cook!" Alif pushed his chair back. "I'm going upstairs."

"Good! Take your plate with you."

Alif jerked his plate off the table, sending the fork skittering to the floor. He stepped over the maid as she bent to pick it up.

Back in his room, he examined himself in the mirror. Indian and Arab blood had merged pleasantly on his face, at least. His skin was an even bronze color. His eyes took after the Bedouin side of his family, his mouth the Dravidian; all in all he was at peace with his chin. Yes, pleasant enough, but he would never pass for a full-blooded Arab. Nothing less than full-blood, inherited from a millennium of sheikhs and emirs, was enough for Intisar.

"A real career," Alif said to his reflection, echoing his mother. In the mirror he saw his computer monitor flicker to life. He frowned, watching as a readout began to scroll up the screen, tracking the IP address and usage statistics of whoever was attempting to break through his encryption software. "Who's come poking around my house? Naughty naughty." He sat at his desk and studied the flat screen—almost new, flawless aside from a tiny crack he had repaired himself; bought for cheap from Abdullah at Radio Sheikh. The intruder's IP address came from a server in Winnipeg and this was his first attempt to break into Alif's operating system. Curiosity, then. In all likelihood the prowler was a gray hat like himself. After testing Alif's defenses for two minutes he gave up, but not before executing Pony Express, a trojan Alif had hidden in what looked like an encryption glitch. If he was half good, the intruder likely ran specialized anti-malware programs several times a day, but with any luck Alif would have a few hours to track his Internet browsing habits.

Alif turned on a small electric fan near his foot and aimed it at the computer tower. The CPU had been running hot; last week he'd come close to melting the motherboard. He could not afford to be lax. Even a day offline might endanger his more notorious clients.

The Saudis had been after Jahil69 for years, furious that his amateur erotica site was impossible to block and had more daily visitors than any other Web service in the Kingdom. In Turkey, TrueMartyr and Umar_Online fomented Islamic revolution from a location the authorities in Ankara found difficult to pinpoint. Alif was not an ideologue; as far as he was concerned, anyone who could pay for his protection was entitled to it.

It was the censors who made him grind his teeth as he slept, the censors who smothered all enterprise, whether saintly or cynical. Half the world lived under their digital cloud of ones and zeroes, denied free access to the economy of information. Alif and his friends read the complaints of their coddled American and British counterparts— activists, all talk, irritated by some new piece of digital monitoring legislation or another—and laughed. Ignorant monoglots, Abdullah called them when he was in the mood to speak English. They had no idea what it was like to operate in the City, or any city that did not come prewrapped in sanitary postal codes and tidy laws. They had no idea what it was like to live in a place that boasted one of the most sophisticated digital policing systems in the world, but no proper mail service. Emirates with princes in silver-plated cars and districts with no running water. An Internet where every blog, every chat room, every forum is monitored for illegal expressions of distress and discontent.

Their day will come, Abdullah had told him once. They had been smoking a well-packed hookah on the back stoop of Radio Sheikh, watching a couple of feral cats breed on a garbage heap. They will wake up one morning and realize their civilization has been pulled out from under them, inch by inch, dollar by dollar, just as ours was.

They will know what it is to have been asleep for the most important century of their history.

That doesn't help us, Alif had said.

No, said Abdullah, but it certainly makes me feel better.

Meanwhile they had their local nightmares to occupy them. In university, frustrated by the gaps in a computer science curriculum taught by the very State servants who policed the digital landscape, Alif had weaned himself on spite. He would teach himself what they wouldn't. He would help inundate their servers with sex videos or bring the soldiers of God down on their heads—it did not matter which came first. Better chaos than slow suffocation.

Only five years ago—less—the censors had been sluggish, relying on social media sites and old-fashioned detective work to track their marks. Gradually they had been endowed with some unholy knowledge. Chatter began on countless mainframes: who had tutored them? The CIA? Mossad was more likely; the CIA was not bright enough to choose such a subtle means of demoralizing the digital peasantry. They were united by no creed, these censors; they were Ba'ath in Syria, secular in Tunisia, Salafi in Saudi Arabia. Yet their methods were as identical as their goals were disparate. Discover, dismantle, subdue.

In the City, the increase in Internet policing appeared as a bizarre singularity. It moved over the weblogs and forums of the disaffected like a fog, appearing sometimes as code glitch or a server malfunction, sometimes as a sudden drop in connection speeds. It took months for Alif and the other City gray hats to connect these ordinary-seeming events. Meanwhile, the Web hosting accounts of some of the City's finest malcontents were discovered and hacked—presumably by the government—leaving them unable to access their own Web sites. Before he left the digital ecosystem for good, NewQuarter01, the City's first blogger, named the singularity the Hand of God. Debate still raged about its identity: was it a program, a person, many people? Some postulated that the Hand was the emir himself—hadn't it always been said that His Highness was schooled in national security by the Chinese, authors of the Golden Shield? Whatever its origin, Alif foresaw disaster in this new wave of regional monitoring. Hacked accounts were only the first step. Inevitably, the censors would move on to hack lives.

Like all things, like civilization itself, the arrests began in Egypt. In the weeks leading up to the Revolution, the digital stratosphere became a war zone. The bloggers who used free software platforms were most vulnerable; Alif was neither surprised nor impressed when they were found and imprisoned. Then the more enterprising geeks, the ones who coded their own sites, began to disappear. When the violence spilled off the Internet and into the streets, making the broad avenues of Tahrir Square a killing field, Alif dumped his Egyptian clientele without ceremony. It was clear the regime in Cairo had outstripped his ability to digitally conceal its dissidents. Cut off the arm to save the body, he told himself. If the name Alif was leaked to an ambitious State security official, a coterie of bloggers, pornographers, Islamists, and activists from Palestine to Pakistan would be put at risk. It was not his own skin he was worried about, of course, though he didn't take a solid shit for a week afterward. Of course it was not his own skin.

Then on Al Jazeera he watched as friends known to him only by alias were taken to jail, victims of the regime's last death throes.

They had faces, always different than the ones he imagined, older or younger or startlingly pale, bearded, laugh-lined. One was even a girl. She would probably be raped in her prison cell. She was probably a virgin, and she would probably be raped.

Cut off the arm.

Alif's fingers glided over the keyboard. "Metaphors," he said. He typed it in English. Dina was right as usual.

It was for this reason that Alif had taken no pleasure in the success of the Egyptian revolution, or in the wave of uprisings that followed. The triumphs of his faceless colleagues, who had crashed system after system in government after government, served only to remind him of his own cowardice. The City, once one tyrannical emirate among many, began to feel as though it were outside time: a memory of an old order, or a dream from which its inhabitants had failed to wake. Alif and his friends fought on, chipping away at the digital fortress the Hand had erected to protect the emir's rotting government. But an aura of failure clung to their efforts. History had left them behind.

A flicker of green out of the corner of his eye: Intisar was online. Alif let out a breath and felt his guts working.

A1if: Why haven't you answered my e-mails?
Bab_elDunya: Please leave me alone

His palms began to sweat.

A1if: Have I offended you?
Bab_elDunya: No
A1if: What is it then?
Bab_elDunya: Alif, Alif

A1if: I'm going crazy, tell me what's wrong
A1if: Let me see you
A1if: Please

For a leaden minute she wrote nothing. Alif leaned his forehead against the edge of his desk, waiting for the ping that would tell him she had responded.

Bab_elDunya: At the place in twenty minutes

Alif stumbled out the door.

*   *   *

He took a taxi to the farthest edge of the Old Quarter wall and then got out to walk. The wall was thronged with tourists. Sunset turned its translucent stones brilliant pink, a phenomenon they would try imperfectly to capture with their mobile phones and digital cameras. Souvenir hawkers and tea shops crowded the street that ran alongside. Alif pushed his way past a group of Japanese women in identical T-shirts. Someone nearby stank of beer. He bit back a cry of frustration as his path was blocked by a tall *desi* guide carrying a flag.

"Please to look left! Hundred year ago, this wall surrounded entire city. Tourist then came not by plane but by camel! Imagine to come across the desert, then suddenly—the sea! And on the sea, city surrounded by wall of quartz, like mirage. They thought was mirage!"

"Pardon me, brother," Alif said in Urdu, "but I am not a mirage. Let me through."

The guide stared at him. "We all come here to make a living, brother," he said, curling his lip. "Don't frighten the money."

"I didn't come here. I was born here."

"*Masha'Allah!* Pardon *me.*" He splayed his legs. The tour group gathered behind him instinctively, like chicks behind a hen. Alif stared past them down the street. He could almost see the corrugated roof of the tea shop where Intisar would be waiting.

"No one cares if a few fat Victorians came across the desert to look at a wall," he blurted. "They're dead now. We've got plenty of live Europeans out in the oil fields at the TransAtlas facility. Give them a tour of that."

The guide grimaced. "You're crazy, *bhai,*" he muttered. He stood aside, holding his brood back with one arm. Alif had invoked a class bond more subtle than commerce. Pressing a hand to his heart in thanks, Alif hurried past.

The tea shop was neither attractive nor memorable. It was decorated with a smudged acrylic mural of the New Quarter's famous skyline, and the owner—a Malay who spoke no Arabic—served "authentic" hibiscus drinks that had gone out of fashion several decades earlier. No native of the City would step foot in such a simulacrum. It was for this reason Alif and Intisar had chosen the place. When Alif arrived, Intisar was standing in the corner with her back to the room, examining a rack of dusty postcards. Alif felt the blood rush to his head.

"*As-salaamu alaykum,*" he said. She turned, jet beads clinking softly in the hem of her veil. Large black eyes regarded him.

"I'm sorry," she whispered.

He crossed the room in three steps and took her gloved hand. The Malay busied himself at a wash basin in the far corner, head down; Alif wondered if Intisar had given him money.

"For God's sake," he said, breath unsteady. "What's happened?"

She dropped her eyes. Alif ran his thumb across her satin palm and felt her shiver. He wanted to tear the veil away and read her face, inscrutable behind its wall of black crepe. He could still remember the scent of her neck—it had not been so long ago. To be separated by so much cloth was unbearable.

"I couldn't stop it," she said. "It was all settled without me. I tried, Alif, I swear to you I tried everything—I told my father I wanted to finish university first, or travel, but he just looked at me as if I'd gone crazy. It's a friend of his. Putting him off would be an insult—"

Alif stopped breathing. Taking her wrist, he began to strip off the glove, ignoring her halfhearted struggle. He revealed her pale fingers: an engagement ring glittered between them like a stone dropped on uneven ground. He began breathing again.

"No," he said. "No. You can't. He can't. We'll leave—we'll go to Turkey. We don't need your father's consent to get married there. Intisar—"

She was shaking her head. "My father would find a way to ruin you."

To Alif's horror he felt tears spring up in his eyes. "You can't marry this *chode*," he said hoarsely. "You're my wife in the eyes of God if no one else."

Intisar laughed. "We signed a piece of paper you printed from your computer," she said. "It was silliness. No state would recognize it."

"The *shayukh* do. Religion does!"

The Malay shifted, looking over his shoulder. Without speaking, Intisar pulled Alif into the back room and shut the door.

"Do *not* shout," she hissed. "You'll cause a scandal."

"This is a scandal."

"Don't be so dramatic."

"Don't patronize me." Alif curled his lip. "How much do you pay that Malay? He's very accommodating."

"Stop it." Intisar lifted her veil. "I don't want to fight with you." A wisp of hair clung to her jaw; Alif brushed it aside before bending to kiss her. He tasted lips, teeth, tongue; she withdrew.

"It's too late for this," she murmured.

"No, it's not. I'll protect you. Come to me and I'll protect you."

One plush lip quivered. "You're such a boy," said Intisar. "This isn't a game. Someone could get hurt."

Alif slammed his fist against the wall and Intisar shrieked. For a moment they stared at each other. The Malay began pounding on the other side of the door.

"Tell me his name," Alif demanded.

"No."

"Your mother's cunt! Tell me his name."

The color seeped from Intisar's face. "Abbas," she said. "Abbas Al Shehab."

"Abbas the Meteor? What a stupid, stupid name. I'll kill him—I'll run him through with a sword made of his own bones—"

"Don't talk like something out of a comic book. You don't know what you're saying." She shoved past him and opened the door. The Malay began shouting in an incomprehensible dialect.

Ignoring him, Alif followed Intisar out through the tea shop. She was crying.

"Go home, Alif," she quavered, jerking her veil back over her face. "Make it so I never see your name again. Please, God, please—I can't stand it."

He tangled his legs between a table and chair and stumbled. Intisar disappeared into the twilight, a black omen against the fading air.

Chapter Two

Sitting in the back of his wardrobe was a box. It was hidden behind a pile of winter clothing the maid had stacked there the previous spring, layers of tissue paper separating sweaters and wool slacks. Alif maneuvered it free and set it on his bed. His throat spasmed; he waited. It spasmed again. He couldn't cry; women would descend on him and ask questions. He disciplined his body. When he was sure of himself, he lifted the lid of the box: inside was a folded cotton bed sheet. Unfolding it halfway, he saw a small stain, now more brown than red, shaped something like the Indian subcontinent.

The stain had appeared during a week when Alif's mother accompanied his father on one of his innumerable business trips. Alif had encouraged the maid to visit her relatives in a nearby emirate while his parents were away, insisting he could manage on his own. The maid was skeptical but needed only a little convincing to agree. Alif gave Intisar a key to the front gate and told her to dress in her plainest robe; if the neighbors saw her, they would assume she was

Dina. When she arrived the first evening, Alif lifted her veil without speaking, struck dumb by the face he had imagined and reimagined for months. In an instant he forgot all his mental projections of Lebanese pop stars and Egyptian movie actresses. She could have no face but this face, with its mercurial dimple, mouth slightly too large, those elegant brows. He'd suspected she was beautiful—she spoke like a beautiful woman. But nothing had prepared him for the force of that beauty.

"What are you thinking?" she'd whispered.

"I can't think," he'd answered, and laughed.

With embarrassed smiles they signed a stock marriage contract Alif found on a Web site that catered to Gulf men seeking to cleanse the sins they planned to commit elsewhere. Though the paper eased his mind somewhat, it took him three nights to work up the courage to uncover more than her face. They were both awkward. Alif was bewildered by her body, so much of which remained hidden to him even when she was unclothed; she in turn seemed equal parts intrigued and appalled by his. Guided by instinct, they had created this stain. The blood was Intisar's, but Alif could not shake the feeling that something of his lay over it, an invisible mark of the ignorance he had shed. In the aftermath, he told her he loved her over and over again until she asked him to stop, frightened of the power she now possessed.

Alif bent and rummaged through a drawer in his file cabinet. Their contract lay in an unmarked folder near the back, carefully pressed between stiff manila folds. He took out the single printed page and ran his fingers over it, tracing the ballpoint indentation of Intisar's signature. His own was a secondary-school scribble. She had laughed to see his legal name, so ordinary, lacking the edgy brevity of his screen name, the only name she had ever called him. The name she would murmur in the faint grainy light of the street lamp that illuminated his room as they lay side by side, whispering through the empty hours before dawn.

Alif put the file back and closed the drawer.

He had discovered Intisar several months earlier, in a digital forum where unwholesome young men like himself heaped bile on the emir and his government from behind clever pseudonyms. Intisar intruded on their conversation like an elegant reproach, sometimes to defend the emir, sometimes to add new levels of complexity to their critique. Her knowledge was so broad, her Arabic so correct, that her lineage was quickly apparent. Alif had always believed that aristocrats avoided the Internet, assuming—correctly—that it was full of riffraff and social disease. Intisar intrigued him. He began to e-mail her quotations on liberty by Atatürk and John Adams; she countered with Plato. Alif was enchanted. He sent her money to buy a second mobile phone so they could talk without being discovered by her family, and for weeks they spoke every night, often for hours at a time.

When they decided to meet, in the very tea shop where she had so recently shattered him, Alif nearly lost his nerve. He hadn't spent time alone with any girl besides Dina since primary school. When he saw Intisar for the first time, he envied her the enfolding anonymity of her veil; he did not know if her hands shook as his did, or if her face was flushed, or if her feet, like his, refused to obey her. She had the upper hand. She could observe him, make up her mind about whether he was handsome, assess his tendency to wear all black and decide whether this offended her or not. He, on the other hand, could do nothing but fall in love with a face he had never seen.

Alif lifted the stained sheet out of its box and breathed in. It smelled of mothballs, having long since lost any trace of Intisar's perfume, or the aching, tender fragrance of their mingled limbs. It baffled him to think that a year ago he did not know her, and in another year it might be as though they had never met. The anger he felt in the Malay's tea shop was fading rapidly into shock. How long had she planned their perfunctory meeting? On what day, as he sat oblivious in front of his computer, had her engagement been performed? Had he touched her, this interloper? That thought was too much. Alif curled around the sheet with a howl, blood churning in his temples.

A frantic knock rattled out on his bedroom door. Before he could answer, his mother came into the room, clutching the trailing end of her scarf to her chest.

"Merciful God, *makan*, was it you who made that terrible noise? What's wrong?"

Alif bundled the sheet back into the box. "I'm fine," he said unsteadily. "Just a pain in my side."

"Do you want paracetamol? Soda water?"

"No, nothing—nothing." He attempted a nonchalant expression.

"All right." His mother looked him over once, lips pursed, before turning to leave. Alif straightened and took a few deep breaths. Taking out the sheet once more, he refolded it neatly, hiding the stain in its deepest layers. Then he rummaged in his desk for a pad of paper, on which he scribbled a note:

This belongs to you. You may need it.

He did not sign his name. He tucked the sheet and the note inside the box and taped it shut, wrapping it in a Saturday edition of *Al Khalij* he found folded up on his bookshelf. Then he tapped on the wall: سطح

* * *

It was ten minutes before Dina appeared on the roof. Alif set the box down beside him and dangled his shoelaces for the black-and-orange cat, which had appeared among the potted plants by some alchemy that did not involve stairs. He jerked his foot in the air and watched her bat at his dirty laces, feeling irrationally oppressed by Dina's tardy response to his summons. When she came out through the door of the stairwell, he was ready for a fight.

"Be careful with this one," said Dina, bending down to greet the cat. "All cats are half djinn, but I think she's three-quarters."

"Where have you been?" he demanded, tucking the box under his arm.

She sniffed. "Praying *maghrib.*"

"God is great. I need a favor."

Dina walked to the edge of the roof and knelt to brush dust from the leaves of a dwarf banana plant teetering in a clay tub. The cat followed her, pressing its body against her leg with a rumbling purr.

"You were mean to me," Dina said without looking at him. "All I wanted to do was talk about your book."

Alif went to sit beside her. "I'm sorry," he said. "I'm a donkey. Forgive me. I need to do something important and I can't ask anyone else. Please, Dina—if I had a sister I'd ask her, but you're—"

"You have a sister. I danced at her wedding."

Alif laughed. "Half-sister. I've met her four times in my life. You know Baba's other family hates me. As far as Fatima is concerned I'm a dark little *abd*, not a brother."

Dina's eyes softened. "I shouldn't have brought her up. May God forgive them for the sins they have committed against you and your mother."

"Sins," Alif muttered, batting at a banana leaf. A plume of dust slid off into the air. "You called my mother a Hindu earlier."

Dina gasped, covering her face with her hands. "I forgot! I was angry—"

"Don't, don't do that. You're an immaculate saint. Don't torture yourself."

She put her palm on the ground, close to his knee. "You know my family has never questioned her conversion," she said. "We love her. She is like my aunt."

"You have an aunt. I've eaten her *qatayyef*."

Dina clucked her tongue. "You always tie my words in knots." She sat back on her heels and clasped her arms around her knees, looking less like a woman than an abstract impression of one, inky and creased. He remembered the day she had announced, at the age of twelve, that she intended to veil her face. Her mother's tears and her father's angry retorts carried easily through the common wall of the duplex. For an upper-class Old Quarter girl like Intisar to veil was one thing; her silken, beaded cocoon was a mark of rank, not religion. But Dina was imported labor—a shabby Alexandrian, expected to become the bare-faced, underpaid ornament to someone's office or nursery, perhaps even discreetly available to whomever was paying her salary. For her to declare herself sanctified, not by money but by God, looked like putting on airs. Even as a pimply fourteen-year-old, Alif had understood why her parents were so upset. A saint was not profitable.

"What's this favor?" Dina asked finally.

Alif set the box in front of her. "I need you to take this to a villa in the Old Quarter and give it to a girl who lives there." A twinge of regret rippled through him even as he said the words. When Intisar saw what he had sent her, she would think him disgusting. Perhaps that was what he wanted: the last word, a final scene more vulgar and melodramatic than the one she had orchestrated in the tea shop. He would remind her of what they had been to each other, and punish her for it.

"Old Quarter? Who do you know in the Old Quarter? It's all aristocracy."

"Her name is Intisar. Never mind how I know her. Seventeen Malik Farouk Street, across from a little *maidan* with a tile fountain in the center. It's very important that you put this in her hands—not a servant's, not a brother's. All right?"

Dina picked up the box and examined it. "I've never met this Intisar," she muttered. "She won't take a strange box from me without an explanation. There might be a bomb in here."

Alif's mouth jerked. She was not far wrong. "Intisar knows who you are," he said.

Dina scrutinized him from beneath her fringe of dark lashes. "You've gotten very odd. I'm not sure I want you talking about me to girls with fussy names from the Old Quarter."

"Don't worry about it. After this errand, we'll never mention her again."

Dina stood, shaking dust from her robe, and tucked the box under one arm. "I'll do it. But if you're asking me to commit a sin without my knowledge, it will be on your head."

Alif smiled bitterly. "My head is already heavy with sins. Such a little one as this will make no difference."

A line appeared between Dina's brows. "If that's true, I will make *du'a* for you," she said.

"Many thanks."

Alif watched her walk across the darkened roof and disappear into the stairwell. When the sound of her footsteps was no longer audible, he leaned his forehead against the rim of the banana plant pot and sobbed.

*　　*　　*

The next day, Alif did not leave the house. He took his laptop to the roof and meditated on a blinking cursor in a blank Komodo code editor, vaguely aware of the maid trudging to and from the clothesline and putting carpets out to air. The cat appeared again, strolling along the concrete balustrade that lined the roof. She paused to observe Alif with something like pity in her yellow eyes. In the late afternoon, Dina and her mother came up to shell peas. Seeing him—his bare feet propped up, his face bathed in the bluish light of the computer—they retreated to the opposite corner and whispered to each other.

Alif ignored them, intent on the coming of evening. He watched the sun flush as it sank into the desert. Entering its most sacred hour, the City began to shimmer in a haze of dust and smoke. Between the irregular rows of duplexes and apartment buildings, Alif could make out a fraction of the Old Quarter wall. Struck by a last volley of sunlight, it was lit to an astonishing hue: not pink, as it was vulgarly called, but salmon-gold, or a bridal shade of old Jaipuri silk. Provided with such spectacular footlights, the call to sunset prayer rose up from the great mosque of Al Basheera at the epicenter of the Old Quarter. It was quickly echoed by a hundred lesser muezzins, each more toneless than the last, in mosques spread across the haphazard neighborhoods outside the Wall. Alif listened only to that first perfect baritone before slipping on his headphones. The great muezzin's voice was like a reprimand: he had coveted what he should not.

When all the light was gone, Alif went inside. He washed, shaved, and accepted a plate of curried fish from the maid; after he had eaten, he went out into the street. He paused at the corner and thought of hailing a taxi, then thought better of it—the evening was pleasant; he would walk. A Punjabi neighbor salaamed him half-interestedly from across the street. Named for the cattle market to which it had once played host, Baqara District was all imported labor from India, Bangladesh, the Philippines, and the lesser Arab countries of North Africa. *El 'abeed.* It was one of a dozen neighborhoods that belonged to nothing, and reached out between the Old and New Quarters as if begging for alms.

Signs flickering to life in the dusk advertised bakers' goods and pharmacies in half a dozen languages. Alif passed them by quickly.

He turned down an alleyway that smelled of ozone; air conditioners working hard in the apartments above dripped Freon on his head. At the end of the alley, he tapped on an unassuming door on the ground floor of a residential building. He heard shuffling. An eye appeared in the peephole.

"Who's that?" came a voice in the throes of puberty.

"Is Abdullah at home?" asked Alif.

The door opened, revealing a nose and a downy mustache.

"That's Alif," said a voice from farther inside. "You can let him in."

The door opened wider. Alif stepped past the suspicious youth into a large room, packed to the ceiling with boxes of computer parts. A welder's bench at the center was strewn with their guts: motherboards, optical drives, tiny translucent microprocessors still in beta. Abdullah straddled the free end of the bench with a laser pen in one hand, working on a circuit board.

"What brings you to Radio Sheikh?" he asked without looking up. "We haven't seen you in weeks. Thought you might have gotten pinched by the Hand."

"God prevent it," Alif said automatically.

"God is greatest. How are you, then?"

"Shit."

Abdullah looked up, wide eyes in a rabbit-toothed face. "Say 'forgive me,' brother. The last time I heard a man answer that question with anything but 'praise God,' his dick was melting off. Syphilis. I hope your excuse is just as good."

Alif sat down on the floor. "I need your advice," he said.

"I doubt that. But go on."

26

"I need to prevent someone from ever finding me online."

Abdullah snorted. "Oh, come on. You're better at this than anyone. Block all his usernames, filter his IP address so he can't get on your Web sites—" Alif was already shaking his head.

"No. Not an IP address, not a username—not a digital identity. A *person*."

Abdullah set the board and laser pen down on the bench.

"I'm tempted to say it's impossible," he said slowly. "You're talking about teaching a software program to recognize a single human personality irrespective of what computer or e-mail address or login he's using."

"Yes, that's what I'm talking about." Alif's eyes flickered. "And it's a she."

"A she! A she! So that's why you're shit." Abdullah laughed. "Brother Alif with girl trouble! You miserable hermit—I know for a fact you never leave your house. How was this accomplished?"

Alif felt his face get hot. Abdullah's face blurred in front of him. "Shut up," he said, voice shaking, "or I swear to God I'll knock those buck teeth down your throat."

Abdullah looked startled. "All right, all right. It's serious. I get it," he murmured. When Alif said nothing, he shifted uncomfortably on the bench. "Rajab!" he shouted at the youth lurking in the corner. "Be a good *chaiwallah* and fetch us some tea."

"Your mother's a *chaiwallah*," muttered the youth, slinking out the door. When the latch clicked, Abdullah turned back to Alif.

"Let's think about this," he said. "In theory everyone has a unique typing pattern—number of keystrokes per minute, time lapse between each stroke, that kind of thing. A keystroke logger, properly

27

programmed, might be able to identify that pattern to within an acceptable margin of error."

Alif sulked for another minute before responding. "Maybe," he admitted at last. "But you'd need a huge amount of data input before a pattern could be detected."

"Perhaps, perhaps not. It depends on how unique one's typing pattern really is. This has never been studied."

"What if you went further," said Alif, getting up and pacing. "Cross-reference the typing pattern with grammar, syntax, spelling—"

"Ratio of language use. English to Arabic to Urdu, Hindi, Malay, whatever. It would be one hell of an undertaking, Alif. Even for you."

They settled into a meditative silence. The youth appeared again with glasses of tea steaming on a metal tray. Alif took one and rolled it between his hands, enjoying the heat against his skin.

"If it worked . . ." he said softly.

"If it worked and word got out, every intelligence agency on God's earth would come to hump your leg."

Alif shivered.

"Maybe it's not worth it, brother," said Abdullah, unfolding his large feet from beneath the bench and standing up. "It's just a *bint*, after all."

Alif looked at the eddies of dark leaf and undissolved sugar in his tea glass. His eyes clouded. "This is not just any *bint*," he said. "This is a philosopher-queen, a sultana . . ."

Abdullah shook his head, disgusted. "I never thought I would see this day. Look at you, you're practically sniveling."

"You don't understand."

"I do, in fact." Abdullah raised an eyebrow. "You have something the rest of us imported Rafiqs do not: a noble purpose. Don't waste it on the whims of your prick."

"I don't want a noble purpose. I want to be happy."

"And you think a woman will make you happy? Son, look in the mirror. A woman has made you miserable."

Alif drifted toward a pile of boxes against the wall. "How much do you want for this?" he asked, holding up an external hard drive. "I could use some more storage space."

Abdullah sighed. "Take it. God be with you."

✻ ✻ ✻

In his room at home, Alif retrieved a packet of clove cigarettes from a drawer in his desk. He opened the window before lighting one, and leaned against the ledge, sending luxuriant trails of smoke into the night air. Dew lay on the jasmine in the courtyard below; its scent met the spicy overture of clove and blew back through the window. Alif took a long breath. Since childhood, he had imagined he could see the sea through this window, shimmering with reflected light beyond the maze of buildings. Now he knew the lights danced not on water, but in smog; nevertheless, the image soothed him. He looked down as the jasmine bushes shook: the black-and-orange cat was picking her way silently across the court. He called to her. She looked up at him, blinking saucer eyes, and made a small sound. Alif held out his hand. The cat leaped onto the window ledge in one effortless movement, purring, and caressed his hand with her cheek.

"Good little *at'uta*," said Alif, using the Egyptian diminutive Dina had bestowed upon her long ago. "Pretty *at'uta*." He flicked the end of his cigarette out the window and turned away, dusting his hands on his jeans. The cat settled down on the ledge with her feet tucked under her body. She regarded him through half-closed eyes.

"You can stay there," Alif said, sitting down at his desk, "but you can't come in. The maid's a Shafa'i and cat hair makes her ritually impure."

The cat blinked agreeably. Alif ran one finger across the wireless mouse pad next to his computer and watched the screen crackle to life. There were messages in his inbox: confirmation for a wire transfer of 200 dirhams from a client; an introduction to a Syrian activist who was interested in his services. A Russian gray hat with whom Alif played virtual chess had made a move against his remaining bishop. After blocking the Russian's advance with one of his pawns, Alif opened a new project file. He deliberated for a few moments.

"Intisar," he said to the cat. "Rastini. Sar inti."

The cat opened and closed one eye.

"Tin Sari," said Alif, typing the words as he spoke. "Yes, that's it. I was thinking in the wrong language. A veil of tin for a wayward princess."

It took him most of the night to modify his existing keystroke logger program with a set of genetic algorithms that might—he hoped—be used to identify basic elements of a typing pattern. He rose only to sneak into the kitchen and brew a *kanaka* of Turkish coffee, adding cardamom pods he crushed against the granite countertop with the back of a spoon. When he returned to his room, the cat had disappeared from the window ledge.

"They all leave," he muttered. "Even the feline ones."

He pulled up Intisar's computer from a drop-down menu. The first time he worked on her machine he'd enabled remote access, allowing Hollywood, his custom-built hypervisor, to track her usage statistics. She never discovered him. Once in a while he meddled benevolently, clearing the malware her commercial antivirus software had missed, running his own defrag programs, deleting old temp files—things the ordinary civilian would either forget to do or never learn properly at all. Whenever there was an increase in Internet policing in one of his client's countries, it was common for him to go without sleep and speech for days; during such periods Intisar often accused him of neglect. It hurt him, yet he never told her about these small acts of affection. She did not know that a copy of her incomplete thesis sat behind one of his firewalls, ensuring her words would survive any event short of the apocalypse. These were the only gestures that made sense to him. So much of what he felt did not translate.

He slipped into her machine and created a node for Tin Sari v1.0, connecting it to a botnet of his clients' computers. The botnet would process the incoming data remotely, sending results to Alif via Hollywood. Alif felt a small pang of guilt for using his clients' machines without asking, and for such selfish reasons. But most of his clients wouldn't notice an extra program running discreetly in the background as they worked, and those who would had known Alif long enough not to ask questions. As soon as Tin Sari started transmitting data, he could begin to refine the algorithms, compensating for errors and adding new parameters. It would take time and patience, but if Abdullah was right, the end result would be a digital portrait of Intisar. Alif could instruct Hollywood to filter any Internet user who fit her specs, making them invisible to each other. He would grant her request: she would never see his name again.

"A *hijab*," Alif said softly. "I am hanging a curtain between us. Dina would say it is not fitting for us to look at each other." Dina would say it, but he would not—his own motives were ridiculous, and he could not speak them. By hiding from Intisar so completely, she could not return to him even if she wanted to, and he was spared the humiliation of knowing she would never try.

Alif blinked as bright spots flickered at the edge of his vision—he had been staring at the computer for too long. His head hurt. Outside, the color of the sky was shifting; soon the muezzins would sound the call to dawn prayer. He shut off his monitor and pushed back from the desk. Without undressing he lay down in bed, overtaken by a sudden rush of fatigue.

Chapter Three

Alif woke the next morning to the sound of a music video streaming from the speakers wired to his flat-screen monitor. As he opened his eyes, the newest Lebanese pop starlet, Dania or Rania or Hania, appeared onscreen bottom-first, lolling on a bed of roses, mouthing autotuned lyrics about the intense longing of the peach for the banana. Alif tugged at the waistband of his boxers. A knock on the door stopped him, and he slouched to answer it, opening up just enough to accept a breakfast tray from the maid.

He ate at his desk. Through the floor he could hear his mother moving about the kitchen downstairs, pulling pans out of cupboards, preparing for the second meal of the day before she'd had a chance to properly digest the first. Squinting, Alif attempted to calculate the number of weeks since his father's last visit. He couldn't remember. As a child he had eagerly anticipated the appearance of his father's leather slippers by the front door, laid out in preparation by his mother, signaling the advent of a long stay. They had been more frequent in those days. Now when his father was in the City he called from the opulent New Quarter flat where his first wife lived, a flat to which he had referred on several occasions as "home." Years ago, when it still mattered, Alif had interrogated him about this, asking why their little duplex in Baqara District was not "home" as well. There was a dissatisfied pause. It's *your* home, his father had answered diplomatically.

Having finished his breakfast and tea, Alif flopped down on his bed again, succumbing to lethargy. Through the wall he could hear Dina talking on the phone, her voice traveling up and down its familiar scale. He put one hand up to the flaking plaster beneath his Robert Smith poster. Dina, too, was an only child—the survivor of a string of false hopes: miscarriages Alif's mother had gossiped about to his father in a sad, insinuating voice in the days when she was still pressuring him for another child of her own. But Alif, like Dina, was to have no sibling—his father already had Fatima and Hazim and Ahmed, the light-skinned progeny of his first wife, and neither his family nor his wallet would tolerate more mottled interlopers. Alif wondered whether Dina had become a reproach to her mother the way he had to his—a single sign of fruitfulness to remind her of barren years.

Dina's voice had ceased; her door opened and closed. Alif took his hand away from the wall. Getting up, he woke his computer and settled down to work.

*   *   *

The first version of Tin Sari failed to tell him anything of substance. Intisar consistently wrote e-mails in Arabic and chatted and microblogged in English, but that could be true of almost anyone in the City. Her keystroke rate varied too much to track. She probably sat for long minutes over certain e-mails and dashed through others depending on the urgency and nature of the message. For weeks she remained elusive, proving, he thought bitterly, that Intisar was made of finer, subtler substance than his programming languages could recognize, or had ever recognized.

As the data streamed in, Alif imagined her sitting at her desk, dark hair pulled off her face in a sloppy bun, wearing only a T-shirt and a pair of jogging pants as she e-mailed her friends to make plans or worked on her thesis. She had been researching and writing it as long as he had known her, and would leave Al Basheera University with the highest honors available to an undergraduate. Thus well-educated and well-bred, she would make a perfect wife for the man whose name Alif hated with an intensity that frightened him.

Without her, he drifted. His life was again reduced to an uncomfortable circle of women inside the house and men outside it; to the chatter of his mother and the maid or the dirty jokes Abdullah and his friends told, all of which seemed insignificant compared to the memory of Intisar's voice going high and soft as he discovered some new latitude of her body. The work he did became like a reproach, a reminder that he was mottle-blooded, unwanted, unfit for any higher or more visible profession. He ran diagnostics and patched firewalls with absent efficiency, wondering if this numbing grief was permanent.

He took out their marriage contract and looked at it almost every day, feeling foolish each time he did so: how ridiculous to think that it meant anything. He had seen too many Egyptian movies and read too many books. The idea of a secret *urfi* marriage filled him with a romantic zeal that seemed naive now. He had imagined a fairy-tale chain of events: Intisar would be thrown out of her father's house with only the clothes on her back, and Alif would manfully assume responsibility, leaving her in his mother's tender care as he prepared their marital household. As the weeks passed the vision atrophied until it was painful to him to remember.

Then Tin Sari returned something he did not expect. On a dusty afternoon, just over a month after he had installed a working version of the program on Intisar's machine, a text box popped up on his desktop as he was reworking a few lines of bugged code.

"What do you want?" Alif muttered at it, clicking on a drop-down arrow. It informed him that a pattern had been identified on HP Etherion 700 Notebook and its orbital devices. Would Alif like to assign a file name to this pattern?

Alif's eyes lingered on the blinking cursor in disbelief. Intisar, he typed.

Create filter for "Intisar" in Hollywood diagnostic software? Enter.

His CPU tower emitted a prolonged series of buzzes and clicks. Alif quit all open programs to free up more processing power.

"Holy God," he breathed. "Holy God." He clicked another drop-down arrow on the text box to reveal a detailed report of Tin Sari's findings. Having watched Intisar for five weeks, it determined that she used Arabic and English at a ratio of 2.21165 to 1, avoided contractions, and, most curiously of all, had in her native language a peculiar preference for words in which the letter *alif* occurred in a medial position. Alif wondered what to make of this subconscious love poem. Mesmerized, he fed Tin Sari e-mails from his cousins in Thiruvananthapuram, text from the sports section of *Al Khalij,* anything he could think of to try and prompt a false positive. Without fail, it sorted Intisar's words from all the rest.

Alif struggled to understand what his algorithms were telling him. Perhaps somewhere deep in the mind was a sort of linguistic DNA, roped helixes of symbols that belonged to no one else. For days Alif wrote nothing—no code, no e-mail—and instead wondered how much of the soul resided in the fingertips. He was faced with the possibility that every word he typed spoke his name, no matter what other superficial information it might contain. Perhaps it was impossible to become someone else, no matter what avatar or handle one hid behind.

The program behaved in a way that made him uneasy. He had written it using a certain amount of fuzzy logic: the commands that acted as gray go-betweens in the black-and-white world of binary computing. Alif knew how to talk to black and white and make them see themselves in each other; this was what made him good at his job. But Tin Sari, full of exceptions and shortcuts though it was, should not have been able to detect a pattern so esoteric—a pattern that remained unclear to Alif no matter how much math he threw at it. For the first time in his life he was using a program without understanding how it worked.

When Tin Sari correctly identified Intisar based on a single sentence—a one-line instant message sent on a day of low computer activity—Alif called Abdullah.

"*Bhai,*" he said. "You have to come take a look at this."

"Which?" Abdullah was chewing noisily on something.

"Do you remember that botnet I told you about? The language filter?"

"The girl trouble botnet?"

Alif made a face. "Yes."

"What about it?"

"It's causing my balls to retreat into my chest cavity. I must have done something wrong. I want you to check my algorithms and tell me I'm not insane."

"Not working out?" There was a vegetable crack followed by rapid chewing.

"No, it's—what the hell are you eating?"

"Carrot sticks. I've started a regime."

"Congratulations. Come over."

Abdullah arrived half an hour later, wearing an old army jacket and carrying a messenger bag over one shoulder. This he threw on Alif's bed without ceremony. Overturning an empty wastebasket, he sat down next to Alif in front of the computer.

"Let me see this beast. What's it written in?"

Alif opened the Tin Sari v5.2 program files.

"C++. But the type system is sort of—new. I've made a lot of modifications."

"That doesn't make any sense, but whatever." Abdullah scrolled through lines of code, eyes flickering in the light of the monitor. His expression changed.

"Alif," he said slowly. "What is this?"

Alif got up and began to pace the room.

"I don't know, I don't know. The first version was a mess. So I kept tinkering with it—by the end I wasn't sure what I was writing anymore. I was just finding ways to solve problems as they came up. Parameters and exceptions became the same thing. I stopped telling it 'this but not that' and started telling it 'this, this, this.' And it listened."

"We are still talking about code, yes?"

"I don't know."

Abdullah tapped his foot in frustration.

"Well, does it *work*?"

Alif shivered.

"It doesn't just work, *bhai*. It frightens me. Today it correctly identified that girl I told you about based on one sentence, Abdullah, one sentence. It shouldn't be possible. No amount of math can identify something as complex as an individual behavior pattern based on so little input."

"It would seem you are incorrect, since you just did."

"But what does it *mean*?"

Abdullah swiveled toward him on the overturned wastepaper basket.

"Is this an elaborate way of asking for a compliment? Do you want me to tell you you're a genius? If I had known you asked me over here to rub your ego, I would have brought some lubricant."

Alif collapsed on his bed with a groan, massaging his closed eyes.

"I don't care about that," he said. "I just want to understand what's happened. I need an outside perspective."

Abdullah pursed his lips over his buck teeth.

"What you are talking about—recognizing a complete, individual personality—is something we do automatically. I recognize your voice on the phone. I could probably recognize your e-mails and texts even without seeing your address or phone number. This is a basic function for anybody who isn't suffering from some kind of mental disorder. But machines can't do it. They need an IP address or an e-mail address or a handle to identify someone. Change those identifiers and that person becomes invisible to them. If what you're saying is true, you have discovered an entirely new way of getting computers to think. One might even say that with this botnet, you have endowed your little desktop machine with intuition."

Alif glanced at Abdullah out of the corner of his eye. He sat with a pronounced slouch, his large feet bent at the toe where the rim of the wastepaper basket met the floor.

"You say that so calmly," Alif said.

Abdullah got up.

"Yes, because I'm not convinced it's actually true. It's impossible, as you yourself said. There must be some other explanation for your botnet's unusual rate of accuracy. Regardless, it's a very, very clever trick, and I salute you." He grabbed his messenger bag off the bed. "You need to get out of the house more often, Alif. You're looking very peaky."

✳   ✳   ✳

He kept his promise: he made himself invisible to her. Using the profile of Intisar that Tin Sari had created, he instructed Hollywood to mask his digital presence. If she tried to visit his Web site—if she even got that far; he hid it in the dark web where it was safe from prying search engines—her browser would tell her it did not exist. She could create a thousand new e-mail addresses and send him messages from each one: they would all bounce. A search for his names, given and professional, would yield nothing. It would be as if he had vanished from the electronic world.

He did not have the heart to turn his weapon on himself. The very thought of making her invisible to him was too much to bear. He left Hollywood connected to Intisar's machine, reasoning that the additional data from Tin Sari might provide an even more complete picture of her digital self, and that this in turn would help him understand these somnambulant patterns, this language-beyond-language he had discovered through her. It was not spying. He didn't read her e-mail, after all, or check her chat logs: he merely studied the patterns Tin Sari detected in her words. He told himself he had moved beyond mourning into pure science. Sometimes he was even convinced.

Midway through October, a sandstorm blew in from the interior. All morning Alif lay in bed listening to a cacophony of female distress on the roof: the maid, Dina, and Dina's family's maid rushed back and forth to bring in the laundry before it was stained by the rich mineral silt choking the air. He ground his teeth and heard microscopic grains of dust pop between them. No matter how well one taped the windows, it inevitably seeped inside, propelled by some unknown and perverse force of nature. Soon he would get up and go over the inner recesses of his computer tower with his mother's hair dryer on a no-heat setting, a trick he'd learned from sandstorms past. He closed his eyes against the gray half-light. It could wait a few more minutes.

A thud against his window pane made him jump. He scrambled out of bed: on the ledge outside sat the black-and-orange cat. She looked at him entreatingly, ears flattened, coated in yellowish dust.

"Oh, lord." Alif peeled his homemade perimeter of duct tape off the glass, opening the window a few inches. The cat squeezed through and flung herself into the room. She landed near the foot of his bed, sneezing.

"Look at you, you're filthy. I barely recognized you. You're going to get sand everywhere."

The cat sneezed again and shook herself.

"You'd better not make any noise or the maid will come after you with a broom. And don't pee on anything." Alif pulled off the *thobe* he'd worn to bed and selected a black T-shirt from his wardrobe. After he was dressed he opened the door to retrieve the breakfast tray of flatbread, white cheese, and tea the maid had left for him. The tea was now cold; Alif drank it in a single swallow. Squatting next to his computer tower, he pulled off the casing and examined the CPU. A thin film of dust covered the blades of the exhaust fan. He blew on it experimentally.

"Not as bad as it could be," he murmured. The cat rubbed her head against his leg. As he reinstalled the casing over the CPU, he heard an alarm chime from his speakers.

"Fuck. *Fuck.*" Alif darted to his desk chair and pounded on the space key until the computer monitor crackled to full resolution. His connection speed was dropping fast. Hollywood's encryption software was reporting a string of errors.

It was the Hand.

Alif felt sweat break out on his upper lip. He forced himself to concentrate: he had to protect the people who depended on him. One by one he severed Hollywood's connection with his clients' computers—it would leave them exposed, but a few unprotected hours were better than certain discovery. His fingers seemed stiff and abominably slow. He cursed. Another alarm went off as the first of Hollywood's firewalls was breached.

"How, how, *how?*" Alif stared at the screen in awestricken panic. "How in all the names of God are you doing this?" Only four of his clients were still connected to his OS. OpenFist99, sever connection? Yes. TheRealHamada, sever connection? Yes. The Hand moved deeper into his system.

"This is not possible," he whispered.

Jai_Pakistan, sever connection? Yes. Alif looked at his client list: the only machine still accessible was Intisar's. He was running out of time.

"Don't worry," he said, "it's not you they're after." He pulled the master plug out of the wall. With a whine, his computer went dark. Alif gazed at his vague reflection in the black screen, breathing in uneven gasps. He heard sand blowing against the window. Little satisfied sounds came from the cat, who had discovered the cheese on his breakfast tray. Time and the world slipped serenely forward as though nothing out of the ordinary had occurred. He shook his head to clear it. What had occurred? A series of timed electrical impulses, on-off on-off. That was all, and it might mean a prison cell for the rest of his life.

Alif waited half an hour before turning his system on again. He ran three sets of diagnostics on Hollywood, whispering a prayer before each one: they returned no anomalies. Reconnecting his clients, he debated whether to send an e-mail letting them know what had happened, and decided against it—what could they do but panic? He would find out how the Hand had managed to cut through his defenses, he would go through the code line by line if he had to.

"I can fix this," he murmured to the screen. A wave of nausea seized him. He leaned forward with a groan, pressing his forehead to the cool metal edge of his desk. Sand hissed around the house, aspirated like some deranged human voice, some haunted voice. Alif heard Dina turn on music in her room—a cheerful *debke* dance song—as though she, too, found the storm unsettling. He got out of his chair and curled up against the wall they shared. When his computer was on and connected to the grid, he never felt as though he was alone; there were millions of people in rooms like his, reaching toward each other in the same ways he did. Now that feeling of intimacy seemed fraudulent. He lived in an invented space, easily violated. He lived in his own mind.

The cat padded up to him and put one sympathetic paw on his knee.

*　*　*

That night he dreamed of a woman with black-and-orange hair. She slipped into bed beside him, unself-consciously naked, and comforted him in a language he had never heard. Her eyes shone in the dark. Alif responded to her without embarrassment or surprise, seeking her mouth and the hollow of her throat while she purred. She ran one hand along his thigh with a look of invitation. He was checked by a feeling of regret.

"Intisar—" he said. The woman made an irritated noise and nipped his shoulder. Urgency overwhelmed him. He covered her slender form with his, shifting his hips as she threaded her legs around him. Delight stole over his body in waves. She cried out when his enthusiasm intensified. Bending to her ear, he whispered in the language she had spoken, telling her they had to be quiet, quiet; obediently, she stifled her moans in his neck. The end came quickly. Alif collapsed against the warm body beneath him, and the woman laughed, speaking a word of triumph. She kissed him with a fond smile. Alif begged her to tell him her name, but she was already receding into darkness, leaving behind a scent like warm fur.

Alif woke to the sound of the cat batting her paw against the window. He felt sated and calm. The storm winds were no longer audible, and the City beyond had descended into a deep, restorative silence. He rose, wincing; his calf muscles were sore. When he opened the window the cat blinked at him once and leaped down into the courtyard. He leaned out and took a breath. The air was purer now, stripped of pollution and heat by the sand. Dawn tempered the eastern horizon. He turned at the harsh sound of a metal hinge followed by feminine coughing: Dina pushed her own window outward, waving one hand to clear the dust that had accumulated on it in the storm. She wore a long green scarf and held it coquettishly over her face with her free hand, like a palace maiden from an old Egyptian film. The image charmed him.

He called her name in a soft voice. She turned to look at him, surprised.

"Oh! What are you doing awake?"

"I had a—" He blushed. "I just woke up, that's all."

"Are you all right?"

"Yes, but not really." He took another long breath. "I wish it was always like this. The air and the light."

"Me, too." She followed his gaze out over the City. The skyscrapers of the New Quarter looked as though they had been built out of pearl and ash. In a few hours workmen would come to clear the dust and return them to their glassy anonymity, but for now they looked like part of the desert, a natural extension of the great interior dunes.

"Like a story," Dina said. "Like a djinn city."

Alif chuckled. "Just like a djinn city," he agreed.

They stood in silence for a moment.

"I'm going to pray *fajr* on the roof," Dina said finally. "Be well."

"God grant you paradise," said Alif. Dina's eyes crinkled in a smile. Her window swung shut. Alif lingered for a minute longer, gathering his thoughts. He would shower and have some tea—there was no point in returning to bed with the day so limpid before him. Redoubling his defenses against the Hand would require all his skill; he might as well begin now, while he felt confident and clear-headed. He would not think about the possibilities that lay before him: at any time a knock might come on the door and reveal a pair of State security policemen in khaki uniforms. Or worse—they might not knock at all. They might appear in the middle of the night and drag him, bound and hooded, to one of the unnamed political prisons that lay beyond the western edge of the City. Alif closed his eyes and banished the thought. He must not lose focus.

Once clean and caffeinated, he sat at his desk and opened one of his code editing programs. Somewhere there must be an explanation for the swiftness with which the Hand had entered his system—a weak or outmoded function in his firewalls, a flaw in his overall design. He wondered uneasily whether the attack had been a coincidence—the result of a roving audit—or targeted at himself. Was his name out in the open? There had been no warning, no chatter on the City's mainframes about any captured gray hat cracking under torture and delivering up identities or locations. His clients were all as safe as he could make them up until the very moment the Hand appeared. No, Alif could not have been the intended target.

"That almost makes it worse," he said to his machine. If the attack was a coincidence, the Hand must be a magician to break through his defenses so effortlessly and with so little information. It was obscene, unbelievable. Alif knew no one with this level of skill. His own ability was childlike by comparison. He leaned back in his chair and rubbed his eyes. "There is always a way," he said. "Know there is a way, and the way will present itself." The words seemed naive as soon as he said them.

He worked steadily until midafternoon, reviewing and adjusting code with an attention to detail that was fanatical even by his own standards. He broke when the maid called him for lunch. Trudging downstairs, he found his mother seated at the kitchen table, washing a bowl of red lentils for the evening meal. She hummed a Bollywood song as she massaged them, sending cloudy trails of sediment up through the water.

"Hi, Mama." He dropped a kiss on her head.

"There's *saag paneer* on the stove," she said. "The maid cooked it specially for you. You still like *saag paneer*?"

The question irked him. "Yes, I still like *saag paneer*." He took a plate from the cupboard and helped himself.

"Your father is in Jeddah," continued his mother. "He sent me a photo on the computer. He is getting tan, out in the sun all day supervising the new natural gas pipeline. A shame to get so dark. I told him to put sunscreen."

"Good. Great."

"You should call him."

Alif snorted. "Why shouldn't he call me?"

"You know how busy he is. Better for you to call."

Alif bent to take a bite of *saag paneer* and studied his mother over the edge of his plate. She pushed the lentils back and forth, her face expressionless aside from a little crease of concentration on her forehead. Alif wondered whether the photo—a perfunctory snapshot of an absent husband; he could see it in his mind—depressed her. There were other photos, prints she kept in a sandalwood box in her room, that she had shown him when he was small. In these she and his father were always together, walking along the Old Quarter wall or buying flowers from one of the stalls in the souk. She looked radiant: an adored, illicit second wife.

Alif wondered at what point the thrill of the marriage had dimmed for his father. He suspected it was his birth. A problematic son with dark-skinned pagan blood in his lineage, the product of a union unsanctioned by his grandparents, impossible to wedge into good society. A daughter would have been preferable. If she was pretty and well-mannered, a daughter could marry up; a son could not. A son needed his own prospects.

Alif heard his phone buzz upstairs.

"I've got to get that," he said, pushing his plate away. "Please tell the maid the *saag* was delicious."

He jogged to his room and picked up the phone: Abdullah's number was flashing on the screen. He held it to his ear.

"Yes?"

"Alif-*jan*. I can't talk. Can you come over?"

Alif felt his heart rate spike. "What's wrong?"

"I just said I can't talk," said Abdullah impatiently. "*Yallah*, waiting for you." He hung up. Alif shoved the phone in his pocket, cursing. He ransacked his cluttered room for a pair of shoes, pulled them on, and went out into the street.

*   *   *

Abdullah was pacing back and forth across the interior of Radio Sheikh when Alif arrived. A young Arab man with bleached hair was with him.

"Alif, thank God." Abdullah crossed the room in two bounding steps and shook his hand. Alif curled his lip.

"A handshake? What are we, third cousins? What's going on?"

"Never mind the handshake. I'm nervous, that's all. Alif, this is Faris. Faris, tell him what you've just told me."

The Arab man looked around restlessly. "Are you sure he's all right?" he asked.

"All right? All right? My dear *sahib*, Alif has been with us since the beginning. It is vital that he be told."

Alif and Faris regarded one another, frowning.

"Fine," said Faris, "here is the story. I work in the Ministry of Information."

"One of my moles," Abdullah explained.

"It's low-level work—mostly I collate documents and answer the telephone. But on Tuesday I sat in on a meeting—"

"With the assistant minister himself," Abdullah said gleefully.

"—and I heard something strange. There were two men from State security at this meeting. They talked about a carnivore program they use for their digital counterterrorism operations, and how successful it has been. They asked the minister to congratulate the man who designed it, and to thank him for spending so much of his own personal time administrating it."

Alif felt his eyes begin to swim. "You're talking about—"

"The Hand," said Abdullah triumphantly. "Is it a program? A man? Now we know: it's both. Hand in glove, so to speak."

"It gets better," said Faris, looking more at ease, "When they referred to this person, they called him 'ibn al sheikh.'"

Alif gaped at him. "He's *royalty*?"

"That's right!" crowed Abdullah, "We're being nibbled to death by a silk-diapered aristocrat!"

"You sound almost happy," said Alif, disgusted.

"I'm not," said Abdullah. "I'm terrified. This is hysteria you're witnessing."

Alif sat down on the welder's bench in the center of the room and put his head in his hands.

"The Hand broke into my machine yesterday," he said quietly.

Abdullah's eyes widened. Faris grunted in sympathy. "It's happening more and more," he said. "You do what you can—change your handle, change all your passwords, switch to a new Internet provider or get a revolving IP address. And do it fast. You've got maybe another twenty-four hours, tops."

Abdullah shook his head, looking pale. "Alif moves in more rarefied ether than the rest of us. His case is not so simple. If the Hand has cracked him, we are all doomed men."

Alif looked up at Faris. "How long until we have a name?" he asked.

Faris sighed. "I'm not sure. There has to be a record of this person's work at the ministry—it's just a matter of finding it. I'm mining their database remotely from my home computer right now."

"Okay." Alif stood. Sweat made his T-shirt cling to his back. "I have to go. Call me as soon as you know anything else."

"Courage." Abdullah gave him a lopsided smile. Alif slapped him on the shoulder.

"Thank you, brother."

*   *   *

He took a detour on the way home in an attempt to calm down. There was a little irrigated plot of date palms at the edge of Baqara District, the remnant of an orchard some wealthy cattle merchant had refused to sell when the City overran its walls. Since no deed to the land could be found, the plot sat untouched, an odd bucolic interruption in the dust-colored rows of apartments. Several years earlier a taxi driver from Gujarat had begun to pollinate the feral trees again. Now people in the neighborhood enjoyed a tiny date harvest every autumn, drying and storing the fruit in their homes like farmers.

The plot had already been stripped of this year's sticky bounty and was quiet when Alif arrived. He skirted along a hillock separating two shallow canals that ran among the trees, breathing in a green stifling scent and imagining himself refortified. He thought of the woman with black-and-orange hair. His groin tightened. A breeze lifted the palm fronds above his head, scattering their shadows across his damp limbs. The trees, like the woman in his dreams, belonged to some other mode of being and were not quite real. Alif lay down on the earth and closed his eyes. He would stay here until the stress and sweat drained from his body and he could think again.

The slapping sound of a woman's sandals from beyond the edge of the orchard interrupted him. Alif recognized Dina's discreet, feminine gait. He rose, jogging along the hillock toward the street until the sound of traffic and machines returned.

"Sister," he called. Dina turned. With an uneasy feeling Alif noticed the box under her arm.

"How funny," she said. "I was just coming to see you. I've been back to the Old Quarter." She lifted the box in her hands.

Alif swallowed. "Why," he asked hoarsely.

"Your friend called me."

"You gave her your number?"

"She asked. It seemed impolite to refuse. Besides, her father was watching."

Alif felt his eyes begin to burn.

"She said she had something to give to you," Dina continued. "So I met her at her house. She looked as though she'd been standing on her head . . . hair a mess, circles under her eyes. She gave me back the box you sent—it feels heavier now—and turned me away. Without offering me tea or anything. It was all very rude."

Alif took the box from her hands.

"I don't like being summoned by rich girls like somebody's maid," said Dina. "I don't understand why she couldn't just call you or e-mail you if she wanted to give you something."

"She can't e-mail me," Alif murmured. Something slid along the bottom of the box. He looked around: women on their way to the souk regarded him curiously.

"Let's go." Alif did not quite touch Dina's shoulder to lead her.

"What? Where?"

"Just into the date orchard. I can't open this on the street." He ducked back in between the palms. Dina sighed and followed him.

"Can't it wait until you get home? People will get the wrong idea if we hide in here together."

"Fuck people."

Dina gasped. Alif ignored her, sitting down on a patch of sunlit dirt and reaching into his pocket for the Swiss Army Knife he carried. The box had been taped shut in a hurry, leaving wrinkled tacky edges. He slit the seams and looked inside.

"What the hell," he muttered.

"What is it?" Dina peered over his shoulder. Alif lifted out a book bound in dark blue linen. It was evidently quite old—brittle to the touch and faded in places. A faint odor emanated from its pages. For a disconcerting moment, Alif was reminded of Intisar's pale arms in the afterglow of their lovemaking.

"It's a book," he said.

"I can see that," said Dina, "but the title's blurred out. I can't read it."

Alif lifted the manuscript into the light and squinted at it. The title appeared to be written by hand in an old-fashioned kind of Arabic calligraphy, with gold ink. It was flaking badly and some of the letters were barely visible. He was startled to discover that the first word was his own name.

"Alif," he said excitedly. "It says Alif!"

Dina snatched the book from his hands.

"No it doesn't," she said after a moment. "It says alf. *Alf Yeom wa Yeom. The Thousand and One Days.*"

Chapter Four

Alif sat back on his heels.

"It must be a joke," he said.

"It looks serious to me." Dina held up the manuscript, turning it one way and then the other. "See how old it is? And it smells like—like—"

"I know," said Alif hastily, flushing. "But what does it mean? Why did she send it?"

Dina rolled her eyes. "You're asking me? I've only met her twice. I could have told you that running around with a stuck-up silk slipper behind her father's back was a bad idea. No wonder you've gotten so strange—"

"All right, all right." Alif jerked the book out of Dina's hands. The sun beat down on his dark hair and made sweat stand up on his scalp. He wanted coffee and the cool of his bedroom, the pleasant familiar hum of his machines. "Never mind. Thank you for bringing this to me. I'm sorry I got you involved."

Dina's eyes looked hurt. She stood, gathering the folds of her robe with offended elegance.

"Here, wait." Alif felt guilty. "I'll walk home with you. If we leave together without shame people will assume we were in here to pick the last of the dates."

"Thank you." Dina walked to the edge of the orchard without looking at him. Alif tucked the book back into the box and followed her. They passed between the jagged palm trunks and were immediately deafened by the late-afternoon traffic that moved down the street in one overheated mass. A skinny man on a moped reached out for Dina's veil as he sped past. Alif cursed at him, running a few steps before Dina called him back.

"It's just a donkey whose mother raised him wrong," she said, adjusting the black fabric over the bridge of her nose. "The City is full of them."

"You should have let me catch up," Alif muttered. "I'd teach him what his mother couldn't."

Dina moved closer to him. They walked in silence, threading through a series of named and unnamed streets until their own block appeared beyond an intersection.

"I'll stop at the pharmacy," said Dina. "Baba's liver is acting up again. It'll only take a minute."

"Okay." Alif waited as she ducked into a white storefront that advertised its wares in Tamil. When they got home he would take a shower and change into the gray house-kurta his grandmother had sent him from India, the one made of cotton so soft it felt like a baby's blanket. Then he would put a cold compress on his eyes and try to make sense of the day's events.

The smell of frying *papadums* wafted down from a cook shop in the next street, mingling with gasoline and dust: a greasy comforting scent he had known since childhood. Their little corner of the City was reassuringly solid, unchanged by what had happened in the past thirty-six hours. Alif's tragedies seemed to spring from some perverse timeline to which Baqara District was not a party.

Alif's gaze drifted to the garden in front of their duplex, half-visible between the neighboring apartment blocks. A man was loitering near the front gate. Alif squinted. He was an Arab, clean-shaven, wearing a white *thobe* and sunglasses. He stood as though he was waiting to meet someone or expected an imminent delivery. Alif had waited at the gate in a similar fashion a hundred times, to receive the butcher's boy, the ironing man, the fruit seller. But that was not strange, because this was his house.

"What's the matter?" asked Dina, exiting the pharmacy with a brown paper bag.

"There's a man standing in front of our place," said Alif. "Looking like he owns it."

Dina peered down the street. "Must be waiting for someone," she said. "Maybe he's a friend of Baba's. Or could he be looking for your father?"

"I don't—" Alif's phone buzzed in his pocket, interrupting him. He pulled it out and touched an icon on the screen: it was a text message from Abdullah. He opened it.

Faris says: Abbas Al Shehab.

Points of light danced in front of Alif's eyes.

"Are you all right?" Dina looked at him in alarm. "You've gone pale!" She said his given name in an anxious voice. He barely recognized it, or her.

"Please—" Her voice came out of a hazy brightness. "Answer me. I'm getting scared."

He mouthed a prayer. Adrenaline shot through his veins like an angelic answer, clearing his mind in one ringing blow. He grabbed Dina's arm. "I need you to do something for me," he said. "Quickly, without any fuss."

Dina looked from his hand to his face. "Okay," she whispered.

"Knock on my door and tell the maid you need to get a novel you lent me. Tell her it's in my room. Go up and get my netbook. It's sitting on my desk next to the main computer. And get—" His throat closed. "Get the gray kurta that's hanging in my wardrobe, on the left."

Dina's chest rose and fell rapidly beneath her robe. "What's going on?" she asked in a low voice.

"That man is waiting for me."

"What have you done? *What have you done?*"

Alif fought to keep his breathing steady. "I'll tell you everything, I swear—I'll tell you whatever you want. Just do this first. It's not safe for me to go home now."

Dina left him without a word. Alif watched as she crossed the street, paper bag clutched tight against her body. He held his breath when the man at the gate stopped her. Dina shifted from foot to foot, gesturing toward the New Quarter at one point with a hand that fluttered and shook. As she turned toward the house, the man grabbed her wrist.

Alif bolted across the street without thinking. As he neared the gate, Dina met his eyes with a look that stopped him dead: a terrible look, a warning, her pupils collapsing into tiny dots. He noticed irrelevantly that her eyes were flecked with green, forming starburst patterns around her pupils, like copper suns. Alif would have reached for the Arab man's arm, or even hit him, but Dina's gaze forced him back with a pressure that was almost physical, and he found himself retreating step by step until he stood at the edge of the street.

Dina twisted deftly out of the man's grasp and continued toward the house. The Arab man turned away from her, pulling a crease from the sleeve of his *thobe* in a gesture of irritation. He looked up and, for a moment, Alif saw his own startled reflection in the man's sunglasses. Alif ducked behind the corner of the apartment block next door, panting. The box containing Intisar's book puckered as he held it to his damp chest. The Arab man did not follow him.

The alleyway between the two buildings was lined with bags of garbage awaiting collection day; pools of reeking yellow fluid had formed beneath them, crisscrossing the unpaved earth to meet one another in rivulets. Alif gagged, straightened, and gagged again, tasting bile. He was still heaving when Dina touched him on the shoulder.

"Don't speak," she whispered. "He's still there. Keep walking down the alley."

Alif stumbled to obey her. They made their way along a thin spit of clear ground that ran through the trash, Dina bundling up her robe to keep it from dragging in muck. When they emerged into the next street, she punched Alif on the arm.

"Ow! *Damn* it!" He glared at her, rubbing the sore spot.

"You stupid, careless, selfish son of a dog," she said, voice shaking. "You've put all of us in danger. Our families, our neighbors. Do you know who that was? That was a detective from State security. Oh, yes." She shoved a backpack into his arms. "Here, take your stuff."

Alif stared at her, slack-jawed. "I can't believe you just said a swear word," he said. "I didn't know you knew any swear words."

"Don't be an idiot and don't change the subject."

Alif flushed and hugged the backpack to his chest. "What's in here?" he asked.

"What you asked for, plus some clean socks and a toothbrush. And a bag of dates."

"Thank you," he said. "Really. You're—I'm sorry about your wrist." He glanced at her black sleeve, feeling ashamed. "This is the second time today I should have protected you and couldn't. I owe you better."

"You owe me an explanation."

"Fine, yes, you're right." Alif glanced around anxiously, bundling Intisar's book into his backpack and letting the box drop. "Not here. We'll go to my friend Abdullah's place."

Dina looked uneasy.

"It's public," Alif reassured her. "At least technically. It's a shop, but only for people who know people. I won't make you break any rules. We'll leave a door open or something."

"Okay."

Alif led her on a circuitous path through Baqara District, doubling back every few blocks. Each time he saw a man in a *thobe* his stomach churned. When they reached the door of Radio Sheikh the sun was setting, and what birds remained in the City made restless sounds as they jockeyed for position in the stunted trees. Alif knocked on the door more forcefully than he meant to.

"Yes?" It opened a crack and Alif saw Abdullah's eyes flashing back at him in the rosy light.

"We need to come in," said Alif. "Now, immediately."

"We?"

Alif pushed the door open over Abdullah's startled protest and ushered Dina inside. Abdullah shrank away from her, glaring at Alif over her head.

"This is Dina," said Alif. "Find your manners."

"*As-salaamu alaykum,* miss," muttered Abdullah, shifting his gaze to the concrete floor.

"*W'alaykum salaam,*" said Dina. Abdullah's expression changed.

"Is this—is she the—" He stopped midsentence, blushing. It took Alif a moment to realize what he meant.

"No! This isn't her. This is the neighbor's daughter."

"Oh. Okay." Abdullah took a deep breath. "Tea, anyone? Dina?"

Alif threw his backpack on the welding bench without answering. "Listen, *bhai,*" he said, "I'm in serious going-to-jail-to-be-raped-by-thugs trouble. It's real this time. I've screwed up in the most profound way imaginable and I am fucked, fucked."

Dina began backing toward the door.

"The Hand again? Has something happened?"

"State security is watching my house. Our house. Dina's family lives in the same duplex. He was very nasty with her when she tried to get inside."

Abdullah fumbled his way toward the bench and sat down. "Go on," he said, feigning composure.

"The girl—Intisar—when the Hand broke into my computer I was connected to her machine. I thought that since she's an aristocrat they wouldn't bother with her, so I wasn't worried, but then Faris—" He swallowed. "It's her fiancé, Abdullah. Abbas Al Shehab—that's her fiancé's name. Imagine his surprise when he found his future wife's computer hooked up to a hacker's. All our e-mails, all our chats—it will be a scandal to end scandals."

"Wait a minute." Abdullah steepled his fingers. "I don't understand what you're trying to say. Slow down and tell me again, because it sounds like you're saying you've been screwing the Hand's bride-to-be."

Alif slumped to the floor and covered his face.

"Alif," said Abdullah in a soft voice, "were you running the pattern recognition program? The one you've been working on?"

"Yes. It was installed on her machine. Functioning perfectly, too."

"So you've delivered into the Hand of the enemy a tool they could use to hunt us down no matter which computer or login we use?"

"Yes." The single syllable crescendoed in a squeak. "Yes."

"And you've given the Hand a reason to cut off your dick as well as your head."

"Yes."

"Then I agree." Abdullah stood. "You are one fucked man, and you've fucked us all along with you."

"Please stop cursing," said Dina.

"What are you going to do?" asked Abdullah, beginning to pace the floor. "You can't stay here. I mean you can, for now, but you'll have to keep moving."

"Thanks. Even one night would be a huge—"

"Don't thank me. This isn't a favor for a friend. I'm so angry I could bash your half-Arab nose right in. But what happens to you now will affect everyone you know. I'd like to keep my own ass out of prison, if it comes to that."

"What about Dina?"

"What *about* Dina?" said the girl herself. "Dina is going home this very moment. I've heard enough."

Alif looked up at her anxiously. "I don't think that's a good idea. Not with the State watching the house. They could get angry and decide arresting you is the best way to drive me insane. You live next door to a terrorist. People have been executed for less."

"What am I supposed to do? Are you saying I can't go back to my own house?"

"Please keep your voices down," said Abdullah, twisting his hands.

"My mother," moaned Alif. "My poor mother."

"You should have thought of your poor mother before you started screwing someone else's prize filly."

"Stop it!"

Alif and Abdullah went silent and stared at Dina. She was breathing heavily, fists clenched at her sides.

"Stop saying such ugly things! You're a couple of boys trying to talk like men—you're not fooling anyone!" She took a few deeper, shaking breaths and relaxed her hands. "We have to think calmly and decide what must be done."

Alif studied Dina over the ridge of his updrawn knees, impressed. A damp flush had appeared on the skin beneath her eyes, but her gaze was steady. She sat down on the welder's bench and smoothed her robe before addressing them again.

"Brother Abdullah, I think we'll take that tea now."

*　　*　　*

For an hour they discussed and discarded Alif's options. Could he flee the country? No: by now his name had certainly been added to a blacklist at every port and border. Could he bribe some Bedouin to take him through the desert, where he could cross into Oman or Saudi Arabia unnoticed? Dina dismissed this as fanciful. Was there no relative or friend with political connections to whom he could appeal for protection? Alif thought of his father's other family: his first wife had a cousin or two in some modest level of government. But she would never help him.

After the evening call to prayer Abdullah left for a quarter of an hour, returning with hot shawarma sandwiches. By this time Alif's anxiety had changed shape: he considered what might happen— or worse, had already happened—to Intisar. Everything hinged on whether her fiancé decided to reveal the scandal to her father or not. The Hand did not yet have formal control over Intisar; her father, on the other hand, was within his rights to beat her to the verge of death. For a brief, fluttering minute Alif let himself imagine the Hand had released her from her engagement and hushed the whole thing up to avoid embarrassment.

"When you saw her," Alif asked Dina as they ate, "Intisar, I mean, did she look like she'd been hurt? Did you see any bruises or marks? Was she limping?"

"No," Dina said curtly. "She wasn't limping. She just seemed upset."

"Maybe it's all right then," said Alif, thinking again of the possibility that Intisar was both free and socially damaged enough to make him look like a suitable match. He could give up his work, take a job at a respectable company, make microchips for morons. They could be happy.

"All right," snorted Abdullah. "You're going to need a bodyguard for the rest of your life. If you even make it to the rest of your life."

"I don't care if I do," said Alif. "All that matters is that Intisar is safe. She shouldn't be punished for what I've done—she's never said a word against the emir or the government in her life. If they hurt her I'll kill myself." He ground the palms of his heels against his eyes.

"Don't be a baby," Dina muttered.

Abdullah crumpled the wax paper wrapping of his sandwich and dragged one hand across his mouth. "Look," he said, "here's my idea. You both stay here tonight. I'll curtain off a corner for Dina and my sister can lend her some night things. Then in the morning you both go to the old part of the souk and look for help. You need protection."

"Look for help? From who?"

"Vikram the Vampire."

Alif burst into an exasperated laugh. "You've got to be kidding me. Vikram the Vampire? Are we ten years old?"

"I used to play that game with my cousins," said Dina. "We'd turn off all the lights and say his name three times and then spit. He never showed up. Of course when I got older I repented."

"He's not *really* a vampire," Abdullah said crossly. "That's just what they call him. After the legend, you know. He's a black market thug. He worked over my friend Nargis, who imports those Chinese hacktops, when he was short on cash one month. Nargis came in here with a broken jaw and two missing teeth, scared to death. Said the guy has yellow eyes."

"So why would we go to him?" Alif asked. "I don't want a broken jaw."

"You pay him, idiot. You pay him to protect you."

"One guy is no match for the Hand, even if he does have yellow eyes."

"Would you just listen? Of course he'll have ideas we haven't thought of. Smugglers, dock workers—who knows what kind of connections those thugs have. They're almost as crooked as the government. And Vikram is the worst of the lot."

"Can't we talk to someone normal?"

"No," said Abdullah, "you're divorced from normal. The further off the grid you go the better."

Alif let out a sharp breath. "Fine, okay. Let's say I find Vikram the Vampire. There's still the matter of the book."

"What book?"

Catching Alif's eye, Dina gave an almost imperceptible shake of her head.

"Nothing," Alif stuttered. "Just thinking out loud. Some research I have to do."

"Well, do it on your own time. Right now you have to think about keeping yourself—and the rest of us—out of jail."

Alif let his head go limp and loll between his shoulders. "Vikram the Vampire. I committed a sin by waking up this morning. That is the only way this day could have gone so terribly wrong."

"What a bizarre thing to say," Dina scoffed.

They cleaned up the crumbs and tea things in the gathering dark. When Abdullah and Dina left for his sister's apartment, Alif took the opportunity to boot up his netbook. He braced himself to find some insidious worm waiting in his e-mail, some miraculous program that would allow the Hand to descend on him out of the ether if he so much as coughed. But there was nothing. Cautiously he enabled remote access to Hollywood; the hypervisor was still online. Alif let out a breath he hadn't realized he'd been holding. Hurriedly he set up a roving IP address—a costly, inefficient way to disguise his location, and far from foolproof, but it would buy him a little time. The Hand would see Alif using his e-mail and cloud computing accounts, but until he could crack his algorithm, Alif would appear to be working from Portugal, Hawaii, Tibet.

Next, Alif set about dismantling his creation. He downloaded what little he could onto the netbook's modest hard drive and dumped a little more—cryptic commands, programs unusable without other programs—into the cloud he shared with a few other City gray hats. Enough to seed a new version of Hollywood when real life reasserted itself. The Tin Sari program files he transferred intact and whole onto the sixteen-gig flash drive he always carried in his pocket. The drive had been blessed, at one point, by a toothless Sufi dervish from Somalia who grabbed

Alif's wrist as he sat in a street café. Alif had yet to discover whether the blessing stuck.

When he was finished he blanked the hard drive of his home computer, leaving behind a program that would cause the CPU to overclock—and, he hoped, melt—the next time it was booted up. He would leave the Hand's agents with a lump of silicon too hot to pick up. They would get nothing from him.

"God, he's *crying!*"

Dina and Abdullah had returned and stood in the doorway staring at him. Alif realized his face was wet.

"It's gone," he said. "I destroyed it. My whole system."

Abdullah knelt beside him with a look of profound compassion. "It'll be all right, *bhai*. You'll rebuild."

"Not in time to help my clients. I have to write a bunch of awful e-mails."

"The threat was always there, Alif—they'll understand."

Alif stroked the white plastic casing of his netbook absently. "In the four years I've been doing this stuff for money, I've had less than forty-eight hours of downtime. Did you know that? And now I'm a ghost in the machine. By next week all the hacks and geeks and hats I call my friends will have forgotten who I am. That is the nature of this business. That is the Internet."

"You still have real friends," said Dina. The two men made identical derisive noises.

"Internet friends are real friends," said Abdullah. "Now that you pious brothers and sisters have taken over half the planet, the Internet is the only place left to have a worthwhile conversation."

"Even if they forget all about you in two weeks?"

"Even so."

Abdullah had brought two thin cotton mattresses and a largish bed sheet. He and Alif strung the latter across one corner of the room, fastening it to the wall with thumbtacks. Alif cleared away computer boxes and put the better of the two mattresses—one had a suspicious stain—in the tentlike space their makeshift curtain had created.

"Here," he said to Dina, "we'll leave while you get ready for bed."

"This isn't right," Dina fretted. "I told my mother I'm staying at Maryam Abdel Bassit's place. If she finds out I'm lying she'll be crushed."

"Live adventurously. See you in the morning." Abdullah left the room with a flourish, one arm slung along Alif's shoulders.

*　*　*

The room was dark when Alif returned. He took off his shoes and lay down on the second mattress, feeling as though he had been through a physical ordeal. His back and legs ached. Intisar reentered his thoughts every time he tried to forget her for a few minutes, bringing with her an unsettling combination of arousal and guilt, foreshadowing a disaster even greater than the one that had already befallen him. Her life was at risk: that much was clear. He felt impotent in the face of the pain he had brought on her, the danger she must now face. He could not save her with a few bracketed commands and C++ programs, but this was the only way he knew.

"I don't like calling you Alif."

He looked over at the veiled corner of the room.

"Why?"

"It's not your name."

Alif looked back at the ceiling. "It might as well be my name," he said.

"But it isn't. It's a letter of the alphabet."

"It's the first letter of Sura Al Baqara in the Quran. You of all people should approve."

He heard Dina shift on her mattress. With the angle of the light from the window, he realized that she could probably see him through the curtain, though he could not see her.

"I don't approve," she said. "Your real name is better."

"*Alif, lam, mim.*" He drew the letters in the air with his finger. "One-digit symbol substitutions: God, Gabriel, the Prophet. I named myself after the first line of code ever written. It's a good name for a programmer."

"Why does a programmer need a second name?"

"Tradition. And it's called a handle, anyway, not a name. It's safer to be anonymous. If you use your real name you're liable to get into trouble."

"You use a fake name and you still got into trouble."

Alif bit back an insult, keeping his teeth shut until he could trust them. "Whatever. Good night, Dina."

He had begun to lose the distinction between his thoughts and his dreams when she spoke again.

"I'm not what you think I am. I'm not trying to be stuck-up and annoying. I'm not what you think."

"I know," he muttered, unsure of what he meant.

✻   ✻   ✻

When he woke up the next morning he had forgotten where he was. Bolting upright, he stared wildly at his surroundings, blinking until his eyes adjusted to the unsaturated light that filtered in through the window. Dina moved along his peripheral vision like a dark bird, humming an Egyptian pop song. The sheet that had protected her while she slept was folded neatly on her mattress. Alif caught the sharp, astringent scent of tea: a tin pot was steaming atop a camp stove on the window ledge, next to a plate of fried eggs and roti.

"Abdullah left some breakfast," said Dina. "We didn't want to wake you. It's nearly ten."

"Where'd he go?" asked Alif, rubbing his eyes.

"He said he had to make some phone calls. We're supposed to lock up when we leave."

They ate without speaking. Alif stared pensively out the window, trying to map his next steps. The day, and the days that would certainly follow it, were unfathomable: too much had been asked of him. He looked at his backpack, wishing he had had more time to consider what he might need.

"Why didn't you want Abdullah to know about the book?" he asked Dina, reminded of the inconvenient article by a rectangular bulge in his bag.

Dina shrugged. "Why does he need to know?" she asked. "The less he knows, the less he has to lie about when they come for him. Your friend obviously wanted to keep the book a secret. There must be a reason for that."

"When they come for him," Alif repeated. "God, I feel sick."

Dina began to tidy the room, clearing away their breakfast things and straightening the boxes they had moved to make room for their bedding. Alif watched her with pursed lips.

"You sing," he said abruptly. "You listen to music."

"So?"

"I thought women who believe the veil is mandatory also believe that music is forbidden."

"Some do. I don't."

"Why? You all read the same books. Ibn Taymiyya, right? Ibn Abdul Wahhab?"

"Birds make music, river reeds in wind make music. Babies make music. God would not forbid something that is the sharia of innocent creatures."

Alif chuckled. "Okay."

Dina whisked his empty tea glass out of his hands and clucked her tongue. "You're always laughing at me," she said.

"That's not true! I laugh when you surprise me."

"How is that better?"

"All right, I laugh when you impress me."

Dina said nothing, but he could tell by the way she refilled his glass that she was pleased. He drank the tea down quickly and helped her finish tidying the room. When they were done Alif shouldered his backpack and opened the door cautiously: no one outside, no one on the rooftop across the way, no one loitering at the corner in an obvious manner. An elderly man in a donkey cart piled with jackfruit rolled past the alley along the street beyond. Otherwise, they were alone.

"Let's go." Alif ushered Dina out in front of him and locked the door from the inside before closing it. They set off down the alley at a nervous pace, wandering too far apart and then too close together. There was an acrid smell in the air—the scent of factory fumes and the overheated sea; cement dust from construction in the New Quarter. Alif headed in the direction of the harbor, following streets that sloped downward to meet the water.

"You're heading toward the souk," Dina observed at one point.

"Yes—I thought that was the plan."

"Plan? We're not seriously going to look for Vikram the Vampire, are we? Even your Bedouin idea was better than that."

Alif kicked a dried clot of dung that lay in his path. "I don't know what else to do, Dina. I really don't know what else to do."

"This isn't a movie, for God's sake. You can't just walk up to a back-alley thug and ask him for a favor. And Abdullah's never even met this man—he could have been making that whole story up!"

"What do you *want*?" Alif turned on Dina with a snarl. "We are down to a small selection of shitty options. Don't harass me." He spun around and continued walking. A minute later he heard sniffling: Dina was trailing behind with one hand over her veiled mouth, head down.

"Oh, God." Alif ducked into a side street, leading Dina by the hand. "Please don't cry. I didn't mean for you to cry."

"Don't touch me." Dina shook her hand free. "You think this isn't awful for me, too? I could have just—" She stuttered to a halt, breath catching in little gulps.

"What?" Alif asked.

"The detective," she answered. "He said nothing would happen to me or my family if we turned you in. You were standing right there. If I had—I didn't—"

Impulsively, Alif took her hand again and turned it upward, pressing a kiss into her palm. They stared at each other. Dina pulled away, rubbing the tears from her eyes.

"It's all right," she said. "Okay. Let's go find Vikram."

* * *

Souk al Medina was close to the wharf, giving vendors easy access to the fishing boats that came in at dawn and sunset. It was as ancient as the Old Quarter, active since the days when the City was only a punctuation mark on the Silk Road, a resting place for merchants and pilgrims on their way to Mecca. Alif had known it since childhood. He remembered clutching the end of his mother's shawl as she bought live chickens and fish heads for stock, or raw spices measured by the gram.

With Dina he wandered down alleys that had never been paved. The footing was half mud and reeked of yeasty animal functions. Every so often the alleys were interrupted by limestone arches, the remnants of a covered market hall long since quarried for newer buildings. The place was impervious to its own history. Women and maids were out resupplying their households in the morning light, a throng of black veils and multicolored *salwar kameez* so indistinguishable from one another that Alif kept glancing over his shoulder to reidentify Dina.

"I think we should look around the wharf side," he said at one point, trying to sound confident. "I know a couple of smartphone importers down there who might be able to help us."

"Importers?"

"Smugglers."

"Oh."

Alif pushed his way toward the wharf, past fishmongers extolling the freshness of their wares in rhyme. Over the sea of covered heads he saw a tiny storefront with a sign advertising mobile phone sales and repairs, and moved toward it. With relief, he spotted a familiar figure—Raj, the enterprising Bengali who had unlocked Alif's own smartphone—leaning in the doorway.

"Raj *bhai*!" Alif tilted his chin up in what he hoped was a jaunty manner. "It's been a long time."

Raj looked up at him with disinterest, then glanced suspiciously at Dina. "Hello," he said in English. He toyed with a SIM card in one hand.

"Listen," said Alif, clearing his throat, "I have a strange question. This might sound strange, I mean. I'm wondering if you know—"

"A man named Nargis," said Dina, cutting him off. Raj's eyes flickered over her cloaked form. Alif shifted uneasily from foot to foot, and elected to say nothing.

"You looking for a hacktop?" Raj asked.

"No," said Dina. "We just want to talk to him."

"No one comes here to talk," said Raj.

Dina sighed with an air of impatience. "We don't have a lot of time," she said. "Do you know this guy or not?"

Raj looked faintly impressed. "I know him. He's usually around in the afternoons. Let me give him a call." He eased himself upright and went into the shop.

"What are you doing?" Alif hissed at Dina. "What's all this about Nargis?"

"Assuming Abdullah was telling the truth, we should talk to the source of the story," she said. "If we go bumbling around the souk asking for Vikram the Vampire we'll look like a pair of idiots."

Alif felt a swell of admiration. She really was as smart as a man. He straightened up as Raj leaned out of the shop door and motioned them inside.

"Nargis is on his way. Come inside. Chai?" He said the last word in a Bengali drawl that verged on sarcasm.

"Hot, please," said Dina, sitting down on a folding chair along the shop wall, "With plenty of sugar."

Raj flushed and skulked away into an inner room. He emerged a few minutes later with two glasses of milk chai, offering them wordlessly to Alif and Dina before retreating behind a desk. Alif sipped his tea in silence, watching Dina as she maneuvered the glass beneath her veil with the dexterity of long practice. A few minutes later, a short, nervous man of indeterminate age appeared in the doorway. Raj rose.

"Nargis," he said, adding something in Bengali that Alif did not understand. Nargis shuffled into the room, glance shifting from person to person as though waiting for a reprimand or a blow. Alif noticed that his jaw was slightly crooked, and sat strangely on his face.

"Hi," said Alif.

"What do you want?" asked Nargis. "I've never heard of you before."

"I'm—we're friends of Abdullah's. We're looking for a certain person and he thought you might be able to help."

Raj said something else in Bengali.

"Would you mind giving us a few minutes?" Dina asked him sweetly. "Thank you so much for the tea. It was delicious."

Unmanned, Raj bolted back into the inner recesses of the shop.

"Abdullah told us you had a nasty run-in with Vikram the Vampire," Alif said to Nargis. "Is it true?"

Nargis touched his jaw. "Vikram the Vampire isn't real," he said.

"We're not interested in getting you into more trouble," said Dina. "We just need to find him."

Nargis broke into a sudden, high-pitched laugh, like a scrofulous hyena Alif had once seen in the royal zoo.

"You must both be insane. He would break you in half if you went looking for him. Do you know what he is? *Do you know what he is?*"

Alif was confused. "A thug?"

"You're insane," Nargis repeated.

"Just give us a location," said Dina. "That's all. We'll never bother you again."

"You don't understand what he'll do to me if I help you."

"He'll thank you. We want to pay him a lot of money to lend us a hand."

Nargis seemed to relax a little. He licked his lips. "That's something else," he said. "If you want to hire him, that's something else. But it will cost you."

"That's fine," said Alif impatiently. "We need to find him first. Right? Yes? So where is he?"

Nargis regarded him for a long moment. "There's a cracked arch on the western edge of the souk. He lives in the alley that runs through it."

Alif suppressed a triumphant smile. He glanced out the corner of his eye at Dina. Her gaze was fixed and calm, betraying nothing. She stood.

"Thank you," she said. "We're grateful for your help." Nodding at Alif, she walked briskly toward the shop entrance. Alif scrambled to follow her, cursing his awkward feet.

"That was great!" he crowed as soon as they were back in the bustle of the souk. "The way you handled them, Dina—it was like you weren't even nervous. For a minute I forgot you were a girl."

Dina made an indignant noise. The sun pressed down as though endowed with physical strength; the day was growing hotter. They moved into the shade of the corrugated shop roofs that extended row after row toward the wharf. At the end of one alley they found a shabby concrete building that had been converted into a prayer room, announcing its repurposed function by the pile of shoes heaped outside. Dina slipped off her sandals and excused herself to perform the midday *salat*. Alif waited idly by the door for her return. The idea of taking off his shoes and socks only to put them back on again was too much in this heat. He leaned against the cool concrete wall and listened to the imam—toneless, weary-sounding—lead the prostrations of his merchant congregation. Dina emerged in the aftermath, a black figure amid the press of men jockeying to retrieve their sandals and loafers from the heap near the entrance.

"*Haraman*," he told her.

"*Gema'an inshallah*," she said. He felt foolish when she did not rebuke him for his failure to pray. They walked silently back through the souk, listing toward the harbor, where the smell of grilled fish and onions announced lunchtime from innumerable food stalls. When Dina suggested they eat before continuing their search, Alif made no protest. An uneasy sensation was building in his middle: a suspicion that he lacked both the will and the competence to see this plan through. He had prided himself on his knowledge of the City's gray market but the thought of a thug, a visceral criminal, made him feel inexperienced and effeminate. He had never held a gun, nor seen one except on television and once or twice in the hands of a border guard.

Alif made a conscious effort to relax his brow and his mouth. When he was nervous he tended to purse his lips; it was a shortcoming Dina herself had identified. He felt her gaze on him now, studying his mood. He would not let her see his uncertainty. He couldn't bear the thought of her familiar sharp sigh, the upcast eyes, the unspoken conclusion that he had once again behaved like a child and it was left to her to make things right. Alif lifted his chin and tried to appear confident.

"Fish kebabs?" he asked her. "Or fish curry?" "Kebabs, please. They let the curry sit in the sun all day."

Alif approached the closest food stall, manned by a boy barely tall enough to fan his charcoal grill, and paid for two nicely charred skewers of red snapper and two cans of Mecca Cola. He gave one of each to Dina, then they threaded their way toward the dock that ran the length of the harbor. Boys and young men patrolled it restlessly, chucking stones at passing seagulls. Alif found space near an antiquated fishing boat and sat down, letting his legs hang over the edge toward the greenish, lapping sea.

"Girls don't sit at the dock." Dina stood over him, shifting from one foot to the other.

"There's no law saying you can't. If one of these donkeys gives you trouble I'll smash him."

"How?"

Alif looked up at her witheringly. Dina murmured something to herself and sat down at a polite distance, lifting the edge of her veil to tuck the kebab underneath. They ate without speaking, licking oil off their fingers, pausing to listen to the bells of the boats that came and went in the harbor. An acne-riddled boy sucked his teeth and moaned at Dina as he capered past; Alif threw a crumpled Mecca Cola can at his head. It caught the boy squarely under his buzz cut. He yelped but did not turn, careening onward down the dock.

"Bastard *desi* dock boys," shouted Alif. "You like making Indians look bad in front of these Arab shits? Do you?"

The boy disappeared into the midday glare.

"Are we all shits?" Dina wiped her hands on a napkin and stood.

Alif waved one hand impatiently. "You know what I meant. Gulf Arabs and all that. Egyptians aren't really Arabs, not in the same way. You're imported labor, just like us."

"You're partly an Arab, too."

"Partly is the same as not at all. Can you see them hiring me at CityCom or the Royal Bank?"

"Yes, as a *chaiwallah*."

Alif swatted at her ankles; she danced out of the way with a squeak. Hauling himself to his feet, Alif surveyed the harbor:

a few fishing boats were bringing their catches home early, struggling in the heavy wake of an oil tanker that was putting out from the TransAtlas slip. He sucked the last of the fish from his skewer and tossed it into the water, where it gravitated toward a buoyant clot of trash. He didn't want to go back to the souk. Dina swayed on her feet, looking philosophical, waiting for him to issue directions.

"All right," he said. "I guess this is really happening."

*   *   *

It was midafternoon before they found an arch like the one Nargis had described. It straddled a row of cloth vendors displaying moth-bitten bolts of cotton and linen, their hands stained with the dye they used to color their goods. The alley was oddly silent: few shoppers wandered past its stalls, giving the whole street a neglected, overlooked air. Alif felt the bile quicken in his stomach as he examined each stall, trying to decide which long-faced merchant might be sheltering a criminal, and how best to approach him.

"Look." Dina pointed to the left foot of the arch. A patchwork tent was set up against it, made from the same material the cloth vendors were selling. An AK-47 lay casually on top of a jerry can near the entrance. Alif hesitated.

"I don't want to do this," he said, ceasing to care whether he looked like an idiot or not. "Let's just forget it. This is crazy, and I can't—I don't know what to—"

"I never wanted to do this in the first place," said Dina, "but you said it was our only choice. We can't just stand here."

They stared at the tent for several more minutes. Alif wondered what the unspeaking merchants in the cloth stalls were thinking as they looked at him. The silence in the alley was unnerving.

"Go," muttered Dina.

Alif edged toward the tent as if approaching an undetonated bomb. He thought he saw movement within. He squinted: the shadow of a four-legged animal, a large dog perhaps, moved against the cloth barrier. He was about to draw Dina's attention to it when he heard her scream.

Alif spun around and was halted by blinding pain. He stumbled forward, dragged by an unseen hand, and saw the dirt alleyway rush toward his face. He flinched. When he opened his eyes again, he was tumbling over Dina into the tent.

Chapter Five

"Alif."

It was a male voice, smooth and low, touched by some untraceable accent. Alif struggled to focus. He put his hand down and felt coarse wool: a carpet, swimming with red and white designs. He blinked rapidly. Dina was somewhere to his left, breathing high, panicked breaths. He flung out one arm with a vague idea of protecting her and heard a laugh.

"She's not in danger yet. Neither are you. Sit up and be a man, since you were man enough to come here." A shadow moved in front of him. Alif saw yellow eyes in a handsome, raceless face, neither pale nor dark, framed by black hair as long as a woman's.

"V-v—" Alif's tongue felt heavy.

"What a drooling mess you are. I didn't even hit you that hard." A hand reached out and took hold of Alif's shirtfront, propping him up. He took a few deep breaths and felt his head begin to clear. The inside of the tent was decorated like those of the Bedouin: a round brass tray on a folding stand, a camp stove, a thin cotton mattress. There was also a stockpile of automatic weapons in one corner. Dina was clutching the hem of his pant leg unconsciously as she stared past him at their host.

"V-Vikram?" Alif managed finally.

"George Bush. Santa Claus." The man grinned, displaying a set of white teeth.

"Are you going to hurt us?" Dina spoke in a wispy voice Alif barely recognized.

"I might. I easily could. In fact, I may without even realizing." The man shifted, and Alif noticed with horror that his knees seemed to bend the wrong way. He looked back at his face and attempted to forget.

"I'm sorry," he said, "sorry to bother you, Vikram *sahib*, I didn't mean to offend you in any, any way—"

"For God's sake, listen to yourself. Your girl is losing respect for you as we speak. You came here to ask me for something. I will probably say no and you may or may not leave with all your limbs. So let's get to it."

Alif forced himself to look the man steadily in the eyes. There was humor there: a predatory, unnerving humor, like the musing of a leopard in a pen of goats.

"I'm in serious trouble," he said. "I'm just a programmer, and I can't—I need someone who can protect me from the Hand. That's what we call the chief censor. We gray hats, I mean. Gray hats are programmers who work for regular people instead of a company. You know? It's a name we made up for him when we didn't know whether it was a man or a program or both. I'm in love with the woman he wants, and he found out, and he could put me behind the sun if he felt like it, I'd just disappear and you'd never see me again—"

The man raised a hand.

"I believe you. No one would come to me with a story so stupid unless it was true. But I'm not going to help. Number one, because you can't afford it, and number two, because my help would get you into even bigger trouble. So out you go."

Alif looked at Dina. Dina looked faint. For a moment worry overwhelmed his desire to scramble out through the tent flap.

"Could she have some water first?" he asked.

The man looked over his shoulder and shouted something in a language Alif didn't recognize. A female voice answered from somewhere just outside. A moment later a woman entered holding a clay cup. She wore the layered robes of a tribeswoman from the south and a red scarf was looped over her head and face. She looked at Alif and gasped. Alif looked back uneasily, discomfited by the recognition in her golden eyes.

"This is my sister Azalel," said the man. "Of course, that's not her real name—Vikram isn't mine, either—but it's as close as we can get in any tongue that you can speak."

"Alif isn't my real name," Alif volunteered, then cursed himself.

"Yes, I know. Your girl told me while you were drooling on the floor. She also told me your given name, which was foolish. Never tell a man your given name if you don't know his."

Azalel handed Dina the clay cup. Dina drank down its contents obediently and murmured her thanks.

"Now you'd better leave," said Vikram. "I haven't eaten all day."

Alif did not stop to ponder this statement. Putting a hand under Dina's elbow, he helped her to her feet. They hurried through the tent flap together and emerged gasping into the afternoon sun. By silent, mutual consent they half-trotted for several blocks before either of them spoke.

"Did you see—did you see—" Dina struggled to catch her breath, as though she'd been running.

"Are you all right? He didn't hit *you*, did he?"

"I don't know." Dina touched her forehead absently. "I thought I saw something awful, and I screamed, and then I was inside the tent. I think I may have fainted. You were lying there opening and closing your mouth like a fish. I was terrified that you might really be hurt."

Alif felt waves of gooseflesh travel up and down his arms. "We have to try not to panic," he said, mostly to himself. "We have to try to think this through and process it. Break it down into its composite parts until it makes some kind of rational sense."

"Rational? Are you mad? That thing was not human!"

"Of course he was human. What else could he be?"

"You unbelievable child—did you see his *legs*?"

The memory of Vikram's leonine joints sprang to life behind Alif's eyes. He felt dizzy.

"That could have been anything. The light inside the tent was strange. We were both upset. When you panic you start to think things that aren't real."

Dina stopped walking and stared at him with knitted brows. "I can't believe this. You read all those *kuffar* fantasy novels and yet you deny something straight out of a holy book."

86

Alif sat down on the concrete veranda of an apartment block. They had passed beyond the western edge of the souk into the outskirts of the New Quarter and were walking down a trim, manicured residential street.

"You've lost me. What am I denying. Instruct me in my religion."

"You don't have to get snotty. Remember: 'And the djinn We created in the Foretime from a smokeless fire.'"

Alif got up again and continued down the street, suddenly angry. He heard Dina make a frustrated sound.

"You lent me *The Golden Compass*! It's full of djinni trickery, and you were angry at me when I told you that made it dangerous! Why do you get mad when religion tells you that the things you *want* to be true *are* true?"

"When it's true, it's not fun anymore. All right? When it's true it's scary."

"If you're so afraid, don't tell me to be rational. Fear isn't rational."

"We can't all be you, Dina. We're not all saints." Alif reached over one shoulder to take his smartphone out of his backpack and discovered he wasn't wearing it. He turned around and looked at Dina in horror.

"The backpack," he whispered.

*　*　*

He let Dina lead him to an Anglo-Egyptian café a few blocks away and listened numbly as she ordered lentil soup, bread, and strong coffee. He obeyed when she coaxed him to eat. The clientele of the café was a mixture of western expatriates and the *desi* professionals who imitated them, moving in the sunlit, sanitized canopy of the

New Quarter rather than on the forest floor with their unskilled countrymen. Alif regarded them uneasily, feeling shabby and adrift without his tools, his ID cards, the few physical artifacts he had been able to carry with him into this strange exile.

Dina was the only *munaqaba* in the place: the western women were bareheaded and barefaced, dressed for the autumn heat in linen slacks and T-shirts. The *desi* engineers and architects were all men. Yet Dina seemed less uncomfortable than he felt, asking the waiter for more ice and an extra napkin with clipped coolness, tucking the folds of her black robe beneath her without embarrassment.

"You're not hot?" Alif asked her.

"Are you kidding? It's freezing in here. They must have the air conditioner turned up all the way."

Alif laughed soundlessly and leaned on his arms against the table. "You're so brave," he said. "It's like you're out shopping for the day. I'm about to collapse. He must have taken the pack when I was half-conscious. My netbook, Intisar's book—everything that could possibly help us."

"I didn't see him take anything," said Dina, "but I was so frightened that I might have missed it."

"It doesn't matter. Without Internet access all I can do is run. Maybe I should just turn myself in and take my chances."

Dina shook her head emphatically. "You can't do that. State security will torture you and then dump your body in the harbor. You know how these things end."

Alif looked around at the elegant lemon-yellow walls of the café and the coordinating flower arrangements on each table.

"Your djinn are real," he said softly. "And this is the fiction."

He could feel her smile. She said nothing as she raised her hand to signal for the waiter and collect the check. Alif sighed when she paid it with her own money, having no other recourse but to sin against chivalry and let her. Dusk had begun to fall as they left the café. A muezzin clearing his throat into a microphone echoed up the street from a nearby mosque and, from much farther away, the pleading melancholy call from Al Basheera was audible. One by one the mosques sent out their melodic demands until the air was thick with sound: come to the prayer, come to the prayer.

"We may have to sleep in a mosque tonight," Alif observed.

"I don't know what I'm going to tell my parents," said Dina. "I haven't even checked my phone. I'm sure it's full of terrified messages."

"Well, don't tell them you're helping me—don't tell them about Vikram, either, or they'll think you've lost your mind."

Dina fretted under her breath, producing a mobile phone from a pocket in her robe. They walked deeper into the residential outworks of the New Quarter, past condominiums and apartment buildings modeled on some architect's fever dream of California and painted contrasting shades of salmon and sea green. This was territory Alif rarely visited. The City, Abdullah had once quipped, is divided into three parts: old money, new money, and no money. It had never supported a middle class and had no ambition to do so—one was either a nonresident of Somewhere-istan, sending the bulk of one's salary home to desperate relatives, or one was a scion of the oil boom. Though Alif came from new money on his father's side, he only saw it in driblets. Baqara District felt closer to the truth of things than the pastel oasis around them.

"I want to go home," he said abruptly. "This whole thing is ridiculous. I'll never take our second-rate street for granted again."

Dina gave an unladylike snort.

A breeze had come up from the harbor, exactly timed, as it always was, with the trailing edge of sunset; Alif smelled salt and hot sand. He took a breath. They had to keep moving: he must find a safe place for them to spend the night. He hoped the mosques in the New Quarter, none of which were more than a decade old, were not so posh that they would go against the established custom and turn out travelers. Alif was following this thought into its contingencies when he noticed a man wearing a white *thobe* and sunglasses. It was odd, he mused, to see a man in sunglasses after dark. A moment later the realization kicked in.

"Go," he whispered to Dina, shepherding her around a corner. "Go, go, go."

"What is it?"

"The detective from State."

She whimpered, then clapped a hand over her mouth, following Alif quickly down a street edged in hibiscus bushes. Alif didn't dare look over his shoulder until they had gone several blocks and then doubled back. He paused in the recessed doorway of a women's clothing store that had closed for the evening. Dina flowed in behind him like a shadow, pressing herself against the locked glass door. Alif peered out through a tangle of mannequin legs: there was no one on the street except for a janitor in a dusty uniform, sweeping out the entryway of an apartment building with a broom made of twigs.

"Is he still there?" whispered Dina.

"I think n—"

A loud crack interrupted him. Glancing down, Alif saw a perfectly round hole in the cement facade of the shop, no more than a few centimeters from his left arm. Dina shrieked. Without thinking, he threw himself over her, and they both tumbled to the ground as the glass display window behind them shattered. He felt her breath against his ear and the rise and fall of her chest, and for one vacant instant was pleasantly aroused.

Three more shots hit the storefront. Alif craned his neck: the white-robed detective was across the street, sighting down a pistol as calmly as if he were hailing a cab. He felt Dina struggle underneath him. She rolled, pushed him off, and half-stood. Alif made a grab for her arm.

"Don't, *don't!* Stay down!"

His heart sank as another shot ended not in a crack but in a gasp, and Dina slumped back down to the ground. There was a noise like a feral animal—Alif thought he himself had made it until he saw a tawny shape dislodge itself from the air and knock the detective flat on his back. Shaking, he gathered Dina's unresisting body and hid his face in the folds of her veil, whispering a prayer directed as much to her as to anything divine. He heard a man scream: a high, terrified gurgling sound, and then it was interrupted by the snapping of bone. The screaming ceased. Alif tightened his grip around Dina's limp shoulders.

"Come, children." The voice was sinewy and sated. Alif felt something close around his neck—a set of talons smelling of blood and shit—and found himself wrenched forward, separated from Dina by brute force. Then he was half-flying down the street, taking longer and longer steps until his feet no longer touched the ground at all.

*   *   *

"Give me your arm."

"No! Leave me alone—"

"Girl, listen to Vikram Uncle. That arm wants dressing. If you keep making this pious fuss I will break it off, dress it, and sew it back on."

There was a rustle of fabric. Alif struggled to sit and was immediately assaulted by nausea; with a groan, he lay back down. He neither knew or cared where he was. Turning his head, he saw Dina kneeling next to Vikram with her robe rolled up to her shoulder, exposing one red-brown arm: a bruised, bleeding bullet wound was visible halfway between her shoulder and her elbow. Relief flooded Alif's body, a sensation so intense that he momentarily forgot to be either nauseous or afraid. She lived. She had lived. His eyes stung.

Vikram was holding a pair of tweezers between his long fingers and peering at Dina's wound with an interest that was not absolutely wholesome.

"You can scream," he said. "It's all right." With no further introduction he plunged the tweezers into Dina's arm. She slumped to one side, balling her hands into fists, but made no sound.

"And there it is." Vikram held up a bloodied bullet in the tweezers. "You see that? That is a piece of your robe clinging to it there. The bullet pulled it in. That would have festered and poisoned your blood." He dropped the bullet into a saucepan

92

sitting near his hyperextended knee. "Now we will clean it and stitch it up. You owe me your life, but your virginity will suffice."

"Try it and I'll kill you," muttered Alif.

"Good God, it's awake." Contemptuous yellow eyes regarded him. "You're threatening me? The girl here has more balls than you do. You'd have pissed yourself just now."

Alif sat up and swallowed hard to keep from vomiting. Dina looked at him blankly, eyes glassy with pain. They were back in Vikram's tent, he realized, which was rosy now with light from several glass lanterns set around the base of the arch. He smelled wood smoke somewhere close by. Vikram was bent on his task, swabbing Dina's arm with a wad of white cotton like some demonic nurse. When he was finished he took a curved needle from a box that looked like a pencil case and threaded it.

"This is the worst part," he said. "I think ten stitches. That means twenty needle pricks and some tugging. You really might scream." There was a plaintive note in the last sentence.

Alif looked away. Dina did scream, short panting yelps that made Alif tense in sympathy.

"Little mud-made *beni adam*," said Vikram, seemingly to himself. "Third-born little *beni adam*. Fragile as a fired clay pot, you are. You can look now, brother."

Alif glanced up: Dina's arm was bound expertly in white linen. She tugged the sleeve of her robe down over it with a hand that shook.

"Thank you," she whispered.

"Why did you change your mind?" Alif tried to look at Vikram without fear. "Why did you come to help us?"

Vikram half-smiled, jerking one side of his mouth to reveal a sharp incisor. "My sister says she knows you."

"Knows me?" Alif began to feel nervous. "I would remember meeting someone like her."

"I should think you would. She says you gave her shelter once during a sandstorm."

Alif stared stupidly at Vikram. He opened his mouth, thought better of it, and closed it again.

"I've been through your things," continued Vikram, putting away his instruments. "As it turns out, you're mildly interesting. You didn't tell me you had a copy of the *Alf Yeom*. There are almost none left in the seeing world. Humans aren't supposed to have it. I assume this is one of the copies transcribed by those old Persian mystics? Naughty of you to be carrying it around this way. I could get you a very pretty price for it."

"You mean the book?"

Vikram loped across the tent on all fours. He stopped in front of Alif and gave him a measuring look.

"Are you saying you don't know what this is?" He pulled Intisar's book out of nowhere and tossed it in Alif's lap. "Strange, as someone seems to have annotated it for you."

Alif frowned, looking from the book to Vikram and back. He opened the manuscript gingerly and leafed through it: tucked between the pages were yellow Post-its covered in Intisar's neat, upright script.

"These must be notes for her thesis research," he murmured. "I don't understand. The girl who sent me this told me she never wanted to see me again. Why would she give me something so valuable, especially if she needed it herself?"

Vikram tilted his head to one side in a raptorlike motion. "Perhaps she wanted to keep it out of someone else's hands."

"I guess." Alif held the book up to the light and began to read the first page.

*　*　*

The kingdom of Kashmir was heretofore governed by a king called Togrul. He had a son and a daughter who were the wonder of their time. The prince, called Farukhrus, or Happy Day, was a young hero whose many virtues rendered him famous; Farukhuaz, or Happy Pride, his sister, was a miracle of beauty. In short, this princess was so lovely, and at the same time so witty, that she charmed all the men who beheld her; but their love in the end proved fatal, for the greatest part of them lost their senses, or else fell into languishing and despair, which wasted them away insensibly.

Nevertheless, the fame of her beauty spread through the East, so that it was soon heard at Kashmir that ambassadors from most courts of Asia were coming to demand the princess in marriage. But before their arrival she had a dream that made mankind odious to her: she dreamed that a stag, being taken in a snare, was delivered out of it by a hind and that afterward, when the hind fell into the same snare, the stag, instead of assisting her, fled away. Farukhuaz, when she awoke, was struck with this dream, which she did not regard as the illusion of a wandering fancy but believed that the great Kesaya, an idol worshipped at Kashmir, had interested herself in her fate and would have her understand by these representations that all men are treacherous. They would return nothing but ingratitude for the tenderest affection of women.

*　*　*

"This is weird," said Alif, skimming ahead. "After that the king asks Farukhuaz's nurse to tell her stories that will encourage her to like men and accept one of the foreign princes. It's just a bunch of old tales like *The Thousand and One Nights*."

Dina rose unsteadily and limped toward the mattress where Alif had been sitting. She lay down on it, curling into a fetal position with her wounded arm held tight against her chest.

"What a rare idiot it is," scoffed Vikram. "*The Thousand and One Days* is not just a bunch of old tales, little pimple. That title is no accident—this is the inverse, the overturning of *The Nights*. In it is contained all the parallel knowledge of my people, preserved for the benefit of future generations. This is not the work of human beings. This book was narrated by the djinn."

Chapter Six

Alif insisted on hanging a bolt of cloth across the tent, dividing it into two rough rooms while Dina slept. He woke her from her doze to tell her she could make herself comfortable; she agreed only after he promised not to leave her alone in the tent with Vikram. Alif retreated as she was taking off her shoes, letting the cloth fall behind him. Vikram was sitting in the opposite half of the tent with a thoughtful expression, flexing his bare, lightly furred toes.

"If she's not safe around you, I need to know," said Alif. "I'll be able to tell if you're lying, even if you are a—a different sort of person."

"I have no intention of raping your friend," Vikram said idly, looking out the tent flap at the shuttered marketplace. "If I had, I would have already."

Alif shuddered. Vikram seemed not to notice his revulsion, and lifted his nose as if scenting something in the violet night air.

"You seem to know a lot about the *Alf Yeom*," said Alif after a tentative silence.

"Enough to price it for what it's worth."

"What did you mean about parallel knowledge? What's all this about djinn?"

"Why should it matter to you? This is more talking than I've done in a month. I'm tired of moving my mouth around air instead of meat."

Alif ground his teeth in frustration. "I need to figure this out," he said. "The girl I love could be in serious trouble. I have to find out why it was so important to her that I have this book, even though she's angry at me."

Vikram stretched out his legs and stood. "Perhaps she was worried about being discovered with it. Your censors only know how to do one thing to books."

Alif shook his head. "The censors don't bother with fantasy books, especially old ones. They can't understand them. They think it's all kids' stuff. They'd die if they knew what *The Chronicles of Narnia* were really about."

"Do you read many of these fantasy books, younger brother?"

"They're all I read."

"And do *you* understand them?"

Alif looked up at Vikram sharply. The lower half of his body seemed less terrifying now, a confluence of man and animal familiar to some inherited memory from another age.

"What is it with you and Dina," he said. "It's like you've formed a conspiracy to convince me I'm stupid. Or an atheist."

"You may be both, but that girl is neither. She saw me this afternoon when you were walking in the alley outside my tent. I was trying to sneak up on you. Most of the tribe of Adam can't see us unless we give them permission, you know. The veil is too thick. When your kind walk in the Empty Quarter, all you see is desert."

"That's because the Empty Quarter is a desert," said Alif.

"It is a desert, but it is also a world turned sideways. Djinn country."

"That's just a myth." Alif began to question the wisdom of spending the night in the company of such a person.

"Myth, myth. Who are you to say? Have you ever been to the Empty Quarter?"

"Of course not. Nobody goes there on purpose. There's no water, no shelter. Not even the Bedouin go there."

"Well, there you are. If you've never been there, you can't say you've never run into a djinn in the Empty Quarter. You can only say you've never not run into a djinn in the Empty Quarter."

"Okay, sure, fine, you're right."

"Of course," mused Vikram, oblivious to Alif's noncommittal demeanor, "there were days when the world was crawling with *walis* and prophets who could stare right at us, but that was a long time ago. Now it's different. Now you are more interested in the veil between man and photon than the one between man and djinn."

"Good," muttered Alif, becoming uncomfortable.

"So you say, but you may think differently when you discover all roads of inquiry end in the same place."

"I'm not interested in your back-alley pseudo-*hikma*. I need straight answers."

Vikram yipped—Alif assumed it was meant as a laugh—and walked out through the tent flap.

"That's right, it has a backbone of sorts," he heard Vikram say as he wandered into the dark. "A small one."

Alif listened to his footsteps recede along the alley.

"Well?" came Vikram's voice faintly on the breeze. "Are you coming or not?"

*　　*　　*

Alif had to jog to catch up with Vikram, who had covered more distance than he would have thought possible for a man strolling at such a pace.

"I don't want to leave Dina alone," he said when he reached Vikram's elbow.

"The girl is perfectly safe. Azalel will keep an eye on her—she's lurking around here somewhere. She prefers to walk with the beasts, you know, at night."

Alif felt a burning desire to change the subject.

"About your parallel knowledge. What did you mean by that?"

"I mean that my race is older than yours—we think about the world differently, and we inhabit it at an angle. We remember the Foretime, when it was just us and the angels, and your tribe had not yet been created from earth and blood. So we tell stories differently. Oh, they might look the same on the outside, but they have meanings that are hidden from you, just as we ourselves are hidden."

Alif could already feel his interest flagging. It was like listening to the babbling of a madman in the marketplace; one feigned attention, then moved away as quickly as possible.

"What does all this have to do with the *Alf Yeom?*" he asked.

Vikram sighed.

"Your kind was never meant to read the *Alf Yeom*," he said. "You have your own stories and your own knowledge. You are seen, and we are hidden. That was the way of things ordained by God before He started the clock on this strange universe. But you *banu adam* are always messing with delicate things and transgressing boundaries. At some point, hundreds of years ago, an unscrupulous member of my tribe allowed one of yours to transcribe the *Alf Yeom*—either under duress, or for a handsome favor, depending on which version you believe. Ever since then there have been copies floating around the seeing world. Many were lost over time, thought to be only, as you said, a bunch of old stories. But a few remain. That book you have is one of them."

Alif thought for a moment. A night bird trilled morosely from a nearby hibiscus bush. They had wandered into the oldest part of the souk, silent now except for the occasional domestic sound of an animal in its berth.

"So the stories aren't just stories, is what you're saying. They're really secret knowledge disguised as stories."

"One could say that of all stories, younger brother."

"How do you know so much about this book, anyway?" asked Alif. He was nagged by the suspicion that Vikram was toying with him. "How do you know what these people were thinking?"

Vikram's teeth flashed in the dark. "I paid attention."

By silent consent they began circling back toward the tent. Alif's mind wandered to Princess Farukhuaz in a Kashmir he had never seen, full of palanquin-bearing elephants and men wearing brocade kurtas like the ones in Mughal miniatures. He tried to imagine a time when his parents' marriage might have been seen as something perfectly natural, removing the dark hint of idolatry with which he had been born.

"You don't believe me," observed Vikram.

Alif flushed. "In what sense?"

"You think I am an ordinary man who has gone a little mad. Well, that's what I get for spending so much time hanging around the periphery of the seeing world. There is danger in being seen as too real."

"I don't think you're ordinary," said Alif with a nervous laugh. He did not know how to proceed. His limbs felt heavy, and the atmosphere was suffused with a sense of dislocation; his room and his bed and his computer seemed to be part of a distant world.

Picked out by lamplight, Azalel's shadow passed across a wall of the tent as Alif and Vikram approached. Alif froze, possessed by an emphatic urge to avoid her, especially while her brother was present. Vikram brushed past him. He spoke a few words to Azalel in their own language, and she answered in kind, saying something that made Vikram chuckle. With relief, Alif watched Azalel's shadow slide off the far end of the tent and disappear. He ducked inside. Vikram was cross-legged on the floor, combing his long hair with his fingers.

"Skittish as a young monk!" he said as Alif approached.

"Where's my backpack?" asked Alif, ignoring him.

Vikram produced it from inside his shepherd vest, where it could not possibly have fit, and let it drop on the floor. Alif knelt to unzip the bag: his netbook, wallet, and smartphone were intact, but the two pairs of socks Dina had packed for him were unfolded, and the bag of dates had been liberally foraged over. Alif made a face.

Pulling out the netbook, he logged on and spent twenty minutes breaking into the nearest encrypted WiFi network, the digital province of some New Quarter entrepreneur. The other gray hats who shared his cloud were online and in a panic: where had he been for the past two days? They had each been infected with a keystroke-logging program none of them had ever seen before—did he know what it meant?

Alif felt sweat spring up on his forehead.

"Goddamn it," he muttered.

"Hmm?" Vikram looked over at him, one eyebrow arched.

"He's found Tin Sari," Alif said. An ache had begun in his temples. "He got it off of Intisar's machine, of course, like Abdullah knew he would. He's trying to figure out what it is and how to use it. He's making a hash of it for now, but that will change."

Vikram snatched the netbook out of Alif's hands.

"Plastic and electricity," he said with a look of disgust. "This is how you people think you will ascend to the heavens. But if you climb too high, younger brother, the angels will ask you where you're going."

"Give me that." Alif struggled to take the netbook back from Vikram, who grinned and held on with two fingers.

"How weak your little fleshy hands are. Have you ever done anything with them but type and fondle yourself?"

"Go to hell." With a jerk, Alif succeeded in wrestling the netbook from Vikram's grip. He turned his back, hunching over the keyboard.

"What are you doing now?"

"Opening Intisar's thesis. I put a copy online, in the cloud. Maybe I can figure out why she wanted me to have this book, and what she expects me to do with it."

Alif pulled up the document on his home screen: it was fifty pages, written in Arabic, and titled *Variations of Religious Discourse in Early Islamic Fiction*. He ran a search for Alf+Yeom and found no mention of it until the last ten pages. Frowning, he began to read.

> The suggestion that the Alf Yeom is the work of djinn is surely a curious one. The Quran speaks of the hidden people in the most candid way, yet more and more the educated faithful will not admit to believing in them, however readily they might accept even the harshest and most obscure points of Islamic law. That God has ordained that a thief must pay for his crime with his hand, that a woman must inherit half of what a man inherits—these things are treated not only as facts, but as obvious facts, whereas the existence of conscious beings we cannot see—and all the fantastic and wondrous things that their existence suggests and makes possible—produces profound discomfort among precisely that cohort of Muslims most lauded for their role in that religious "renaissance" presently expected by western observers: young degree-holding traditionalists. Yet how hollow rings a tradition in which the law, which is subject to interpretation, is held as sacrosanct, yet the word of God is not to be trusted when it comes to His description of what He has created.
>
> I do not know what I believe.

* * *

Through his growing confusion, Alif felt pained: why had she never spoken of this to him? Why had she not revealed her spiritual crisis? Clearly the *Alf Yeom* had moved her in some deep and troubling way, yet she had been mute. If there were clues, Alif had failed to pick up on them.

The last few pages of the thesis were a degeneration: stray thoughts and bullet-pointed arguments Intisar had not yet organized into prose. They seemed to have less and less to do with the work itself and more with her own fragmented thoughts, and ended in a series of pseudo-mathematical logic exercises, one of which, written in English, Alif recognized.

GOD=God Over Djinn. GOD=God Over Djinn Over Djinn.
GOD=God Over Djinn Over Djinn Over Djinn.

"Hofstadter," Alif muttered.

"What now?" In the dappled lamplight of the tent, Vikram seemed to have congealed into shadow; Alif had forgotten he was there.

"Douglas Hofstadter," he repeated. "Intisar has one of his recursive algorithms in her thesis. God equals God over djinn. It's a mathematical model in which God sits on an infinite pillar of djinn who hand our questions up and up, and the answers down and down. The joke—or maybe it's serious—is that GOD can never be fully expanded." Alif scratched at a patch of dandruff on his scalp, frowning. "I think I may have lent her that book."

Vikram said nothing. Alif looked up at him and found he had trouble focusing. When he tried to make out Vikram's features his thoughts shimmered, anesthetized as though he was half-awake and remembering a dream. For one disorienting moment he was convinced he had been talking to himself.

"Could you not do that?" he said, closing his eyes. "Whatever it is that you're doing. It's really weird."

"It's not me, it's you," came Vikram's voice. "You're tired. Your mind is getting sick of dealing with things it's taught itself not to see."

Alif did feel tired. He closed the netbook and lay down on his side with one hand over his eyes. The last thing he heard was an exasperated sigh. A blanket unfolded itself over his body. With a feeling of profound relief, Alif wriggled into a more comfortable position beneath it and fell immediately asleep.

* * *

There was the scent of fresh water. A sparkling blue smell, absent any tang of dust, accompanied by a splash and a gasp. Alif opened his eyes. Beneath the hem of the tent he saw two pairs of feet: one a pharaonic red-brown, the other honey-colored, topped by stacks of silver anklets. Rivulets of water ran under them through the dirt. He heard scrubbing sounds, another splash, a woman laughing.

"It's cold!"

Dina's voice. Alif sat up and tilted his head from side to side; his neck was stiff from sleeping on the ground. Azalel was crooning in a low, affectionate warble, like a well-fed house cat, her inarticulate noises arranging themselves in his mind as sentences in a half-remembered language. She was calling Dina her precious child, her brown-limbed little girl who had grown up so well, whom she had loved since she first saw her playing

among the jasmine bushes in her garden. Alif didn't know how
he comprehended Azalel's meaning until, feeling freshly ill, he
remembered that he had understood her when she spoke to him
in his dream.

The maternal caress of her voice aroused him. Racked with
conflicting spasms of shame and desire, Alif turned away. He was
hungry. He fumbled in his backpack for a clean pair of socks and
what was left of the dates. After eating as many of the sticky fruits
as he could stand, he pulled out the *Alf Yeom* and opened it to read,
knowing it would be unwise to leave the tent until the women were
finished bathing. He found the spot where he had left off under one
of Intisar's yellow sticky notes.

*Princess Farukhuaz settled down in her bower, supplied with sweets and
delicacies and rose water with which to bathe her face in the heat of the day,
and prepared to listen to what her nurse had to say. She knew full well that
her father, a kindly but unsubtle man, had sent the nurse to ply her with
stories that would frame her mind toward marriage. But the dream of the
hind and the stag and all it portended was still fresh behind her waking eyes,
and she hardened her heart against any persuasion the nurse might offer.*

*"I'm ready, let's get on with it," she said with a yawn when her nurse
arrived.*

"Ready for what?" the nurse asked innocently.

*"Your stories. You're here to convince me to marry some prince of whom
my father approves. It won't work. I have been given a vision of the true
nature of men, and I shall never subject myself to marriage."*

*"That's as you like," said the nurse. "My stories are stories, not whips to
turn you this way or that."*

"If you say so," said Farukhuaz.

"I do," said the nurse. "Shall we begin?"

Haroon and the Wise Judge of Abouzilzila

Once upon a time in the land the Arabs call Al Gharb, there was a town called Abouzilzila. It was so named because of its frequent earthquakes, brought about by the great traffic of djinn through that area. Abouzilzila was a rocky, mountainous place with many caves. In one of these caves lived a highly respected *hakim* or judge from among the djinn, whose counsel was so sought after that he was often consulted by humans as well as by his own kind.

Abouzilzila was also home to an unfortunate farmer named Haroon. Haroon, never a very clever man, was the frequent butt of pranks by both his djinn and his human neighbors. The humans would leave his laundry in knots and hide his shoes; the djinn would cause his animals to go mad and copulate with mates from inappropriate species. One day, they went too far: Haroon woke to find his new crop of turnips entirely vanished. Since this was a great part of his livelihood, Haroon was fuming with anger and decided to take decisive action. Packing up his elderly mule with supplies for a day's journey, he rode into the mountains and up to the cave in which the wise judge lived. At the threshold, he dismounted, took off his hat, and called out in his most respectful voice:

"Oh, wise judge! I have come from the village below with a terrible case to lay before you and humbly ask your judgment."

"I hear and sympathize," came a voice from inside the cave. "Do go on."

Haroon explained the escalating pranks of which he had been a victim, culminating in the theft of his turnip crop.

"This is indeed a grave matter," said the voice from inside the cave. Haroon thought he glimpsed a pair of yellow eyes floating in the darkness. "One to which I will gladly lend my trifling expertise. Send word to your neighbors and tell them to present themselves tomorrow night at my cave. If they refuse, the wise judge will come and fetch them himself, which will not be pleasant."

Haroon thanked the wise judge profusely and hurried home, rapping at each of his neighbors' doors, in turn, to deliver the judge's message. He did not bother to conceal a note of smug triumph in his voice, nor the look of gloating when he saw the dismay on his neighbors' faces.

With the threat of the wise judge in their minds, Haroon's neighbors, both human and djinn, presented themselves at the entrance to the cave the next evening with the greatest alacrity. Haroon came as well, eager to see for himself what the judge had planned.

As darkness fell, a great creature lumbered out of the cave, one part shadow, one part beast, one part man.

"Here is what you will do," it said. "All of you will spend the night in my cave. At the center of the cave, I have placed a copper vessel housing a terrible night-seeing demon. It can read the thoughts of men and djinn, and will place a mark on the back of the thief. In the morning, we will know without doubt who has stolen Haroon's turnip crop. Haroon and I will spend the night right here at the entrance to make certain no one is tempted to wander off."

The neighbors did as they were told, though each of them quaked with fear as they entered the cave, alarmed by the thought of the demon residing in the large copper kettle they found inside. Haroon bedded down next to his mule, casting furtive glances every now and then at the wise judge, who stood very still and upright all evening, and did not appear to sleep.

In the morning, the judge herded Haroon's neighbors out of the cave. One man, the butcher who lived down the road, lagged behind with an anxious expression. When he finally left the cave, he threw himself at the wise judge's feet—or what passed for feet—and burst into tears. A large black stain was visible on his back.

"Forgive me, wise judge, and forgive me, brother Haroon," he wept. "I have indeed stolen the turnips. It was only a joke. I intended to give them back. That is, I sold them at the market to pay off my gambling debts, but I will repay you."

"Well, Haroon?" said the wise judge. "What would you ask of this man in recompense?"

"The money he received from the sale of the turnips will do," said Haroon, immediately cursing his sense of charity and wishing he had asked for more.

"Very well. Sir, you will surrender your ill-gained profit, and thank the Maker I have not decided to take one of your hands as well, as the law decrees."

The man stuttered an incoherent and relieved thanks, vowing never to molest Haroon again. He returned to the village with Haroon's other neighbors, all of whom were much shaken by the night's events.

"So a mind-reading demon was the secret to your wisdom all along," said Haroon to the wise judge when they had gone. "How fortunate that you possess this magical copper kettle."

"There's no magic to it whatsoever," said the wise judge, with something curiously like a snort. "It's an ordinary kettle. I smeared the walls of the cave with soot. The innocent men slept soundly but the guilty man sat all night with his back pressed against the wall so the demon couldn't mark him."

"Astonishing," said Haroon.

"Whether djinn or man, a wise person need never call on anything more arcane than his wits," said the judge. "Remember that, Haroon, and keep a better eye on your crops."

Haroon returned to his village, satisfied, and from that day on extolled the virtues of the wise judge of Abouzilzila to anyone who would listen, taking care never to reveal the secret of his methods.

"And that," said the nurse, "is why you can never trust your neighbors, and must always read verses against the evil eye when you encounter copper pots."

Princess Farukhuaz raised a delicate eyebrow.

"Surely you've got it wrong, nurse. The moral of the story is that the guilty will always reveal themselves, and that wit is superior to superstition. Clearly by this you mean to convince me not to listen to my dream, and instead take the path of common sense."

"Perhaps you're right," said the nurse. "But a story is a story, and one may glean from it what one likes. Good sense need not enter into it."

"What a bunch of *hagoo*," muttered Alif, closing the book with a snap. The unsettling scent of the resin-covered pages wafted up toward his nose. He felt his face go red and fumbled for his smartphone.

He powered down the device and pried off its outer shell, revealing the battery and SIM card. He slid the latter out with his thumbnail and bent it back and forth until it snapped in half. Then he dug in a side pocket of the backpack, looking for the stash of spare SIM cards he kept hidden in an empty dental floss dispenser.

"Good morning," said Dina, coming into the tent.

"Rosy morning." The Egyptian response came to him automatically after years of listening to her dialect. "Give me your phone and I'll swap out your SIM card. Safer for us that way, since we're obviously being tracked."

He glanced up as she handed him her cell phone: she was wearing a blue cotton robe embroidered in geometric patterns of red and yellow yarn. Instead of her usual veil she had a black scarf wound over her head and face. Her eyes were rimmed in thin lines of kohl.

"You look—" Alif struggled for a word that wouldn't sound ridiculous.

"Like a film extra on the loose? I know. I feel silly." Dina sat down slowly, favoring her wounded arm. "It was all she had, and I've been living in that abaya for two days straight. It's still got some of my blood on it. She offered to wash it for me. Your clothes, too, if you don't mind borrowing some of her brother's."

"I do mind," said Alif, shifting uncomfortably. "I'll stick with what I've got." He bent over the two phones—Dina's was an older model, without a touch screen, encased in one of the girlish pink skins that were fashionable—and installed a new SIM card in each.

"Dial seven eights," he said when he was finished, handing Dina back her phone. "When you hear a beep, enter whatever phone number you'd like to use. Make it something you'll remember. Then hit *pound* and hang up."

Dina made an incredulous noise. "How do you set all this stuff up?" she asked. "This is crazy."

"This isn't my grid," said Alif. "I don't do phones much. I just know people who do."

He glanced at her again, furtively, as he closed his smartphone. Dina seemed unruffled in her borrowed robe, as cool and self-possessed as a native tribeswoman. Only her arm, held at a tender angle against her body, belied the shock she had endured.

"How is it?" he said, gesturing to her right side.

"God be praised," she answered. There was a half-note of exhaustion in her voice. It was enough to trigger all his protective instincts, and he made her sit down, fussing around her with the blanket he had slept under until she fended him off with her good arm.

"I'm hurt," she said, "not disabled. You make me feel like someone's grandmother."

"You were *shot*, for God's sake. You've got to rest. I—"

He stopped when Azalel slipped in with a copper tray of tea things and bowls of minted yogurt. Her face was concealed beneath a cream-colored veil held in place by an elaborate chain circlet of some dark metal; her robe, a pagan shade of saffron, failed to hide the curve of her hip. Unable to speak, Alif backed away from her without a word, ignoring Dina's curious expression. Azalel seemed amused by his discomfort. She turned and walked back through the tent flap, glancing at Alif over her shoulder with a look that went straight to his groin. He sat down hastily.

"Tea?" asked Dina, reaching with her left hand for the steaming kettle on the tray. Alif blessed her discretion.

"Let me get that," he said. "You take it easy." He poured two glasses and set one of the bowls of yogurt in front of her. They ate in silence punctuated by the sipping of tea, staring pensively past each other into middle space. Alif felt as though he should take charge and announce some kind of plan that did not involve continued reliance on the hospitality of Vikram the Vampire. He cursed Abdullah and his wild ideas. Clearly they had exchanged one kind of trouble for another. And Azalel—Alif banished her from his thoughts.

"Good, it's awake." Vikram appeared before them, framed by sunlight as he stooped to enter the tent. "How did it sleep? And how is little sister's arm?"

"My arm is fine," said Dina in a cold voice.

Vikram sat down next to Alif and helped himself to tea.

"Here is what we are going to do," he said. "We are going to take your copy of the *Alf Yeom* to a well-connected *gori* I know and see if she can trace it. There aren't many left, and how your woman came by it might tell you something about her motives. We'll also shake off all the tails you have collected, one of which is even now skulking at the corner of the alley, waiting for you to appear. Then we will talk about getting you and little sister safely out of the City."

"Wait a minute, wait a minute." Alif felt his face go hot. "I wasn't consulted about any of this. What *gori*?"

"An American."

"No. No way. I don't want foreigners involved in my business. Djinn are one thing but I draw the line at Americans."

"Foreigners," snorted Vikram. "Neither of you are properly native. You are obviously a wretched mongrel, and little sister, unless I miss my guess, is Egyptian."

"Whatever. The point is I don't want to talk to this friend of yours, and I'm not leaving the City until I know Intisar is safe."

"I don't want to leave the City at all," said Dina, clutching her bad arm. "This has gone far enough."

"Suit yourselves. You'll be in a State political prison within the week. And for little sister here, I think we know how particularly unpleasant that will be." Vikram raised one arched black brow. "She'll wish she'd given it to me after all. At least I would have made it good for her."

Dina gasped.

"What the hell is wrong with you?" Alif snapped. "Don't you dare talk like that in front of her."

With a laugh, Vikram stood. "What a prickly little monk it is. I'm only telling the truth." He stepped out of the tent into the intensifying sun. "Gather your things, children, we're leaving."

Alif spat an insult at the tent flap. Dina was sitting with her knees drawn up and her eyes down, silent.

"I'm sorry," said Alif, clenching and unclenching his hands. "We'll get out of here. This was a mistake. He's not a—he's not—"

"No." Dina looked at him. "We should do what he says. It's too late to change the plan now."

Alif jerked his backpack over one shoulder. "I just feel like this whole thing is getting out of control."

"We live in a city run by an emir from one of the most inbred families on earth, where a few censors can throw someone in jail for writing things on the Internet and falling in love with the wrong person." Dina reached out to be helped to her feet. "It went out of control a long time ago."

Alif lifted her by the hand and held on as she got her balance. "It's not like you to be so philosophical," he said.

She tilted her head. "How do you know?"

An impatient growl from outside the tent made them both jump. Alif hurried out, inwardly chastising himself for failing to show Vikram more resistance, more nerve. Dina followed behind him.

"You can stay behind if you prefer," Vikram said to her. "That arm is tender and we are going to do a lot of walking."

"I do not prefer." Dina's chin shot up beneath her black scarf.

"Very well." Vikram padded down the alley on his silent, unshod feet. "Stay close behind me. I am going to play a little trick on our friend in plainclothes up ahead."

Alif peered over Vikram's shoulder: at the end of the alley was a short, husky man with a mustache, wearing a polo shirt that clung in the heat and slacks that poorly concealed the pistol bulging in his waistband. To his horror, he saw the man turn and begin walking toward them, mouth set in a grim line.

"Vikram—"

"Calmly, calmly."

The man's hand went to the bulge in his slacks. "You two," he said. "Stop there. Set down the backpack."

Alif froze. Vikram loped straight up to the man, who did not appear to notice him.

"These are not the *banu adam* you're looking for," he said.

The man blinked. His face went placid and slack, as though he had recalled some pleasant memory. He smiled.

"Quickly now, children," said Vikram, loping onward. "This trick wears off pretty fast."

Aghast, Alif stumbled to obey. He heard Dina stifle a giggle. When they had turned the corner and emerged into a larger thoroughfare of the souk, she began laughing in earnest.

"Dina!" Alif had never heard her laugh in public; had, in fact, heard her censure women who did.

"I can't, I can't help it." She bent forward, pressing the wounded arm to her midsection, her laughter ending in squeaks. Vikram looked pleased with himself. He began humming a *raga* appropriate to the hour of the day, interweaving it with some strange feral tune Alif didn't recognize, until the music was one hybrid melody, without form, without origin, trailing along the street on motes of dust.

Chapter Seven

They were deep within the New Quarter before Alif thought about getting nervous.

"I don't want to see this *gori*," he said, lagging behind as Vikram galloped past the sterile edifice of a fast-food outlet. "Can't we keep the book to ourselves? You seem to know everything about it anyway. Why do we need to go dragging Americans into the whole thing?"

"A boy as stupid as you shouldn't do so much thinking. I know plenty about the *Alf Yeom* but nothing about this particular copy. The American is a sort of book scientist—if you're serious about wanting to know where your lady friend got the manuscript, and where it originated, and you aren't simply wasting my time, she may be able to help. You'll hate her. She wears the most awful-looking polyester robes, like a country housewife who has given up on herself. These western sisters never know how to dress. It's all exotic costumes to them."

Sullen, Alif ground his molars, feeling too hot and too tired for such an early hour.

"Does this convert have a name?"

"Most probably." Vikram halted in front of a trim, freshly painted apartment complex with wide glass doors, attended by a defeated-looking provincial man in a dirty turban.

"Here we are," he said, and twisted inside as the turbaned doorman held the glass door wide for a girl whose black veil was patterned in rhinestones. Alif and Dina shuffled in after him, flinching under the doorman's malevolent squint. Inside was a cool marble-tiled lobby lined with a bank of elevators. The Arab residents who whisked in and out regarded Alif with blank disregard, making him feel unwashed and shabby and too dark; the smattering of pale foreign professionals regarded him not at all, chatting to each other with dogged good nature in voices two octaves too high.

Following Vikram with downcast eyes, Alif found himself in the entranceway of an apartment on the tenth floor—how, he was not entirely sure; Vikram had entered without appearing to produce a key. Dumbly, Alif fixed on the one feature of the well-appointed living room that was most familiar: a Toshiba laptop, a three-year-old model by the look of it; probably no more than two gigs of RAM. A vinyl decal of the crescent and star—something only a westerner could conceive of or get away with—was plastered on the lid. Alif gazed at the machine with mild contempt.

The woman sitting behind it seemed nervous, looking from Vikram to Alif to Dina with pallid, flickering eyes. She wore a head scarf rather than a veil. One lock of blonde hair had escaped it and lay simmering against her forehead.

Vikram disconcerted her by asking for her hand in marriage as soon as they walked through the door.

"You could do much worse," he was saying now. "And probably will. I know what happens to you foreign women—your own men have forgotten how to treat you, so you fall into the arms of the first brown man who gives you a compliment. Since you are a converted sister, he will have to prefix that compliment with a *bismillah*, but otherwise he will be just the same."

"This is very rude," said the convert. Her Arabic was foreshortened, accented. Vikram waved his hand dismissively.

"You enjoy it. Otherwise you would never allow me to drop in on you like this." He ran a finger along the edge of her hand. Alif was shocked when she made no effort to pull away or rebuke him. "I've made a study of you. A convert may be forgiven all her prior sins, but she does not forget them, does she. She still misses the feel of a man."

"For God's sake!" Dina's eyes flashed. "Ridiculous animal! You're not fit to be among people."

The convert looked pained but said nothing. She seemed afflicted by a kind of ambivalence that Alif could not place, and it made him uneasy. He roused himself, realizing it fell to him to defend the honor of this woman in whom he had no stake.

"Apologize," he ordered Vikram. "You are deeply sorry, and you beg her forgiveness."

"Thank you," said the convert, without quite looking Alif in the eye.

Vikram grinned, leaning back in his faux-French brocade armchair, one of several that adorned the convert's apartment. A bristling landscape of steel and glass was visible outside the window behind him, stretching toward the oil fields in the west.

"I am deeply sorry, and I beg your forgiveness," he said. "But I've only spoken the truth."

The convert leaned against her desk, rubbing her temples like an old woman.

"What did you come here to ask me," she questioned in a monotone.

Vikram gestured toward Alif's backpack, which sat on the parquet floor near his feet.

"Show her," he said.

Alif unzipped the bag and pulled out Intisar's book, careful not to put stress on the binding as he lifted it free. The convert sat straighter.

"What's that?"

"This," said Vikram triumphantly, "is a genuine copy of the *Alf Yeom*. See, now you do forgive me."

"Forgive you? I believe you not." The convert stepped out from behind her desk and knelt to take the book from Alif. She opened it on her knees, skimming the text with a slim index finger. Her nails, Alif noticed, were bitten raw.

"Paper," she murmured. "Real paper. Not parchment. Bound by hand. Some kind of pasting here, too. What a smell."

"We can talk in English if you prefer," said Alif.

"Oh, God, really?" The convert looked up at him, relief evident on her face. "Awesome. Thank you. My Arabic is so—I understand pretty well, but when I talk I sound like an idiot." She looked back down at the book. "This is amazing. Just amazing.

It's sewn into the binding with silk thread, see? That's how it's lasted so well. I think that smell is from some kind of preservative resin, but it's not one I've ever seen before." She bent over the book once more, tracing the letters that curled from right to left and sounding out each word in a way that was at once childlike and elderly.

"Are you an expert in books?" Alif knew his own spoken English, a mottled interplay of Anglo-Indian and Arab accents, sounded strange. He could read and write the language well enough, but avoided speaking it when he could. Dina watched in silence. She had given up on English several years earlier, since she could not seem to speak it without resorting to Urdu loan words every time she forgot something. It came from living in Baqara District, where the residents were mostly subcontinental. Urdu and English, she said, went in the same category of foreignness in her mind, and she found it difficult to separate them.

"Not an expert yet, no," said the convert, interrupting Alif's thoughts. "But I study history and I like books. I came here to get my PhD in archival science."

"At Al Basheera?"

"Yes—in the American University exchange program." The convert had a self-conscious grin. "I know, I know. Classic *ajnabi*. Go to an exciting new country to hang out with people just like you." She blinked myopically, hunching over the *Alf Yeom* as if to protect it with her body. Alif wondered what she thought of Vikram's improbable knees. He'd drawn himself into a kind of half-lotus, looking particularly demonic against the tawdry brocade of his chair.

"She can't quite see me as I am," he said. "It's an American quirk. Half in, half out. A very spiritual people, but in their hearts they feel there is something shameful about the unseen. You'd be right at home there, younger brother."

Alif was startled by the precision with which Vikram had guessed his thoughts. Perhaps he had been staring too openly.

"That's not fair," said the convert in English. "We're really not that bad." She looked at Alif for support. "He does this to me because I tried to psychoanalyze him once for an article. I was so fascinated by the idea that a back-alley fixer from the souk thinks he's Vikram the Vampire. So I tracked him down. And now I can't get rid of him."

Alif caught Dina's eye. Her expression mirrored his discomfort.

"I am Vikram the Vampire," said Vikram.

"Then you're very well-preserved for a two-thousand-year-old Sanskrit legend," the convert said tartly.

"What about this book?" prompted Dina. The convert flushed and rippled through several pages of the manuscript.

"Well, if it's real, it's extraordinary," she said. "The general consensus is that *The Thousand Days* were made up by a seventeenth-century Frenchman named de la Croix. He was trying to cash in on the *Arabian Nights* craze. He was commissioned to study in the Orient by Louis XIV—the *Roi Soleil,* the Sun King. And when the Sun King gives you marching orders, you march. He had to come back with something spectacular. So he brought home a canon of stories he claimed were dictated to him by Persian dervishes who, in turn, had heard them from the djinn. That part's nonsense, of course. But the consensus is that he was lying about the whole thing, and never met with any Persian mystics at all."

"That's not the consensus," said Vikram. "That's the consensus of academics."

The convert made a sour face.

"You said this Frenchman claimed to have heard the stories from the Persians," said Dina, "but our book is in Arabic."

"After the Muslim conquest, Arabic became a scholarly language throughout the Persian empire," said the convert. "It could be that whoever wrote these stories down saw them as some kind of advanced knowledge, appropriate only for sheikhs and learned people, and so recorded them in Arabic rather than Persian."

"Data encryption," murmured Alif.

"I'm sorry?"

"Nothing."

"This all presumes one thing," continued the convert, tapping the spine of the book. "Namely, that the manuscript is an original, and not an eighteenth- or nineteenth-century translation from the French or even the English version. It happens, you know—one culture invents something and claims it's from somewhere else, and then the people of somewhere else adopt it as their own. History is full of palimpsests like that."

Alif felt strangely insulted. "Intisar believed it was an original," he said. "She wrote like she was certain of it."

"Who is Intisar?"

"The young man's young woman," said Vikram. "She's the one who sent him the manuscript."

The convert shrugged her shoulders. "It's possible she was mistaken. If this is the genuine article, it's the first Arabic edition ever to surface in a hundred years of scholarship on the subject."

"Western scholarship," Vikram interjected.

"I beg your pardon, but is there any other kind? I mean, aside from the City, the Arabian Peninsula has been an intellectual black hole since the Saudis sacked Mecca and Medina way back in the 1920s. Palestine is a wreck, so there goes the scholarly tradition of Jerusalem. Ditto Beirut and Baghdad. North Africa still hasn't recovered from the colonial era—all their universities are in the pockets of autocrats and westernized socialists. Persia is up to its neck in revolutions. If there's any native scholarship on the *Alf Yeom*, it'd be the first I've heard of it."

Silence followed the convert's pronouncement. Dina fidgeted restlessly with her sleeve, looking at no one. Alif struggled with a rising dislike for the woman sitting across from him. She looked unmoved. Touched by a faint, sour breeze coming through the window, the edge of her lavender head scarf fluttered against her chair like a flag.

False colors, thought Alif.

"Look, I don't mean to be a buzz kill," said the convert, trying again to catch Alif's eye. "I'm just—if this is real, I'd be surprised. That's all." She straightened a little in her chair.

"You've made me look foolish in front of my young friends," Vikram said. Something in his voice made Alif look up in alarm. "I don't thank you for that."

"I'm sorry!" The convert dabbed sweat off her brow with the back of one hand. "I didn't mean to. You brought this book to me and I've given you my opinion. It looks at least a hundred and fifty years old—it's not a modern forgery or anything—but unless we can prove for certain that it predates de la Croix's French edition, all we know is what has already been agreed upon."

"How can we discover exactly how old it is?" Alif asked in careful English.

The convert sighed. "I could take a sample of the paper and look at it in our archival forensics lab—that's a fancy way to say 'under a microscope.' The way wood pulp is processed into paper has changed a lot over the centuries. That would give us a good idea. Then I can work on figuring out how your friend got her hands on it in the first place."

"I wish I could just speak to her," said Alif, half to himself. "I wish I could just ask her why she sent this to me and what she expects me to do."

"Why can't you?"

An impassioned refusal to tell the convert anything was forming itself in his mind when he was struck by a realization.

"I can," he said. "My God, I can. Hollywood is gone. There's nothing to stop her from writing to me if she wants—I could make a new e-mail address, get on some public network. She has to speak to me now." Forgetting his animosity, he turned to the convert with eagerness.

"Could you get us into one of the computer labs at Al Basheera?"

"Yeah, sure—"

"That's a bad idea," said Vikram. "Basheera is upper-crust territory. I can handle one or two fat State security agents, but not tens of them, and not in a closed space. If Alif is asked for his ID at the gate, that will be the end of it."

"Don't go," said Dina anxiously.

"You're forgetting something." The convert flashed an ironic little smile. "You'll have the ultimate escort: a white American with a blue passport. No one is going to ask you for your ID. In fact, no one is going to remember you were ever there."

*　*　*

It took nearly half an hour to convince Dina to stay behind at the convert's apartment and rest. She was anxious not to be left alone. Only after Alif swore to call her every half hour did she agree to take a couple of ibuprofen and lie down on the couch. When she was settled, Alif and Vikram followed the convert down a set of service stairs that led to an alley behind the apartment complex. The alley, Alif noticed, was better kept than his own street in Baqara District; the bags of garbage were discreetly confined to wooden stalls and dumpsters, the ground recently repaved.

The convert led them around the far edge of the apartment building and into a busy street. Alif saw a McDonald's and an American coffee franchise with a round money-green logo, incongruous against the dusty view of the Old Quarter glimmering on a rise in the distance. There was a scent in the air like newly minted paper. He sidled a glance at Vikram: the man looked solemn and preoccupied. His expression was so human that Alif felt suddenly insecure, wishing back his predatory confidence, needing it to bolster against their sanitized surroundings.

"Let's get a taxi," said the convert.

"Will they take us together? We're obviously not related." Alif looked dubiously at the convert's pink skin.

"In the New Quarter they will. They're used to foreigners doing all kinds of weird things here." The convert stepped into the stream of cars, bicycles, and mopeds and raised one arm. A black-and-white cab drew up alongside her.

"You get in front, Alif," murmured Vikram.

Alif obliged, wincing as he lowered himself onto the overheated vinyl seat next to the driver, a Sikh man whose yellow turban brushed the underside of the roof. Climbing in through the back door, the convert gave him directions in accented but passable Punjabi. They sped off into the white glare of midday traffic.

"Wait—where's Vikram?" The convert turned to look out the back window, dismayed. Alif felt the same needling dysphoria he had experienced the night before, when Vikram was like a word he once knew or an errand he had forgotten to run, facts just beyond the pale of memory.

"I think—I think he's meeting us there," Alif said, though why he thought so he did not know. He shook his head to clear it. Half in, half out.

"But he doesn't know where we're going! This is ridiculous." The convert gave a forced little sigh and leaned back into the seat cushions, which groaned in agreement. Alif shrugged.

"Vikram knows everything."

"Do you believe him? I mean about what he is?" The convert's eyes were narrow in the rearview mirror.

"I don't know what I believe."

"If you don't know, it means you think there's a possibility that he is actually an evil spirit."

"Evil?" Alif turned to look at her. "You think so?"

129

"Ha! You really believe him, don't you."

The corners of Alif's mouth twitched. He thought of half a dozen veiled insults, and despite himself, the worst one came out.

"Why did *you* become Muslim?" He found himself elongating the pronoun with a hostile sneer, forgetting for a moment that he shared some of her foreignness, some of her skepticism.

The convert seemed unsurprised by his implication. "Islam was presented to me as a system for social justice," she said carefully. "I converted in that spirit."

"God never came into it, then."

"Well, of course *God* came into it, but as a—as an—"

"A side issue? A thought experiment? Or something for one of your papers?"

The convert jerked as though she'd been slapped. "That's not fair," she said in a quieter voice. "That is really, really not fair."

Alif felt chastened. Thinking of Dina and what she might say to him if she were there, the feeling deepened to shame too heavy for an apology. He turned his burning face toward the window: they were speeding through the indifferent neighborhoods between the New and Old Quarters. Baqara District was not far away. If he leaped out at this street corner, he could reach his house in a fifteen-minute walk. As the cab slowed for a passing microbus, Alif actively considered it. The frantic confusion of the last two days was settling into something else: a malaise, a desire for nothing more than to sleep in his own bed, even if it meant waking up to the police. Was not capture inevitable anyway? Alif could think of no other dissident, religious or political, who had successfully evaded State. He was no different—no smarter, no better equipped.

The cab jerked forward again. Alif watched regretfully as familiar streets slid away one after the other. The convert's silence was becoming oppressive. He unzipped his backpack and removed the *Alf Yeom* once more, thumbing through the delicate pages until he found his place.

Once upon a time, the king of the birds had an urgent message to impart to the prince of the salamanders. A great wave had been spotted by his lieutenants at sea, and the bird king, eager to curry favor wherever he could, thought to warn the prince of salamanders of this threat to his people. There was only one obstacle: custom prevented birds from speaking directly to salamanders. The bird king couldn't possibly relay his message to the salamander prince himself, or even send another bird as intermediary; to do so would go against all good form and propriety.

"What to do?" the bird king asked his wisest vizier.

"If I might make a suggestion," said the vizier—who was a large black grackle, "perhaps your majesty might consider sending an emissary from among the insects. We can speak to them, after all. A hearty dragonfly, or even a locust, is almost as good as a bird."

"A tremendous idea," said the bird king. "Send for the commandant of insects at once."

The commandant of insects was delighted to receive an invitation from the king of birds, and arrived with all haste.

"Tell the prince of salamanders to warn his people," he told the commandant. "A great wave is coming from out at sea and if they do not move their burrows they will surely drown."

"Never fear," said the commandant. "I will send my speediest wasp to communicate your message."

Back at his palace, however, the commandant of insects was distraught. Insects could no more speak to salamanders than birds could—such a thing was shocking even to consider.

"What to do?" he asked his wisest vizier—who was a heavy-looking bumblebee.

"If I might make a suggestion," said the vizier, "why not send a messenger from among the crustaceans? A stalwart lobster, or even a crab, is almost as good as an insect."

"Famous," said the commandant. "Send for the premier of crustaceans at once."

The premier arrived as soon as he was able.

"With all good speed," said the commandant, "send someone from among your people to warn the salamanders that a great whale is coming in from the sea, and if they don't hurry, it will surely be beached upon their burrows."

The premier agreed to do so. But as soon as he arrived home, he collapsed in distress. It was impossible to conceive of a crustacean stooping so low as to speak to a salamander.

"What to do?" he asked his vizier—who was a fat-clawed crayfish.

"If I might make a suggestion," said the vizier, "why not send a go-between from among the turtles? A clever leatherback, or even a box turtle, is almost as good as a crustacean."

"Fantastic," said the premier. "Send for the chairman of turtles at once."

The chairman was delighted by the invitation, and arrived that very day.

"Make it a priority," said the premier. "Send someone from among your people to warn the salamanders that a great wind is coming in from the sea, and if they don't take care, they'll miss their chance to harvest all the debris it will blow upon the shore."

The chairman promised to do so at once. The salamanders were great allies of his people. He went himself to dine with the prince of salamanders.

"By the way," he told him, "the king of birds told the commandant of insects to tell the premier of crustaceans to tell me to tell you that a great window of opportunity has arrived for your people, and if they don't hurry down to the sea, they'll miss it."

The salamander prince was delighted by this news, thinking perhaps a merchant ship had been wrecked and spilled its treasures upon the beach, or perhaps a tasty dolphin carcass had washed up on the shore. He hurried down to the sea with his people, who were promptly drowned by the great wave, which had just come crashing in from out at sea.

"And that," said the nurse, "is why crustaceans and salamanders are no longer on speaking terms."

Princess Farukhuaz frowned.

"You mean that is why one should never let antiquated custom stand in the way of progress, or why one should never send a third party to relay information better communicated in person," she said.

"Oh, well, yes, that, too," said the nurse.

"Dear nurse, much as I love you, you are terribly muddled when it comes to the morals of stories."

"Dear child, some stories have no morals. Sometimes darkness and madness are simply that."

"How terrible," said Farukhuaz.

"Do you think so? I find it reassuring. It saves me from having to divine meaning in every sorrow that comes my way."

Alif came to with a start. He frowned, wondering at what point he had fallen asleep. The pages beneath his fingers were beginning to pucker with sweat; hastily, he closed the book and put it away in his backpack. The cab was circling up toward one of the ancient gates in the Old Quarter wall. He glanced at the convert in the rearview mirror: she was leaning against the car door on one elbow, frowning out the window.

"You must know the Old Quarter very well by now," he hazarded, "Better than most foreigners."

She said nothing.

"Your Punjabi is also very good. I barely speak any at all."

"For God's sake, don't make it worse."

Mortified, Alif slumped in his seat until the rearview mirror reflected only off-white sky. They passed through the Old Quarter wall—a mundane color in the midday light—and rattled on to cobbled roads lined with gracious stone houses. Wooden shutters over the windows protected the residents from the staring of passersby. Here and there, low-slung harem balconies extended out over the street, their latticed arches reminders of a time when architectural mercies were the extent of an aristocratic woman's public life.

The cab shuddered to a halt at the western edge of the Al Basheera campus. The buildings here were modern: glass boxes designed by some French architect with a perverse sense of humor who, now that women were permitted to attend the university, apparently desired to put them on display. Classes were in session. Students went in and out of the glass doors in tight groups, the foreign ones visible as clots of bare skin against the uniform banner of *thobes* and veils. A lone *chaiwallah* hawked his milk tea from a cart drawn up alongside the glass edifice, making him look shabbier and it more pretentious than either could hope to do alone.

"Let's go." Straightening her head scarf, the convert stepped out of the cab. Alif was gratified when she let him pay—if she was really angry, he reasoned, she would have tried to pay herself. He followed her toward the nearest building: outside were two security guards flanking a metal detector, searching students and their bags as they went inside. Alif felt adrenaline bloom in his body.

"This is where it gets tricky," the convert muttered. She pushed back her shoulders. "Give me your backpack. It's too nice for a menial."

"Excuse me?"

"Just give it to me for a minute. I'll give it back."

Frowning, Alif handed the convert his backpack. She slung it over one shoulder.

"Okay. Now look like a bored, downtrodden migrant worker." The convert strode confidently up to the younger of the two guards, her passport in hand.

"Excuse me," she said in English, with an exaggerated, high-pitched American accent, "I'm so sorry, but my driver left his keys downstairs when he came to pick me up—can we run back in and get them?"

The guard leered at her. "You are Muslim?"

"Il hamdulilah."

"You looking nice Muslim husband?"

"Inshallah." With a modest, downcast smile, the convert walked through the metal detector. Alif shuffled after her, not daring to look either guard in the eye. No one stopped him. When he glanced over his shoulder, the guards were rummaging lazily through a veiled woman's large Prada bag. No tension shadowed their faces; no indication that they had even noticed him. He was simply a rich woman's accessory.

"Well, well," came a voice at his ear. "You do have a talent or two of the hidden folk."

Alif brightened. Vikram bobbed along beside him as they made their way down the hall. The students hurrying to and from classrooms swerved around him without looking.

"Did you see that?" The convert bustled toward them, flushed with triumph. "Wasn't I right? They didn't even ask for your ID! They—"

She stopped short when she noticed Vikram. He grinned at her wolfishly.

"How did *you* get in here?" she demanded.

"Through that door, the same as you did."

The convert drew a breath as though preparing for a retort. Instead, she let it out again and turned away.

"Fine. Whatever. I don't want to know. The lab is down this way." She let Alif's backpack drop at his feet. He shouldered it and followed her. At the end of the hall was a glass-enclosed room with modish recessed lighting and row upon row of flat-screened monitors, about half of which were in use. Along the wall were workstations with embedded clusters of electrical outlets and data ports. The scent of working metal and the whir of machines greeted Alif as the convert opened the door. He sighed with sheer joy, quickening his steps to catch the door before it swung shut behind her.

Vikram chuckled as he slid into the lab in Alif's wake.

"So happy to see so much dead wire. Tell me, younger brother, do you get this excited about living flesh? I will judge you on your answer."

"I don't care," said Alif. He tossed his backpack onto a chair at an empty workstation. "And it's not dead. It's just another kind of alive." He took out his netbook and examined the data ports in the wall.

"TNova," he said reverently. "They've got TNova. The connection speed is so fast that a Web site practically loads before you've had time to type the whole address."

"Well, I'm glad you like it. They jacked up tuition to pay for this place." The convert stood over him with her hands on her hips, looking mollified. "If you give me the book, I'll take it down to the archival science department. I'll have to take paper samples, but I'll make them as small as I can."

Alif extracted the book from his pack and handed it to her.

"Be careful," he fretted.

The convert sniffed. "You should be careful. You're the one who's lugging it around in the heat and the dust like a high school biology textbook." She tucked the manuscript under her arm and turned to go.

"Thank you," said Alif to her retreating back. She didn't answer. He pursed his lips in frustration.

"Don't worry about it," said Vikram, crouching at his feet. "I'm sure you haven't been more of an ass than usual."

"You're the ass," Alif muttered. He plugged in his netbook and waited for it to identify the TNova connection. Five muscular bars appeared at the top of his screen, alongside a megabytes-per-second ratio among the highest he'd ever seen. Within a few clicks he was inside the cloud. It hummed with information, half-finished programs posted for feedback, jokes written in code—the electrical thoughts of isolated people. Alif felt his shoulders relax. All problems are simply interruptions in the transmission and preservation of data, he reminded himself. He had been projecting needless fear and anxiety onto his situation: he must stay calm and rationally eliminate the barriers between himself and his return to normal life, one by one.

As he studied the cloud's community portal, his serenity evaporated. On an ordinary day data turnover in the cloud was rapid, but Alif saw that many of his friends' posts were several days old. Some had logged on only to leave cryptic messages in leetspeak, many of which were directed at him.

On 26/10 at 18:44:07, Gurkhab0ss *left you a message*:
Alif u fuk were getting pwned where are u
On 27/10 at 00:17:35, Keffiyagiddan *left you a message*:
pwned pwned pwned

"Shit," said Alif. A blinking chat box opened in the bottom right corner of his screen.

NewQuarter01: Alif?

Alif stifled a cry of surprise. After his dramatic retirement, NewQuarter had disappeared off the face of the blogosphere and was now spoken of only in terms of hushed awe and contempt. Some said he had been arrested, others that he didn't have the stomach for real danger. Alif had remained aloof and cultivated no opinion, ashamed that he could feel abandoned by someone he had never met.

A1if: NQ! Thought youd gone 4ever

NewQuarter01: I have. Im a ghost now. Ur speaking to the dead.

A1if: . . .

NewQuarter01: U need to tell me how to stop this program the Hand nicked from ur comp. EveryI keeps getting reinfected.

A1if: Can't sweep for malware and delete?

NewQuarter01: New delivery method evry day. Homograph attacks on some of our own sites. Can't keep up w/the tricky bstard. With u gone everybdy's panicking. Ur friend RadioSheikh even called me on the damn phone. STupid.

A1if:: He told u it was my program?

NewQuarter01: Yes. Dont be mad. Too late for mad. Now focus on fix.

A1if: Can't fix.

NewQuarter01: Wat u mean can't fix? U wrote the damn thing.

A1if: I don't know how it wrks, NQ. It shouldn't wrk the way it does. I don't understand.

NewQuarter01: wat the hell u saying?

A1if: Saying can't fix.

NewQuarter01: Wat is this bullshit? Im supposed 2b RETIRED u understand

A1if: dunno wat to say. im sorry. wrking on fix IRL.

NewQuarter01: were talking about *comp* issue Alif, is no fix In Real Life.

A1if: this is different. something else going on IRL. Wrking on it.

NewQuarter01: whtvr. all i can say is if this gets really bad u better do the right thing. U know what im talking abt.

A1if: *i know.*
NewQuarter01 is now offline.

Alif ran his fingers through his hair and tightened them until he could feel tension against his scalp.

"Shit, shit, *shit.*"

Several students turned to shoot him looks of near-identical disgust. Alif hunched his shoulders and ignored them. A hissing cackle came from beneath his desk, where Vikram had somehow managed to cram himself.

"Listen to this foul language. Were you raised in a brothel?"

"Would you get out from under there?"

"No."

Alif ground his teeth and opened up a new browser window. Logging on to a large, generic Web mail provider, he created a new e-mail address using a random string of letters and numbers. When he typed Intisar's address in the "To" field of a blank message, an unexpected rush of tenderness overcame him. To think that she might be nearby—that she might be in class at this very moment, or shopping at one of the small boutiques they had passed in the cab—was too much for his rational mind. He felt himself disappear into his heart and guts, ignoring the risk of detection and capture that even this anonymous contact would pose. *Hayam,* his mother would call it: love that stumbles over the earth in broken ecstasy.

He remembered a thousand things at once: the subtle turns of phrase that convinced him she was different in the same way he was different, that she had a superior mind and fought the same internal battles against the monotonous demands of daily life. There was not

140

one e-mail from her that he had not read a dozen times over, not one pretty compliment, delivered with just the right level of modest reserve, that he could not recall. No other woman had ever flattered him. Occasionally his mother would propose one or another of the dull-eyed neighborhood girls as a potential match, but when Alif met them they inevitably responded to his nervous, polite questions with one-word answers and he would leave feeling depressed. With Intisar it was different. She had pursued him as passionately as he pursued her, employing a kind of arch, feminine elusiveness that made her interest all the more maddening. He had, despite himself, been intrigued by her wealth. He spent so much time deriding the elite online that his relationship with Intisar seemed doubly transgressive, and the idea that a girl—a woman—with money wanted him was not unwelcome to his ego.

The need to see her again overwhelmed all other considerations. *3:30 pm at the chaiwallah's in the new campus,* he wrote. *I love you.*

He hit *send* before giving himself time to think. Pushing his chair back from the workstation, he stretched, nervous muscles shuddering in his arms and legs. He had two and a half hours until the appointed time. Hunching back over his netbook, he ran a query for de la Croix on a black hat-built search engine. The first few results were about a nineteenth-century painter; he discarded these. He clicked on an entry labeled *Les Mille et Un Jours*:

Having worked six full months on the Shahnama, together with Mullah Kerim, the extreme dedication made me fall into an illness lasting two months—on the brink of death—from which I hardly recovered to find that, notwithstanding the twenty volumes of books I had read, I still had

141

to learn from a certain theological and very difficult book called Masnavi
*(comprising at least ninety thousand verses—the good people of the country
have it that it contains the Philosopher's Stone). I looked for someone who
knew the book, but against payment I found no one and was obliged to
turn to a great superior of the Mevlevi. A friend conducted me there and I
had hardly paid my respects when he offered me his services for the understanding of the* Masnavi *and he allowed me during four or five months
to see him very frequently to study. His name was Dervish Moqlas. Since
he was capable of leading a party I knew he was under observation of the
court and so I had to take my precautions. I did not hestitate to inform
Monseigneur Murtaza, brother-in-law to the king, and Myrza Ali Reza,
also from the king's family, and Cheikh al Islam, the head of the law, that
I only went there to read the* Masnavi, *which they approved.*

"Vikram," Alif said to the form under the workstation, "what do
you know about a Persian guy named Moqlas who might have been
up to no good in the seventeenth century?"

"Moqlas the dervish?" Vikram's eyes reflected light like a cat's.
"He was a scholar of sorts. Very interested in the insides of books."

"What reason would the Shah have to be upset with him, or have
him watched?"

"He was what you would call a heretic."

"But a learned heretic."

"Some might say. Why do you care?"

"This de la Croix the convert was so worked up about studied
with him. He believed one of the books Moqlas was helping
him study—the *Mathnawi*—contained the Philosopher's Stone."
Alif looked back down at Vikram, who had managed to work his

ankles over his shoulders like a circus acrobat. "But that doesn't make any sense. The Philosopher's Stone is supposed to be a physical substance, right? An alchemy thing. Like some kind of miraculous chemical that turns stuff into gold, or the water of life, or something. Not a book."

"The distinction is relevant only to a fleshy idiot like you. The Philosopher's Stone is knowledge, pure knowledge—a fragment of the formula by which the universe was written."

Alif rubbed his eyes. "And this thing is in the *Mathnawi*?"

"Well, it's in a mathnawi, or so the theory goes."

"What do you mean, *a*? Wasn't the *Mathnawi* written by Rumi? Is there more than one?"

Vikram snorted. "Of course there's more than one. Plenty of morons who thought they'd reached some great understanding of the cosmos claimed to have written one. But most of them were terrible. Rumi's was the only one that stuck."

"You don't think the Philosopher's Stone was in Rumi's *Mathnawi*, though."

"If I did, I would be out conquering time, not sitting under this desk. What would happen if I pulled on that green wire?"

"Don't, don't!"

Vikram cackled gleefully.

"Would you just concentrate for two minutes?" snapped Alif. "I need to figure this out."

"You've already figured it out. Obviously the mathnawi to which this de la Croix refers is the *Alf Yeom*. Ninety thousand verses is about right, length-wise. Obviously Moqlas the dervish is the Persian mystic who initiated him into the study of the text, just as he was initiated by his teachers, and they by theirs, and so on, all the way back to whatever fourteenth-century rapscallion first heard it from the djinn. Obviously Moqlas believed he could somehow decode it and come up with the Philosopher's Stone and thereby empower himself to manipulate matter and time."

Alif made a skeptical face.

"Is that true?" he asked. "Can reading the *Alf Yeom* really do that?"

Vikram shifted, craning his neck in an unnatural way to meet Alif's eye.

"A human being with a lust for forbidden knowledge might certainly think so. Whether he would ultimately succeed—no, that has never happened. Nor will it do you any good, if that's what you're wondering."

"I'm not wondering. I'm not interested in cosmic powers. I just want to figure out where Intisar picked this thing up and what she expects me to do with it."

By way of response, Vikram sank his teeth into Alif's ankle. Alif closed his netbook, cursing, and kicked the arm that reached out for his power cord. The convert appeared in the doorway of the computer lab and motioned to them. Vikram extricated himself from beneath the desk, bending in ways that made Alif vaguely sick, and stood to greet her as though lurking under desks was something ordinary. The convert had a strange expression: chin tucked, mouth pursed, brows drawn into a brooding look. She held the *Alf Yeom* in both hands like a platter. It had been wrapped in some kind of protective film and sealed with surgical tape.

"How was archival science?" Alif hazarded.

The convert ran one thumb along a corner of the book, making the plastic film crackle. "Do you want the short answer or the long answer?" she asked.

"The long answer, naturally," said Vikram. "You can tell us while we are sniffing out lunch. You do have such a thing as shawarma in this upper-class pile, don't you?"

"I can take you to the cafeteria."

"Splendid."

"I have to meet someone in a couple of hours," Alif interjected. "At the *chaiwallah's* we passed near the front entrance."

Vikram looked interested. "What's this? Meet whom?"

"The—my—the girl who sent me the *Alf Yeom*."

"Why didn't you say so?" Vikram's yellow eyes were merry. "We'll all go and bear witness to your little tryst. It will be more romantic entertainment than the convert has had in years."

"Bastard," the convert muttered.

"No one is going," said Alif. "I don't care what else you do, but I see her alone."

"Well, whatever. The cafeteria is back that way in any case." With a frigid glance at Vikram, the convert led the way out of the computer lab and down the hall. Radiant air hit Alif in the face as they emerged into the overheated afternoon. He regretted the loss of the climate-controlled lab, so solicitous of both body and machine. Outside everything warred with everything else: heat against skin, skin against propriety, propriety against nature. Alif rubbed sweat from the back of his neck, irritated.

The convert wove through clusters of chatting students toward a low building near the campus entrance. The scent of fry oil and chickpea flour wafted from its windows. Alif felt his stomach rumble and wished he had eaten more of the minted yogurt Azalel had given them in the morning. He trailed behind the convert as she pushed through a pair of double doors and into a large hall. Long tables and benches were set up on one end; on the other, sour *desi* women in uniform served food from behind metal counters.

"It's campus food, but it's hot," said the convert, handing Alif a tray. He needed no more prompting, and loaded the tray with vegetable *pakoras, naan,* and *kabsa* with chicken that smelled as though it had been sitting on a hot plate for many hours. The convert found an empty table and sat down, setting the *Alf Yeom* on a bower of clean napkins.

"Careful with that tray!" She slid the book farther along the table as Alif sat down across from her. "You'll get grease on the manuscript."

"Sorry."

"Where's mine?" Vikram pounced on the spoon Alif was reaching for, helping himself to the *kabsa*. Alif curled his lip.

"Okay, so here's the deal." The convert paused and steepled her hands beneath her chin like a Catholic icon. "I took a five-millimeter-by-five-millimeter sample from one of the pages in the middle that had some blank space. I had my advisor look at it. Because the pages are paper instead of vellum and the condition of the book is so good, I assumed it couldn't be more than a couple hundred years old."

Vikram smiled through his food, looking, Alif thought, like a man anticipating the punch line of a joke.

"My advisor—and I didn't tell him anything, just asked him to look at the sample—disagrees. He thinks it's no less than seven hundred years old."

Alif quickly swallowed the lump of *pakora* in his mouth.

"He says the paper was made using a process that went out of vogue in Central Asia by the fourteenth century. It's almost certainly Persian, too, or at least the paper itself was made in Persia. He thinks that awful-smelling resin is what has kept the book in such good condition, though he can't tell offhand what it's made of. He wants to have the lab analyze it."

"So . . ." Alif trailed off, unsure of what he wanted to say.

"So I was wrong." The convert smiled wryly. She looked tired. "This is the genuine article. De la Croix wasn't making it all up. The *Alf Yeom* is real."

Vikram leaned back in his chair with a satisfied purr. The convert gazed at him steadily, mouth twisting in exaggerated contempt. He seemed amused by her silent fury. His eyes shone, reflecting the blue in hers as he stared back, unflinching, and it seemed to Alif as though he was saying something, though his lips did not move. Whatever it was, it caused the convert's pout to evaporate. She blushed and looked away, biting her lower lip in a way that was almost coy, and it occurred to Alif that she was almost pretty when she didn't scowl.

"Now I'm really interested to know how your friend got her hands on this," she said, clearing her throat self-consciously. "This is not the kind of artifact you find lying around in a used bookstore. Or in a rare bookstore. Or in the Smithsonian. I ran searches on all the major lending libraries in the City, and called up a couple of the antiques dealers who sell stuff they shouldn't. No one's ever heard of it."

Alif studied the plastic-shrouded manuscript on its bed of napkins. It could not weigh more than half a kilogram, yet it felt like an unbearable load—an unasked-for, ill-defined responsibility, an unknown unknown. How like Intisar, he thought, to drop this in his lap in her imperious way without thought for his broken heart. He was seized with contempt.

"I'm sick of guessing what all this means," he said. "I want some facts."

The convert shrugged. "I've told you all I know," she said. "The lab will come back to us with the results of the resin test in a few hours. But I can't tell you where the book comes from."

"I may be able to do as much," mused Vikram, stroking his goatee. "But it would involve taking you someplace you shouldn't really go."

"Where's that?" asked Alif, suspicion roused.

"The Immovable Alley. There's an entrance to it in the City, but I haven't used it in years—it's probably moved by now."

"But . . ." Alif attempted to collect his thoughts. "Alleys don't move. So how could the entrance be somewhere other than where it used to be?"

"It moves."

"But it's called the Immovable Alley!"

"The alley is stationary. That's the whole point. The world moves around it. So entrances and exits can pop up anywhere." Vikram smiled, evidently pleased with himself.

"What a bunch of bull," said the convert, wrinkling her nose. "Immovable Alley my ass. He wants to get us down some dark side street and rob us. Then when we call the police we can tell them we were following a dude who thinks he's a genie to a place that doesn't exist, and they can lock us up in jail for being nuts."

"My dear woman, how long have we known one another? I am hurt by your lack of confidence." Vikram pulled his handsome face into a pout.

"I don't care. I'm not falling for your tricks." The convert crossed her arms and set her mouth in a thin, masculine line. Vikram imitated her. She pretended not to notice.

"I'll go," said Alif, feeling emboldened. "Any alley, immovable or not, as long as there's someone there who can tell me what I need to know."

"Alternately," said the convert in a slow, condescending voice, such as one would use with a child, "you could just wait until you meet your friend and ask her where she got it and what she expects you to do with it."

Alif rubbed *pakora* grease on his jeans, wilting under the convert's scrutiny.

"I could," he mumbled, "but I don't even know for sure that she's going to show up. Or what she'll say when she does."

The convert sighed, tucking a loose strand of hair beneath her head scarf.

"Okay," she said. Narrowing her eyes at Alif, she stood. "But if I end up beaten, raped, or robbed, I'm blaming you. You are officially responsible for my well-being. Let it be known that I'm only doing this under duress."

"Nonsense," scoffed Vikram. "You're doing this because you're curious. Come along, children."

He loped toward the door of the cafeteria, humming. Alif and the convert followed, keeping a brittle distance between themselves. Outside, Vikram turned downhill, toward the edge of campus and the Old Quarter wall beyond it. They threaded their way into the Old Quarter proper, beyond the university, along stone-paved streets that threw curious echoes. Everything here felt older, grander, wealthier than the City Alif knew; there were trees that had been carefully cultivated against the dry desert air for a century or more, dust-caked and wide-rooted, spreading their leaves over the arched entranceways of town houses and villas. Gone were the stocky apartment blocks and duplexes like the one he and Dina inhabited. Baqara District was indifferent to taste or beauty, and if one wanted either, one had to look further than the outsides of things. Here were both in abundance.

"I wish I had money," said Alif. "Money buys beauty."

"What a cynical thing to say," said the convert.

"He's right," said Vikram, cavorting a few steps. "However much we may wish to deny it. Money smooths the path for many things."

"It's different back home." The convert spoke with a kind of offhanded confidence Alif associated with foreigners.

"I doubt that very much," said Vikram. "America is a country like any other, with rich and poor. If you asked a poor American whether he'd rather remain so, or wake up with a million dollars under his pillow, I guarantee you would get the same answer every time."

The convert raised a skeptical eyebrow.

"Have you ever even been to the States?"

"In what sense?"

"Is there more than one?"

"But naturally."

"God, you're ridiculous." Flouncing her long skirt, the convert pulled ahead of Vikram, walking down the street with a purposeful gait. Vikram laughed.

"I didn't mean to offend your vanity, my dear," he called. "Slow down. I meet so few westerners that I forget how prickly your little consciences are."

"Do you know how many words for foreigner I know?" the convert asked. She didn't turn to speak; her voice seemed to float from the back of her silk-clad head. "Many. *Ajnabi. Ferenghi. Khawagga. Gori. Pardesi.* And I've been called all of them. They're not nice words, no matter what you people claim."

"Wait a minute, who is *you people?*" called Alif.

"Easterners. Non-westerners. Whatever you want to call yourselves. It doesn't matter to you what concessions we make— whether we dress respectfully, learn the language, follow all the insane rules about when to speak and how and to whom. I even adopted your religion—adopted it, out of my own free will, thinking I was doing something noble and righteous. But it's not enough. You'll always second-guess every thought and opinion that comes out of my mouth, even when I talk about my own fucking country. I'll always be foreign."

Alif was taken aback by this bitter outpouring. He glanced at Vikram and was surprised to see genuine concern on his face. Stooping low in a doglike fashion, Vikram cantered ahead until he had caught up with the convert, and took her arm.

"Enough," he said softly. "Forgive me."

The convert looked away, staring at a dead Taif rosebush that clung to a wall, mummified in dust.

"I don't understand why you keep showing up," she said. "I can't be the only person you know worth harassing. I'm not pretty, I'm not charming, I'm not available, and I've made a strenuous effort not to be interesting to you. I don't know why you come back again and again."

Vikram plucked at her sleeve, drawing her toward him.

"You're the only person I've ever met stupid enough not to fear me," he said, "and yet you aren't stupid. It drives me mad. Does that please you?"

"You're lying."

"I never lie."

The convert did not respond. Vikram murmured something too low for Alif to hear. It seemed to have the desired effect, for she looked up at him and smiled a little sheepishly.

"Come along, younger brother," said Vikram with a wave of his arm. "Keep up."

Alif jogged to meet them. The convert seemed mollified, and had slowed her steps again.

"What I don't get," she said in a more conciliatory tone, "is how non-westerners can move back and forth between civilizations so easily. I think westerners never get the hang of it. It's not in our cultural DNA to be adaptive. I mean, look at all the eastern writers who've written great western literature. Kazuo Ishiguro. You'd never guess that *The Remains of the Day* or *Never Let Me Go* were written by a Japanese guy. But I can't think of anyone who's ever done the reverse—any westerner who's written great eastern literature. Well, maybe if we count Lawrence Durrell—does the Alexandria Quartet qualify as eastern literature?"

"There is a very simple test," said Vikram. "Is it about bored, tired people having sex?"

"Yes," said the convert, surprised.

"Then it's western."

The convert looked crestfallen, then laughed.

"God, I'm afraid you're right. Whatever. I'm being silly."

"Not at all." Vikram made a gallant half-bow in her direction. Alif glanced from one to the other, feeling somewhat left out. He had known only a handful of westerners in his life, most of them instructors from Britain or America who taught at the shoddy private schools he had attended. His classmates had been other *desis* from India, Pakistan, or Bangladesh, along with a smattering of Malays and the odd Arab from less oil-rich North African lands—the children of migrant laborers with enough saved up to educate their children in a fashionable way. He had always assumed his Anglo teachers belonged to some other, more ethereal, way of being, free from the anxieties of identity and displacement he suffered. To see the convert distressed by such things unnerved him. He studied her out of the corner of his eye. A smile played around her mouth and disappeared; one eyebrow quirked upward and settled. Evidently she did have a sense of humor.

"Ah. Let's see now." Vikram paused in front of a garden wall surrounding a villa. It was limestone, the sort quarried in the desert a century earlier by wealthy merchants who bought and built on the last parcels of land left in the Old Quarter.

"What are we looking at? Why have we stopped?" asked Alif.

Vikram lifted his nose and sniffed.

"I smell vagrant air," he said. "And water in pools of quartz. And possibly garlic. I think we're in the right place."

"Sorry, what?" said the convert.

"This smells right," said Vikram patiently. "There must be an entrance to the Immovable Alley near where we're standing."

Alif sighed in irritation. "You mean you've been leading us around by *smell*? Are you kidding me?"

"What did I tell you," said the convert, contempt settling on her face again. "He's tricked us. Now he'll ask for money."

Making a growling noise deep in his throat, Vikram stalked back and forth in front of the wall.

"I'm beginning to lose my temper," he said. "I offer to bring you to a place few of your kind are ever allowed to travel, to meet people in front of whom I pray you will not embarrass me, and you stand here bickering."

"Vikram, this is a *wall*!" Alif felt the last of his patience give out. "There's no entrance to anything here. A wall is meant to keep people *out*."

"By God, why should that matter?" With a haughty glance, Vikram walked toward the limestone edifice, turned right, and disappeared, as if the wall was not a single structure at all, but two overlapping panes of stone with a narrow passage between them.

Alif and the convert stood staring at the spot where he had vanished. The convert's mouth was hanging open in a way Alif found unattractive but that mirrored the slack sensation in his skull: he struggled to make sense of what he had seen, and found he could not.

"Are you coming or not?" Vikram's voice came from an indeterminate point within the wall. The convert shook herself.

"Yes," she called faintly. Alif forced himself to string an intelligent answer together.

"It must be some sort of optical illusion," he suggested in a chastened voice. "Vikram has good depth perception."

"Yes," repeated the convert. She took a step forward, then another. Arriving at the wall, she turned right, looked surprised, and vanished between the blocks of stone the same way Vikram had. Alone, Alif was suddenly nervous, and trotted in her wake, blinking once when he saw that there was in fact a slender opening. The wall was actually two walls, close together, so perfectly aligned that head-on one blended seamlessly into the next.

The passageway between them seemed to extend much farther than its outer appearance suggested. Alif followed it for what seemed like a full city block, then another; when it continued even farther he began to panic.

"Vikram?" His voice was shrill.

"Down here, you idiot."

Alif peered at the stone-flagged ground and stopped himself just before tumbling down a set of stairs as invisible as the passageway had been. The only reason he could tell they were stairs at all, and not a continuation of even ground, was because Vikram and the convert were standing at the bottom, looking unusually small. Collecting himself, Alif walked down the steps to meet them. He attempted to appear nonchalant.

"Hi," he said. "Hello. I thought I'd lost you."

Vikram laughed. "You see? It's as I said. Don't you regret giving me so much grief?" Moving aside, he revealed the strangest tangle of architecture Alif had ever seen: it was an alley, certainly, but it did not behave like one. The central corridor, lined by two walls and overhung with canopies of bright cloth, ran away from them into the distance. Stone staircases led from street level halfway up the walls, then stopped or turned in odd directions; staring at them for too long made Alif's head hurt. Doorways perched ten feet above the ground or stretched out at perpendicular angles into the main thoroughfare, such that you could see either side at once.

The alley was crowded with people: circles of men perched on cushions in the dust, arguing with one another over rings of nargileh smoke; women wearing veils or robes or very little at all hawking goods from the stalls that hugged either wall. Then there were those who resembled neither man nor woman but errant shadows moving against the light, coalescing every so often into bipedal forms. The noise of it all, a blend of languages Alif could not entirely follow, rose and fell like a tide on a seashore. The effect was hypnotic.

Vikram led them through the crowd toward a shop built into the left wall several hundred feet away. A woman with dark brown hair bound up in an elaborate network of braids stood within it, leaning against a wooden counter fronting the street. Her eyes, like Vikram's, were yellowish; her features lacked any discernible ethnic trait or distinction. She smiled at Vikram as he approached, with the easy familiarity of long acquaintance.

"*As-salaamu alaykum,*" he said to her, touching his forehead.

"*W'alaykum salaam*," she replied. Her voice was low and liquid. She examined Alif in a way that made him blush, letting her eyes roam briskly up and down his figure with a look of concentration.

"Why have you brought them here?" she asked Vikram in Arabic. "The Alley isn't as safe as it used to be, you know. And I don't think the girl is taking it very well."

Alif glanced at the convert: her eyes were glassy and she kept swaying back and forth as though falling asleep and catching herself each time she dozed off.

"She's an American," said Vikram, apparently by way of explanation.

"Ah." The woman gave the convert a look of pity. "Half in, half out. She may not remember much of what passes here."

"She'll remember enough. The boy is the chief reason we've come, anyway, doubter though he is. Alif, this is Sakina. Sakina, this one calls himself Alif."

"Alif." Sakina narrowed her sun-colored eyes. "A single stroke of the pen from top to bottom. The original letter. An interesting name."

"Thanks," said Alif, feeling unnecessary.

"Why have you come?" Sakina looked at him, raising one expectant eyebrow. Alif glanced at Vikram. Vikram was watching him and smiling a little.

"I—well. I've got a book and I'd like to know where it comes from," said Alif, when it became clear Vikram would deliver no explanation himself.

"Oh? Let's see it."

Alif lowered his backpack to the ground and unzipped it, lifting out the *Alf Yeom.* He set it on the wooden counter in front of Sakina. Her eyes widened. She looked up at Vikram in dismay.

"Vikram, Vikram—you've always been a troublemaker, but with this you have outdone yourself."

Vikram shrugged. "I'm getting old," he said. "I let the wandering earth guide me where it may. If it brings me to grief, what does it matter?"

Sakina clucked her tongue and glanced up and down the alley.

"You three had better come inside," she said, swinging the counter outward to admit them. Alif filed inside behind Vikram, the convert following in his wake. The interior of the shop was pleasant and light-filled, with arched stone walls and deep windows. A mottled gray cat was napping in one of them and raised its head briefly when they entered.

Alif was surprised to see that the wooden shelves lining the shop were packed more or less equally with books and computer parts: old tomes bound in leather, paperback novels in several languages, clumsy motherboards from the early nineties, third-generation optical drives less than a year out of beta.

"Is this a bookstore or a computer store or what?" he asked. "Who shops here?"

Sakina laughed without unkindness.

"What third-born questions," she said. "This is neither a bookstore nor a computer store, Alif. I trade in information, no matter what form it takes. People come here when they wish to buy or barter knowledge."

"Oh." Alif wished he hadn't spoken. He gazed pensively at a quad-core processor sitting on a shelf at eye level. Sakina looked at Vikram.

"Computers and books," she said. "Does that mean he can't see the other things?"

"Probably not," said Vikram, giving a fond slap to the back of Alif's neck. "He's still made of mud, after all."

With a curse, Alif twisted away from Vikram, rubbing his neck. "Stop talking about me like I'm not here," he snapped.

Sakina gave him a pretty smile.

"Forgive us. It's only that you aren't quite here, you see. Or to put it another way, we're not wholly visible to each other. It's as if you and I are talking on the phone, but Vikram and I are talking in person. It makes it tempting for us to speak over you."

Helpless, Alif sat down on the floor with a sigh.

"Fine, whatever," he muttered. "This was all Vikram's idea to begin with."

"What a beautiful space," said the convert in English, speaking up for the first time. "Thank you for inviting us here."

Alif felt the need to make up for her absurdity, and therefore his own—to justify their incompetence in some way.

"I think the convert's phone is getting a bad signal," he jested weakly.

Sakina laughed again in a polite, accommodating way.

"It's all right," she said. "It is this way for many of the tribe of Adam. If her sight was entirely veiled she wouldn't have been able to come here at all. So that's something."

Alif nodded as though he understood what she was talking about. Sakina sat on the floor and placed the *Alf Yeom* in front of her, giving it a quizzical look, as though she had divined from it some hidden meaning. Vikram slid to the ground next to the convert, observing her blank face with wolfish amusement.

"So it's true—it's been found. This is the Moqlas manuscript, is it not?" Sakina asked Alif.

Alif was glad to field a question he could actually answer.

"Yes," he said, "Or at least, that's what the small amount of research I was able to do suggested."

"I believe you were correct in your findings," said Sakina. "When the *Alf Yeom* was first dictated to a human being by one of our kind, many hundreds of years ago, that man—his name was Reza— made four copies. He was a member of a heretical sect called the Battini—they lived in Persia and were connected to the Assassins. Perhaps you've heard of those. Anyway. The manuscripts were passed down through the Battini from master to student. Each generation attempted to discover what they believed was secret knowledge hidden within the text, through which they expected to gain supernatural powers. None succeeded."

"Is it possible?" Alif interrupted. "Do you get superpowers if you figure out what the trick is? I mean, if there *is* a trick?"

Sakina chuckled. "There is no trick—it is simply that your kind and mine see the world differently, and that is that. The transcendent aspect of *The Thousand Days* is apparent only to the hidden folk. Although—" She paused, glancing up at a microprocessor on a shelf above her.

"Although what?"

"I have often wondered whether you are getting close," she said slowly. "Most of my people disagree with me, but I believe that with the advent of what you call the digital age you have breached a kind of barrier between symbol and symbolized. It doesn't mean the *Alf Yeom* will make any more sense to you, but it may mean you have grasped something vital about the nature of information. You are the chosen race, after all—our ancestors were commanded to bow to your progenitor in the Foretime. And it was one of your kind who brought forth the *Criterion*, not one of ours."

"What *Criterion* is that?" Alif leaned forward, intent on her serious face.

Sakina looked bemused.

"Surely you must know, given your real name."

"But I thought—how do you know my real name? I didn't hear Vikram mention it."

"I didn't need to," said Vikram, playing with the hem of the convert's skirt. She appeared not to notice. "Since I know what it is, it is implied by your chosen name every time I say it. That's why it's dangerous to tell a djinn your real name if you'd rather he didn't know."

"That's Dina's fault," muttered Alif. "She refuses to call me anything else."

"It's a blessed name," said Sakina. "I don't see why you should be ashamed of it."

"It's common. It's everybody's name. I wanted to be different."

"Even so."

Alif ran a hand restlessly through his unkempt hair.

"Whatever. That's not the point. What's this *Criterion*?"

Sakina pointed to a shelf behind his shoulder. "*Al-Furqan*, of course. *The* book."

Alif turned and looked: in a cradle, bound in green leather, was a copy of the Quran.

"Oh," he said.

There was a pause in which Alif felt sheepish and small. Sakina and Vikram looked at one another in catlike communion, saying nothing, smiling in one simultaneous instant.

"I'm sorry," said Sakina, breaking the spell. "We got lost in thought. Where was I?"

"The Battini," said Alif. "And Moqlas."

"Yes. Two of the four copies were destroyed in Isfahan when Shah Abbas shut down the Battini school there in the early seventeenth century. Another was lost in a fire fifty years later at the Battini outpost in Cairo. By the end of the seventeenth century only a single copy remained, and it was this copy that Moqlas inherited. It's said that he dictated the stories to a Frenchman, who translated them into his own language, though I am told the translation is not taken very seriously."

"De la Croix," Alif said. "Everybody thought he'd made it all up."

"Made it all up," echoed the convert.

"All translations are made up," opined Vikram, "Languages are different for a reason. You can't move ideas between them without losing something. The Arabs are the only ones who've figured this out. They have the sense to call non-Arabic versions of the *Criterion* interpretations, not translations."

"So the French translation," said Alif, "that doesn't qualify as a real version of the *Alf Yeom*?"

Vikram gave him a disgusted look. "Is *anything* real in French?" he asked.

"When Moqlas died, the remaining manuscript of the *Alf Yeom* went missing," Sakina continued. "The Battini school died out, ending their days as hashish-addled wanderers bemoaning their bad luck. No word was heard of the manuscript again—that is, until several months ago."

Alif's left leg had gone to sleep. He shifted, feeling pins and needles break out in his calf and foot.

"What happened then?" He felt like a child listening to a bedtime story.

"There was a rumor that a young noblewoman from one of the emirates had identified the manuscript through a rare bookseller in Damascus and paid a small fortune for it. No one was able to confirm this. But there was a man—one of your tribe, a *beni adam* they call *falling star*—who was convinced enough to recruit some very dangerous company to look for it, and her."

"Intisar." Alif felt his face grow hot. She was menaced by so many things beyond his control. He had not done enough to protect her. The name *falling star* meant something to him, but he could not remember what. He was impotent, here as in the outside world, his utility confined to punching commands into computers. Beyond the bedroom where he sat day after day like an idle spider in the midst of a digital web he was boneless, protected only by a black carapace of T-shirts and jeans, unprepared for physical danger. His mind struggled against the limits of his body.

"She must have sent the book to me because she got scared," he said, mortified when his voice shook. "Whoever this *falling star* guy is, he clearly threatened her. So she sent the book away to protect herself." He gave a brittle laugh. "Though why she would think I could keep it safe is beyond me. I've fucked it up already, getting hacked by the Hand and going on the run. I have plenty of my own problems. I've been careless and stupid."

Sakina touched his foot with a sympathetic hand. Alif felt an immediate calm descend on his body, soporific and cool. He wondered if the effect was born of his own suggestible mind, or the result of some arcane ability the woman possessed. Either seemed possible.

"Who is this man who wants it?" Alif asked her. "The book I mean. Where does he come from? Who are these people you say he's recruited?"

Sakina's eyes flickered.

"I have never seen him," she said, "Though it's said he came to the Alley on his own. No guide, no map. He has some kind of authority among humankind—an enforcer, a law-giver, a dealer of punishment. How he reached this place no one knows. But he was able to convince certain elements among our people to help him."

Alif looked at Vikram. The man seemed intent, even uneasy.

"What does she mean?" he asked.

"There are many kinds of djinn," Vikram said in a quiet voice. "As there are many kinds of *banu adam*. Some good, like Sakina, some less good, like me. Most are scuttling moral cowards, like you. But there are a few who are very, very bad indeed."

"As bad as—as what?"

"Well, the outcast Shaytan is a djinn. From there you may elaborate."

Alif balled his fists against his face.

"I can't handle demons," he muttered.

"No, you can't," said Sakina. "But no one has asked you to. Leave the book here with us. It's safer in the Alley than it is in the seeing world. Your kind was never meant to possess it in the first place—you are too careless with your tools, too hungry for progress to consider its cost."

Alif looked with relief at the manuscript sitting between them. If he got rid of it, Intisar would be no less unsafe, but he would be a great deal safer indeed. It was an honorable thing, returning a lost artifact to its rightful owners. He would be able to look her in the eye and tell her he had done something, anything, to prove himself worthy of what she had withdrawn from him.

"The man who came looking for the book," said Alif. "He doesn't know I've got it, does he? I mean, how could he? If I left it here, that would be the end of my part in this whole thing. I'm anonymous."

Sakina's mouth quirked into a doubtful frown.

"I'm not sure that's true," she said. "The man in question may be mud-made like the rest of your kind but, as I said, he is not without resources. His allies may already have informed him that you are here. And if he was able to reach the Alley on his own, he must have considerable access to information in the seeing world as well. If I were you, I would assume nothing."

The familiarity of the man's name, kicking around in the back of his mind since Sakina had spoken it, came into chilly clarity.

"My God," said Alif. "It's a meteor. A falling star is a meteor. Al Shehab. Al Shehab means *falling star*."

"So?" Vikram yawned, revealing too many pointed teeth.

"It's the Hand." Alif felt like laughing. "His real name is Abbas Al Shehab. The Hand is coming for the *Alf Yeom*."

Chapter Eight

Though Sakina urged him to stay, Alif bundled the manuscript back into his pack and slung it over one shoulder.

"I've got to meet Intisar and warn her," he said. "I should have left ages ago. I'll be late."

"Allah, Allah!" Vikram exclaimed. "Yes, be manful! Take up your destiny!"

"Don't encourage him," said Sakina. "He could be in terrible trouble."

"He's already in terrible trouble. A little more won't hurt," said Vikram.

"It's true." Alif gave them a wan smile. "It makes a lot more sense now. The Hand must already have known that Intisar was planning to smuggle the book to me when he broke into my computer. The attack was too surgical—I knew there was no way it could have been random. He was looking for something that would tell him whether

I had received the book, or where I had stashed it. He doesn't care about Intisar or about Tin Sari—he wants the *Alf Yeom*."

"Made it all up," said the convert. Alif looked at her doubtfully.

"I still think you should leave the book here with us," said Sakina. "It would be wise."

"I don't know if it's wise or not, but if the Hand is mixed up with this book, I need to find out why. I'm responsible for a lot of people he could hurt." With a pang of guilt, Alif thought of all the clients who had been exposed when he pulled the plug on Hollywood.

"Very wise," said the convert.

"Can you take care of her?" Alif asked Vikram.

Vikram pressed one hand over his heart. "Like my own eyes," he said. "But where shall we meet you after your little tryst?"

"I don't know." Alif flipped open his smartphone. No messages. He snapped it shut again. "Call me. The convert has my number, if you can get her to remember how to work a phone."

Vikram waved him off. "She'll be fine once we get her back to the City proper," he said. "The effect of this place wears off quickly. She'll think we spent a charming afternoon in some corner of the Old Quarter she's never seen before."

It occurred to Alif that he had no idea how to escape.

"Where's the, uh—exit?"

Sakina shrugged. "Back the way you came, I imagine," she said. "Vikram will guide you if you can't make out the way yourself. I can look after your friend until he returns. But remember that whatever entrance you used will probably spit you out in a different spot than where you entered."

"How different? Middle of Tibet different?"

"Difficult to say."

Alif looked dubiously at Vikram.

"That's it? Difficult to say? You don't have some kind of cryptic advice?"

"None," said Vikram, in a voice with more forced cheer than was natural. "If Sakina is right about the kind of folk the Hand has recruited, you've got much more to worry about than a little detour. Gather your things."

Alif elected not to think too hard about Vikram's warning. He saluted Sakina, who pressed a hand to her heart, and turned on his heel, trotting briskly to keep up with Vikram as he ducked into the street. Men and women and things in between stared at him as he followed in the wake of Vikram's swaying dark hair. The colors of buildings and clothing seemed overbright. Alif's feet began to drag. He felt sluggish as he skirted a messenger boy with an enormous jar of butterflies riding on his head.

"You're losing the narrative of things," came Vikram's voice. "Here—take hold of me."

Dutifully, Alif reached for his arm. His fingers brushed something warm and soft, like the pelt of an animal. For a moment, sleep descended over him, and he couldn't see.

"Cousin. Last-born. This won't do."

Alif felt himself lifted like a baby and cradled against a furred, feral-smelling shoulder. He resisted a long-buried urge to suck his thumb, roused by the memory of a time when the darkness at the edge of sleep was peopled with beasts.

"Wake." Vikram's voice was low and urgent. "You aren't safe."

Alif forced his eyes open. Half-shadowed figures stared at him with eyes like lamps. An elephant lumbered past, her painted face scarcely clearing the saffron-colored shades of the shop fronts. He came fully awake and struggled out of Vikram's grip, feeling overwhelmed.

"You don't have to do this," he said, tugging at his rumpled shirt. "You don't have to hang around if it's really going to get as bad as Sakina says. *God.* All I did was let a cat wait out a sandstorm in my room. A normal person would kill me for sleeping with his sister."

"Normal people must not love their sisters as much as I do." Vikram's face had regained its usual expression of contempt. "What an ungrateful little creature it is." He spun on his foot and continued down the Alley, so fast that Alif nearly lost sight of him.

"Wait—I didn't mean it." He ran to catch up. The sight of a girl with silver chains looped through piercings scattered across her face arrested him and he stared; she looked back and smiled, revealing a row of pointed teeth. Horrified, Alif ran on. The near-invisible staircase came into view, detectable only as a sudden collapse of the near horizon. Vikram paced in front of it like a restless lion.

"Normal people," he muttered to himself. "Idiot. After I've done everything but swaddle it in linens when it shits."

"I'm sorry," said Alif guiltily. "It's just that I don't know what to do. This place is so funny and bright—it hurts my eyes. I can't think. I'm freaking out."

"Your eyes, your eyes. Better leave before something else offends them. There are the stairs." Vikram's head seemed to sink below his shoulders as he stalked back toward the main thoroughfare of the Alley until he resembled something ghoulish and obscene. Growling noises of complaint issued from his retreating form. Dazed, Alif watched him for several moments before steeling himself for action. He sprinted back and caught Vikram by the shoulder. The man turned with a snarl. Awkwardly, Alif kissed him on both cheeks, as he would a brother.

"I meant to say thank you," he said. "That was what I meant to say."

Bewilderment spread over Vikram's face, quickly replaced by a careless smile.

"Go away, younger brother," he said, walking a little straighter. "I'll see you later, God willing."

Alif hurried back toward the hidden staircase, hearing the noise of the Alley die away behind him. Squaring his shoulders, he climbed to the top and soon enough found himself jogging along the narrow passageway between the limestone walls of the Old Quarter garden where he had started out.

When an opening failed to materialize, Alif told himself not to panic. He slowed his steps. Reaching out one hand, he ran his fingers along the chalky stones as he walked past, like a blind man taking his bearings. One block passed, and then another. Finally his fingertips fell away into empty air. Turning, he squinted: the barest shadow informed him that here, too, was a nearly undetectable gap, where the wall became two overlapping walls. He threaded his way through, and in a few steps found himself on an unpaved street, choking on the smoke of burning garbage.

"Damn it," he muttered. "Damn it all." He wheeled in a circle, trying to determine where he was. Behind him loomed a concrete wall—intact and without interruption when he put his hand to it—against which were built a series of shabby lean-tos. Barefoot men in the uniforms of the City garbage disposal service were throwing sacks of trash onto a smoking pyre in the middle of the road, heedless of the Datsun mini-trucks that tried to pass. Women, barefoot and up to their ankles in mire, waded through a second, as yet undisposed pile of garbage, picking up reusable fragments of glass and plastic with their fingers. The stench was terrible.

"Uncle," he called to the nearest man, an elderly fellow with a stoop and a thatch of yellowing white hair. "What district is this? Where can I get a taxi?"

The man smacked at what remained of his teeth, cackling a little.

"No proper district at all," he said. "We just call it the Place of Trash. Where do you need to go?"

"The Old Quarter," said Alif, looking desperately up and down the street for the black-and-white glimmer of a cab.

"That's a ways. I'll take you there myself for thirty dinars."

Alif glanced at the man's unshod feet, feeling skeptical.

"In what?" he asked.

"Apricot." The man pointed to a donkey cart hitched to a disagreeable-looking animal, presumably Apricot herself.

Alif bit his lip in despair. He would be late.

"Fine," he said, throwing up his hands. "Let's go."

* * *

Half an hour later, Alif arrived at the Old Quarter wall, thoroughly polluted by the dueling scents of refuse and donkey. He paid the driver in a rush, hurrying away before the old man's gnarled hand had a chance to close completely over Alif's crumpled bills. Sprinting up the stone-flagged road that led toward the university and the heart of the Old Quarter, he did not pause for breath, thinking with each footfall of Intisar. The memory of her perfume was so intense that he believed he could smell it over Apricot's more insistent odor. He ducked left down a side street toward the university entrance. Students were leaving their afternoon classes in talkative groups, taking out cell phones and cigarettes and stowing notebooks in their messenger bags. To Alif, they seemed unnaturally relaxed, unaware of the impending disaster he felt hovering all around him, marking him as a doomed, unfortunate, foolish man who had taken on burdens he had no hope of discharging.

In the distance, Alif could hear the *chaiwallah's* voice over the babble of students, his song punctuating their academic jargon. Sweet milk tea, joy for the tongue and health for the body; when you consider that Foucault defined the postmodern discourse, consider also his own experiential bias; sweet milk tea, if it runs out, I can't be blamed; obviously you believe social capital will eventually have a market value; sweet milk tea, a heavenly drink for a worldly price; you suffer from the colonized mind, dude. The last was from a boy who looked *desi* but wore cargo pants and a T-shirt advertising some floppy-haired western band. Alif brushed past him, following the *chaiwallah's* cry.

Intisar was not there when he arrived. He bought a cup of tea and tipped the *chaiwallah* excessively. While drinking it—hot, soupy with ground-up spices—he wondered if she might not come at all. She did not check her e-mail as frequently as he did. She might be afraid to see him. Perhaps she enjoyed being so capricious, rejecting him one day, sending him dangerous artifacts the next. It was for her that he had put himself and his friends in danger, for her that he had written the program that could send them all to prison. And she remained maddeningly aloof.

When he tried to rehearse what he would say, two separate scenes played themselves out in his mind: in one, he shouted accusations; in the other, he took her in his arms. Both ended with Intisar trembling against his shoulder, apologizing and professing her unbroken love. He drank the rest of his tea too fast and felt his stomach protest. He must not hope; the hope alone would kill him.

Alif shook his head to clear it and willed his innards to settle. The afternoon was getting hotter, the sun approaching its most unforgiving angle. A man had wandered up to the *chaiwallah* from around a corner. He ordered tea and paid with a small bill, waving his hand when the *chaiwallah* offered him change. Turning away, he discreetly dumped the hot liquid on the ground. Alif tensed. Two more men, trying too hard to look nonchalant, approached from the cobbled street that ran up to the campus entrance. One of them reached for something buckled into his belt.

Alif did not wait to see what they would do. Throwing his empty cup on the ground, he bolted past the *chaiwallah's* cart. Voices followed him, ordering him to stop and put up his hands. He did neither. Gulping air into his lungs, he sprinted toward an alley that led between the edge of campus and the closest private house. It was narrow—didn't Amitabh Bachchan escape into a narrow alley in *Sholay?*—and they would have to follow single file. He clattered past a splintered pile of boards, the detritus of a construction project, and prayed a loose nail would find its way into one of his pursuers' feet. Alif's own feet smarted—he was not used to exercise. Gasping, he emerged out the other end of the alley.

The street on which he found himself was broad and genteel, its stone-flagged surface recently washed. It sloped upward toward the heart of the Old Quarter. Squinting along its length, Alif saw the outline of the great mosque of Al Basheera against a white sky, fronting the original, medieval campus of the university. Alif scrambled up the street, legs aching, with a wild idea of seeking sanctuary. Surely they could not drag him out of Al Basheera in handcuffs. His phone buzzed in his pocket. He ignored it, continuing up the punishing incline toward the top of the hill. Footsteps rang against the stone behind him, and shouts: a man's voice called for backup. Alif blinked back tears of frustration.

"You! Boy! Why are you running?" At the gate of an ornate villa, the rotund, officious belly of a doorman blocked his path. By way of a uniform, the man wore a pseudo-Ottoman robe and a feathered turban that gave him the air of a circus performer or a waiter at some touristy restaurant. The simulacrum was unbearable. Alif was seized by a desire to strike the man, or trip him, or plunge a foot into the soft underside of his enormous belly, anything to get him out of the way. But courtesy stopped him, and the doorman grabbed his arm.

"Damn you to hell!" Alif shrieked, feeling betrayed. The doorman puffed out his cheeks. Alif struggled, but his abductor's meaty hand tightened around his arm until Alif could feel his own pulse. State agents were closing in behind them, sweat stains visible beneath the arms of their sport jackets.

"Is this your life, dressing up like a monkey for a bunch of rich fucks?" Alif bellowed at the doorman, baring his teeth. "Is this your life? Is this your life? Do you think they're going to stop treating you like shit if you turn me in?"

The doorman looked stunned. His cheeks fluttered. The grip on Alif's arm slackened, and he twisted free. Bolting up the street, he paused long enough to look over his shoulder, guilt and contempt warring in his chest as he saw the doorman staring after him, shoulders slumped, the feather in his absurd turban drooping in the heat.

Near the top of the hill, the street branched into two. Alif swerved left and stumbled over a traffic bump, then again on a loose flagstone, cursing all the while. Something buzzed past his ear. He yelped and flinched, convinced it was a bullet. Women's voices floated out the open door of a shop on his right. Without thinking, Alif changed course, rushing inside to shrieks of dismay. A profusion of ladies' gear greeted him: shoes on stands, purses on racks, gloves on tables. He knocked over a jewelry display as he stumbled on, seeking the back exit; a fresh volley of shrieks followed him and he felt a stinging blow on the back of his head.

"I just need the back door, damn it!" he screamed, fending off more blows with his arm.

Unseen hands shoved him toward a door marked EMPLOYEE propped open with a rock. He rushed through it, half-leaping over the lintel, and found himself in another alley. The backs of buildings obscured his view of the mosque. He spun in a frantic circle, hoping for some landmark to guide him, and found none. Weeping openly now, he sprinted onward in the first direction that presented itself, past a row of cats watching coolly from a garbage heap.

He turned one corner, then another, rushing through clusters of men in tailored white *thobes*. He had neither changed nor shaved in two days, and knew full well he looked like someone's thieving garden boy on the run. These men, these women, would have no qualms pointing the security police in the direction he had gone, would complain to each other about how dishonest maids and drivers had become these days. He could not stop now. In Baqara District it might be different; in Baqara District people knew about injustice. Here he was alone.

"Stop him, stop him!"

Alif turned to see his three pursuers panting up the street. He surged on, given fresh momentum by fear, and nearly toppled an old man fondling a string of prayer beads.

"Sorry," he gasped. The man made a private remark to God. Alif took a wrong step and fell. As his knee came down hard on the flagstones, he wondered if the man had evil-eyed him.

"Damn it," said Alif, uncertain if he was addressing the old man or the Almighty. "It's not my fault!" Bursts of pain flared in his right knee, keeping time with his heartbeat. He lurched to his feet and ignored them. The men from State would surely catch him now. He staggered around another corner, under an old carved arch, and sent up his own prayer in half-formed desperate thoughts.

The mosque appeared in front of him at the end of a narrow street, reaching toward the sun stone by stone, as if summoned. Alif cried out in relief. He jogged toward it and winced, limping the last few feet to its massive copper doors. Age had turned them a flat shade of green, such that the old songs about Basheera's shining gates no longer made sense, but Alif greeted them like lost friends. He pushed his way inside.

The interior of the mosque was dim. The only illumination came from five circular skylights built into the dome, letting geometric columns of sun and air into the prayer space. All the electric lights were switched off—the midday prayer had been over for an hour, and no worshippers remained. Alif quieted his breathing and slipped along one wall. There was noise coming from somewhere in the murk—the incongruous sound of an old violin recording. It was an Egyptian folk song in a wry, diffident key, and for an instant Alif was reminded of the way Dina shrugged when confronted with a question for which she had no answer.

"God forgive us, man! Your shoes!"

Alif spun around in terror. A leathery sheikh wearing a turban and a brown cloak was coming toward him from the opposite end of the room.

"What do you mean by this disrespect? Are you mad?" The sheikh halted in front of Alif and squinted at him indignantly. His eyes were a rheumy, unfocused blue. "Are you a Muslim, sir?" he asked, switching to Urdu.

"I'm sorry," Alif stuttered in Arabic. "Yes, I am, but I'm in terrible trouble and shoes are the last thing on my mind."

"Trouble?"

Someone pounded on the outside of the main doors. Alif froze. The sheikh considered him for a fraction of a second.

"Keep moving," he muttered. "My office is through the arch on the far side of the *musala*. When you get there, ask our Lord's forgiveness for your dirty feet."

Alif hurried to obey him. As he slipped through the arch he heard the great doors open and a terse voice ask whether the sheikh had seen a young man in a black T-shirt come into the mosque. Flattening himself against the rounded edge of the archway, Alif listened.

"My eyes are not the best anymore," said the sheikh, "and I'm afraid I have just closed up the *musala*. You'll have to come back for the midafternoon prayer."

"Nonsense. We have the authority to search the whole mosque anytime we please." The voice was fat and guttural.

"Whose authority?" the sheikh asked.

"State's, you impudent old man—what other kind is there?"

"God's," he answered serenely. There was a pause.

"Maybe we should clear this with Religious Oversight first," said a second voice in a quieter tone.

"Search the place now if you like," the sheikh's voice continued, "but I must insist you take off your shoes and make ablution first. This is a place of worship. I won't have it polluted with unclean feet or unclean thoughts."

"He didn't mean to insult you, Uncle," said the second voice apologetically.

"Really? Well, he must have a natural talent."

There was another pause. Alif heard shuffling feet.

"Is that *music*?" came the fat voice.

"And if it is?"

"Music in a *mosque*?"

"How convenient that you have suddenly found your piety," the sheikh snapped. "Basheera has been under my care for longer than you've been alive and I've never had any complaints. Now, I've told you the prayer hall is closed and my eyes are failing. Clearly I can be of no help to you. I hope you find whoever it is you're looking for."

"If we don't, we're coming back with a warrant from Religious Oversight," said the fat voice. "And God help you then."

"He often does," said the sheikh.

The doors rumbled shut. Alif slid to the floor with his back against the arch, realizing how dangerously close he had come to soiling himself. It was over now. He wiped his sweating, tear-streaked face on the hem of his T-shirt. The sheikh walked swiftly toward him across the faded carpet of the *musala*, bending once with a sigh to examine a clod of dirt left behind by Alif's shoe.

"Your path of destruction will need to be scrubbed," he said as he reached the far end. "I hope I can count on you to volunteer."

"Of course," said Alif. "Anything."

The sheikh peered down at Alif through his milky eyes.

"You're just a boy!" he exclaimed. "Or barely a man, at any rate. What have you done that's got State security so worked up? Are you a terrorist?"

"I'm a computer programmer. I help—I help whoever asks me."

"Meaning the Islamists?"

Alif let his head drop miserably to his knees.

"Islamists, anarchists, secularists—whoever asks."

"God have mercy upon us. A man of principle. My name is Bilal—Sheikh Bilal, they call me. Don't tell me your name, it's better I not know. Come into my office—you need a wash and a cup of tea."

*   *   *

The sheikh's office was an old stone room off the *musala* with a wooden-latticed window that looked onto a courtyard. A roll-top desk stood against one wall, piled high with books and forms and loose paper clips. It was called the Morocco Room, the sheikh said, because in the old days madrassa students from North Africa gathered there to listen to lectures in their own dialect. After Alif stowed his backpack in a corner the sheikh showed him to a small washroom down a corridor.

"Make sure to wash your feet!" he said, handing Alif a towel. "Use the lower tap, that's what it's there for. Do you take sugar? I make tea the Egyptian way: dark, with mint. None of this womanish milk chai you *desis* brought with you. I'll wait for you down the hall."

He turned, gathering his robes about him, and went back toward the office. Alif rolled up the cuffs of his pants and turned on the tap, letting tepid water gush over his hot feet. It was so pleasant that he stripped bare and performed a sketchy wash of his entire body, watching the accumulated dust of the past two days run off his skin in rivulets. He pressed his forehead against the dingy tile wall. There was a fresco of octagonal stars picked out in green at eye level—an institutional mosque design, ordinary, reassuring. He allowed himself to feel safe. Strains of the sheikh's violin recording echoed from the corners of the washroom, growing louder or softer depending on how Alif turned his head to listen.

Cooler and cleaner, Alif re-dressed, carrying his shoes gingerly by two fingers as he padded barefoot down the corridor. Sheikh Bilal was in his office, measuring out spoonfuls of sugar into two tea glasses. A tin pot let off steam as it boiled on a hot plate in the corner. Alif moved a stack of newspapers off a chair near the sheikh's desk and sat down.

"There! Much better." The sheikh handed Alif a glass of dark red tea in which a sprig of mint was steeping. "You look less like a ruffian and more like what you claim to be. I thought you might be trying to fool an old man into letting you rob the joint."

"I'm not a thief," said Alif.

"I believe you. But what made you come here of all places? Surely it would have been wiser to find a good lawyer."

Alif laughed soundlessly. "I'm past needing a lawyer, Sheikh Uncle. I'd be better off arranging my funeral rites. I thought—well, it's silly."

"Possibly so, but tell me anyway."

"I thought there was no way they could drag me out of a mosque. Especially this mosque."

Sheikh Bilal's expression grew serious. He took a sip of tea, sucking the liquid between his teeth before swallowing.

"There was a point in history when you might have been right about that," he said. "But not now." His eyes wandered to the wood-latticed window. Strong sunlight cast a woven shadow across the floor and the hem of his robe.

"For many centuries the emirs answered to us, you see," he continued. "To the *ulema* of Al Basheera. Back then the protection of this mosque would have meant something. We ran the university and acted as judges for the common folk—during the Middle Ages they say we even ran a well-respected bank. Credit, my boy! Invented by the Arabs."

"I'm half Arab," said Alif, irritated.

"Oh?" Sheikh Bilal blinked at him. "Yes, perhaps you are. At any rate. The emirs were enforcers. They protected the City, protected us, sent the young men off to war when they got too rambunctious."

"What happened?"

"Oil." The sheikh shook his head. "The great cursed wealth from beneath the ground that the Prophet foresaw would destroy us. And statehood—what a terrible idea that was, eh? This part of the world was never meant to function that way. Too many languages, too many tribes, too motivated by ideas those high-heeled cartographers from Paris couldn't understand. Don't understand. Will never understand. Well, God save them—they're not the ones who have to live in this mess. They said a modern state needs a single leader, a secular leader, and the emir was the closest thing we had. So to the emir went all the power. And anyone who thinks that isn't a good idea is hounded down and tossed in jail, as you have so recently discovered. All so that some pantywaist royal nephew can have a seat at the UN and carry a flag in the Olympics and be thoroughly ignored."

"This is treason," said Alif with a nervous giggle.

"Don't I know it! Never fear, I'm completely domesticated. I don't give Friday sermons anymore, but when I did, I glossed over the latest jailed journalist or disappeared dissident like everyone else, and prayed for the health of the emir, and the princess to boot. Yes, I know what's good for me." Sheikh Bilal tossed back the last of his tea and set the glass on his desk with a loud clank.

"Now, if you're finished, I will find you a bucket and some soap and you can get to work on the carpet."

* * *

Sheikh Bilal sat in a chair and directed Alif as he scrubbed at his footprints with a horsehair brush, pointing out debris he had missed. Alif hadn't realized his shoes were so dirty. With growing mortification, he thought back to the mud and donkey shit of the Place of Trash and the well-watered soil of the little date palm grove in Baqara District. His path had taken him across more than a dozen prayer niches printed on the wall-to-wall carpet of the *musala*, prefabricated substitutions for the hand-woven mats men once brought with them from home. His knees quickly grew tired and damp as he worked his way backward toward the mosque's main doors.

"I don't see why this needs to be such a production," he muttered, leaning into the brush. "It's just some dirt. The people who come to pray walk through it to get here."

"Spiritual technology, my boy!" said Sheikh Bilal. "The dirt on your shoes is ritually unclean even if it is practically unavoidable. Ritual law is not required to make sense to us mortals, it is enough that it makes sense to God. When you pray all your actions must fit together like gears in a great machine—like one of your computers."

"Computers don't have gears."

"Don't be obstinate. It's not attractive in someone so young. I know you understand what I mean. Two hundred years ago, would anyone, even the most learned scientist, believe you if you told him one day men would walk on the moon and send information through the very air? I will supply my own response: *no*. But today these are unremarkable events. Perhaps the same is true of ritual—perhaps on the Day of Days the schematic of God's great machine will be as obvious to you as the code in your programs."

Alif sat down and stretched his legs.

"It's not always like that. The reason I came running in here is because—" He paused, then elected to tell a half-truth. There was no need to bring djinn into the equation. "I wrote a program and I don't really understand why it works, and now the government has it."

Sheikh Bilal leaned forward. "Now that is interesting. What does it do, this program?"

"It can tell who people are by analyzing what they type."

"Yes, that is just the sort of thing the State would love. But there is a girl mixed up in all of this, I have no doubt. In a lovely silk veil, whose modesty does not prevent her from using more eye makeup than several Fifi Abdous."

Bewildered, Alif's gaze skittered from the soapy carpet to the sheikh and back again. He wondered if the old man might be a spy, and whether the wet horsehair brush could serve him as a weapon while he made his escape.

"Don't look so startled. You have that sullen expression young men get when they've been jilted. It's why men are meant to have beards—growing all that hair leaves no energy for moodiness. Much more dignified."

Alif touched the stubble on his chin doubtfully. Sheikh Bilal chuckled, folding back the sleeves of his robe and dabbing his wrists with oil from a small glass vial.

"Lotus oil? It helps in this heat. Am I right about the girl?"

"I never noticed that she used too much eye makeup," Alif mumbled. "She looked fine to me."

"I'm sure she did. What, did she say she wouldn't marry you? Not enough money, apartment not big enough, and that skin—well, it is a shame you take after the *desi* side. Girls these days are a frivolous bunch."

"It was her father," said Alif. "He's forcing her to marry someone else. Someone who doesn't love her—someone who only wants to use her to increase his own power."

The sheikh's expression changed. "Hmm. That may be—or it may not. In my experience, a treasured daughter can usually get her way when it comes to these things."

"I know Intisar doesn't want this man," Alif said hotly. "She was crying when I last saw her, crying—"

"All right, all right." Sheikh Bilal leaned back in his chair. "She is betrothed to this other man and breaks it off with you. What do you do next?"

Alif flicked a soap bubble with his finger. When framed so bluntly, his reaction to Intisar's betrayal seemed hysterical, unnecessary. Why had he bothered to write Tin Sari? Why had he not simply erased her number from his phone and deleted her e-mails? It would have been easy enough to avoid her.

"She said she never wanted to see my name again," he said. "So I wrote this program that would identify her no matter what computer or e-mail address she might use. Then I told my system to block her whenever it found her, and make it look like I didn't exist."

"And the government censors found this program, and your goose is cooked."

"Something like that." Alif elected not to mention the other reason for the Hand's vendetta.

"Well, well. You have pious instincts for someone who looks like such a heathen. Not many men use the Internet for so high-handed a purpose as discretion."

"I'm not as good as all that," said Alif, chucking his brush back into the bucket of soapy water. "I could still see her. Online I mean. I still had access to her machine."

"That was very wrong of you. It is only given to women to see without being seen—men must act in the open, or not at all."

"You've gone metaphysical. Can I stop scrubbing? My knees ache."

Sheikh Bilal examined the trail of suds leading back toward his office. "No, no. You've got another six feet until you reach the door. If you rally your energy you could be done in ten minutes."

Alif slopped more water on the floor and dragged the brush in circles over another footprint.

"You don't need to be sulky—you'll be done before you know it. Tell me more about your work. At what point will I be able to write an e-mail to my grandson in Bahrain merely by thinking it?"

"Thinking it?" Alif smiled contemptuously. "I expect never. Quantum computing will be the next thing, but I don't think it will be capable of transcribing thought."

"Quantum? Oh dear, I've never heard of that."

"It will use qubits instead of—well, that's kind of complicated. Regular computers use a binary language to figure things out and talk to each other—ones and zeroes. Quantum computers could use ones and zeroes in an unlimited number of states so, in theory, they could store massive amounts of data and perform tasks that regular computers can't perform."

"States?"

"Positions in space and time. Ways of being."

"Now it is you who are metaphysical. Let me rephrase what I think you have said in language from my own field of study: they say that each word in the Quran has seven thousand layers of meaning, each of which, though some might seem contrary or simply unfathomable to us, exist equally at all times without cosmological contradiction. Is this similar to what you mean?"

Alif looked up from his work, surprised.

"Yes," he said. "That is exactly what I mean. I've never heard anybody make that comparison."

"Perhaps you've never put yourself in the way of hearing it. You look like the sort of boy who shirks his religious education."

"Why does everyone keep saying that?" Making a face, Alif dunked his brush in the soapy bucket once more. "You, Vikram, Dina—"

"No names, please!" Sheikh Bilal put his hands over his ears. "If those chubby idiots from State come back here, I want them to find me in total ignorance. They are not above taking a lighter to an old man's ass hairs if they think it'll make him talk."

Anxiety pinched Alif's midsection. He felt tired and sick, unwilling to be the cause of such potential humiliation. "I'm sorry," he said.

"No matter. In God's eyes whatever will happen has already happened. You don't need to look so guilty."

"I don't know another way to look." Alif bent over yet another footprint. He was nearing the great copper doors where his muddy path began. For the first time he became aware of the profound silence of the place, insulated by stone and metal from the noise of the street outside. It gave the mosque a sympathetic air, as if it could speak but chose instead to listen. An early memory surfaced: he was six years old and his father, still often at home in those days, deemed him big enough to attend Friday prayers. They h.. come here, hand in hand, and prayed in this *musala*—perhaps it had even been a younger Sheikh Bilal who gave the sermon, of which Alif remembered only a deeply intoned *ameen* resonating from the domed roof. He had been happy. He put down the brush and curled up on his side, overwhelmed. The carpet was damp and soapy beneath his cheek.

"My poor dear boy. This won't do at all." Alif heard cloth rustle and felt Sheikh Bilal's hand on his shoulder. "You mustn't despair. Much too early for that. You're clearly exhausted—here, get up. Leave that last bit. I'll have one of the cleaning women do it. You need to rest."

Alif let the old man propel him out of the *musala*. Sheikh Bilal smelled of napthalene, lotus oil, and laundry detergent—grandfatherly scents that put Alif at ease. In a room across the hall from the office where they had taken tea, he unfolded an old camp bed that left a rusty streak where it had been leaning against the wall, muttering to himself as he wrestled it open.

"There. Lie down. Let's say that you are safe here. It's functionally true, for the moment. The sunset prayer will start in a few minutes— I'll lock the door on my way out."

Alif nodded, already on the verge of sleep. When he heard the click of the lock in the door, he burrowed into the musty camp bed and closed his eyes. Sleep did not come. His heart beat erratically, stimulated by adrenaline and the sheikh's black tea. Reaching beneath the bed, he pulled the *Alf Yeom* from his backpack and flipped through its pages with idle restlessness. His eyes fell on a strange transliteration of a familiar word.

"*Feh-kaf-reh-mim,*" he muttered. "Vikram."

The Vampire and King Vikram

In the land of Hind, which in our language means a sword so sharp it cuts without a sound, there lived a great king named Vikram. He was both handsome and noble, as kings ought to be. His people loved him when he was successful in war and lowered taxes and hated him when he was not and did not, as people are wont to do. For many years his realm was prosperous and his reign fruitful.

One day, however, a troupe of villagers from a far province came to him with their faces full of fear: a vampire spirit from among the djinn, which the people of Hind call a *vetala*, had taken up residence in a banyan tree outside the town and terrorized the villagers at night. They begged King Vikram to intervene. Being both humble and brave, the king promised to dispatch the *vetala* himself.

"That's silly," said Princess Farukhuaz. "A king would never risk his own life to get rid of a single evil spirit in some smelly provincial town."

"Ah," said the nurse, "but this one did. Not all kings are cruel immoral men who send others to do work they are too frightened to carry out themselves."

"You're trying to trick me into softening my heart toward marriage," said Farukhuaz. "It won't work. But please continue."

"Very well," said the nurse.

King Vikram took his fastest horse and rode at once to the village in the far province. At midnight, under a full moon, he confronted the *vetala* as it hung by its feet from the banyan tree.

Though the creature was a terrible thing, more shadow than substance, with the countenance of a jackal, King Vikram was master of his fear.

"You are not welcome here," said King Vikram. "As lord of this village, I order you to return to the unseen lands from which you came."

The *vetala* laughed.

"I recognize no lord," it said. "And I find this tree and this village rather pleasant. I think I'll stay."

The king drew his sword. The *vetala* merely laughed the louder.

"Don't bother," it said. "I would kill you before your blow fell. But since you have proven yourself both brave and stubborn, I will agree to leave this place if you can best me in a game of wits."

"I will gladly try," said King Vikram.

The *vetala* folded one ankle against its knee, assuming the yogic position of the Hanged Man, in order to better channel its wits.

"Very well," it said. "I am a mighty fortress, sheathed in stone."

King Vikram thought for a moment.

"I am a catapult," he said. "Stone-breaking, fortress-sundering."

"I am a saboteur," countered the *vetala*. "Oath-breaker, weapon-disabler."

"I am ill luck," said King Vikram. "Upending plots, dismaying plans."

The *vetala* was favorably impressed.

"I am fortune," it said. "I crown luck with destiny."

"I am free will," said King Vikram. "I challenge destiny with choice."

"I am divine will," said the *vetala*, "to which choice and destiny are one and the same."

"I am myself," said King Vikram. "The only thing that is mine to give, by choice or by destiny."

The *vetala* was silent. It stretched out its legs and dropped from the tree, moving to stand in front of King Vikram.

"How very clever you are for a human," it said. "You've won, but you've also trapped yourself. Which I feel you must have known would happen."

"I was prepared for that possibility when I came here," said the king. "Otherwise I would not have come at all."

"Then you are honest as well as clever," said the *vetala*. "A pity you've given yourself to me."

"You will uphold your end of the bargain?"

"You have my word. I will leave this village and never return. But then again, neither will you."

King Vikram took off his sword and attached it to his horse's saddle and with a sharp whistle sent the animal cantering back down the road that led to the capital city. He then faced the *vetala* once more.

"Do what you are going to do," he said.

"Very well," said the *vetala*. "I honor you, King Vikram, as will all my race, for you have demonstrated true nobility: the willingness to sacrifice the greatest of your possessions for the least of your dependents."

With that, the *vetala* entered King Vikram's body and assumed its shape. True to its word, it left the village, traveling west to the land of the Hyksos, known today as the Arabs. King Vikram's memory was ever after honored among both djinn and men, and many histories were attributed to his name.

"How ridiculous," said Princess Farukhuaz, reclining upon a pillow. "A waste of a perfectly good king, all to pacify a few villagers who might have fared as well with a decent exorcist. Nobility is overrated."

"Perhaps," said the nurse. "On the other hand, Vikram might have a greater part to play as a vetala *than as a king. The right thing to do and the smart thing to do are not always the same. Only the Lord of Lords knows all, and He created the world three-parts unseen."*

Alif closed the book with a laugh that verged on hysterical even to his own ears. A strange admixture of fatigue and giddiness ran through his body as a tremor. It was too late to war with belief or disbelief; all he felt was exhaustion. He curled up on his side like a baby, succumbing at last to sleep.

He dreamed he wandered in the desert. Milky dunes spread out beneath his feet, under a sky from which stars and moon were absent. He had been on a road: the elevated highway that ran west out of the City, into the oil fields. But at some point he had lost his way, and now not even the lights of the New Quarter were visible in the advancing landscape. At this time of night the sand was glacially cold. Alif wasn't wearing any shoes. The desert stole warmth from the soles of his feet, then his ankles and shins, until he was dead from the knees down and dragged his limbs like a sleepwalker.

He was waiting for someone. She appeared on the lip of a dune, wearing one of Intisar's jet-trimmed black veils.

"Princess!" Alif waved his arms, not trusting his icy legs to carry him up the dune.

Princess Farukhuaz turned and looked, eyes crinkling with recognition, and slipped gracefully down the sand toward him. She was barefoot also, her feet pale and white-gold.

"You're wrong about a lot of things," Alif told her. "There is nothing you can do with a sphere that you can't do with a straight line."

She shook her head. The beads in her veil quivered musically.

"I could do it," said Alif, growing impatient. "I could out-program your book. I know all the right codes, even if I don't understand them."

Her laugh seemed to come up from the frozen sand.

"And we're not all like that," Alif continued. "I would have done anything for Intisar. Her love was like three kebab meals to me, with tahini and hot peppers. I never took her for granted. Never."

"You're always talking about her when I'm trying to talk about something else."

Alif realized with surprise that the woman underneath the veil was Dina. The feet peeking out from beneath her robe, which had been palest gold a moment earlier, were now a ruddy copper.

"What do you mean?" he asked, baffled.

"I won't let him in," she replied, in a voice not hers. "If you are really his friends, fine, but that—that *thing* is not setting foot inside this mosque."

There was a pause.

"I said stay out!" Dina screamed.

✳   ✳   ✳

194

Alif jerked awake on the camp bed. There was a commotion outside his door. Blinking rapidly, he attempted to clear his head. He heard raised voices: Sheikh Bilal's, and those of two distressed women. Over all three boomed a malicious, sarcastic laugh.

"Don't worry, old man. I promise not to eat you. The walls will not bleed. The Messenger walked among us in our own country, and we heard the Warning. Let me in."

Alif stumbled toward the door of his room and jiggled the lock, still half-asleep. It jerked open from the outside. Sheikh Bilal stood in front of him, all color drained from his face.

"Some girls are here to see you," he whispered. "And they've brought—God protect us from Satan—"

Alif pushed past him into the hallway and jogged across the *musala*. It was very dark. The great skylights cut into the dome above admitted only thin, pinkish streams of illumination from the street lamps outside. The copper doors were open a crack and Alif recognized the convert's pale, puffy face in the gap.

"Alif!" she hissed. "Jesus Christ! Why haven't you answered any of my texts?"

"Hello," he muttered in English.

"You see? I told you he was here." Vikram's yellow eyes glowed, floating in the dark above the convert's head.

"How did you find me?" asked Alif incredulously.

"Your smell," said Vikram. "You reek of electricity and hot metal. I've never smelled anything like it. Little sister was hysterical when we lost you so I went sniffing around the City hither and yon until I caught your scent."

Dina, damp strands of black hair trailing out from her veil, squeezed through the opening in the doors, into the *musala*, with a frightened cry. She was wearing her own clothes again; the black robe and veil looked freshly laundered.

"Don't do that!" she quavered. "Don't leave me with people I don't know and disappear."

"I'm sorry! Those men from State ambushed me when I was waiting for Intisar—"

Dina shrieked. Alif turned in time to see Sheikh Bilal swing a broom through the open door, toward Vikram.

"Stop, stop!" Alif batted at the broom head with his hands. "He's all right! He's helping me!"

Panting, Sheikh Bilal dropped the broom.

"I don't know what you're mixed up in," he said in a low voice, "but if it means letting young girls run around the City at night unchaperoned, with this—this *creature*, then I'm not sure I can offer you my protection any longer."

Eyeing the broom, the convert squeezed into the *musala*. Alif looked from Vikram to the sheikh.

"What do you mean, creature?" he asked.

"This! That thing in the doorway! Dogs are not meant to speak, or go on two legs when they should be on four."

"You seem to have found a holy man," said Vikram blithely.

"He's not as bad as he looks," said Alif, a note of pleading in his voice. "He saved our lives."

"I'm sorry, did you say a *dog*?" the convert interjected. "The Arabic of mine is not a hundred in a hundred."

Sheikh Bilal mopped his brow with one sleeve.

"All right," he said. "Recite the Fatiha, oh, hidden one, and I will let you in."

"In the name of God, the Beneficent, the Merciful," purred Vikram. "Praise be to God, Lord of Worlds. The Beneficent, the Merciful. Master of the Day of Reckoning. You we worship and to You we turn for aid. Show us the straight path, the path of those whom You have favored, not of those who earn Your anger, nor of those who go astray. *Ameen.*" He grinned. "You see? It hasn't burned my tongue."

"That means nothing," muttered Sheikh Bilal, pulling the door wider. "The Devil is said to be wise."

"I'm not the Devil," said Vikram. He bounded inside. "Here, old man—is this better?"

Sheikh Bilal pressed a hand to his forehead as though he felt faint. Coming to again, he frowned at Vikram in surprise.

"You can take the shape of a man," he said. "How did you do that?"

"I turned sideways."

Sheikh Bilal shook his head. Crossing the *musala,* he muttered something about brewing more tea. Alif went to kneel next to Dina, who had taken off her shoes and sat on the carpet with her knees pulled up.

"How is your arm?" he asked tentatively.

"It hurts," she said. "I want to go home."

"I don't know if it's safe yet."

"I don't care anymore. This is crazy. If they come for me I'll tell them everything. Maybe they'll be generous when they realize I had nothing to do with your schemes."

Alif felt stung. "You would really hand me over to State? Just like that?"

Dina looked up at him. Her eyelids glistened with sweat. Alif realized in alarm that she might need real medical care, that being stitched up in a tent by Vikram could hardly be sufficient for a bullet wound. He told himself she was overtired.

"You still need rest," he said. "Here—there's a cot in one of the offices. It's not bad. I was asleep when you all showed up."

Dina followed him across the *musala* without saying a word. He led her into the room across from Sheikh Bilal's office, from which issued the scent of boiling mint. Dina collapsed on the cot, digging her toes into the musty fabric, and let out a sort of half-moan.

"I'm sorry," said Alif. "If I had known any of this was going to happen, I wouldn't have—"

"You keep saying *sorry* without really meaning it. I was so worried, lying there alone in that girl's apartment—and then when they came back looking like death and saying they'd lost you, I thought I would faint. Or scream. It was terrible. And you're not sorry."

Alif felt his patience giving out. "Whatever. Believe what you want. I've been trying my best. It's not like you haven't made mistakes, even though you pretend to be perfect. If you stayed down while that guy was shooting at us, you never would have gotten hurt."

"I panicked!"

"So did I, but even I know not to *stand up* while bullets are hitting the wall over my head."

"You were lying on top of me! I had to do *something*."

Alif was incredulous. "I can't believe what I'm hearing. I was trying to protect you from getting shot. Are you seriously telling me you stood up because you'd rather be killed than touch me for five seconds? Am I as disgusting and sinful as that?"

A choked, exhausted sound escaped her throat. "No! You don't understand, you don't want to understand."

"You're right. I don't care." Alif walked out the door and slammed it shut on her heartbroken sobbing.

*   *   *

In the *musala*, Sheikh Bilal was pouring out cups of tea on a copper tray. Vikram sprawled on his side while the convert sat with her knees tucked beneath her, looking nervous.

"How is the other sister?" Sheikh Bilal asked as Alif came into the room. There was a note of coolness in his voice. Alif clenched and unclenched one hand.

"She needs a good night of sleep," he said curtly.

"She's welcome to it. Our sister here can join her on the cot in the storeroom. You will have to sleep here in the *musala*. And you—"The sheikh looked up at Vikram with an unfriendly expression.

"Don't worry," said Vikram, smiling. "I don't sleep."

"As you like. You all must be gone before the noon prayer tomorrow."

Alif knelt on the floor next to the tea tray. "I'm sorry, Sheikh Uncle," he said in a thin voice. "I didn't mean to make such a mess of things. Vikram really isn't all bad. And I didn't know they were going to show up in the middle of the night. You've been so nice to me—I don't want to get you in trouble."

The sheikh's expression softened. "*Khalas*. It's all right. I'll go to my rest—the dawn prayer is in three hours. You'll hear the call go up." He tucked his robe about him and walked toward the rear of

199

the *musala*, throwing a last look at Vikram before disappearing down the corridor toward his office.

"Why do you always have to make such a scene?" Alif snapped when the sheikh had gone. "Why did he think you were a dog?"

"In his eyes, I was one." Vikram lounged on his side, sipping tea. "You're ridiculous."

"Could we talk English again?" asked the convert.

"Okay, fine," said Alif, rubbing his eyes.

"Thanks. I'm worried about Dina," she continued. "I think she's starting to crack. I mean, she was *shot*. She might need medicine or something."

Vikram laid his head on the convert's leg. "You've hurt me. Do you doubt my abilities as a nursemaid?"

The convert jerked away. "Yes, frankly. I think there need to be doctors and a game plan in place at this point."

Though he agreed, Alif felt a need to change the subject. "Did you hear anything else from your advisor? About the book, I mean?"

The convert flushed. "You didn't get my first message?"

Alif's hand went to the pocket where he carried his phone. It was warm from the pressure of his body. Strange to think that until very recently he had depended on this little sheath of silicon more than his own limbs.

"I haven't been checking my messages," he said.

"Oh. Okay. The gist is—the basic thing is—they've decided what that awful-smelling resin is made from."

Alif waited. The convert seemed unwilling to continue.

"And what is that?" he prompted.

She cleared her throat. "*Pistacia lentiscus,* which is mastic sap. That's not an uncommon ingredient in ancient resins, though it's a little weird to see it used to treat paper. But they also found traces of amniotic material. Human amniotic material."

"*Anioteek* what?"

"The birth caul," supplied Vikram in Arabic.

Alif made a face. "That's disgusting! Who would do such a thing? I've been carrying that awful book around and touching it and holding it for three days now. I'm going to burn my backpack."

"I wouldn't do that. This book is tremendously valuable. I bet you could sell it to some western research institute for half a million bucks."

Alif thought of something horrible. "This anioteek," he said, "you don't think it means the babies were——?"

The convert gave him an exasperated look. "What? Sacrificed? Eaten? No way, not in medieval Persia. They probably just thought the amniotic sac would protect the book the same way it protected the baby."

"That is *extremely gross.*"

"Don't be such a presentist."

"It was common, back then," said Vikram, rolling his tea glass between his palms. "Living books. Alchemists were always trying to create them. There was the Quran, which shattered language and put it back together again in a way no one had been able to replicate, using words whose meanings evolved over time without the alteration of a single dot or brushstroke. As above, so below, the alchemists reasoned—they thought they could reverse-engineer the living word using chemical compounds. If they could create a book that was literally alive, perhaps it would also produce knowledge that transcended time."

"That's pretty blasphemous," said the convert.

"Oh, very. Heretics, my dear. They made the *hashisheen* look orthodox."

"What do you mean, words whose meanings evolved?" asked Alif. "That doesn't make sense. The Quran is the Quran."

Vikram folded his legs—Alif did not watch this operation closely—and smiled at his audience.

"The convert will understand. How do they translate ذرة in your English interpretation?"

"Atom," said the convert.

"You don't find that strange, considering atoms were unknown in the sixth century?"

The convert chewed her lip. "I never thought of that," she said. "You're right. There's no way *atom* is the original meaning of that word."

"Ah." Vikram held up two fingers in a sign of benediction. He looked, Alif thought, like some demonic caricature of a saint. "But it is. In the twentieth century, *atom* became the original meaning of ذرة, because an atom was the tiniest object known to man. Then man split the atom. Today, the original meaning might be hadron. But why stop there? Tomorrow, it might be quark. In a hundred years, some vanishingly small object so foreign to the human mind that only Adam remembers its name. Each of those will be the original meaning of ذرة."

Alif snorted. "That's impossible. ذرة must refer to some fundamental thing. It's attached to an object."

"Yes it is. The smallest indivisible particle. That is the meaning packaged in the word. No part of it lifts out—it does not mean smallest, nor indivisible, nor particle, but all those things at once. Thus, in man's infancy, ذرة was a grain of sand. Then a mote of dust. Then a cell. Then a molecule. Then an atom. And so on. Man's knowledge of the universe may grow, but ذرة does not change."

"That's . . ." The convert trailed off, looking lost.

"Miraculous. Indeed."

"I don't understand," said Alif. "What does this have to do with *The Thousand and One Days*? It's not a holy book. Not even to the djinn. It's a bunch of fairy tales with double meanings that we can't figure out."

"How dense and literal it is. I thought it had a much more sophisticated brain."

"Your mother's dense," Alif said wearily.

"My mother was an errant crest of sea foam. But that's neither here nor there. Stories are words, Alif, and words, like ذرة, sometimes represent much grander things. The humans who originally obtained the *Alf Yeom* thought they could derive immense power from it—thus, it was in their best interests to preserve these manuscripts the best way they knew how. That way, even if they never cracked the code themselves, the books would be vital and healthy for future generations, who might have more success."

The convert yawned into the hem of her scarf.

"I can't function anymore," she said. "I'm going to sleep. Is the spare room through there?"

"Yes," said Alif, distracted. A verging, half-formed thought stood on the edge of his mind, plaguing him. Vikram faded from his vision. He curled up on the floor, pulling his knees to his chest and closing his eyes. The thought could wait; he was still exhausted. If he slept now he could get another hour or two of rest before the dawn prayer. The convert's footsteps ended with a door creaking shut and a murmured *good night*. He didn't answer.

A doe leaped across his eyelids, pursued by a stag; the landscape they traversed was a Linux platform. He knew there was a snare waiting for the doe—*The Days* said so—and watched passively as the creature stumbled, its leg crushed in a hidden vise of slash commands. A Trojan, thought Alif, a cleverly hidden trap. In all probability the doe had invited it in without knowing; perhaps it had executed some kind of dubious content from a foreign land. The stag ran on obliviously. It was a utility program, incapable of responding to the doe's anguished cries, built for more basic purposes than empathy.

Alif cursed it. Idiotic animal. Little packet of ones and zeroes—it was all he was; this was his problem. Dina needed help with her little hoof shattered in the trap. It was his fault. Why couldn't he turn around? A doctor, a doctor—

"Alif."

Vikram's voice seemed to come from inside his own head.

"Wake up, you silly meat puppet. Something is wrong. Stop thinking about forest animals and move your feet."

His eyelids were slow to open. He felt hot breath on his cheek. With great effort, he moved his fingers, batting at whatever was breathing down his neck. He encountered fur.

"Fuck!" Alif sat upright, staring: a large dog—or jackal, or ghastly thing—crouched in front of him with an intent look in its yellow eyes.

"For God's sake, don't be such a baby." The figure shimmered like a mirage, resolving into Vikram. "You were dreaming."

"Don't do that," Alif croaked, rubbing his eyes. "Please, I'm serious. Don't ever do that again."

"I haven't done anything. You need to pay attention. There is a woman here to see you. You've got to send her away."

"What?"

"She's being followed by something terrible. If she leads it here we can all put our beards in our asses. I can't protect you from everything, Alif, or the girls for that matter. Do you understand?"

Alif struggled to his feet. The look on Vikram's face alarmed him. He shuffled toward the great copper doors, willing himself awake. He undid the lock and heaved the crossbar upward, pushing on the left door with his shoulder. It slid open without a sound. Outside on the steps of the mosque stood a woman with her back turned, wearing a black veil. Night air floated past her to touch Alif's face; it was damp, smelling of the sea and the oncoming dawn. Little lights were visible in the windows of the villas and shops down the street.

"Hello?" called Alif tentatively.

The woman turned and looked at him through familiar ink-black eyes. Alif stopped breathing.

It was Intisar.

Chapter Nine

"Peace be upon you," she whispered.

Alif could not speak. He didn't return her greeting.

"What the hell are you doing here?" he asked finally.

"I can't stay," said Intisar, ignoring his question. "I got your message. I was going to meet you at the university, like you wanted, but Abbas—Abbas found out. He finds out everything. All the things I write in e-mails or say on the phone. You shouldn't try to contact me again."

"I wasn't going to," said Alif. His voice cracked. "I tried to leave you alone. But the book—"

Intisar's eyes flickered, unable to hold his gaze. "I should have just given it to him. I took all the notes I need for my thesis—I didn't understand why he was so interested in it. But I was angry, so angry, at him, at my father—I thought if I gave it to you, you might be able to figure out why he wanted it so badly. You're clever about these things. I wanted to punish him."

"Do you know?" he asked her. "Do you know what it is? Do you know who—what—wrote this book, Intisar?"

The eyes peering out from above her veil were very black.

"I don't know what I believe," she whispered. "I only found out about the *Alf Yeom* by accident—it was mentioned in an article I read about French Orientalist translators. I wanted to see if I could find a copy in its original language. But as soon as I began to search for it, things got—strange."

Alif held his breath.

"I was contacted by a bookseller in Syria who said he had a copy to sell for fifty thousand dinars. I was skeptical—that's a lot of money. I asked him if the book had been out of print for long, thinking I could find another copy and get a different price. He just laughed at me. He said it had never been in print to begin with. He said the original wasn't even written by human hands. I thought he was crazy. But I was so intrigued that in the end I agreed to pay his price."

"And you read it." In spite of himself, Alif's eyes lingered on her slim shoulder. The fabric of her gown was so fine that he could detect a hint of collarbone beneath it, and ached, longing for permission to kiss the enrobed skin.

"I read it," she said. "It became clear to me that this was not an ordinary collection of stories. When I got to the last chapter I almost panicked, it was so disturbing. And then one night I woke up all of a sudden and saw a man sitting in the desk chair near my bed. Just sitting, looking at me. He had yellow eyes. And I realized he wasn't quite a man at all. He was something else.

When I turned on the light, he was gone. The next day, Abbas came to ask my father for me."

"A spy," said Alif. His heart rattled in his chest. "Sakina was right. He's got allies. That's how he found you. Intisar—" He seized one of her hands. "He doesn't need you anymore. You got rid of the thing he really wanted. You could leave him. I'll give the *Alf Yeom* back to the people who know what to do with it, and you and I will go somewhere, anywhere, together. Screw the City. We could see Istanbul or Paris or fucking Timbuktu. I'd live in a hut if it meant I could see you every day."

He could see the interest draining from her eyes. The first ripples of despair began somewhere in his gut.

"It's not that simple," she murmured. "He's already paid part of the dowry—a very generous dowry. I think he's serious, Alif—it isn't just about the book. If it was he could have thrown everything back in my face after I betrayed him by sending it to you. But he didn't. If anything, he's been nicer to me since then. Just today he came and sat next to me and told me how beautiful our children would be, because I was so beautiful, and asked me about my thesis and told me how happy he was to have an educated wife. He cares about my mind. None of the other men my father has suggested have given a damn what I think, or whether I think at all."

"He's trying to bribe you." Alif attempted to quell the searing sensation that was burning up his veins, the onset of a rage that would be the end of his self-control. "He thinks if he pampers you you'll hand me over to him and he'll get everything he wants—the book, the girl, and the hacker he's been trying to squash for years."

209

Intisar said nothing.

"Tell me," said Alif, breathing hard. "Tell me you still want me and not him. Tell me you meant it when you said you loved me all those times."

"Of course I meant it," snapped Intisar. "But love isn't everything, Alif. Where would we live? What would we live on? I can't spend the rest of my days in a two-room apartment in Baqara District, doing my own laundry."

Her words fell on Alif like stones, leaving bruises.

"Is that what you were thinking about when we were together?" he asked. "When we were lying in my bed and counting streetlights out the window like they were stars, is that what was going through your head? That you couldn't believe you'd agreed to slum it with an imported Rafiq from Baqara District?"

She jerked away, her pretty brows knitting together above her veil.

"Of course not. I wanted to be with you. I fought my father when he told me he was marrying me off to Abbas. I hid the *Alf Yeom* from him, remember? I sent it to you. To hurt Abbas. It's just that . . ." She trailed off, looking restlessly out into the deserted square.

"It's just that I've been thinking about things since then," she continued in a more moderate voice. "And talking with my father, and with Abbas. They're not going to force me to do anything I don't want to do. But they've convinced me that marrying outside your own people can only lead to trouble. You know that better than anybody. Look at your parents."

Her reasoning sounded stilted, rehearsed. Though he could not refute her logic, the insult was too great to bear. It was one thing for him to criticize his parents—which he had done on more than one occasion while Intisar listened in what he had assumed was sympathy—but quite another to have that criticism thrown back in his face. He felt her betrayal of his confidence more keenly than he had her betrayal of his body.

"What about me?"

Intisar dropped her eyes entirely. Her face was unreadable behind the black drape of her veil.

"What about me?" Alif asked again, more agitated now. "You get engaged to this monster behind my back, you saddle me with this awful-smelling old book, and while I'm running around like a criminal in my own city, you're doing what exactly? Do you know what I've been through in the last few days?"

"I'm sorry," Intisar whispered. "I thought—but it doesn't matter now. I'm frightened for you. I don't know what he's planning. He told me that even without the *Alf Yeom* he had enough evidence of your illegal activities to put you behind the sun for the rest of your life. What's Tin Sari, Alif?"

Alif swallowed. "A program," he said hoarsely.

Intisar looked at him. "He says you were involved with criminals, real criminals. Is it true?"

"No." Indignation began to override his anger. "That's a lie. My clients aren't criminals. They're just trying to escape from this gold-covered shit we live in, like everybody else. The only difference is that they have the balls to stand by what they believe."

"You said you loved me," Intisar said softly. "How could you get mixed up with these people when you knew I would get dragged in, too?"

211

He found the question bizarre. The strangeness of this meeting—the late hour, the steps of the mosque, the absence of Intisar's car and driver anywhere he could see—crept up on Alif like nausea.

"Intisar," he whispered, "how did you know I was here?"

She backed down the steps.

"I was supposed to make you come out," she said. "Where they could see you. They needed to be sure. They made me, Alif—I didn't want this to happen—"

The red beam of a laser sight danced near Alif's temple. With a screech, he ducked back inside the great door and slammed it shut. The crossbeam slid down into its cradle with a loud clank.

"You bitch," he shouted through the dense metal. "You've sold us all to the Devil!"

The lights inside the *musala* flickered and shadows began to move across the underside of the dome in strange patterns, against the light. Alif felt chilled. Vikram appeared behind his shoulder.

"Get the girls and the old man," he said. "Lock the rest of the doors."

Alif looked up at him wildly. "What do you mean? What are we going to do?"

"We are going to stay exactly where we are for as long as possible. Your friend's new buddies can't come inside a mosque, but that won't stop them from trying. I have to warn you—this can only end one way."

"What? What way?"

"With you in their custody."

Alif ran a trembling hand through his hair.

"Is it better if I just turn myself in?" he asked. "Do you think they'd be merciful if I cooperate?"

"I doubt that very much."

"Mother *chode*." Alif sat down on the floor.

"I told you," said Vikram, scaling the far wall and the underside of the dome with his claws. He stopped, hanging batlike from the smooth stones, to examine one of the dome's five skylights. The curling shadows retreated when he approached. "I can't protect you from everything. At least, not permanently. However, some time is more useful than no time, so I will give you all that I can." His voice bounced through the room and landed in Alif's ears half-muffled.

Something occurred to Alif.

"Vikram," he called up. "Can you die?"

Vikram landed soundlessly on the floor.

"Oh, yes," he said.

"How?"

"The same ways as you. Starvation, thirst, old age, decapitation, a bullet wound, a broken heart."

"People don't die of broken hearts," said Alif.

Vikram snorted. "You are at this very moment," he said.

Alif looked down at his chest in horror. There was nothing out of the ordinary. He pressed his temples with his fingertips until he felt pressure building in his head; the parameters of the world felt off, his processing speed compromised.

"Get the girls and the old man," Vikram repeated. "If they haven't been awakened already by your cursing."

213

Alif got up and half-ran toward the rear of the *musala*. Sheikh Bilal was coming out of his office, buttoning the collar of his long robe with fingers that trembled.

"What is this unholy racket?" he hissed. "Why is the *musala* empty? Where are the worshippers for the dawn prayer?"

"I don't think they're coming today, Sheikh Uncle," stuttered Alif. "The Hand—the men from State, and maybe some worse things—are here for me. Vikram wants us to lock all the doors."

Sheikh Bilal puffed his cheeks. "I have been caretaker of Al Basheera for thirty-two years," he said. "Never have I turned away a Muslim at prayer time. This business of yours—"

"I've been betrayed," wailed Alif, the last of his self-control slipping away. "She tricked me and now we're all fucked, Sheikh Uncle, fucked—"

"God forgive us! How dare you use such language here? Is this *Hamlet*? Are we onstage? Stop blubbering and go perform your ablutions—we will do the dawn prayer ourselves, if nothing else."

Alif made a face at the elderly sheikh, aghast. "How can you possibly think of prayers at a time like this?"

"How can you afford not to? Get out of here and wash your feet."

Incredulous, Alif stumbled toward the washroom to obey. He heard nervous female voices coming from the room with the camp bed. A gust of air hit him as the convert yanked open the door and looked out wildly.

"What's going on?" she asked in English. "We heard shouting."

"We're surrounded," moaned Alif, rolling up the hems of his pant legs with great energy.

"Surrounded by what? What are you doing?"

"Washing for prayer."

"Jesus—hold on." The convert ducked back into the spare room. She emerged again with Dina, who was hastily pulling her veil into place over the bridge of her nose.

"What have you done now?" Dina asked in a leaden voice.

"Nothing. That bitch sold me out to State."

Though he could not see her face, Alif detected a faint air of satisfaction.

"I told you she was trouble. Any rich girl willing to run around behind her father's back in Baqara District is trouble."

"I know she was slumming it by being with me," snapped Alif. "You don't have to rub it in. She was going to be my wife—she did it for love—"

"If you say so."

Alif cursed again and half-hopped across the cold tile at the perimeter of the washroom. The water that splashed out of the tap in the wall was frigid; he yelped as it hit his perspiring skin. A muddle of voices came from down the hall and split as they echoed against the washroom walls, creating a kind of operatic harmony: Sheikh Bilal's loud indignation, Vikram's musical contempt, the convert's nasal protests. Dina was silent but he could guess what she was thinking. A wave of guilt passed over him. He had no right to bring her into his perverse orbit, so far removed from the little duplex in Baqara District where she performed the hidden offices of her sex. She would be tainted by his infamy—he had, perhaps, put the nice young suitors with trim beards and reasonable salaries out of her reach. All this he had done by sending her to Intisar's house with that wretched sheet, and by walking back from the date grove with her on a hot afternoon. It took so little to destroy a woman.

Sheikh Bilal was calling his name. Alif finished his ablutions and hurried back down the hall toward the *musala*. The sheikh stood in an ornamented niche facing Mecca, sunk two steps below the floor to demonstrate the humility of the prayer leader. Dina and the convert stood shoulder to shoulder in the rear of the room, near the great doors. Alif hurriedly turned his back; Dina would not be able to lift her veil for prayer with him looking. He stood just behind Sheikh Bilal, looking around furtively for Vikram—who had disappeared— before bowing his head.

Someone pounded on the great doors from the outside. Sheikh Bilal ignored the noise and cleared his throat. The call to prayer came melodiously up from his lips in a voice that suggested a much younger man: confident, well-trained, unwavering. For a moment Alif was distracted by the force of the familiar words praising prayer above sleep. It was not singing, exactly, but some occult scale, the music of the spheres. The pounding arose again. Alif gritted his teeth, forcing himself not to look back. He realized with alarm that anyone who came through the doors would get to the girls first. It was ludicrous to stand there and do nothing, he thought, like the sheep that crowded the streets on the eve of the Feast of Sacrifice, wagging their little heads and making plans for the following week.

In front of him, Sheikh Bilal was bowing; Alif hurried to copy his movements. The commotion outside the great doors grew louder. Abruptly the noise stopped, replaced by a terrified howl. The hair stood up on Alif's neck. He knelt and touched his forehead to the musty carpet, fighting back the bile that rose in his throat. As he stood for the second *raka* the noise outside redoubled, punctuated by the sound of a police siren. Sheikh Bilal raised his voice. "And on the Elevated Places shall stand men who know all things by their signs; they shall call out to the dwellers of the Garden: peace be upon you! They shall not have entered it yet, though they hope."

On his knees, Alif greeted the angel to his right; when he turned to his left he saw Vikram kneeling next to him. He yelped.

"Quiet," said Vikram. "You sound like a little girl."

"Did you just *kill somebody outside?*"

"No. I thought the old man might be upset by guts on his doorstep. I gave them all a good scare, though. One or two are catatonic."

"How many are out there?"

"They've cordoned off the whole street. That should give you an idea. The other things—well, it's difficult to guess how many there are. They move as one. I'm not sure anybody besides the man who summoned them can see them. The people from State don't seem to realize they're there."

Dina crept up from the back of the room and sat down several feet away from Alif.

"If I go out there and tell them I've been held hostage by a terrorist, do you think they'll let me go home?" she asked Vikram. Miserably, Alif attempted to catch her eye. She ignored him.

"Since you deliberately misled a State agent in order to protect your abductor, I doubt it." Vikram cocked his head at her. "How is your arm, little sister? I smell blood."

"It's fine. I'm fine."

The convert walked toward them, twisting her hands. The face above the hem of her violet scarf was pale and puffy.

217

"I really don't know about this," she said in English. "I had no idea you were in this much trouble. I shouldn't even be here—I've got class today—" Hysteria pressed at the edge of her words. Alif gave an inarticulate cry of frustration.

"Sit down." Sheikh Bilal's voice left no room for refusal. He carried a folding chair under one arm and a volume of *tafsir* under the other. "Enough sniveling. You will all listen quietly to the lesson I prepared for the *dars* that would be taking place at this moment had your escapades not prevented my students from attending."

"What? Why?" Alif looked from the sheikh to the great doors. The sound of groaning metal suggested State had moved from man power to more forceful methods. "This is crazy. They're cutting through the doors and you want us to sit here at your knee like a bunch of pimply madrassa students? We're done if we stay."

"We're done if we leave. At least this way you can tell them I gave you nothing but tea and religious instruction. My skin will be safe." The sheikh sat down on the folding chair, arranging his robe around him. Vikram loped across the carpet and scuttled up the far wall once more, disappearing out of a skylight. A pale, unsaturated luminescence, the false start of dawn, came down through the opening in his wake.

Sheikh Bilal opened the *tafsir* to a marked page.

"We will begin with a question," he said. "It is particularly appropriate to this context. God, in His mercy, tells us that a good deed is recorded as soon as a person decides to perform it, while a bad deed is only recorded after it has been performed. But the world today is more complicated than it once was. So I present you with the following dilemma, posed to me by a young boy of my congregation: when one is playing a video game and his avatar consumes a piece of digital pork, has a sin been committed?"

Alif waited. "You're asking me?" he said when Sheikh Bilal was silent. "You're the *alim*. How am I supposed to know?"

"I'm interested in your opinion. I know very little about video games. It is my understanding that this boy is very involved in something called World of Battlecraft."

Alif sighed in exasperation. "I don't know. It doesn't matter." The great doors shrieked as though under pressure from a saw. "I really can't concentrate."

"It mattered very much to this young person. I was inclined to tell him that if he was worried, it probably *was* a sin, or at the very least, would weigh on him as one. For God also tells us that when you perform an action you believe to be a sin, it still counts as a sin even if it is proven to be permissible. Conscience. Conscience is the ultimate measure of man."

"All right, it's a sin," moaned Alif. "I don't care. I don't play Battlecraft. It's for teenagers."

"I'm not looking for any particular answer. Don't feel you must agree. I want to know what you think."

"I think people need a break. It's not like they're out there selling bacon and booze. They want to pretend for a few hours a day that we don't live in this awful hole getting squeezed by State on one side and pious airheads on the other, all while smiling our shit-eating grins so that the oil companies keep shoveling money into our pockets. Surely God wouldn't mind people pretending life is better, even if it involves fictional pork."

"But isn't that a dangerous precedent? Fictional pork is one thing—one cannot smell it or taste it, and thus the temptation to go out and consume real pork is low. However, if we were to talk about fictional adultery—I know there are many people who do and say all kinds of dirty things online—then it would be another matter. Those are real desires manifesting themselves on the computer screen. Who knows how many adulterous relationships begin on the Internet and end in the bedroom?"

Alif blanched.

"And even if they don't," the sheikh continued, "who's to say the spiritual damage isn't real nonetheless? When two people form a relationship online, it isn't a fiction based on real life, it's real life based on a fiction. You believe the person you cannot see or touch is perfect, because she chooses to reveal only the things that she knows will please you. Surely that is dangerous indeed."

"You could say the same thing about an arranged marriage," said Alif.

Sheikh Bilal smiled a little ruefully. "Ah. Yes. You have me there."

The noise of the saw rose several decibels, screeched, and stopped. Voices yammered outside, high and confused.

"Those doors are four hundred years old," said the sheikh in a wistful voice. "The gift of a Qatari prince who passed through the City while on hajj. They are irreplaceable."

"It's my fault." Alif wiped his brow with the back of one trembling hand.

"Yes, that's true. But. You are likewise irreplaceable." Sheikh Bilal leafed through his *tafsir*. "I believe your friend has disabled their saw."

The convert, who had been pacing back and forth across the *musala*, came to stand next to the sheikh's chair.

"This is making me to worry, a lot, a lot," she said in Arabic. "I can't stand it anymore. I want to leave."

"Yes, I'm sure you do," said the sheikh. "But that does not seem possible at the moment. Would you mind if I asked you to boil some tea and fetch the tin of biscuits sitting in my office? Bless your hands."

The convert stared at him for a moment, then shuffled off to do as he asked. Dina rose from the floor and went silently after her, pulling her robe tight against her wounded arm like a sling. Alif watched her with deepening anxiety.

"I have to end this," he murmured. "I have to get her out of here." He remembered NewQuarter01's parting words: *if this gets really bad u better do the right thing. U know what im talking abt.*

Sheikh Bilal sighed and closed his book. "So much fear and doubt over a computer program," he said. "One does not even need to commit a crime in order to commit a crime anymore. We live in a simulacrum. I've got djinn in my mosque and State agents at the door—fah! Who could believe it? Soon we will lose the thread of history, and the birds and the beasts will be telling us what is real and what is not."

The sheikh's words prompted a memory. He had been asleep in the spare room, on the camp bed, and begun to dream. Birds and beasts. A stag and a doe—like the story in the *Alf Yeom*. But the stag had not been a stag, not really. The stag was an avatar, a stand-in for a—

"Utility program," whispered Alif. His face felt hot and he began to perspire. The thought that had been lurking in the back of his mind, just out of reach, rushed out like a back-alley thief ready to mug him for his wallet. It filled him with commands and equations, cascading tiers of information, coding platforms. He looked at the sheikh with glazed eyes.

"Sheikh Uncle," he said hoarsely, "do you remember that thing you told me when I was trying to explain quantum computing?"

"What's that?"

"That thing, that thing! About the layers of meaning in the Quran—".

"Ah. Each word has seven thousand layers of meaning, all of which exist without contradiction at all times?"

Alif was flooded with euphoria.

"I know what he wants to do with *The Thousand and One Days*," he said. "I know why he's so desperate to get his fists on it."

"Who do you mean?"

"The Hand," said Alif. "He's trying to build a computer."

Chapter Ten

Mercifully, Sheikh Bilal had a DSL line in his office. He ran it into a Toshiba desktop that was several years old and clogged with malware, but which had enough RAM to suit Alif's purposes. After swearing to back up his Word files and archived e-mails in the cloud, Alif convinced the sheikh to let him blank the hard drive, leaving a tabula rasa, a clean void of machine into which Alif could pour himself. He installed a Linux platform off of his netbook, feeling an almost erotic surge of excitement when the familiar home screen loaded, accompanied by a series of energetic clicks from the guts of the CPU. Alif propped the *Alf Yeom* against a half-empty case of bottled water that sat at the back of the sheikh's wide, cluttered desk, opening the book to the story of the hind and the hare: the origin point. He took a breath.

"I'm sorry, my boy," said Sheikh Bilal from the doorway, "I still don't properly understand what you are attempting to do. You said this censor is trying to *build* a computer. My computer is not only built, but becoming a little out of date."

"If I'm right, it shouldn't matter." Alif squinted against the pink dawn that flowed slyly inward through the latticed window. "I'm going to teach it how to think all over again. I will give it a second birth."

"I beg your pardon?"

Alif looked over his shoulder at the old man with a feeling of beneficent tenderness. He shouldn't be impatient; he was on fire with meaning, with light colder and purer than the ruddy dawn. He could explain anything.

"You remember our conversation about quantum computing?"

"Yes, roughly."

"A quantum computer would theoretically perform data functions using ions—which are difficult to get, control, and manipulate. That's why real quantum computing is still mostly a dream. Not even the Hand has that kind of hardware. But. But."

"But?"

Alif's eyes gleamed. "But you could do almost the same thing if you could get a normal silicon-based computer to think in metaphors."

The sheikh's rheumy gaze sharpened. "If each word has layers of meaning—"

"Yes. You do understand, you do. I knew you would. It was that analogy you made to the Quran that got me thinking in the first place. Metaphors: knowledge existing in several states simultaneously and without contradiction. The stag and the doe and the trap. Instead of working with linear strings of ones and zeroes, the computer could work with bundles that were one and zero and every point in between, all at once. If, if, if you could teach it to overcome its binary nature."

"That sounds very complicated indeed."

"It should be impossible, but it isn't." Alif began typing furiously. "All modern computers are pedants. To them the world is divided into black and white, off and on, right and wrong. But I will teach yours to recognize multiple origin points, interrelated geneses, systems of multivalent cause and effect."

He could hear the sheikh shifting on his feet.

"When we spoke about the Quran, I was only trying to understand what you wanted to tell me about computers," he said. "I didn't mean for you to use it so literally—"

"I'm not using the Quran," said Alif tersely. "I'm using the *Alf Yeom*. The Quran is static. You aren't supposed to change a single dot. You have to be trained to recite the words correctly, because if you mispronounce a single one, it's not the Quran anymore. The *Alf Yeom* is something dynamic, changing. I think—I think *it* changes, I mean the book itself, depending on who reads it. The dervishes saw the Philosopher's Stone, but I see code."

"Knowledge must be fixed in some way if it is to be preserved," said the sheikh. "That's why the Quran isn't meant to be altered. There were other prophets sent to other peoples, but because their books were altered, their knowledge was lost."

"I can compensate for that," said Alif, feeling less sure than he sounded. "It must be possible. The Hand believes it is. He was going to translate the strings of metaphor into strings of commands."

"But the book is ancient! Its writers couldn't have known anything about computers."

225

"They didn't need to. It's not what they said that matters, it's the method they used to say it—the way they encoded the information. They threw everything they knew into one pot and developed a system of transmitting knowledge that could accommodate the contradictions. It's that system I want to replicate in your computer."

Alif's fingers paused on the keyboard. A vision pressed itself against his sinuses from inside his head: Dina, outlined in black against their rooftop in Baqara District, her veiled face a floating interruption of the dust-pale minarets strung out along the horizon. She held his copy of *The Golden Compass* like an enemy flag. Alif blinked rapidly. The screen in front of him came back into focus.

"I'm still not sure how it all connects," he admitted.

"If that is the case, I would be very careful," said Sheikh Bilal. "The greatest triumph of Shaytan is the illusion that you are in control. He lurks on the forking paths, lying in wait for those who become overconfident and lose their way."

"I have to code," said Alif. He heard the swish of cotton robes as Sheikh Bilal withdrew. The sun had grown more persistent, throwing an intricate pattern of light and shadow on the floor as it came in through the wood-latticed window. His head began to ache as he bent to his task. Every so often he could hear the sound of rifles, and once or twice something heavier, a dull boom like distant thunder. The noise always ceased abruptly, replaced by the desultory calls of sparrows in the courtyard outside. Once he heard the static-laced sound of a megaphone, and a voice, faint by the time it reached his ears, announced that anyone who laid down his weapons and came out would not be harmed.

"—think that we have weapons?" Dina's voice, muffled by stone, carried through the door, along with the echo of her sandals as they slapped against the floor of the corridor outside.

"I don't know, my daughter," came Sheikh Bilal's weary answer. "Perhaps your friend—well. They can't get in, at any rate. This place was built to withstand Bedouin raiders . . ."

The voices faded down the hall. Alif squeezed his eyes shut until they smarted and then, opening them again, he was assaulted by pinwheels of light. Despite the sun, he had the sense of some malevolent pressure in the air around him, a sentience he recoiled from investigating too closely. The feeling came in waves, and each time it receded, Alif could half-see Vikram, who appeared to his fevered consciousness like a coil of dark matter uncurling itself against the invisible threat. Alif could tell Vikram was tiring.

He worked steadily. His fingers knew what he needed to do before his mind did. Pieces of the fragmented Hollywood hypervisor were still useable; he plugged lines of the familiar code into the sheikh's machine, watching with satisfaction as algorithmic towers grew before his eyes. Every so often he paused to reread a portion of the *Alf Yeom*, separating the frame story into two threads of code: Farukhuaz, the dark princess, became a set of Boolean algorithms; the nurse, her irrational counterpart, non-Boolean expressions. There was nothing he could not interpret numerically. The numbers themselves, like stories, were merely representative, stand-ins for meaning that lay deeper, embedded in pulses of electricity within the computer, the firing of neurons in Alif's mind, events whose defining elements blurred and merged as he worked.

The sunlight strengthened until nearly midday, when the lattice over the window served its purpose, folding a matrix of shadows into one flat stretch of shade. Alif marveled as the sheikh's office went suddenly cool and dark. Centuries ago, a woodworker had measured the changing angle of light against this room's east-facing wall and built a wooden screen that would provide shade in the hottest part of the day without interrupting a scholar's view of the courtyard. It was simple, elegant. Alif felt a pang of envy—his own creation, when it was finished, would be neither simple nor elegant. It would be a lumbering, evolving miasma, a vastness, perpetuated by the sheer pressure of information. It would be capable of functions beyond counting, but on its own it would be meaningless.

*   *   *

Dina appeared in the late afternoon. She brought a glass of tea and a plate of *ful* that had obviously spent a long life on the inside of an overheated tin can. Alif sniffed at it before taking a bite.

"It's all there is," said Dina. "We can't exactly send out for food."

Alif studied her. She kept her eyes downcast; the translucent skin of her eyelids was discolored, as if from bruising or sleeplessness. He held out the plate.

"You eat it," he said. "You need your strength. You should be lying down anyway."

Dina made a restless motion with her good arm.

"I've eaten. It's gone quiet outside—Vikram says the street is still blocked and there are snipers on the rooftops. We're under siege."

"Are we on the news?"

"You are. And they're using your fake n—your handle. They're calling you a terrorist."

Alif let his head roll back, closing his eyes. His name. He thought of Intisar breathing it in the dark, sanctifying it. To see it made so ugly and public was worse than the terrorist label, which he had seen applied to loftier and better men.

Dina pressed the tea glass into his hand. "You never told me you work for Islamist groups."

"I don't work for anybody. I work against the censors."

"But you've helped the Islamists."

"I've also helped the Communists. And the feminists. I'll help anybody with a computer and a grudge."

"Okay, well, I'm just telling you that the newscasters on *City Today* haven't been making such fine philosophical distinctions."

"Of course they haven't. They never do." Alif shoveled a spoonful of *ful* into his mouth. Dina lingered, glancing around the office at the piles of file folders and books.

"What is it that you're doing?" she asked after several moments.

Alif set his mouth in a thin line.

"The Hand stole my greatest idea," he said. "Now I'm stealing his."

"What's the point? The only way you're leaving this place is in handcuffs, with a black bag over your head."

"It doesn't matter. By that time I'll have bombed out their entire system. All the data they have on me or my friends or anyone else in the City will look like scrambled eggs. He won't be able to use Tin Sari to hurt anybody else. They can kill me if they want—I'll still have won." A thrill went through his body. The scent of the *Alf*

229

Yeom roused something unfamiliar in him, a dormant athletic instinct that made him want to run and rend and rip until his opponent was beaten. A small part of him was frightened by the ferocity of his own aggression. He quelled it.

"I don't like it when you talk like that," said Dina. "Like you're some kind of hero from one of those novels you're always reading." There was a quaver in her voice that made Alif look up. Moisture rimmed her lashes. Guilt replaced his aggression. He half-stood, bungling his feet in the legs of Sheikh Bilal's desk chair.

"I'm sorry," he said. "I didn't mean to upset you. Please don't cry. You have no idea how unfair it is when you cry—I can't do anything but what I'm doing."

"I can't help it," Dina whispered, little catches in her voice. "I'm so tired. I don't want to be here. I'm scared of whatever is going to happen next but I want it to happen—not knowing is even more terrible."

"Dina—"

"And when you talk like that, like you don't care about what happens to you, like there's no one who would miss you and worry about you, it makes me want to scream. You can be so stupid about these things."

Alif sank back into the chair, feeling bereft. He swallowed the remainder of his tea. In the thrall of some mysterious impulse, he kissed the rim of the glass twice before handing it back to Dina. Her fingers closed around the imprint of his mouth.

"Bless your hands," he said hoarsely. She turned and left the room.

* * *

By the time evening fell, Alif had begun to shiver. The air was not cold; the stone walls of the office radiated a pleasant warmth accumulated during their long hours in the sun, but the combined pressures of coding and fear and a night without real sleep weighed on his body. Alif knew he was dangerously tired. He was alarmed by the thought of making a mistake, creating a digital tick buried too far within layers of code for him to find without serious effort. On an ordinary day his own fastidiousness would have kept him from reaching this point; many times he had interrupted himself on the downward slope of a coding jag and slept or eaten or washed, reasoning that time was less costly than error. Now he felt the pressure of each minute. Some higher brain function recognized the absurdity of spending his last hours of freedom alone in front of a computer at a task he might not even finish but he ignored it, struggling instead to maintain the trancelike level of focus he needed to continue.

As night drew on he began to dream. He imagined the columns of code on his computer screen were instead a tower of white stone, growing up and up as he typed. He adorned the tower with the climbing jasmine and dusty yellow hibiscus that grew in the garden of the little duplex in Baqara District. He imagined himself at the top of the tower, surveying his domain like a general. At midnight a golden foot appeared on the edge of his field of vision.

You've come back, said Alif.

I'm back, said Princess Farukhuaz. The foot retreated beneath a gauzy black robe. He regretted its passing. Farukhuaz knelt next to the desk, or on the white stone of the parapet—he had lost the ability to distinguish between them. She put one hand on his knee, her slim fingers laden with gold and tipped in red henna. His shivering increased.

You are building a tower, she said. *Up and up and up, and at the very top I am waiting. All things are possible at the top. All things take whatever form they like. They will call you a transgressor but I will call you free.*

Yes, said Alif, *that's what I want.*

You're very close, said Farukhuaz.

He accessed the State mainframe almost without thinking. The firewalls that had been erected to protect their official intranet seemed trivial to him now, as decorative and breachable as the Old Quarter wall that surrounded their literal fortress, a tourist attraction. Alif felt as though he was looking down at it from a great height. Grids of code spread out within the wall, representing government e-mail accounts, municipal security, the City budget office. Largest of all, occupying an almost satirical amount of RAM in a well-cooled room full of blade servers somewhere, was the intelligence bureau.

Alif was bewildered. For years he had written off his own bravado; he and Abdullah and NewQuarter01 and all the rest were, at the end of the day, hacks, not revolutionaries. As much as he hated State, the idea of physical confrontation made him ill. All his efforts had been the product of fear, an anonymous finger in the face of men he would never have to confront face-to-face. He had always assumed State crushed people like him because it could, not because it saw them as a real threat. The vast, energy-leeching intelligence grid told him otherwise. This was a government terrified of its own people.

The Hand lurked there, a scavenging mathematical mass, unleashing worms in their millions upon the digital City. Alif recognized the payload they carried. Tin Sari was bundled in their guts, ready to be injected into dissident hard drives like parasitical DNA.

Alif took a moment to marvel at the craftsmanship that had gone into creating the Hand. To call it a carnivore system was insufficient—one might as well call the pyramids a collection of headstones. It functioned out of a single, central ISP. The usual packet-sniffing protocols had been replaced with something much more dynamic: software that could learn and adapt to the usage patterns of each individual target, eliminating the false alarms that often occurred when search terms were used with a negative bias. The mark of a single personality was clear throughout its design: the man who had programmed it was inventive, surgical, with a mind that melded orthodoxy and innovation. That he understood the metaphorical capacity of machines was obvious; he had intuitively incorporated some of the basic elements Alif was using to build his tower.

That's how he broke into my machine, said Alif. *He was speaking a language none of my firewalls understood. He was speaking a language I myself did not understand, not then.*

Yes, said Farukhuaz, *but you have something he does not. Something he covets. I have the Alf Yeom.*

You have me.

Alif looked down into the digital plain below him. It was easier to strike here, from above; the binary world was still flat. He stood apart from it, ears ringing with the music of the spheres. The tower churned beneath him.

Unleash it, said Farukhuaz. *Destroy it all.*

Alif typed in a series of execution commands. Immediately the plain began to glow with activity. Alarm after alarm was tripped as antimalware programs rushed in to contain the damage, attempting to shut down noncritical functions to block Alif's progress, creating a kind of burn perimeter between him and State's most sensitive code blocks. He laughed; Farukhuaz laughed. It was so easy now. He was above. The perimeter was a smudged circle beneath him, a child's pencil drawing on a piece of paper, devoid of any depth. He sent himself into the heart of the State intranet.

The Hand roused. It lumbered to its feet, reeking of ionized air and dry metallic bones, revealing a level of functionality Alif had not detected. He reeled backward, recalibrating. Breaching the confines of the State intranet, the Hand began to attack the base of Alif's tower, slicing away layers of code through a mirroring protocol of a kind Alif had never seen before.

Break him, whispered Farukhuaz.

I don't know how! Alif felt a swell of panic as his creation began to shudder. Desperate, he began an elaborate code-switching operation, changing the state of the data the Hand was attacking faster than it could attack. The shuddering lessened. Alif steadied his breathing. The panic in his chest, born of adrenaline with nowhere to go, turned swiftly to a sulfuric, thwarted rage. The Hand had taken his love, his freedom, his name; yet those things mattered less to him now than destroying the man who had taken them. They were an acceptable sacrifice.

Alif turned on the electronic beast. It had weak points. There was no system that did not. His creation altered itself and its methods until it found them—errors that Alif now recognized not as computational limits but as failures of imagination. His creation was better, higher, operating in a realm of near-consciousness, unbound by dualities. The tower rose. It spread its roots into the guts of the Hand itself, injecting the beast's most basic infrastructure with multivalent statements it could not process. The Hand fell back with a silicon scream, retreating behind the burn line of the intranet.

Elated, Alif turned to pursue it, but found the entire edifice looked smaller now—alarmingly small. The height made him giddy. Farukhuaz's arms were around his back, her veiled head resting on his shoulder. She coaxed him in words he only half-heard, but he couldn't breathe; the altitude, her arms, the lack of oxygen in this electrified stratosphere, everything pressed down on him at once. He began to see spots of light. He shook his head to clear them, but instead they coalesced into something that spanned the horizon, arcing upward toward an improbable nexus—not a face, not eyes and ears and a mouth, but a bright mass unnervingly akin to all those things.

Alif was pierced by a memory: he floated in a skin-bound pool, naked, curled upon himself. His mind was sluggish, as if unformed; he could not distinguish between his body and the saline world around him. Suddenly the pool was lit from all sides by this very object, this nonface: time had begun then, and he had known himself to be alive.

The nexus grew brighter. Alif cowered before it, overcome by an emotion he could not identify.

Where are you going? it asked.

Alif couldn't find his voice. He had made a grievous error. The code was unstable. As he traveled dizzily upward, no longer certain of his control over what he had created, he realized that in his zeal for innovation he had sacrificed the integrity of his knowledge. The base of the tower was blurring as data failed to cleanly replicate itself, leaving uncertainties, gaps in its theoretical DNA. The tower could not hold long. He was approaching some kind of ceiling, a point at which the super-adaptable nature of his coding scheme would no longer compensate for its inherent instability. If you told knowledge it could be anything it wanted, there was a risk it would degenerate into nothing at all.

You tricked me, said Alif to Farukhuaz, trembling. Farukhuaz didn't respond, but tilted her head to the sound of the tiny bells that shivered in her veil. She was a cipher. Alif fought for something real, something to make him remember the earth that looked so tremulously small below him. He tried thinking of Intisar. But Intisar, too, had become an ashen idol. He saw his own life polluted with her ambivalence, first about their uncertain marriage, then about this uncertain book, the purpose of both clouded by pointless secrecy.

He had mistaken that secrecy for something elite, evidence that he had been initiated into a greater truth than the unseeing people around him could understand. At this altitude his self-importance seemed tawdry. He did not hide because he was better, he hid because he was afraid. It was not Intisar's fault—it had begun with his name, the name behind which he had concealed himself, a single line seemingly as straight and impregnable as the tower rushing skyward around him. The name without which he would never have had the courage to approach her. Yet he blamed Intisar nonetheless.

It occurred to him that he might not love her.

The nexus was drawing nearer. The light it emitted penetrated Alif's skull even when his eyes were closed, and he wailed, overtaken by fresh panic.

Where are you going? the nexus repeated.

The tower began to crack.

*　　*　　*

Alif heard the door to the sheikh's office crash open. There was a smell in the air like burning flesh. He gasped, wrenching away from the keyboard: it glowed hot and blisters were already forming on his fingertips. The computer monitor was a molten heap, revealing mechanical guts that crackled with a bluish static charge. Pain overcame the protective veneer of adrenaline. Alif moaned, balling himself around his injured hands. There were voices in the doorway. The smell of burned skin was replaced by that of sweat, fur, and blood; a dark-pelted shape, now jackal-like, now human, limped toward the desk chair and regarded Alif at eye level.

"You've made quite a mess, younger brother," it rasped. Fluid trickled from one side of its mouth.

Alif turned sideways in the chair and buried his face in the furred shoulder closest to him.

"I've screwed up so badly," he whispered. "Dina was right—the sheikh was right—you were right—"

"I usually am." A cough vibrated through the chest beneath Alif's cheek.

Alif looked up. "You're hurt!"

Vikram was favoring one limb, which ended in a paw, or hand, that bent inward at a sickly angle. Blood streaked his coat.

"There are a lot of them now," he said, "and they're on their way inside."

Sheikh Bilal appeared behind Vikram's looming shoulder, with the convert and Dina close behind. Alif instinctively reached for Dina; she stopped short of touching his hand, but let her fingertips linger in the air above it.

"God save us! What on earth has happened in here?" Sheikh Bilal surveyed the simmering wreckage on his desk. "Did you light my computer on *fire?*"

"Hellfire," said Vikram, with a hissing laugh that ended in another cough. "The boy has been dabbling in some very naughty things. That's sulfur you're smelling." He cackled at his own joke.

"There's no time for idle talk. We've got to get the women out. God knows what might happen to them if they're arrested."

"I'm an American citizen," said the convert in a voice that shook. "I'll show them my passport—they can't interrogate me without someone from the embassy present—"

Alif did not take his eyes from Dina. The sight of her, concealed though she was behind yards of black, drained some of the fear from his chest. She looked at him steadily, the green solar flares around her pupils bright and tearless.

"I won't let anything happen to you," he told her.

"You most certainly will not, because you are going to turn yourself in," said the sheikh. "You will explain to the authorities that these girls were coerced into aiding you and have had no part in whatever schemes you are involved with."

Alif uncurled his hands, wincing. "Where are they now?" he asked.

"They've gotten through the outer doors," said Sheikh Bilal. "I barred the back entrance of the *musala* to buy us a little more time. I think, perhaps, if the girls were hidden in the cellar—"

"What a stupid idea," said Vikram. "They'll be discovered within an hour. No, I'll take them with me."

"Take us where?" The convert's question ended in a shriek. Her face was very white.

Vikram sighed. "Into the Empty Quarter," he said. "Into the country of my people."

"What are you talking about? *What is he talking about?*"

"Is that safe?" asked Dina quietly. Vikram shook his head.

"It's said that only holy folk can walk there without going mad," he said. "And it's very difficult to get your muddy little bodies through intact. Very difficult." He winced. More fluid dripped from the side of his mouth and splashed on Alif's knee. "But it's better than what will happen if you stay."

Alif searched for the origin of the blood on Vikram's pelt. He thought he saw a red wound between two ribs, opening and closing with each breath like a hideous mouth.

"Are you—well enough to do that?" he asked.

Vikram's head drooped a little.

"On a good day it would cost me my life. Today it may cost me significantly more."

"No!" said Dina. "No—"

"Don't squeak at me, little sister," said Vikram irritably. "Let me choose my own final deed, so the angels have something impressive to write down on the last page of my book."

The voices of men, angry and low, echoed down the corridor from the direction of the *musala*.

"I want five minutes," said Alif. "Do I get five minutes? With Dina. Alone."

Vikram hauled himself to his feet.

"You'll be lucky to get three," he said, and padded toward the door. Sheikh Bilal ushered the convert out in front of him.

"I will wait for you outside," he said to Alif. "Plan your next actions very carefully. *As-salaamu alaykum.*"

The door closed behind him. Alif knelt at Dina's feet.

"It's so bright in my head," he stuttered. "There are so many things I want to say but it's so bright I can't think—help me, please. You're the only one who knows what to do. Just—just make it less bright—"

Dina hesitated. Then she knelt in front of him, knee to knee, and threw her veil over his head.

*   *   *

The darkness soothed Alif's dazzled eyes. After a moment his pupils adjusted, lessening the smarting pain in his head. He could not have guessed the world she had created for herself. Sewn into the underside of her long outer cloak were patches of bright silk: patterned, beaded, spangled with points of light; they hung above him like a tent, supported by her bare, bandaged arm. They lay on the floor facing one another. He rested his forehead in the curve of her neck, taking in the scent of her hair. She watched him. She was not beautiful, not by the measure of the magazines hidden beneath his bed at home. Not like Intisar. Her nose was as large as he remembered. She was unfashionably dark, leading

240

Alif to guess she had never bothered with the skin-bleaching creams so many girls used to poison themselves. Of course she had not. She had pride.

"What are you thinking?" she asked.

"I'm thinking that you are all good things in one place," he said.

She blushed. Her mouth was tender, expressive, her red-brown skin unflawed. He realized with something like humility that her most striking feature had always been visible to him. The greenish, upswept eyes, set against the palette of her flesh, were even more appealing now.

No, not beautiful, but a face that was not easily forgotten.

"I've been unfaithful to you," he murmured. "Forgive me."

"I forgive you." The delightful mouth curved upward. He wanted to kiss it, but held back. He would not touch her until she permitted him, until he had spoken to her father and made it all right. He had to take leave of her and go.

"Please stay alive," she whispered.

"You, too. I'm coming back for you."

"Say it again."

"I'm coming back."

*   *   *

Sheikh Bilal was waiting in the hallway with a grim expression. Vikram, like an oversized dog, lay panting at his feet, damp with clotted blood and sweat. He rose unsteadily when Alif and Dina emerged.

"You go wait over there, little sister," he said to Dina. "Keep the other one quiet. She's gotten a bit hysterical." The convert was leaning against a wall farther down the corridor, whimpering. Dina gave Alif a searching look before turning to do as she was told. Alif watched her go with a dull ache in his throat.

"If you are ever cruel to her, I will come back and haunt you," said Vikram. "Guard her like your own eyes. She is probably circumcised, which means you must be very patient and very gentle when you take her to bed."

"God forgive us, man!" Sheikh Bilal stared at Vikram in dismay. "At least leave this world with some manners."

"I'm only telling the boy what he needs to know," Vikram said sullenly. Alif put his arms around the broad, blurred shoulders, which shifted between man and animal and shadow in a way that betrayed pain.

"Thank you," he muttered, embarrassed by his own ragged affection. Vikram clapped him on the back with his good limb.

"Keep your wits sharpened, younger brother," he said. "I don't believe we'll meet again in this life."

Alif gave a curt nod, hoping his lip didn't tremble.

"I'll see you in the next, then."

"God willing."

Vikram limped down the hallway toward Dina and the convert, who stood watching him with clasped hands, as though waiting for a train that might not arrive. Alif looked away, sensing he could somehow damage what was about to happen by observing it. He sent up a wordless prayer for Dina's safety. As an afterthought, he prayed for the convert as well, with the uncharitable feeling she needed it more.

"I am going to unbar the door," said Sheikh Bilal, looking likewise away from the scene at the end of the hall. "I would take my hands

242

out of my pockets if I were you. These are the type of men who will never spend a day in jail for shooting you on sight. *Bismillah.*" He lifted the creased wooden bar from the door between the *musala* and the classrooms and offices beyond it.

"Wait!" Alif called out. "What will happen to you? They wouldn't shoot the imam of Al Basheera, would they?"

Sheikh Bilal snorted. "This will be an entertaining way to find out."

Alif took his hands from his pockets and wiped them on his pants. The wooden door slid open, revealing two rows of riot police in full uniform, all of whom began to smash their batons against their polycarbonate shields in a coordinated rhythm. Alif fought the urge to giggle. His nerves, shot and exhausted, couldn't summon the chemical wherewithal for fear. He looked over his shoulder: Vikram and the girls were gone. The only evidence of their passing was a thin trail of blood, smudged in several places by what looked like the footprints of a very large dog, footprints that halted abruptly three feet before the stone wall at the end of the hallway.

Turning toward the police, Alif put his hands back in his pockets.

"Hi," he said in English. The rows of men parted as three State security officials with handguns at their hips came rushing forward. Alif heard Sheikh Bilal shout. Before he could look back at the old man, a baton came down on Alif's skull. Pain shrieked through his head and neck. He brought up the contents of his stomach, gasping.

"Little faggot's thrown up on my shoes!" The voice was fat and familiar. Alif recognized it as belonging to one of the men who had trailed him from the university.

"Stupid shit. I should make you lick it up. It's the last meal you'll have for a long time."

"F-f—"

"What's that?"

"F-fuck you." Alif spat the remaining bile from his mouth. Then, suddenly, he couldn't see. A black bag had descended over his eyes and the world collapsed into a flat void.

Chapter Eleven

He awoke in darkness. Blinking revealed nothing: he could make out neither shapes nor depth nor any kind of light. Clawing at his face, he discovered the black bag was gone; this darkness was something more complete. For a moment he thought he had been buried alive and shrieked, flailing his arms. He touched only air, and heard the shriek echo off of a wall some distance away: not in a coffin, then. Was he blind? He rubbed his eyes experimentally and saw spots. This reassured him, but only for a moment; he realized he did not know what a blind person could and could not perceive. Was it like seeing darkness, or was it the complete removal of all visual sense? The question kept him occupied for several haggard minutes. Fear had returned, fresh and rested, and poured through his limbs in a stew of adrenaline.

Air on several sensitive parts of his body told him he was naked. He ran his hands down his torso and was relieved to find himself intact. His head was sore, and a painful exploration of his scalp revealed the skin had split where the baton had met resistance. The cut had not been treated; it stung under his fingers. Blood was matted in his hair. He moved forward, shuffling his feet, and reached out with both arms until he met a chilly wall. He followed it around several corners, coming at last to a hinge and an expanse of metal that might be a door. Pounding on it and shouting yielded nothing. He slid to the ground with his back against the metal facade, succumbing to a loud, wet bout of weeping that left him exhausted.

When the tears stopped, he curled up on the floor facing the door. A tiny breeze touched his face, telling him there was a gap, small but existent, where the door met the ground. Try as he might, he could divine no light from it. Either the space beyond the door was dark as well, or he truly was blind. The thought threatened to bring on fresh tears. He wanted Dina, he wanted her consecrated darkness, so unlike this hostile absence of light. She was dark the way the hour before dawn was dark, a time ordained by God for prayer. He wanted the lemon scent of her hair and the stars that glimmered in the secret interior of her veil. He thought of what she had risked by comforting him and was overcome by urgency; he knew her exasperating sense of decorum would not permit her to take any other partner now that she had shown him her face. He had to return to her. He began pounding on the door again.

There was no answer. When his hands were raw he stopped and withdrew to the opposite side of the room, restlessly aware that he had created a third problem to go along with his wounded head and blistered fingertips.

"I'm doomed," he said to the unlistening air. The sound of his own voice startled him. He needed to urinate. Feeling his way along the wall, he halted at the first corner he encountered. He deliberated for several moments before relieving himself into it, shuddering with humiliation. All the stories he had read online about the prisons of the western desert had seemed so theoretical, a goad for his outrage against the government, not real in and of themselves. They were part of the fiction in which he lived. But there was nothing fictional about this room, no tangible evil against which he could prove himself brave. There was only the stifling black silence, which amplified his thoughts in a way that stirred dread in the recesses of his mind.

He backed away from the corner, hoping he would remember which one it was to avoid stepping in his own mess. The air around him was growing uncomfortably warm. Was it daytime, then? There seemed no better option than to try and sleep. Alif felt his way to the door again and lay lengthwise in front of it. The tiny draft it admitted was an iota cooler and fresher than the stuffy rebreathed air inside the room. He took long, slow breaths of it, eyes closed, and willed himself to relax.

The speed with which he lost track of time alarmed him. When he woke he couldn't tell whether he had slept for minutes or hours; making his way to the corner, which was going fetid in the heat, he urinated again, and wondered whether the recurrence of this bodily function told him anything about how long he had been confined. He was getting thirsty. He tried to go back to sleep and couldn't. Lying awake, he wrote code in his mind, tapping out key sequences on the metal door to make a little noise. At some point, he drifted off again.

The sound that awoke him was difficult to identify. At first he thought it was steam escaping from somewhere, perhaps a vent or a pipe hidden in the ceiling. For a moment he was afraid they were gassing him. But the sound was syncopated, irregular, halting at organic intervals and, after listening for some time, he realized with horror what precisely he was hearing.

It was laughter.

He searched wildly in the gloom for its source but the darkness was too thick to be certain of anything. Terrified, Alif began to pant, pressing his back against the door and drawing his knees to his chest. The laughter grew louder. There was something familiar about it. Alif was possessed by a wild hope.

"Vikram?" he whispered.

The laughter stopped.

"No," came a voice, hissing, neuter, disembodied. "Not he. You are not saved. Vikram is dead. Quite dead."

"Who are you?" Alif's voice broke on the last syllable. There was movement across the room, the dry noise of fabric being dragged along the ground.

"You don't recognize me?" The voice drew closer. "After all that we built together, Alif."

He heard the sound of small bells. The edge of something soft, like silk, slid across his foot. His head throbbed.

"Farukhuaz," he breathed.

The laughter began again. Alif pressed his hands over his ears.

"You're not real," he said. "I made you up to help me finish the code—you're a fantasy, you're in my head—"

"I am very real," said the voice from between the bones of Alif's skull. "And I am also in your head."

Alif ground his hands against his eyes until he saw spots once more.

"I could have made so much of you," the voice continued, "if you'd let me. You were so close. A few minutes more and you would have pierced the veil of Heaven itself. All things seen and unseen would have been laid bare in front of you."

"It was the wrong way," said Alif, pressing himself more tightly against the door. "It wouldn't have worked. The code was too unstable."

"You are afraid of your own power." Alif felt a hand slip between his bare knees. He jerked away.

"It wouldn't have worked," he repeated. "It started to decay in front of my eyes. You saw it. The information had no integrity, no guiding principle. The whole project was collapsing when the computer fused."

"Coward," said the voice. "Fake. You lacked the nerve to see it through."

Alif struggled to escape Farukhuaz's questing fingers. Shuddering currents of revulsion passed through him.

"Stop it," he gasped. "Please stop."

"What, not a man either? A little piglet."

Alif lashed out at the void. His hands encountered cloth, trembling bells, and something awful, like slime; he cried out and fought with greater strength, shoving the viscous thing farther into the darkness. It occurred to him to recite the *shahada*. The thing began to shriek. Encouraged, Alif bellowed every talismanic holy verse he knew, testifying to the oneness of God, the indivisibility of His nature, the perfidy of Satan. The shriek rose to an unnatural decibel, rattling through the room in fading reverberations until it became indistinguishable from the tinnitus inside his own ears.

Alif ran out of breath. Light flooded the room, sending arcs of pain through his already tender skull. He doubled over, shielding his face with a gasp.

"Babbling already? That doesn't speak well of your fortitude. Get up."

It was not Farukhuaz's voice. Squinting, Alif peered toward the speaker: a man stood in the doorway, wearing a *thobe* so white Alif's retinas ached to look at it. He was tall, with a neatly trimmed goatee and a bearing that suggested long-held authority. Alif had trouble focusing, and could not guess the man's age; tears seeped out when he held his eyes open for more than a moment or two.

"Get up. I want to look you in the face."

Alif struggled to his feet. The room, he now saw, was a bare concrete box, whitewashed with some kind of cheap paint that bore the smudged and foul-looking imprints of dirty fingers and blood and perhaps worse. There was a drain in one corner—not, he realized with regret, the corner he had been using as a urinal.

The man in the white *thobe* watched him with a critical air.

"You look younger than I expected. I know your birth date, naturally—nevertheless, I anticipated you would appear mature for your age. But you haven't even really filled out yet."

Alif remembered his nakedness and flushed, attempting to turn away and hide his most vulnerable parts. There was no manful way to go about it.

"Please don't bother," said the white-robed figure. "This is standard operating procedure. Very effective—isolation, no light, no clothing. We don't even have to touch people much, these days. Of course, there are exceptions. Some of the more emphatic religious types have been through psychological training, quite rigorous stuff. Impressive really. But every man has his limits."

Alif blinked at him stupidly.

"Every woman as well," the man continued, running one finger along the wall and rubbing the chalky residue of the paint against his thumb. "But then, God made woman perversely easy to brutalize, didn't He? It does seem unfair. Don't you agree?"

Alif opened and closed his mouth, wondering whether there was some sort of implied threat in the question.

"I wouldn't know," he said finally. His voice was hoarse. He was afraid he might start crying again, and gritted his teeth.

"You wouldn't know." The man chuckled. "You're quite a boy. I'm a little disappointed—one wants to feel respect for one's enemy. Especially one as talented as you have proven yourself to be. I'm surprised she became attached to you. I would expect her to have better taste."

"She?"

"I can see the mental lethargy has begun to set in. Well and good. Intisar, Alif. You do remember Intisar? I hope you do, since you have had from her that which was due to me by right. One of us ought to have gotten some pleasure or pride out of it."

Alif felt his heart jump. He felt thwarted, standing there ridiculous and unclothed; he had always imagined this moment with his hands around the throat of the man standing before him.

"It's you," he rasped. "You're him. You're the Hand."

The man smiled.

"If you wish. I've never liked that name, flattering as it is. It's a little overblown. You dissident types do enjoy your amateur theatrics."

"You—you're—" Alif shook with fury. He knew no curses vile enough.

"The son of a dog, a whore, or what? I've heard it all. Let's skip that and be civil. There will come a point, very soon, when your anger will burn off and be replaced by desperation. You'll be groveling at my feet, and in such an attitude you'll wish you'd kept a polite tongue in your head. I'm doing you a favor by warning you now."

"I don't need any warning, you pig-eating ass-coveter."

"Creative, very creative. You see how fast one's mental faculties return when the lights come back on? Light stimulates all the hot spots in the frontal lobe. Without it, even the most civilized philosopher is at the mercy of his primitive brain. I've seen respected university professors lose the power of speech after a few months in here. It even works on the blind, if you can believe that. They can't see the light but their brains still perceive it at some level. Unless they've been recently blinded—no long-term neural adaptation in that case. Speeds things up tremendously."

Alif felt several of his bodily organs recoil.

"How long have I been in here?" he asked in a different tone.

The Hand chuckled. "If I told you that, it would undo all the good work you've already put into your own psychological deconstruction."

252

"What do you want from me?"

The Hand's smile faded. "What a banal question," he said softly. With one hand he adjusted the pointed edge of his head covering. He held it between his fingers for a moment with an expression Alif couldn't read, examining a crease in the white cloth. "How long have we been playing this game, Alif? Back and forth, State and insurgency, firewalls and viruses. Your entire adult life. Many precious years of mine. No progress, no victory for either side. Finally, I thought I had an edge; I knew *The Thousand Days* was real, and I had a powerful intuition—a vision, almost—about what I could do with it. Those hash-smoking medieval mystics didn't really understand what they meant when they talked about the Philosopher's Stone. They didn't have the same intellectual or technological resources we do. The human mind isn't set up to make as many calculations as you would need for a multivalent coded manuscript like *The Days* useful in any way. But a computer is."

"It didn't work," said Alif.

The Hand ignored him. He studied Alif with detached curiosity, his eyes lingering on the younger man's nicked, stubbled chin.

"We all get off on the same thing, that's the problem," he said. "You don't really care about revolution, I don't really care about the State. What gets us hard is the code itself. I created what I believed to be the most beautiful suite of security programs ever made, a continuation of the sinews of my own flesh, in some way. I thought that was winning. It certainly helped me track down a lot of your friends. But never you—you remained maddeningly hidden. And then you stole the greatest idea I'd ever had, and used it to destroy my life's work."

"I'm better than you," Alif said, slurring his words. He wondered whether the Hand was right about the effect of light on his mind.

"I think you're probably right," said the Hand, without apparent offense. "For me programming was never an intuitive process. I studied very hard while all my classmates slacked off, knowing that government jobs were waiting for them whether they did well in school or not. I wasn't different because I had any special gift for computers—I was different because I had ambition. I was as angry at the State as you are, once—not for the same reasons, but angry nonetheless. I had no desire to lie around a villa and screw an endless parade of terrified housemaids, or sit in an office with a bunch of fat, lethargic princes, pretending to run an emirate. I saw what kind of security apparatus our vast resources were capable of creating and I decided to unleash them. God knows no one else would have taken the trouble."

"You're a fucking tyrant," said Alif.

"What other kind of man do the peasants respect in this part of the world? Come on, Alif. Tell me what you honestly envision for the City. A democracy? Plato's Republic? You've imbibed too much western propaganda. Give the citizens of our fair seaport a real vote and they will do one of three things: vote for their own tribe, vote for the Islamists, or vote for whoever paid them the most money." The Hand's eyes twinkled. "Would you like to cast bets about the kind of treatment a person like you would get if the Islamists came to power?"

"They'd probably make me caliph," muttered Alif. "I designed their whole e-mail encryption setup from scratch."

"They'd stone you to death for adultery. Don't imagine for a moment that they'd bother with the nicety of four witnesses to prove your guilt."

Alif felt his anger returning. "I've never committed adultery," he said. "Intisar is my wife in the sight of God." The words sounded profane as soon as he said them. He did not love her. The promise he had made to Dina, the promise she had prompted from his guts and his loins and his heart by showing him her face, was greater than his furtive union with another woman.

"Oh, you've signed a precious little piece of paper. I don't suppose you bothered with witnesses either."

Alif was forced to admit he had not.

"You see? You're as much a hypocrite as your bearded friends. Your marriage isn't valid in the eyes of God or anyone else. This is what kills me—why can't we be honest with ourselves? Why must we drag God into each of our sins? You wanted to go to bed with Intisar, so you did. Better to be an honest fornicator than a false pietist."

A retort died on Alif's tongue, killed by a grudging sense of relief.

"Am I supposed to admire your honesty?" he said finally. "Is that it?"

"I had hoped you would." The Hand looked a little sad. "I imagined our first conversation playing out in a very different way. I thought you would divine the purpose of my bringing you here more readily."

Alif blinked away tears in the bright light.

"You're here because I've won," said the Hand. His mouth settled into an unfriendly line. "You asked what I want from you—I should think it would be obvious, but since it isn't, I'll tell you. I've won. Even though you took my trump card and used it against me, I've won. I want that realization to settle over you like a premonition of death. I want your defeat to seep into your bones as you sit naked in the dark, watching your life and your sanity spool away before you into nothingness. I want to watch each of your intellectual powers drop away one by one until you are a quivering, pissing mess at my feet. By then I will have gotten what little information I require from you to rebuild my system. You will become useless to me. At that point, I will allow you to die. Perhaps I will even have you executed, though most probably I will starve you to death instead. The idea of watching you eat your own fingernails in desperation is appealing."

Alif's breathing became labored. He looked the Hand in the face, ignoring the tears that streamed from his smarting, dilated eyes. The fear was so intense that it was indistinguishable from euphoria, and gave him strength.

"I will live to watch you thrown to the dogs," he said quietly.

The Hand laughed.

"You wish." He turned to leave, rapping on the door in the far wall of the room. It opened from outside with a loud clank.

"Next time," he said over his shoulder, "we will talk more about the book."

* * *

After that, they began to feed him. Every so often a slat would open in the door—no light accompanied it—and a tray was shoved through into Alif's cell. He did not believe that these meals, usually bread and lentils, came at regular intervals; sometimes he was still full when the next one arrived, yet at other times he was ravenously hungry for what seemed like days before the slat opened again. He suspected the uncertainty was part of the Hand's procedure, designed to keep him anxious, or to further elide his sense of time. Alif learned to jump up at the sound of the slat opening; if he did not, the tray would clatter to the ground in an inedible mess. A paranoid certainty settled over him and he was convinced that each meal was his last, inaugurating the Hand's threat of starvation.

A beard grew on his face. He tried to guess the number of days of his confinement by the length of the hair, but it proved impossible; the only time he'd ever had more than a few days' worth of growth was when he had coded Hollywood. It simply grew, and at one point he woke to discover a full fist-length under his chin. Very soon after, the lights came on again and revealed two State security agents, who dragged him down a corridor to another bare room to hose him down and scrub him with a wide brush meant for the floor. Alif had howled in pain, heedless of his dignity; he howled again when they took a razor to his head and face, removing all hair from both and leaving him nicked and bleeding. For a time he fantasized that they had read his mind, and did not touch his face to judge the length of the hair there.

He began to speak to himself in an attempt to stave off the lizardlike haze fast settling over his mind. It started, he thought, as a rational exercise, a method of self-preservation. He recited song lyrics, as many as he could think of, jogging his sluggish and increasingly nonverbal memory for fragments of things he'd heard on the radio once he had run through several albums of Abida Parveen and the

Cure. He would stop when his voice was hoarse, satisfied by this quota of mental exercise. Soon enough, however, the tenor of these monologues changed, and he would wake from a half-daze at the sound of his own babbling, halting in the middle of pronouncements that did not seem to contain words.

Panic returned then; slow, oozing panic that seemed to emanate from his pores in a foul-smelling sweat. He found himself calling for Vikram, in the insensible hope that the creature would appear from between the cracks in the wall and free him amid a volley of insults. But Vikram did not come, and with a dread that originated in some uncorrupted part of his soul Alif knew Farukhuaz had spoken the truth. He mourned, grateful to be shaken by a feeling that fed on something higher than animal adrenaline. Supplications for Vikram's soul flew out of the darkness, and for the woman he had taken with him. He did not say her name, worried that the Hand might be listening, but he projected the image of her naked face with all his might, until he believed he could see it hanging in front of him, a truer darkness than the one that blotted out his sight.

Farukhuaz he could sense. She—or it, the primordial thingness of her, invented yet eternal—lurked at the edge of his perception like a cautious predator waiting for its prey to tire. Of Farukhuaz he was most afraid, certain now of what she truly was, and when he could remember, while he could remember, he recited holy verses under his breath. He felt like a charlatan; he knew it could see the indifference of his faith. As his verbal self declined, he felt it getting closer, a fetid presence that stalked his shrinking perimeter of sanity.

When the Hand appeared again, Alif was glad to see him.

"Thin and disgusting," the Hand said approvingly while Alif wept in the bright light, unable to keep his eyes lubricated against its sudden luminous influx.

"Alive," Alif croaked.

"Yes, for as long as it suits me. Look, I've brought you a chair." He unfolded a metal object and placed it in front of Alif. Alif peered at it, and deciding it was what the Hand claimed it to be, sat down. The laminated seat was cool against his cramped muscles.

"So." The Hand produced another chair, sat, and folded his hands in his lap. "What have you been doing to occupy yourself? The guards say you sing. And spout nonsense."

"Keeping busy," said Alif.

"Yes, a good idea. Hallucinating yet?"

"I'm being watched by the Devil."

The Hand chuckled.

"Naturally. He's a very common guest down here. A lot of inmates see him. Then again, the really crazy ones see Gabriel, and the ones even crazier than that see God."

"Saw the Devil before you locked me in this shit hole. He came out of that book of yours."

The Hand looked displeased.

"Don't be such a pietist. There is no such thing as evil knowledge."

"I used to think so, too," said Alif.

"Then you've begun right and ended wrong. I was the opposite —when I began to discover the unseen, I had as many spiritual qualms as my childhood Quran teacher could have wished. Then again, my introduction to the hidden folk was mostly an accident. I began researching magic as a purely intellectual exercise. I hoped

259

it would broaden my understanding of code. Our impulse to store and access data through coding languages predates computers by thousands of years, and that's really all magic is. I was simply looking for a fresh perspective. The first time I tried to summon a demon, I wasn't expecting anything to come of it."

"What happened?"

The Hand's smile was mechanical. His teeth gleamed like polished metal in the strong light.

"What do you suppose? It worked."

Alif jerked as a chill gripped his body. The Hand hooked one foot under the crossbeam of Alif's chair and pulled it closer.

"Now, I need you to pay attention," he said. "There are things I need to know."

"I've already told you what you need to know," said Alif, feeling belligerent. "The *Alf Yeom* is not what you think it is. Or maybe it's exactly what you think it is. Either way, it's dangerous."

"Of course it's dangerous. That's the entire reason I want it. The way you were able to trample over my lovely security system tells me the code-writing methodology embedded in the *Alf Yeom* works even better than I dared hope. I was so impressed with what you managed to get out of it that I couldn't find it in my heart to be angry. Well, that's a lie. But my anger was tempered by respect."

"It doesn't work as well as you think," said Alif. "It's too unstable. When you ask information to adapt to new parameters that rapidly, the fundamental commands get lost. There's a huge data decay issue. The whole system forgot what its original function was supposed to be and collapsed. It fused the machine I was working on. I've never seen a computer run that hot."

"Yes, I saw. It was a useless lump of elemental metals when we got to it. Totally unrecoverable. But in my opinion the breakdown had more to do with the truly idiotic amount of RAM you were using. That little desktop was never meant to handle such a data load."

Alif shook his head emphatically.

"Nothing to do with RAM. I made sure each of the programs were running at peak efficiency. And I stripped out all the original software before I even started."

"Wouldn't have made a difference. In the final analysis, you were working on a computer too unsophisticated for what you were trying to achieve. If you'd had access to a suite of our machines, all wired into a blade server, your little science experiment would have changed the future of computing."

"No."

The Hand made a gesture of irritation.

"If you're still trying to fight with me about this, you clearly haven't been down here long enough. I'm not interested in false humility and dire warnings. I know you're trying to put me off so I don't build on your work and outdo your own efforts. You're still playing the game, Alif. You haven't yet realized that the game is over and I have won."

Alif sawed his jaws back and forth.

"I'm not playing anything. I'm telling you the *Alf Yeom* is ideological cancer. The djinn were right—we can't really understand their way of thinking, and we make a mess of it when we try. If you tried to use that methodology on a system that was really important—the City's electrical grid or something—you could end up with chaos. No light, no phones, people going crazy."

The Hand sighed. His eyes reflected the light strangely, as if they were all pupil. Alif felt queasy.

"Let's talk as colleagues for a moment," said the Hand. "Surely you see the limits of binary computing. We are rapidly approaching the ceiling of its utility. After that, what? Is this the peak of civilization? Is there nowhere to go but down? Quantum is a pipe dream. If human progress is to continue, we have to relearn how to use the tools we already have. Reteach our machines. Look what the ancient Egyptians were able to achieve using rudimentary wheels and pulleys. That's what the *Alf Yeom* allows us to do, Alif. Build a pyramid with wheels and pulleys. The djinn be damned—they've got something powerful and they don't want to share it. That's all their shadowy warnings amount to."

Alif said nothing. He recalled the feeling the Hand was describing, the sense that he had, for bare instants, seen through to the sinews of the code, the bones of language itself, and known them in some profound way. But that feeling was not attached to the *Alf Yeom*.

"You're wrong," Alif said. "We haven't exhausted the possibilities of binary computing. There's more left to do."

"What makes you say so?"

Alif thought of the letter his name represented, repeating in a pattern over and over in Intisar's words, unseen even by her. "Sometimes when you ask God for more, He moves the horizon back just a little. Enough to let you breathe."

The Hand grimaced.

"Are we still talking about computers, or have you come down with ergot poisoning? That slop they feed you is none too fresh."

262

"I'm talking about things that matter."

The Hand stood in one abrupt motion, causing his chair to skitter backward away from him.

"All right, I'm done. I didn't come here for a philosophy lesson. I thought you might be grateful for a little shop talk. I only want one thing before I leave: where is the *Alf Yeom* now? State couldn't locate it in the mosque where we found you."

Alif frowned. "I don't know," he said. "I had it next to me while I was working. I didn't move it."

"Not even after your computer crashed? Not to get it out of the way?"

"My fingertips were all burned and I hadn't slept in two days. I wasn't thinking about much of anything else."

"If you're trying to prevent me from re-creating your code, this is not the way to do it. I've got my people reverse-engineering it from the mess you left on the State intranet as we speak."

"Be my guest. You'll just end up screwing yourselves. I don't know where the book is and I don't care."

"How sad. This means we'll have to keep interrogating the sheikh. I'm not sure how much longer he'll last at this rate. He's not a young man."

Alif felt the blood drain from his face.

"You've got Sheikh Bilal in here?" he asked. His voice had grown hoarse.

"Oh, yes. Right down the hall. I'm surprised you can't hear him. He makes quite a bit of noise when we start in with the electric prods. I suppose the walls must be thicker than I imagined."

Alif began breathing rapidly. "He doesn't know anything," he said. "I'll swear it on whatever you put in front of me. He doesn't even know my name. He's just an old man with a conscience."

"A conscience is something old men who harbor terrorists cannot afford, I'm afraid."

"I'm not a terrorist. I've never been a terrorist. All I do is protect people who want the freedom to say what they really think."

The Hand stepped back toward the door. His eyes still shone oddly in the light, black discs that reflected only fluorescence.

"What naive garbage. People don't want freedom anymore— even those to whom freedom is a kind of religion are afraid of it, like trembling acolytes who make sacrifices to some pagan god. People want their governments to keep secrets from them. They want the hand of law to be brutal. They are so terrified by their own power that they will vote to have it taken out of their hands. Look at America. Look at the sharia states. Freedom is a dead philosophy, Alif. The world is returning to its natural state, to the rule of the weak by the strong. Young as you are, it's you who are out of touch, not me."

Alif passed a hand over his eyes. His head ached.

"Please leave the sheikh alone," he said in a small voice. "I'll say whatever you want me to say. I'll say you've won. I don't care. Just don't hurt him anymore. It's on me if he dies. It's all on me. I can't bear it."

The Hand's eyes widened. His expression made Alif nervous: a blank, menacing, almost sensual readiness—the look of a rapist.

"What were you thinking," he murmured, "when I came in today? What went through your mind when you saw me?"

Alif began to shake.

"I was glad to see you," he said. "I was relieved to see you. I wanted you to stay. I still want you to stay. I don't want to go back to the dark."

Exhaling, the Hand closed his eyes. His face slackened.

"Very good," he said. "Yes. Very good. I have been waiting for this."

Alif wondered what he was meant to understand from 'this.' Bile rose in his throat at the thought of what the Hand might ask him to do, to which he himself might acquiesce without complaint. Anything was better than another stretch in the void with the thing-that-was-not-Farukhuaz padding around him in the darkness in ever-shrinking circles.

But the Hand merely turned and rapped on the door.

"I'm glad you felt you could share your true feelings with me," he said. The door opened. "I wanted our relationship to end on exactly this note. I hope you ate well at your last meal—you'll never have another."

Alif swallowed. The Hand regarded him with something very like sympathy.

"Good-bye, Alif. In a way, I feel as though I'm losing a friend. I'll think of you every time I have Intisar on her back. What a strange coincidence that we should want the same woman, but for two very different reasons. Fitting, somehow, but strange."

*　*　*

Alone in the dark again, Alif was almost immediately hungry. He paced the room with one hand on the wall to guide him,

avoiding the slop corner, and attempted to take his mind somewhere else. He thought of daylight. He thought of sitting in the
window of his room in Baqara District on a spring afternoon, his
limbs cooking pleasantly in the heat of the sun-warmed cement
ledge. He thought of Dina in a summer robe, gray or green in
contrast to her usual black, sandals slapping against her feet as
she came through the courtyard laden with bags of fruit from
the market. That would make it a Saturday. He was baffled to
remember that there had been a time when such a scene would
have filled him with existential dread, agony at the quiet female
rhythms that encompassed him, prompting him to flee back into
his computers, the cloud, the digital world populated by men.

Now the idea of such an afternoon seemed exquisite. He had
let too many pass with too much indifference. In his mind he
made himself get down off the ledge and go outside to help Dina
with her bags, then see if there was anything his mother needed;
he spoke to the maid in complete sentences, and remembered
to clean the dust from his own shoes when he came back inside.
Naked in the dark, with the memory of the Hand's reptilian
eyes, he realized that the ritualized world he had dismissed as
feminine was in fact civilization.

As time began to blur again, he occupied himself by rewriting
more of his own history. He did not shrink from his father, and
did not hate him; instead he politely demanded that his mother
be given equal time, reminding the man of all she had given up
to marry him and raise his son. He was helpful and active around
the house. He contributed more money toward their monthly
expenses. Finally, he presented himself to Dina's parents as soon

as he knew what she wanted—which he should have known years earlier, when they were still almost children and Alif remained the only boy she would seek out and speak to alone. He ached then, ached for their conversations on the roof, cursing himself for treating her intimacy in such an offhand way. Her decision to veil had irritated and alarmed him as it irritated and alarmed her family, and he had been too absorbed in himself to realize that her continued friendship was a kind of plea, a thread back to the life she had left behind.

The necessity of returning to her kept his survival instincts alive. He drank all the water he was given, making no effort to speed his death by adding thirst to hunger. The knot in his stomach turned into a sharp, continuous cramp, and sitting became painful; it felt as though his hip bones bruised the flesh beneath them. He gripped his waist with his hands to keep the pain at bay. He had expected to feel afraid, but did not; his thoughts, though sluggish, were clear. His body remained relentlessly alive. He marveled at it, a machine more elaborate and efficient than any computer he had ever used. This was where the echoes of God lived: not in his mind but in his cells and sinews, the parts of him that could not lie. He felt his flesh transcend itself.

Farukhuaz came to him for the last time when he was lying on his side to relieve the pressure beneath his hips.

"Bones, bones, bile, bones, locked away to die alone," it rasped. "You are digesting your own insides."

"I'm alive," said Alif. "And I know what you really are. You're not Farukhuaz at all. That's just the illusion you projected to sway me into doing what you wanted. You're something much worse."

"I am I. End it quickly, neatly."

"I'm not planning to die."

The hissing laughter started up, bouncing off the invisible walls of the room as though it had no precise origin.

"You're a fool," said the thing-that-was-not-Farukhuaz. "You are already dying. There is no one here to commend you for bravery or witness your sacrifice. Your death will go unseen. Have a little pride and end things on your own terms."

Something wet and warm slid along his foot. Alif jerked away, feeling, for the first time, a sense of unease about his determination to survive. Even if he held out for some miraculous stretch of time, the door to his cell would still be locked. He did not, strictly speaking, have a plan.

"There is another way," whispered Farukhuaz. "I could get you out."

Alif searched the darkness in alarm, certain the thing had read his thoughts.

"It would be easy enough," Farukhuaz continued. "All you would have to do is tell your captors you have something they want. Give them your friend Abdullah, or any of the dissidents you know. Give them access codes, handles, passwords. You have many things with which to bargain for your life. They are surprised that you haven't offered already."

Alif curled up into a ball.

"I would help you." The voice was very close to his ear. "I would tell you how best to sway them. It would be a simple thing for me."

He thought again of daylight. He thought of returning to Dina and lying under her starry veil and feeling safe.

"No," he heard himself say.

"Why not?" The voice kissed the small hairs on the back of his neck. "You seem determined to live."

"I am," said Alif. "But if my only way out is through you, I'd rather keep starving."

The sudden rush of anger through the room made him yelp. He felt it as a physical force, like the recoil of earth after a tremor.

"Who are you trying to impress?" The voice came from inside his head, louder than any thought. He clapped his hands over his ears and screamed.

"You really think the One who is birthing stars and eating up the bowels of dysenteric infants cares whether you live as a traitor or die as a martyr? You think any of this matters?"

Alif fought back tears. He could not answer *yes*. His doubt was exposed in front of him, like a wet mewling thing, a diffidence that had never matured into belief or disbelief. He did not have the wherewithal to fight.

"Poor little creature." The voice softened. "I'm only here to keep you safe. You think we've just met, but I've been with you all your life. I have been the little whispers in your veins, numbing you, keeping you between the walls of your room when the world seemed too big. I have been the ringing in your ears, waking you in the small hours of the night to remind you of your wretchedness. You are alone, and I am the only real partisan you have."

Curling into himself, Alif attempted to steady his breathing. The air in the room seemed dense, like one collective exhalation from which all sustenance had been drained.

"I don't believe you," he said.

"You don't know what you believe."

"Whatever I believe, your bullshit isn't part of it."

A hiss.

"Be sensible. The only way out of this room is through me."

"Then I'll stay in this room until I'm a disgusting smear of muck on the floor. I'm sick of listening to you."

"A part of you still hopes there is another way. A part of you still hopes that the door will open and you will walk out of it free in body and in conscience. It is this part of yourself that you must kill if you really want to survive."

Alif felt his heart rate rise again, and with it, a new thrill of anger.

"No. No. That's the only part of me I still want."

The room grew colder.

"Suit yourself."

He strained to listen for several more minutes, ready for the renewed sound of laughter, the soft scuffling of feet. But the room felt empty in an emphatic, unfamiliar way. He shivered in the sudden lack of warmth. Exhaustion warred against his underfed muscles. The thing had been right: he was profoundly alone. An unpleasant kind of self-pity washed over him, bringing with it no solace. He wanted to sleep. Closing his eyes, he spoke to the indifferent, artificial night.

"Please," he said. "Please don't let it be right. Please open the door."

For a moment he actually expected something to happen. But the silence and the darkness remained complete and unyielding and, with a feeling close to despair, Alif allowed himself to drift off.

It was the sharp sound of a metal hinge grinding against itself that woke him. Scrambling to his feet, he blinked: a flashlight bobbed in the darkness, illuminating a figure in a white robe and headdress.

"Good God," it said in an amused tenor. "It reeks of piss in here. I'd hate to be the janitor who comes in after they wheel out your corpse."

"Who are you?" croaked Alif, shielding his eyes against the light.

The figure drew itself up stiffly and raised the light a little: it shone on a young, haughty face with a patrician nose and a fashionable scattering of stubble across its cheeks and chin.

"Who are you, *sir*," it said.

Alif attempted to process this correction.

"You're royalty?" he asked, skepticism slurring his words.

"Yes, I am," said the bearer of the flashlight in a cool voice. "I'm Prince Abu Talib Al Mukhtar ibn Hamza."

Deprivation made Alif bold; there was nothing they could do to him that they had not already done.

"Is that name supposed to mean something to me?" he challenged.

"No, I suppose not." The young man smiled sheepishly. "There are twenty-six other princes in line before me for the throne. You know me as NewQuarter01."

*   *   *

Alif felt like his mind had thrown a gear, leaving it to spin uselessly, without traction.

"You can't be NewQuarter. NewQuarter is a—he's a—"

"A peasant, like the rest of you? Oh, good. I was hoping I'd managed to fit in. I didn't want to seem like some kind of poser.

Even though I suppose that's what I am." NewQuarter put one hand under Alif's elbow and helped him sit back down.

"You really look a mess. I didn't expect them to have taken your clothes—I'll have to go back for some. My stuff will probably be too short for you but it'll do until we've sprung you out of here."

"We've what?" Alif shifted to take the weight off his bruised buttocks.

"Don't be dense. I've come to rescue you." NewQuarter set the flashlight on its end, throwing a bluish glow across the ceiling.

Alif gasped, bit his lip, and began to bawl. NewQuarter's mouth twisted into an expression of repressed horror. He patted Alif's shoulder awkwardly.

"I don't—I'm not really good with crying, I have to warn you. Especially not when the guy in question is naked and filthy."

"I'm sorry," sniffled Alif. "It's only that I thought I was going to die in here."

"If you don't eat something, you still might." NewQuarter produced a bar of chocolate from the pocket of his robe. "Here, take this."

Hands shaking, Alif unwrapped the chocolate bar and bit off one corner. The substance was rich and almost too sweet to swallow.

"Thank you," he said around a mouthful.

"I'll bring something more substantial next time," said NewQuarter. "I should go now before the guards come back."

"How many are there? How'd you get them to leave?"

NewQuarter sat back on his heels with a tense smile.

"There are five stationed in this corridor. Two on either end and one in the middle. Fortunately they keep women in the cells opposite you—I told them I wanted some time alone with one of them. They just gave me the keys and took a cigarette break."

Alif shuddered.

"They let you do that? Just like so?"

NewQuarter looked away. The cynical set of his mouth made him seem older than he probably was.

"There are some very well-paid sheikhs who say captive women—prisoners—are like slaves, from a shariah point of view. So their liege-lords have the right to fuck them. If you've got a title you can pretty much walk in and out of this place whenever you want."

The thought of Dina being forced to submit to some aristocratic lecher made Alif nauseous. Vikram had been right to take the girls into hiding, despite the risk—and the cost. Alif swallowed the syrupy liquid that rose in his throat. How awful that the man's nobility was apparent only now that he was dead.

"I know," said NewQuarter in a quiet, distracted voice, watching Alif catch his breath. "Makes you want to break things. That's why I started hacking. I didn't want to be on the wrong team." He stood and gingerly shook out his robe, looking around himself with faint disgust.

"I hope you haven't picked up some horrible disease in here, because you're not bringing it home with me. I'll be back tomorrow. Your job is to stay alive until then."

Alif looked at him with speechless gratitude. NewQuarter smiled and touched his forehead in an old-fashioned salaam, turning toward the door. As he left, Alif remembered something.

"Sheikh Bilal!" he called. "We can't leave without him. Please—"

NewQuarter paused, frowning.

"What's this? Who's Sheikh Bilal? I didn't plan for more than one person."

Alif rose to his feet again, swaying a little, and looked NewQuarter in the eye.

"He's the imam of Al Basheera and very old, and they've been torturing him for information he doesn't have. The Hand said he's down the hall. The man risked his life protecting me—I can't possibly leave him behind."

"Can't possibly?"

Alif shook his head.

"Can't possibly. Not an option."

NewQuarter sighed in irritation.

"All right. Let me recalibrate a little. I'll see you tomorrow." He turned again to leave.

"What time of day is it?" Alif asked him in a rush. "What month? What's the weather like?"

NewQuarter smiled sweetly.

"It's about ten p.m. on a balmy winter evening in late January."

Alif closed his eyes, face slack with relief.

"Thank you," he said.

*　*　*

Alif's perception of time returned with excruciating suddenness. If it was late January, he had been in the Hand's custody for almost three months, a period that seemed by turns unthinkable and blessedly short. The day that remained until NewQuarter's return ballooned before him, longer than any of the undifferentiated periods of sleep and wakefulness he had experienced in the dark. The sugar in his stomach made him jumpy and his pulse raced; sleep would not come to him. He paced the room, walking back and forth on sore feet.

An attempt to count seconds quickly frustrated him. He focused instead on his breathing, remembering some rubbish or other he'd seen on Rotana about relaxation techniques, and thought with bliss that he might be very close to that life again, to the privilege of waking up to trivial nonsense on television. He made a mental list of the Egyptian daytime dramas he would watch when he was free. All the mother-daughter cat fights, melodramatic close-ups, and plot lines so wretchedly thin you could recite whole monologues before the actors spoke them. They had disgusted him once, convinced him of the superiority of his mind, now they were humbling reminders of a safer world.

As the day drew on, he grew tense. He imagined it was almost dawn, but still could not sleep; though he could finally guess what time it was, the vagaries of the sun had long lost their impact on his body. He began to sing again. He sang the old Alexandrian fishing songs Dina liked, about painted boats and the safety of the ancient harbor and, beyond it, the once fruitful Mediterranean. She would sing these to herself on the roof when she set out the laundry and thought no one was listening; Alif would hear her voice drifting down through his window, deepening and softening over the years as she grew to womanhood. He wondered how it was that she still felt such a connection to Egypt, a place she had not lived since she was an infant. Perhaps they should spend some time there together after they were married. They could rent an apartment overlooking the port in Alexandria, with a balcony where Dina could sit in the sun bareheaded. He would ask her. There were, perhaps, parts of her he still did not understand, desirous of things he could not guess, though he had known her all his life.

Daydreaming about Dina and a country he had never seen, Alif drifted off. He woke again with a prescient feeling, and moments later heard a key turn in the lock. NewQuarter slipped inside.

"Thank God," breathed Alif. "I don't think I've ever been as happy to see anyone as I am to see you. I'm so—"

"Yes, yes, you're welcome. Let's not get carried away." NewQuarter set a loaded backpack on the floor. "There are clothes in here. I brought an extra set for your friend. Both *thobes*. I hope you don't mind. We don't wear much western clothing in my family."

"I'm not about to complain." Alif unzipped the backpack and pulled out a white robe similar to the one NewQuarter was wearing. It smelled dazzlingly clean.

"There's a head cloth, too—better wear it, you look like a homeless person. If I'm going to drive you out of here in a BMW we need a certain amount of plausibility."

"We're driving out of here in a BMW?"

"I thought about bringing the Lexus," fretted NewQuarter without irony, "but a BMW is more anonymous. All the princes drive them."

"Oh."

"Hurry, will you? If we're going to pick up this sheikh we need to move."

Alif pulled the robe over his head. It felt like a bandage on his abused skin, which had gone scaly in some places and tender in others.

NewQuarter briskly arranged the head cloth over Alif's brow and held it in place with two circlets of black braided cotton.

"Good God," he said, "you still look a mess. Oh, well. Just keep the edges of the head cloth low around your face and don't say anything. Your accent will give you away. There's a whiff of Indian menial in your Arabic."

Alif nodded obediently. NewQuarter slipped through the open door and glanced down the hallway, holding his flashlight at shoulder height.

"Okay," he said. "Let's go."

Alif followed him into the hall. A desperate euphoria rushed over him as NewQuarter quietly shut the door of his cell. The uncertainty of being free and not yet safe was too much. He steadied himself, blinking to dispel the onset of dizziness.

"Know which cell this guy is in? Are we really going to wander up and down calling his name through the food slots on every door?" NewQuarter swung the flashlight in an arc along the doors lining the corridor.

Alif prodded his still-sluggish brain.

"You said there are women on the other side, right? So that narrows it down."

"I suppose so. There are still six other doors on this side, though."

Alif glanced up and down and bit his lip.

"We couldn't just open them all up? On both sides. The women—"
He couldn't finish his sentence.

NewQuarter tapped the flashlight against his leg.

"I know," he said quietly. "But to be honest with you, Alif, the more we play liberating heroes the less our chances of getting out of here ourselves. If only two of you go missing, the guards may not notice for several hours. If we instigate a jailbreak there will be immediate chaos. How are we supposed to extricate ourselves from that?"

"For God's sake," said Alif, "isn't this what we're meant to do? Or what was all our messing around with computers *for*? Fun? Aren't we meant to believe in something?"

"They'll all be caught again anyway. You can't just walk out of here, Alif—there are walls six-feet thick topped with razor wire, and beyond that, eighty kilometers of desert between us and the City. And as you well know, most of the people in these cells are probably not in the best of health."

Alif gazed at the rows of steel-doored cells that flickered in the beam of NewQuarter's flashlight. He felt light-headed.

"We're really going to leave them?" he asked in a softer voice.

"We don't have a choice. You're of more help to these people out of jail than in, *akhi*." NewQuarter moved down the hallway and tapped on the cell door next to Alif's.

"Sheikh Bilal?" he called softly. A voice inside murmured a timid negative. The next two cells yielded similar results. When he tapped on the fourth, a familiar voice rasped out a curse in flowery, classical Arabic.

"That's him," murmured Alif. NewQuarter produced a large ring of keys and sorted through them, flashlight balanced in the crook of his arm. Selecting one, he turned it in the lock and pulled the heavy door open. Alif crowded over his shoulder to look inside: Sheikh Bilal, wrinkled and emaciated, blinked bloodshot eyes in the glare of the flashlight. Alif felt a rush of embarrassment for the older man, whose rank made his nakedness somehow more grotesque. The sight of his bare head made Alif wince; to see the spotted, balding pate of a sheikh, fringed with white hair, bereft of the dignity of even a skullcap, unnerved him. He could not bring himself to speak.

"Here, Uncle," said NewQuarter, awkwardly holding out his backpack. "There are clothes inside. I've got water and food waiting. But we don't have much time."

Sheikh Bilal took the backpack with shaking hands.

"What is this?" he croaked. "Is this one of your dog-cursed tricks?"

"It's not a trick, Sheikh Uncle," said Alif, voice catching in his throat. "NewQuarter is from the royal family. He's here to spring us."

Sheikh Bilal attempted to spit. A clot of drool ran down his chin.

"Any shred of loyalty I might have felt to the royal family died in this cell," he said. "I don't want anything from those inbred bastards."

"And you won't get anything," said NewQuarter with a wry smile, "just me. One inbred bastard with a vendetta."

The sheikh peered up at NewQuarter.

"How do I know you won't simply deliver me to a worse fate than this?" he asked.

NewQuarter shrugged. "You don't. I didn't come here for you, I came here for Alif. He's the one who insisted he couldn't leave without you."

The sheikh turned his bleary eyes on Alif.

"So you're alive," he muttered. "Much good may it do you."

"I'm sorry, Sheikh Uncle," said Alif. "I'm so sorry."

Sheikh Bilal said nothing. NewQuarter glanced from the younger man to the elder one and slipped his arm under the sheikh's elbow.

"You can scream at him later. Right now we've got to leave. Let me help you get dressed."

*   *   *

They slipped down the corridor in single file. Alif ached at each door they passed, thinking of the silent inmates behind them. He thought he heard a muffled cry issue from a food slot near the end of the hall and stopped.

"We can't just—"

"Yes we can," said NewQuarter firmly. "There is nothing we can do for them, Alif, nothing, not from in here."

Alif trailed after him, straining for another sound, but heard none. At the end of the hall, NewQuarter paused with his hand on the lever of a large metal door.

"The guards will be waiting at the bottom of the stairs," he muttered. "That's the way out. Wait here while I send them for my car. I'll knock on the outer door when it's safe."

Alif was incredulous.

"The prison guards are going to bring your car around like a bunch of valets?"

"You'd better believe it." NewQuarter grinned and disappeared into the stairwell on the opposite side of the door. Sheikh Bilal quaked, wobbling on his feet; Alif took his arm to steady him.

"Forgive me," Alif whispered.

The sheikh snorted.

"I have no breath left to waste. Talk to me again when I've eaten."

Alif looked away, face burning. They stood in silence for several more minutes, jumping at echoes from other wings of the prison. Finally the sound of a well-oiled motor became audible. Three sharp knocks followed, rattling up the stairwell beyond the door. Alif felt his palms begin to sweat.

"Let's go," he said, pushing open the door. Sheikh Bilal needed help getting down the soldered metal stairs. Alif prevented himself from screaming in frustration, gamely lending the old man his hands. At the bottom of the stairs, Alif pushed open a very heavy door, tasting night air, deep and clean and cool.

"Now," hissed NewQuarter from the interior of a black town car. "Now now now."

Alif bundled the sheikh into the backseat before climbing in the passenger door.

"In the name of God, the Beneficent, the Merciful," said NewQuarter, gunning the motor. Alif slid down in his seat, heart pounding. NewQuarter pulled the car around the exterior of a windowless, dun-colored building. It took Alif a moment to realize that this was where he had been living for the past three months, that this was the shape of his lightless hell. It seemed both surreal and alarmingly ordinary, like an office building that had blinked, obscuring visual access to its innards.

The building was surrounded by a paved courtyard that ended at the foot of a high wall, two stories perhaps, topped with ugly jumbles of wire. Pairs of security personnel patrolled the inner perimeter on horseback. With detached anxiety, Alif observed that the horses of each duo matched: a pair of black ones, a pair of reddish ones, a sandy-colored pair with white manes and tails. This seemed, to him, the final perversity: matched horses at the gate of an abattoir. He closed his eyes. His head was pounding, as if the blood vessels in his brain had swelled.

"Here we go," murmured NewQuarter. They were approaching a barred metal gate. There was a guard on either end, each armed with an automatic rifle. NewQuarter slowed the car.

"Oh, Captain!" he called through his window, snapping his fingers at the guard on the left. "Open up, I'm finished here."

The guard scurried up to the driver's-side window of the car.

"Yes, sir. Right away, sir," he said. His eyes flickered over Alif in the passenger's seat. Alif looked dead ahead.

"I'm sorry, sir—these men—"

"Are my personal attendants," NewQuarter snapped. "You think I drive around by myself like some delivery boy?"

"No, sir, of course not. It's only that—there is a certain *smell*—"

"Who wouldn't smell after spending an hour in this filthy place? Open the gate."

The guard backed away, muttering into the walkie-talkie hanging from his shirt front. Motioning to the guard opposite, he pressed a series of numbers into a keypad on the edge of the gate. The metal bar began to rise.

"Thank God," said NewQuarter. "I swear I've sweat all the way through my *thobe*."

As the gate opened, NewQuarter inched the car forward. Alif heard Sheikh Bilal breathe out a sigh. Alif's shoulders ached; he realized he had been tensing them since before they left the prison.

"And that, my friends," said NewQuarter triumphantly, pressing a button to roll up his window, "is how you break out of prison."

There was a flicker of black in the rearview mirror. Alif frowned: a guard was running toward them from the direction of the prison complex, waving his arms angrily. Through the tinted, insulated glass, Alif couldn't hear what he was saying. He turned his head to see the guard at the gate jamming a red button on the bottom of the keypad.

The gate began to close.

"Shit!" There was a squeal of rubber as NewQuarter jammed his foot against the accelerator. The car shot forward. Alif heard a series of loud pops. Swiveling in his seat, he saw the guard on the other end of the gate level his rifle at the car.

"They're shooting at us!" Alif shrieked. He fell back in his seat as the car swerved, skidding on sand that had blown across the road that rose in front of them. NewQuarter was hunched over the wheel, gritting his teeth. From the backseat, Alif heard Sheikh Bilal begin to mutter an incantatory prayer, asking God to protect them from the evil of His creation.

Another loud pop put a fractal pattern in the glass of the car's rear window. The sheikh threw himself across the seat.

"*Allahu akbar!*" he shouted. "*Allahu akbar!*"

"Fuck! Are you hurt?" Alif leaned toward the old man and was rewarded by being half-choked by his seatbelt when the car swerved again.

"I'm not shot, if that's what you mean," said the sheikh, clinging to his head covering.

Lights flashed on the road: two Peugeots painted matte black were speeding toward them.

"Screw this." NewQuarter yanked the steering wheel to the left, running the car off the road. They bumped along soft veins of sand. High dunes loomed against a star-patterned sky. NewQuarter accelerated toward one of them.

"What are you doing?" Alif wailed. The car began to tilt upward.

"Going on a safari, you tremendous ass-coveter. How's the view?"

Alif clamped his hands around his head as the car crested the top of the dune. For a moment he saw only sky. Dark and speckled with shimmering points, it seemed to surround them, separating them in some essential way from the earth, gravity, dust. Alif gasped. His stomach turned.

With a crash, the car tipped over the crest of the dune and began to slide down the opposite side. NewQuarter pressed on the brakes. The car fishtailed, its rear wheels sliding back and forth on the sand.

"Hold on!" He gunned the motor. They raced down the dune, slamming into level ground again. Alif's head hit the ceiling.

"Where are we—"

"Away, just away. Maybe they'll crash or get lost." NewQuarter wheeled around the foot of another dune, sending a spray of sand against the back windows. Alif saw a black shape crest the dune behind them and begin sliding down. A second followed.

"They're still behind us!"

"Okay, okay." They raced along a narrow corridor between two hills of sand. The ground grew unexpectedly rocky and the car shuddered as it crushed the remains of fossilized shells beneath its wheels, remnants of an ancient sea. Alif looked over his shoulder again. The two Peugeots slid around a bend and pursued them into the corridor. NewQuarter shifted gears, accelerating, and turned toward another dune. It loomed in front of them like a pyramid, massive and unshakable, the survivor of hundreds, perhaps thousands of years of windstorms. Alif's mouth fell open.

"We'll never make it up that one!"

"Your mother's cunt! Neither will they."

The car roared up the side of the dune at a terrifying angle. Alif leaned forward, with the vague notion that the counterbalance of his weight could keep them from tipping. Sheikh Bilal began slapping his head rhythmically.

"Oh, God," whimpered Alif. "Oh, God."

The upper edge of the dune came into view. They were now perpendicular to the ground, preserved only by momentum. The wheels of the car threw sand in every direction. The engine struggled. Cursing, NewQuarter shifted gears again. With a burst of speed, they slid over the top and dangled into space.

For a moment Alif thought they might be all right. The front wheels of the car touched down on the far side of the dune almost gently, in a modest puff of sand. Then physics caught up with them. In a sudden rush, the car began to spin, whipping around in circles as it slid downward. NewQuarter took his hands off the steering wheel, eyes wide. Alif felt pressure building in his bladder and squeezed his legs shut in alarm. It felt as though he had no control over his muscles; he was in free fall, voiding all unnecessary weight. The car continued to spin.

When they hit the bottom, Alif felt his bones shudder. A ripple swept through the car, shattering all the windows; metal groaned as the front fender crumpled into the sand. Someone was screaming. Alif shielded his face against bits of glass that seemed to fly at him from all sides, stinging his arms through his thin white robe. He thought of Vikram. He thought of Dina. He shut his eyes.

The silence came suddenly. Night penetrated the car through its empty windows, touching Alif's face with a crisp, assertive breeze. He lowered his arms. They were sitting diagonally across the gap where the dune met flat earth, back wheels propped up at an incline, nose collapsed like a crumpled can. NewQuarter was pale and blinking.

"Wow," he whispered.

There was a cough from the backseat: Sheikh Bilal cleared his throat, shaking fragments of glass from his robe.

"Well, my son, I promise never to ask to see your driver's license," he said, sounding, to Alif's relief, more like himself.

"Thank you, Uncle," said NewQuarter, still staring straight ahead. Alif struggled with his seatbelt and pushed open the door. Ruined, the hinges made an embarrassed noise as the door swung out. Alif limped into the sand. It was soft and cold beneath his feet, glinting in the reflected light of the sky. A moon hung low over the horizon.

"It's so dark," complained NewQuarter, shuffling out of the driver's side.

"No it isn't," murmured Alif. He was overwhelmed by color: deep navy and purple in the sky; silver and black on the ground. "It's not dark at all."

"Where are we, at any rate?" asked Sheikh Bilal. He leaned on Alif's shoulder with an arm that trembled. Alif wondered if he should interpret this as a sign that he could be forgiven.

NewQuarter pulled off his head cloth and let it drop on the ground, running a hand through a crown of well-oiled dark hair.

"I believe we're on the edge of the Empty Quarter," he said.

"Merciful God. That far?" The sheikh turned in a slow circle, ogling the landscape.

"Uncle, that prison fronts the deep desert. They built it there on purpose, so that any idiot who managed to escape would die of thirst or exposure before he saw anything resembling civilization." NewQuarter kicked a rapidly deflating rear tire. "As we will doubtless do."

"Have faith," the sheikh said in a tone Alif could not identify.

NewQuarter made a derisive sound and jiggled his keys in the trunk of the car.

"Yes, faith. Here. I brought water and food. If we're going to starve we'll start starving tomorrow." He lifted out a bottle of spring water and a cooler. Opening it, he revealed grapes and oranges, flatbread rolled around slices of cured meat, and a brick of feta cheese quivering in an oil bath inside a Tupperware bowl.

Alif threw his arms around NewQuarter with a strangled yelp.

"Thank you," he said. "A thousand thank you's. You have no idea what—"

"Yes, you're right, I don't." NewQuarter unhooked Alif's arms and brushed at his robe. "It's okay. I've never done anything really brave in my life outside a computer. This seemed a good place to start."

"But you've risked your life!"

NewQuarter looked surprised.

"*Akhi*, you're a hero. There are a thousand dissidents and hacktivists in the City who would line up for a chance to meet you, let alone help you. Your arrest was all over the news. State media called you a terrorist, of course, but it's not like anybody believes what State says. Holing up in Al Basheera of all places—that was a master stroke. Claiming our most famous mosque as a symbol against tyranny. Genius. Your Communist friends and your Islamist friends probably had tears in their eyes at the same time. Wonder if that's ever happened before."

Alif flushed.

"I didn't mean to do all that," he said. "I was running away from a bunch of State agents on foot, and Basheera seemed like the safest place to go."

NewQuarter raised an eyebrow.

"Well, it worked, at any rate. The whole City was talking about you for weeks. Since you disappeared, though, a lot of people assume you're dead."

Alif thought in horror of his mother.

"What? They do? What about my family?"

NewQuarter shrugged.

"Couldn't tell you. I wasn't sure you were alive myself. Had to pull a lot of strings to figure out where you were. It was really only luck that I found you at all."

"How do you mean?"

NewQuarter began making a plate of bread, fruit, and cheese, squatting in the sand next to the open cooler.

"As it turns out, we're sort of related," he said. "Your father's first wife comes from rather a good family. She's my mother's sister's niece by marriage. I guess that makes me kind of like your uncle. Just think—we've known one another by reputation for years and never knew how close we really were."

Alif made a wry face. "But that—that's twice removed from no blood relation at all. I thought you were going to tell me I was secretly the heir to the throne or something."

"Ha! You wish. No, all this means is that certain pieces of gossip came through my family that might not otherwise have reached me. My aunt's niece by marriage was in hysterics, worried that her husband, your father, would lose his position, or the family would have their assets seized by State or something. Because of the royal connection, neither of those things happened, but it still gave me a good lead to go about tracking you down."

Alif sat down in the chill sand, mulling over these pieces of information.

"What a happy coincidence," he murmured.

"All things are named destiny," said Sheikh Bilal, accepting the plate of food from NewQuarter. He tucked into it with evident relish, eyes half-shut, a dribble of oil seeping into his beard. NewQuarter handed a similarly loaded plate to Alif. The scent of edible things made him light-headed. He popped a fragment of cheese into his mouth, letting it dissolve, the pungent flavor spreading over his tongue. He felt giddy; the grinding despair that had beset him before NewQuarter's appearance now seemed unreal. He had been liberated. He had the sense that something profound had occurred, yet he had no words to attach to it. His senses, reawakening, were saturated with simple and immediate things: the scent of the air and the food, the vastness of the landscape. Overwhelmed, he set his plate down and knelt with his forehead to the sand, breathing inarticulate thanks.

"What is he doing?" came NewQuarter's voice.

"I believe he is attempting to pray," said Sheikh Bilal.

"But he isn't clean. He hasn't performed the ablution or checked the direction of Mecca, or begun in the correct position."

"My dear sir," said the sheikh. "God likes catching His servants unprepared. The boy has set down what is obviously the first plate of food he has seen in a long while in order to thank his Creator. There are few acts of piety more honest than that."

"Or more ramshackle. You can see the man's bones through his skin. I wish he would just eat and address his Creator when he's clean and civilized."

Alif heard the sheikh chuckle.

"I have had much experience with the unclean and uncivilized in the recent past. Shall I tell you what I discovered? I am not the state of my feet. I am not the dirt on my hands or the hygiene of my private parts. If I were these things, I would not have been at liberty to pray at any time since my arrest. But I did pray, because I am not these things. In the end, I am not even myself. I am a string of bones speaking the word *God.*"

Alif lifted his head and sat back down on the sand. Sheikh Bilal handed him his plate in one long, deliberate gesture, as though he had aged considerably, or was in great pain. Alif accepted it with a pang of concern.

"They hurt you," he said.

"Yes."

"You're angry at me."

"Very."

"I don't know how to apologize."

"You might start by telling me where that damnable book is. That's what they were after."

Alif rolled a grape between his fingers.

"I have no idea where the book is," he said. "I don't remember moving it after the computer melted down. There was a lot going on at once."

"I'm sorry," said NewQuarter. "What book is this?"

Alif and Sheikh Bilal glanced at one another.

"It's called the *Alf Yeom*," said Alif. "It was written by genies."

NewQuarter snorted with laughter.

"They must really have roughed you up in there," he said. "Jumped by the Hand for a book written by genies? You're hallucinating."

Alif shook his head.

"It's real," he said. "The Hand wanted it to create an entirely new programming method. The djinn think about knowledge in a different way than we do, so their books are sort of like long sets of encoded metaphor and if you translate that methodology into the world of computing—"

"You've clearly gone mad," said NewQuarter, munching on meat and flatbread. He looked at Alif with disdain. "The Hand's been after you for years, just like he's been after all of us gray hats. We're enemies of the State. It's got nothing to do with any book."

"But why now, NewQuarter? Why did he wait until now to strike? It was because I had something he wanted urgently—something he didn't want anyone else to have, especially not someone who could figure out what he intended to use it for."

NewQuarter grinned.

"What's funny?" asked Alif.

"You called me NewQuarter. I've never heard it spoken aloud before."

"Well, your other name is too damn long."

"Only to a peasant." NewQuarter handed him more meat and cheese. "Keep eating. Let's feast today and not think too hard about what's to become of us when we are either found by State or die of thirst."

Getting to his feet, Alif looked out at the receding dunes. They seemed clean, innocuous, free of dirt and debris and malice—so unlike the landscape of the City. The low-hanging moon made the horizon shimmer like glass. Yet Alif remembered his school-age geography lessons: there was no water for hundreds of miles in all directions save the City. The desert was as implacable as it was beautiful, and it had claimed many lives. Or at least, many human lives.

"If this is the edge of the Empty Quarter," he said, "in theory we should only have to wander into it for the djinn to find us."

"Again with the djinn," said NewQuarter, beginning to look nervous.

"Djinn is in the final verse of the Quran," said Alif impatiently. "Don't look at me like I'm nuts. You believe the Quran, don't you?"

"Well, yes, but—just because there are djinn doesn't mean one meets them in the street. They're like—they're simply—"

Alif got up and started wandering away. He remembered Dina's admonishment the first time they met Vikram, and his own anger when she asked him why it was so hard for him to believe what he wanted to believe. When it's real it's not fun anymore, he had said. When it's real it's scary.

It felt good to stretch his legs, to walk for more than a few steps in any direction. His stomach was reacting strangely to food after having gone so long without it, and protested; he wanted to be far enough from Sheikh Bilal and NewQuarter so they wouldn't see him if something embarrassing happened. He stopped at the lip of a small rise in the sand, where the earth fell away into a depression glazed in darker, heavier sand. He felt like running but his heart leaped feebly at the idea; who knew but he might drop dead if he attempted it.

"I'm an old man," he muttered to himself. Every sinew of his body felt stretched and used, as though the three-month stint in prison had aged him by decades. Only his mind remained clear. He took several deep breaths of the clean, dim air and turned back toward the wreckage of NewQuarter's car.

NewQuarter had lain down near the crumpled hood and thrown his head cloth over himself like a blanket.

"I've got to get some sleep," he muttered when Alif approached. "I wasn't expecting the day to end like this. If you can believe it, I thought we would all be camped out at my flat in the Dahab District by now. This is what comes of being raised to believe that money can fix anything. Clearly I am a failure."

"But very handy behind the wheel of a BMW."

"Thanks. I suppose that's something."

Alif lay down a short distance away from NewQuarter, wriggling in the sand to create a body-shaped hollow. Sheikh Bilal was leaning against the still-warm corpse of the car, snoring gently. Alif found himself succumbing to the silence of the place, a quiet so open and broad that it seemed almost to roar, as though it was not silence at all but music in some ancient inaudible key. His eyes drifted shut and he slept without dreaming.

When he woke again, it was to Sheikh Bilal poking his shoulder.

"Hmm?" Alif rolled over, unsure of where he was.

"Look," said the sheikh.

Alif opened his eyes. The sky was full of colored light: blue, white, reddish-gold. He began to breathe very fast, overcome by a joy that ached.

"What is it?" he asked.

"Dawn," said the sheikh. "It's the dawn."

Chapter Twelve

Though it was winter, and warm as opposed to hot, the sun quickly asserted its supremacy. There was no shade except that which they could make with their head cloths and a little more lent by the shadow of the car. The dunes that had seemed unearthly at night became stark, the sand soft but unyielding, ready to mummify the unprepared and unwary.

"Isn't there an entire Persian army lost out here somewhere?" joked NewQuarter at one point while he sorted through their provisions. His voice was brittle.

"They got lost in the Sahara," said Alif. "Not here." He squinted out at the dunes. The sky was reflected in the bowl of sand he had seen the previous night, creating a near-perfect mirage. It appeared as a tiny, very blue lake, as real as the junked BMW behind him. He noticed that the other two avoided looking at it, as though the pressure of false hope made them nervous.

"I think we've got enough water for two days," said NewQuarter, "maybe three. I didn't plan for this little expedition. I wonder if State will show up. We can't have gone that far off the main road."

"I doubt even State could get anything smaller than a tank over those dunes without crashing," said Sheikh Bilal. "Perhaps they can't come at all. Perhaps they will simply wait at the road to see if we appear, and if we don't, assume we've perished."

"A fair assumption," said NewQuarter, digging in the cooler. He looked pale.

"Perhaps. I will choose to believe that our lives have been spared for a purpose, until I am proven wrong." The sheikh held his head cloth out over his face, fanning himself with the loose ends. Alif was encouraged by the color coming back into the older man's cheeks.

"Not much purpose in dying slowly rather than quickly," NewQuarter muttered, repacking the cooler in the trunk of the car.

Wandering toward the mirage, Alif considered their situation. He was not frightened or anxious; his fear of death had dulled during the weeks he had spent awaiting it. He thought about what Vikram had said, about the Empty Quarter containing not just desert but a world turned sideways—the abode of the djinn. He had said it was difficult to get a human through intact. There was a moment's anxiety when Alif thought of Dina and the convert and wondered whether they had made it out alive, and if they had, where they were now. The thing in the prison had said that Vikram was dead. Did it follow that the girls had died as well? That thought propelled him forward, and he slid down the embankment toward the illusion of blue.

The mirage was so complete that for a moment he believed he could hear the sound of water lapping at the sand, and caught the scent of evaporating mist. He laughed at himself and at his own helplessness, leaning back against the declining sand.

"You've failed her," he said aloud. "If anything's happened to her, it's your fault. She trusted you."

"I beg your pardon?"

Alif scrambled upright. A man was standing in the midst of the mirage, bare-chested, his dark skin beading up with water. It was as though he had been swimming. Alif made a strangled noise and scurried backward up the embankment like a crab.

"Please don't. I was only wondering whether you were addressing me. I'm afraid I don't know who this woman you've accused me of neglecting is, however. Perhaps you have me confused with someone else?"

Opening his mouth to respond, Alif made a shrill, inarticulate sound, and blushed. The man climbed out of the water—for it was water, or something very like it—and stood at the bottom of the sandy incline to look up at Alif. He wore a wrapper of black cloth around his waist, like a fisherman.

"Damn it all," he said, frowning. "I took you for one of us. I shouldn't have spoken. How is it that you can see me?"

"I don't know," stammered Alif. "I came down to look at the mirage, and I thought I heard water . . ."

The man stared hard at Alif. There was something distorted about his face, as though Alif was looking at him through an old, warped window. When Alif concentrated too hard on one feature, it would shiver and run, resembling a shadow or a spot in his eye caused by the sun.

"How interesting," said the man, half to himself. "It's got a strange whiff of the unseen about it." He shook his head and seemed to recover himself. "You'd better go back to wherever you came from, third-born. It isn't quite safe for you on the borderlands, if you can see us."

"I can't go back," Alif blurted as the man turned away. "We've wrecked our car—we'll die out here if we can't get to water and shelter."

The man seemed to weigh this statement for a moment.

"Sorry, can't help you," he said finally, and splashed back into the mirage.

"I was a friend of Vikram's," called Alif. "He died trying to rescue two women I know. He would have brought them into the Empty Quarter with him."

The man turned, surprised.

"The one your legends called the Vampire? I'd heard about his death. Nothing about two humans, though. But the Empty Quarter is a big place."

"It's dangerous, isn't it? That's what Vikram said. Dangerous for humans. Do you think—do you suppose two healthy women could get through all right?"

The man shrugged. "It's difficult to say. The tribe of Adam is fragile, this is true. It would depend on the disposition of the particular people involved. You used to walk among us quite frequently, and we among you. Now things are different."

"Why?" Alif wanted to keep the man talking. Perhaps he could convince him to help.

"Belief," said the man. "It doesn't mean the same thing it used to, not for you. You have unlearned the hidden half of the world."

"But the world is crawling with religious fanatics. Surely belief is thriving."

"Superstition is thriving. Pedantry is thriving. Sectarianism is thriving. Belief is dying out. To most of your people the djinn are paranoid fantasies who run around causing epilepsy and mental illness. Find me someone to whom the hidden folk are simply real, as described in the Books. You'll be searching a long time. Wonder and awe have gone out of your religions. You are prepared to accept the irrational, but not the transcendent. And that, cousin, is why I can't help you."

"I know someone who believes exactly what you have described," said Alif. "She may still be in the Empty Quarter. Help me find her."

The man stood hip-deep in the mirage and studied Alif for a long moment.

"If there really are two humans stuck in the Empty Quarter, there could certainly be trouble," he said at last. "And that won't do. If you promise to leave as soon as you've found them, I suppose I could help you get in."

"I promise," said Alif in a hurry. "I swear it on my life, or what's left of it. But there are two others I have to bring with me, otherwise they'll die out here—an elderly sheikh and a younger man who saved both our skins. Please let me get them."

The man sighed and looked over one shoulder, as though fearful of being watched.

"Hurry then," he said. "The longer we stand here talking, the more attention we'll attract."

Alif bolted off through the sand toward the BMW. NewQuarter and Sheikh Bilal were lying in the tiny stripe of shade that remained, fanning themselves with the hems of their robes.

"We've got to go," said Alif. "I've found someone who can help us."

NewQuarter scrambled to his feet.

"Praise God. You've got some luck, *akhi*—who is it, a Bedouin running hash? One of those awful dune-bashing tour groups?"

"Never mind who," said Alif. "Just come quickly. He's in a bit of a rush."

NewQuarter helped the sheikh to his feet and took his cooler of food from the trunk of the car.

"Poor car," he lamented. "That's the second one I've totaled this year. Father will not be pleased."

Sheikh Bilal made a derisive noise but said nothing. Clinging to NewQuarter's arm, he shuffled as fast as he could, tailing Alif as he made his way back toward the mirage. Alif half-expected the man and the illusory pool to have disappeared by the time they returned. When he saw blue over the lip of sand where his tracks led, he let out a long breath. The man stood where Alif had left him, both arms crossed over his chest.

"That one is going to be trouble," he said, pointing to NewQuarter. "I can tell already."

"What's that?" called NewQuarter. "Look, man, where's your car? I was expecting something a little more impressive." He glanced at

Alif. "For God's sake, what were you thinking? This guy isn't even wearing any *pants*."

"Neither are you," the man retorted. NewQuarter raised his chin.

"Yes, but I'm *dressed*," he said. "I'm wearing a proper robe with underwear and everything."

Sheikh Bilal touched Alif's arm.

"My boy," he rumbled in a low voice. "I am starting to be concerned about the number of—of dubious people you seem to attract."

"It's a recent thing," said Alif. "Sort of an accident. But they seem to be awfully handy in a crisis."

"All right, let's go," said the man, beckoning. "One by one."

"Into the mirage?" Feeling dubious, Alif looked down into the shimmering blue bowl.

"Yes, if that's what you'd prefer to call it. Send the old man first."

Alif helped Sheikh Bilal down the short slope of the depression, handing him off to the man at the bottom. The glare of the illusion increased, like sun reflecting on glass, and the two vanished into it. After a pause, the man reappeared, without the sheikh.

"What the hell?" NewQuarter peered down at him, opening and closing his eyes rapidly, as though attempting to focus.

"You next," the man said to him. "Since you're the trickiest."

"Tricky my left one," said NewQuarter, voice high with alarm. "You're the one who just disappeared an entire sheikh."

"Fah. He's standing right over there, waving at you. *Yallah*." He reached out his hand. After a moment's hesitation, NewQuarter took it and half-slid down the sand, evaporating when he reached the bottom. Alif paced at the top of the incline as he waited for the man to return. The daylight he had so missed seared his exposed face and he was grateful for NewQuarter's head cloth, which kept the sun off the back of his neck. To be free and still not yet safe: there was something maddeningly incomplete about it. He kicked at the sand, which belled upward and blew against him in a scudding breeze, smelling of hot glass.

"Where are you?" he muttered at the mirage. A moment later the man reappeared, looking exasperated.

"That was unnecessarily difficult," he said. "Your friend may need to be talked down a little. He's having a bit of a fit."

"I'm sorry," said Alif. "He's had a long couple of days."

"Not my problem. Here, down you come."

Alif took the man's outstretched hand and skittered down into the blue. He was assaulted by the scent of ozone, and a static charge rippled over his skin, causing the hair on his arms to stand on end. When he opened his mouth to breathe he became convinced there was no oxygen, and began tearing at his throat with his free hand. The ozone smell seeped into his nostrils, his mouth, the pores of his skin, until he felt he would dissolve in it, becoming a cloud of stratospheric particles. He went limp. There was a tug on his arm and when he blinked again he was standing on a shoal of stardust.

"What?" Alif looked around, panting to catch his breath. A few yards away, NewQuarter was kneeling in a hillock of luminous powder, babbling, while Sheikh Bilal stood over him and spoke in a low, soothing voice. The man who had ferried them across brushed more of the strange dust from Alif's shoulders, looking him over with brusque concern.

"All right?" His form was even more indistinct here; his ears stretched into pointed tips, then became tufted with fur, then shrank again into a shape more human; his hair seemed to float around his face like ink in water.

"Fine," said Alif faintly. He moved his legs, testing them, and was glad when they obeyed him. Straining against the limits of his vision, he studied the landscape. Though the sand had been replaced by the finer, paler material in which they stood, it was still a desert of sorts: dunes washed away into the distance, shedding clouds of crystal vapor in the light wind. The sky above was many-hued, like an early twilight. Sun and moon were both visible, along with a few stars, giving the impression of a day that had never begun or a night that had never ended. The sight awoke something primitive in Alif's brain: a sense that he had strayed into a place where he did not belong and had become prey among predators.

"What is this?" howled NewQuarter. "What is this?"

The man shrugged as if the question was banal.

"The edge of the Empty Quarter, near the road to Irem," he said. "Exactly where you were a minute ago, only different."

"Irem, as in the City of Pillars?" asked Sheikh Bilal, looking, to Alif, absurdly unshaken. "The city built by djinn in the old legends?"

"The very same," said the man. "Though it's fallen out of fashion in recent times, I'm afraid. Many of us prefer to live in places abandoned by humans. Less work for us. Detroit is very popular."

Alif knelt in the dust next to NewQuarter and put one hand on his shoulder.

"Snap out of it, *bhai*," he said. "You're all right. Think of it as a computer game. You used to play World of Battlecraft, didn't you?"

"This," said NewQuarter with a squeak, "is way too real to be Battlecraft. This is realer than high definition. This is realer than real life."

"We should get going," said their guide. "There will be others moving through here, and not all of them will be as understanding as I am. Vikram had plenty of enemies."

"Will you tell us your own name?" asked Alif, getting NewQuarter to his feet.

The man made a musical series of sounds that slid off Alif's hearing like oil.

"I'll never be able to pronounce that," he said. "Do you use another name? Vikram said he does. Did. I mean, Vikram wasn't his real name."

The man snorted. "I don't deal with your tribe often enough to warrant a second name," he said. "I see no point. You couldn't possibly use my name against me if you can't even pronounce it." He set off in the direction of the moon, kicking up a haze of dust as he went. Alif followed, tugging NewQuarter after him. The sheikh trailed behind, moving more slowly across the yielding ground. The man led them over a series of small dunes that shifted in the wind, reshaping themselves like the surface of the sea. As Alif struggled to keep up, it seemed to him as though the man was walking on water and the dust that sprang up in his footsteps was the salt spray of a dry ocean. The idea had a soporific effect on his mind. He found himself lulled into a kind of trance as they walked and his eyes began to flutter, heavy-lidded.

"Careful back there," called their guide. "If you fall asleep I may lose you. Keeping your bodies intact here is a lot of work."

Alif shook himself, opening his eyes wide. He heard Sheikh Bilal take several deep breaths behind him.

"The air here doesn't help," the sheikh said. "It has a very strange effect on one. It's like that gas they give you at the dentist's."

Alif gave an experimental sniff. The ozone scent that had almost overwhelmed him at the mirage was still detectable, though fainter; or perhaps he was becoming accustomed to it.

"What's so bad about sleeping?" he heard NewQuarter ask. "Sleep is God's mercy. I could use a nap."

"Borderlands are treacherous," said the man. "You're drowsy because your mind wants to return to the world you know. But it would never get there. The sleeping mind wanders between seen and unseen without settling in either. If you slept here you might never wake again, at least not in any fashion you could understand. You can sleep once we get to Irem. It's so deep in our territory that you can't wander far, even in dreams."

Alif remembered Vikram's concern when he had nodded off in the Immovable Alley and felt a pang of regret for the way he had reacted. Lost in thought, he followed the trail of footsteps the man left behind in the soft powder. He led them over dune after dune, pausing with impatience at the crest of each one as they toiled through the glittering, overyielding earth, each step a struggle. The man seemed not to sink into the dust as they did, treading lightly over it as though it were as springy as grass. Finally, at the rim of a dune that curled like a wave, he pointed: below, in a rough valley between the hills of dust, was a road.

"There," he said. "This will take us to the city. Once we reach Irem, I suggest you make yourselves someone else's responsibility—I can't be held accountable for what may happen to you there."

"Fine," said Alif, with a confidence he did not feel. NewQuarter was stalking back and forth at the top of the dune, rubbing his temples.

"Road," he said. "That's not a proper road. I've never seen a white road. Why is the road white?"

Alif peered down at it: the road was paved with blocks of milky crystal that picked up the shifting colors of the sky. It reminded him of something.

"Quartz!" he exclaimed. "Like the Old Quarter wall in the City."

The man nodded. "Quarried from the same mountain, in fact. Quartz is favored by the djinn. One of our people built your wall, many centuries ago."

"Sidi Abdullah al Jinan," said Sheikh Bilal, and broke out in a wheezy chuckle. "The genie who brought religion to the City. I confess I always assumed he was a myth, and that tomb where they keep his turban a clever way to pump more money out of tourists."

"A fellow's turban is a serious thing," the man said gravely.

"Oh, of course," said the sheikh. NewQuarter looked from one to the other and squawked with hilarity.

"I'm not going anywhere," he said, sitting down in a puff of luminescent powder. "Not one more step. Take me home. I want a good meal and a bath with overpriced salts from some exploited indigenous locale. I want my old life, by God. You understand that, surely?" He looked up at Alif in desperation.

"Not the thing about the salts," said Alif, "but about your old life, yes. You won't get it back, *bhai*, not ever. Even if you could snap your fingers and teleport back to your flat, you couldn't avoid being changed by this. That's the price you pay for thinking you've got an angle on things, that you've managed to figure out a way around the ordinary world because you're so clever. God help you if it's true."

"I admit that my plans for heroism had serious flaws," said NewQuarter with a glare, "but the genies are entirely your fault."

"We aren't dead," said Sheikh Bilal, "so I am tempted not to find fault with either heroism or genies. *Yallah*, boys, let's go."

"Yes, let's," said the man. "As I've been trying to tell you, it isn't safe out here."

Alif followed him down the dune toward the road, with NewQuarter and the sheikh close behind. As they stepped onto its glassy surface, the road seemed to straighten, and the winding valley between dunes became a sculpted, planned channel. The road reached toward the horizon with military perpendicularity. It was less of a road, Alif thought, and more of a triumphal march or processional, the work of people who desired to impress. It had an abandoned air now, a melancholy elegance made stark by the strange light and the silence of the dusty hills.

"Once upon a time," said the man, walking at a brisk pace, "you'd never see this road so empty. I suppose it isn't really empty even now—for there are things in heaven and earth that we can't see either, and are known only to God. But for argument's sake: Irem is not the place it used to be."

"Why's that?" asked NewQuarter, scuffing the surface of the road experimentally with one foot.

"I'm afraid it's mostly your fault," said the man, without malice. "It was left to Adam to tell all the birds and beasts and angels and djinn their rightful names, but his heirs have forgotten many of them. Irem is passing out of memory."

"I thought djinn are supposed to like abandoned places," said Alif.

"We like places abandoned by men," said the man, "not by history. You should have seen Irem five hundred years ago, when our peoples still acknowledged one another. Caravans, poetry competitions, trade in all manner of bizarre knickknacks you third-borns kept inventing. It was a sight to be seen. The toilet—now that will never be equaled. We all thought the toilet was pretty hysterical."

"I would love a toilet just now," said NewQuarter.

"You have such an odd relationship to your environment," mused the man. "Such a paranoid relationship. You seem intent on existing in smaller and smaller spaces, filled with more and more gadgets, with the mistaken impression that this will give you more control over your lives. There's something a little impious about it."

"Nothing wrong with gadgets," muttered Alif.

"No, except that they're not magic," said the man, "and a lot of you seem to believe they should be."

Silence followed this observation. They walked for what seemed to Alif like a very long time, though the ineffable position of the sun and moon made time difficult to tell. This depressed him, and again he was hounded by the feeling that he did not belong here and had traded one kind of danger for another. He longed for a full day of sun followed by a full night without it, and wondered how something so basic should come to be denied to him. He felt there must be some lesson locked up in his celestial dislocation, first in the

Hand's lightless cell and then in the Empty Quarter, but he could not determine what it was.

A quiet sound was the first hint he had of trouble. The desert of the djinn, like the banal one he knew, was silent, lacking water or trees or the critical mass of living things necessary for noise. So a sound was something. It was innocuous in and of itself, like the distant cry of a fox or some other small plaintive creature. But their guide stiffened when he heard it, halting in midstep on the quartz road.

"You must be very calm," he said, his own voice low and deliberate. "Do not cower or run, and do not under any circumstance answer its questions."

NewQuarter opened his mouth to respond, then clapped it shut, eyes bulging as he stared at the thing that had appeared in the road.

It was a beast, though unlike any other animal Alif had ever encountered: massive, reddish, indistinct, a bloodstain on the pale paving stones. Fur hung down in clumps over the goatish pupils in its gas-blue eyes. There were no teeth in its primitive jaws; instead, row after row of knives receded into the darkness of its gullet. It was a child's nightmare, the fantasy of a mind too innocent to encompass human evil, but capable of imagining something far worse. Alif heard a high, thin cry, and was mortified to realize he had made it.

"*Banu adam*," the beast said in a voice like grinding metal. "*Banu adam* on the road to Irem."

"They're nothing," said the man. "A couple of children and an old man."

"That's three more things than nothing," said the beast.

"Not to you," said the man. "To you they are nothing. Let us pass."

The beast gave another foxlike cry, all the more terrible to Alif because it was so soft and seemed to come from somewhere else.

"If they're in here, it means someone out there is looking for them," it said. "That's the only reason for three third-born not-nothings to be on the road to Irem at such an hour in history, when the war drums of the Deceiver are all their kind remember of the unseen."

"So? That still doesn't mean they're worth anything to you."

Alif detected an edge in their guide's voice.

"But they are worth something to *someone*," said the beast, lumbering toward them, "and that makes them interesting." It stopped in front of NewQuarter, who had gone as white as his robe.

"Tell me, mud-boy, how would you like to die?"

"At the age of ninety," said NewQuarter shrilly, "on a bed made of money in a villa overlooking the sea, while at least three wives beat themselves bloody with grief."

The beast roared with laughter.

"Imbecile," hissed their guide. "I told you not to answer its questions."

"I'm *sorry!*"

"Let the boy speak." The knives in the beast's mouth rang as it smiled. "What's your name, little friend?"

To Alif's horror, NewQuarter seemed on the verge of replying. Alif seized his arm and jerked him back.

"Not your name," he breathed. "For God's sake, not your name."

The beast's gaze shifted, alighting on Alif's face.

"So. This one knows a thing. Or two." It snapped its mouth shut, the knives in its jaws slamming together like a trap.

"He doesn't know anything." The man glared at Alif with unconcealed fury.

"I'm an idiot," Alif agreed meekly.

"No. This one has a tang about him." The beast sniffed the air near Alif's neck. "Copper wire and rare earth elements and electricity. He barely smells of mud at all. Why are you here, chemical man?"

"I'm—" Alif fought the terror that made answering seem like the easiest way out. He retreated into the things that he knew. Diminishing helixes and parabolas appeared in his mind, and he remembered that one could avoid faulty output by adding a new input parameter.

"Who wants to know?" he hazarded. When the beast merely blinked, he grew bolder. "Why should I answer your questions if you won't answer mine? Why should my friend give you his name if you won't give him yours?"

The beast gaped at him, looking almost hurt.

"I liked them better when they were forgetting," it said in a small voice. Seeming to shrink, it shuffled off the road into the dust, fading slowly from view. For several moments the only sound was labored breathing. Sheikh Bilal was shivering visibly, his eyes vacant. Alif slipped a supporting hand under his elbow.

"That was well done," said their guide in a mollified tone.

"But I didn't do anything at all," said Alif.

"You answered questions with questions. That's more presence of mind than most *banu adam* would have in front of a demon." He

311

laughed. "The look on its face—like a fox chasing a rabbit when suddenly the rabbit turns and bares its teeth."

"That was a demon?" NewQuarter reeled in a circle, clutching his head. "Oh, God, oh, God."

"Yes, a demon." The man gave a musical sigh and continued down the road at a faster pace. "In times of ignorance they grow bolder."

NewQuarter's high, unbridled laugh made Alif nervous.

"Who knew demons were such cowards?" he said in a manic falsetto. "Alif chased it away by looking at it funny."

"They are cowards," said Sheikh Bilal quietly, breaking his silence. "As the Enemy of Man is a coward. We are not meant to fear them because they are powerful, but because we ourselves are so easily misled."

They walked for what seemed to Alif like a very long time, though the altered paths of the sun and moon, which seemed to revolve around the sky without rising or setting, made it difficult to tell. A glimmer on the horizon was the first sign of the djinn city. As they grew closer, Alif saw slender pillars of the same mineral that made up the road, rising to some indefinite height above the dunes. They were illuminated by a light whose source was unclear and appeared to generate from within the pillars themselves, casting shadows of amber and pink across the dust. A large, arched gate was visible among the pillars, carved with geometric patterns resembling starbursts. The road ran beneath it, into the city itself.

As they approached, Sheikh Bilal and NewQuarter fell into an awed silence. Alif became nervous. Figures began to appear on the road around them, most of which seemed not to notice the human migrants in their midst: some were simple shadows, walking upright and independent of any surface; others, like their guide, were blurred amalgams of man and animal. One creature made Alif fall back with a cry of alarm: it was the height of a two-story building, hairless and muscular, with a torso that fell away into mist as it moved along the road.

"What—what is—"

"It's a *marid*," said the man, his tone disinterested. "Like the lamp genie from your Aladdin stories. Don't worry, you're much too puny to be worth his bother."

Alif was not comforted by this reassurance.

"The ones you should be worried about are the *sila*," said their guide. "You won't find a *marid* hiding in your basement, but the *sila* can take many forms, and they like to live around human beings. They're all female, you know. They might look less terrifying but they're twice as dangerous. Remember that when you go home."

"As if we see female spirits every day," snorted NewQuarter. Their guide shrugged.

"You probably do."

As they approached the first pillars of the city, the activity around them increased and Alif could hear a low murmur of voices speaking in a language—or languages—he could not understand. He was reminded of the cacophony of voices in the Immovable Alley, and thought at once of Sakina.

"I think I know a way for you to get rid of us," he said, turning to their guide. "Do you know a woman, an information-trader in the Immovable Alley, whose name is Sakina?"

The man started in surprise.

"You've been to the Alley? Who took you? Why?"

"It was Vikram. He was trying to source something for us," Alif hedged, hoping the man did not share Vikram's uncanny ability to read into half-truths.

"You seem intent on getting into a lot of trouble," said the man, though his tone was admiring. "I don't know this Sakina woman but it would be easy enough to track her down. Let me stash you somewhere first, and then see what I can sniff out."

He led them under the archway and into a teeming thoroughfare. Quartz buildings lined the street, their windows covered in wooden tracery like mansions in the Old Quarter of the City. Whether they housed dwellings or shops Alif couldn't tell; their inhabitants were screened behind the wooden window-lattices and visible only as interruptions in the light that spilled out into the street. Around them, Irem bustled with nameless activity, none of it clearly identifiable to Alif as commerce or socializing or work: just speech and movement. There was, he thought, a numb quality to it all. It was as though the city remembered the pageantry of its former self and, failing to replicate it, had lapsed into indifference.

"In here." The man ushered them through the wooden double doors of a large, square building. Inside were long tables where a scattering of strange figures sat in conversation. There was a tall, slim, coal-orange individual who looked like a moving candle flame, two women with the heads of goats, and a creature the size of a large toad that sat on the table itself, gesticulating with a pair of fat glistening hands. Their voices rose in laughter and died down again, backlit by a bluish fire burning in a metal grate at one end of the room. The grate was molded to look like a man and a woman engaged in an act Alif himself had never performed. As he watched, unable to look away, the fire dancing behind the carvings seemed to animate them, bringing them to lurid life and throwing their images across the ceiling.

A shelf nearby was stocked with bottles of liquid in an array of unnatural-looking colors. Alif was surprised to see a large flat-screen television affixed to the opposite wall, tuned to Al Jazeera, and was struck by sudden recognition.

"Is this a *bar*?"

The man laughed.

"You could call it that. We come here to eat and drink and discuss things. Sit in the corner there—they'll bring you something to fill your stomachs." Before Alif could protest, the man was off across the room, vanishing through the doorway. Sheikh Bilal and NewQuarter, looking profoundly out of place, sat down on a bench at the table the man had indicated. Alif perched across from them. He opened his mouth to speak, intending to diffuse his embarrassment over the suggestive grate by making a joke, but a loud squeal interrupted him. At the table across the room, the toadish creature had seized the candle flame by what Alif assumed was its throat, and with strength alarming for something so small, proceeded to throttle it violently. One of the goat-headed women snatched a bottle from the shelf and, with a summary swing, broke it over the toad's head. The toad went belly up on the table with a loud croak.

"This looks suspiciously like a den of vice," the sheikh muttered.

"Does it?" NewQuarter made a nervous study of the room. "I can't tell what it looks like. It might not look like anything. Who is this woman you've sent that guy to find? How do you know these people?"

Alif rubbed his eyes. His body was making feeble complaints, demanding food and rest.

"I don't know them," he said. "I'm not sure it's possible for people like us to know them. It's only—there was a man who died helping me and my friends, and he was one of them. He told me about this place. He took two girls I know here to hide them from State, and I'd like to find out what happened to them."

NewQuarter broke out into a high, helpless laugh.

"Is this what it takes to escape State these days? Is there literally nowhere on earth that is safe, leaving Never Never Land the only logical place to flee? I've gone mad, Alif. I've gone mad."

"I'm sorry," said Alif. It occurred to him that he had done more apologizing in the last few months than in all previous twenty-three years of his life put together. It seemed absurd that in his attempt to put a few simple things right he should have made such astronomical miscalculations. A girl he loved had decided she did not love him—at least, not enough. How was such a problem usually addressed? Surely not with the clandestine exchange of books and computer surveillance and recourse to the djinn. He struggled to fix on the exact moment when he had run his life off the rails.

A shadow appeared carrying a platter of food and glasses filled with greenish liquid. It set these down on the table between Alif and his companions without a word, as NewQuarter stared in silent horror. The sheikh touched the glass in front of him with a frown.

"Is this alcohol?" he asked, as though accustomed to speaking to wraiths.

No, came a voice in Alif's head. *Alcohol is not something we can make or consume. But it is certainly an intoxicant, if that's what you meant to ask.*

"It was, thank you," said the sheikh, pushing the glass away with two fingers. "Might I have some plain water?"

"Me, too," said Alif.

If you wish. The shadow moved away.

"I'll stick with the intoxicant, by God," said NewQuarter, clutching his glass. "After the day we've had I think I deserve it."

"*Khumr* is *khumr,*" said Sheikh Bilal. He gave NewQuarter a severe look.

"*Khumr* is booze, Uncle," said NewQuarter. "And that thing just said this isn't booze."

"Nonsense. *Khumr* is any substance that clouds the mind for recreational rather than medical reasons. This is clearly forbidden."

"Well, I think our fiasco qualifies as a medical reason." NewQuarter tipped his head back and took a long swallow of the phosphoric drink. Alif watched, fascinated in spite of himself, as the younger man's face went pale and broke out with sweat.

"Well? How does it taste?" he asked.

"Like Windex," rasped NewQuarter. He coughed, and a thread of smoke issued from his lips. "Oh, God."

Alif was reminded of his first and only experience with alcohol: Abdullah had been given a half-empty bottle of Scotch in exchange for a DVD-R drive and they had done shots together in the storage closet at Radio Sheikh. It had taken all of Alif's willpower not to vomit the burning liquid up again.

"You don't drink!" he exclaimed, divining the source of NewQuarter's bravado.

"No," said NewQuarter miserably, clearing his throat. "I don't. But when you put something in front of me, I panic—you have no idea how many awful parties I've been to, with princes and hired women getting wasted everywhere once the help is gone and the liquor cabinets are unlocked. They practically pour vodka down your throat. If I don't take at least one swallow and pretend I'm into it, my manhood is suddenly in question."

Sheikh Bilal laughed—the first real, unguarded laugh Alif had heard him make since their escape.

"You're wrong," he said. "It's *their* manhood that is at stake, and this is why they bully you. If you were to refuse, you would make them look weak. You should be proud to abstain."

NewQuarter belched, one hand over his stomach.

"Making a prince seem weak is a bad idea," he said. "Especially if you're another prince. It looks like competition. One of these days one of those bastards is going to find out whose side I'm really on and then it will be you coming to rescue me from a prison in the desert."

"Is that why you retired?" Alif asked.

"Yes," said NewQuarter, wiping the sweat from his brow. "The thing was—when I figured out that the Hand must be someone in the aristocracy, I couldn't shake the feeling that I probably knew him. Had met him at a family lunch, Ramadan, Eid—hell, maybe he was one of the weekend vodka-swillers. It made me nervous."

Alif hesitated, suddenly self-conscious.

"I've seen him," he said in a quiet voice. A shudder ran down his back. He did not know how to speak about the Hand except with intimacy, drawing on the grotesque bond between jailer and prisoner. "I know his name."

NewQuarter leaned forward, setting his elbows on the scuffed wooden table, eyes bright.

"At last. Oh, this is a good day. Who is he?"

"Abbas Al Shehab."

To Alif's surprise, NewQuarter began to laugh.

"Impossible," he said. "Not Abbas. I know the man—he's my uncle-by-marriage's third cousin, or maybe a second cousin once removed. One or the other. Anyway, he doesn't have it in him. He's a geek, like us. I don't think I've ever seen him standing somewhere other than in a corner, trying and failing to make charming conversation. I didn't think you could be born Arab and not inherit that skill. He must have been swapped at birth with some dour mountain Turk or something. Unmarried, if you can believe it, though he's plenty rich. That's how bad it is. No, Abbas couldn't say *boo* to a dog if his life depended on it."

Indignation and shame warred in Alif's chest. He found he didn't like to talk about the Hand now, though the man had once been a mainstay of his conversations with City malcontents.

"I know what I know," he said stiffly.

"I don't doubt that you've—that in prison, you—I just wonder if you've got the name right, that's all." NewQuarter fiddled with a piece of bread between erratic fingers. Alif ignored the younger man's tipsy, earnest attempt to catch his eye.

"Anyway," continued NewQuarter when the silence grew awkward. "Leaving aside the question of identity. I'm not the most durable person on earth—if the Hand had gotten me in a room and so much as nicked my chin with a close shave, I'd have rolled over on everyone. You. Radio Sheikh. GurkhabOss. I couldn't live with that constant reminder of my own spinelessness, so I quit."

Alif was touched in spite of himself. "You're not spineless," he said. "You came and boosted me from prison in the middle of the night. In a BMW."

"I did do that, didn't I." NewQuarter brightened. "Good for me. Now I'm just as fucked as the rest of you. I'm not even scared. This green stuff must be working."

Sheikh Bilal nudged the offending glass away from NewQuarter's hand. The shadow arrived again with three cups of water and set them down on the table.

Eat, it said. *The food won't hurt you. I'm not interested in having a trio of human corpses on my hands.* It floated back toward the other end of the room.

Alif turned his attention to the platter in front of him: it contained, or so he was fairly confident, stewed meat and saffron rice, along with a cooked green that might have been spinach. A pile of warm flatbread sat beside the food on the edge of the tray. Tearing a loaf in half, he scooped up meat and rice and took an experimental bite. The flavors of cardamom and pepper and gamey meat bloomed on his tongue.

"Goat," he said. "Or at least, that's my guess."

"A relative of one of those ladies at the other table, maybe," muttered NewQuarter.

Sheikh Bilal pulled back his sleeve and tucked in without further prompting. NewQuarter leaned forward and sniffed before plucking a single piece of meat from the stew. Chewing it, he nodded his approval. They ate in silence. At intervals, they smiled somewhat wryly at each other, enjoying the camaraderie of dislocation, like tourists stranded together at some nameless outpost. At the table across the room, the toad was gathered up by the presiding shadow and deposited in a heap outside the door; his table companions continued their conversation without any appearance of either sympathy or distress. Alif caught NewQuarter's eye and made a face. NewQuarter snickered, ducking behind one hand when one of the goat women looked at him sharply.

After filling his belly—which did not take long, leading him to wonder if his stomach had shrunk during its prison hiatus—Alif was sleepy, warmed by the spices in the food. He leaned back against the wall and let his eyes drift shut.

"I wonder if there's such a thing as a bed in this pile," he muttered. He heard fingers snap. NewQuarter called out to the shadow, demanding to know whether it could provide them with a place to sleep. Alif smiled without opening his eyes, hoping the return of NewQuarter's imperiousness meant he was feeling better. A hand shook his shoulder: he rubbed his eyes, rising, and shuffled after Sheikh Bilal and the shadow toward a staircase at the back of the room. At the top of the stairs was a hallway lined with doors painted the same range of colors as the sky outside: dusky rose, dark blue, lavender. Set in the milky quartz wall, the effect was like looking through nothing, into the sky itself; Alif had to blink several times to make the scene resolve itself into something he could fathom.

You may take the blue room, said the shadow, bowing them through the midnight-colored door. Inside was a small room with an oil lamp in the window and a few sleeping mats against the wall. The ceiling was painted to look like an arm of the Milky Way, silver-painted stars popping and fading in the lamplight.

The shadow wished them good night. Alif barely heard it, his mind already thick with sleep. He kicked off his sandals and lay down on the nearest mat, pulling down his head cloth and wrapping it around himself like a blanket. NewQuarter yawned conspicuously. Alif heard the low murmur of Sheikh Bilal's voice in prayer and the scrape of the man's feet as he knelt in supplication. The familiar words comforted him. He was asleep before the sheikh saluted the angels to his right and left.

*   *   *

"Alif? Is that really you?"

There was a scent like jasmine and, beneath it, something more bestial. Alif rolled on to his back and blinked sleep-encrusted eyes: a tawny, feline figure hovered over him, looking concerned. He propped himself up on his elbows. It was Sakina, her dark braids looped atop her head, gold dangling from her ears. She set a cloth bag on the floor beside her.

"You look half-dead," she observed. "What happened?"

"Prison," he said, at a loss for some more elegant way to put it.

Her sympathy and alarm were so obvious that Alif found his throat closing and began to suspect there were parts of his mind and his body that were truly unwell. The glory of his rescue felt as profound as ever but beneath it lay the damage of the dark and all that had kept him company there. A small, frightened sound escaped his throat.

"No, please don't get upset—I'm sorry. Here." She rummaged in her bag and produced a vial of thick purplish substance, pressing it into his hand. "Take a sip of that."

Obediently, Alif uncorked the vial and tipped it back between his lips. The viscous liquid tasted of honey and dark fruit, leaving behind an herbal tang. A pleasant sensation, like the anticipation of a holiday, put distance between his waking mind and the residue of his three-month night.

"That's nice," he said. "What is it?"

"An elixir against heartache," said Sakina, showing a row of delicately pointed teeth. "Keep it." She crossed her legs beneath her and sat. Alif felt his cheer increasing as he looked at her; she was proof that he was not without resources, even now.

"You know that Vikram is dead," she said in a lower voice.

The effect of the elixir faltered for a moment.

"Yes," said Alif. "He knew he was dying when I left him—he's the only reason the convert and Dina didn't end up in jail, like me. He saved them."

Sakina's smile was melancholy. "Poor Vikram," she said. "He could be quite unpredictable and dangerous—you didn't know how dangerous, or you'd never have traveled with him. But when he felt like it, he was capable of noble things."

Alif remembered the fatal wound in Vikram's side and touched his own, feeling a twinge of imagined pain.

"He lived a long life. A very long life—as long as an age of the earth, it seemed. I imagine that by helping you he was hoping for a chance to die on his own terms. He knew the history of that manuscript you'd gotten your hands on. The people who come into contact with it do not tend to die in contented old age."

"I lost it," said Alif, head drooping. "The *Alf Yeom*. I lost it."

Sakina's eyes went wide.

"Lost it? How? Who has it now?"

"I have no idea who could have taken it. The Hand doesn't have it. Sheikh Bilal doesn't have it. I was holed up in Basheera, using it to code, and then everything went to hell——"

Sakina leaned forward and pressed her hands together beneath her chin, fixing Alif with an urgent, sun-colored stare.

"Say that again. What do you mean you were using it to code?"

Alif struggled for the right words to explain.

"I figured out what Al Shehab——we call him the Hand——wanted to do with it. He believed all those mystics who'd been trying to understand the *Alf Yeom* for centuries were going about things from the wrong end. He thought that since the book can be understood as a symbol-set, there was an obvious application for computing. He thought, in other words, that he could use the *Alf Yeom* to create a totally new coding methodology, a sort of supercomputer built out of metaphors."

Sakina sat back and studied Alif in a way that made him slightly uncomfortable.

"And you did it," she said. "You made it work."

"Sort of. The code was only viable for a few minutes before the computer I was using crashed. You have to remove too many parameters to work like that. It causes a lot of errors. Computers are like angels——they're built to obey commands. If you give them too much interpretive leeway they get confused."

"Hmm." Sakina worried the end of one of her braids with a claw-tipped finger. "I'm impressed you're willing to admit as much. Most people who become convinced that kind of power is within their grasp stop believing in the possibility of failure. I'm also worried that the book is now out in the open, and that more of your kind will attempt to use it for the same ends. Not all of the *banu adam* are as farsighted as you."

Alif twisted his hands anxiously. Behind him, NewQuarter and Sheikh Bilal were stirring on their sleeping mats.

"I'll find out who took it," Alif said, lowering his voice. "And when I do I'll get rid of it."

"I don't have the authority to tell you what to do with it," said Sakina with a slight wince. "But I don't like the idea of getting rid of books. That manuscript is a legacy of your race, for good or ill."

"Mostly ill," said Alif.

"Even so. The *Alf Yeom* is not evil in and of itself—for the djinn it is history. Like so many things, it becomes corrupt in the hands of man. But if we were to destroy all the things that man has made corrupt, the earth would be barren in a day."

"I wouldn't be destroying the *Alf Yeom*," Alif pointed out. "Just the man-made copy. The djinn will still have all of theirs. You'll lose nothing."

Sakina responded by looking away, as though considering some eldritch facet of their conversation. Though she had complimented him on his intellect, Alif felt outmatched even by her silences. He attempted to steer her back toward his most immediate concern.

"Vikram said he was taking the convert and Dina here, to the Empty Quarter. Do you know—is there any way to find out if they made it, or where they might be if they did?"

Sakina roused herself from her reverie.

"We could look for them," she said, "but I have to tell you, Alif, any *beni adam* without a protector in the Empty Quarter is not likely to survive for long. You're not meant to be here, and your minds are not equipped to interpret what you see. It's taxing on the sanity of all but the most spiritually elite. You'll start to feel the undertow of this place yourself soon enough."

"Then we have to go now." Alif was haunted by the image of Dina undone by madness. He needed to see her.

"Go where?" NewQuarter sat up, rubbing his frowzy head and yawning.

"To find my friends," said Alif. "They may have been stranded here after everything went down at Al Basheera."

"Good God, you brought a woman." NewQuarter noticed Sakina for the first time. He hastily ran a hand through his sleep-tousled hair.

Alif introduced NewQuarter and Sheikh Bilal, who stuttered out a greeting while arranging his rumpled head cloth, still not fully awake. Sakina smiled at them, seeming not to notice their furtive glances at her eyes and teeth and hands. When they had made themselves presentable, they followed her downstairs into the main room of the bar, or inn, or whatever it was; the tables were less populated now and only a few uncanny patrons could be seen around them. The candle flame from the night before appeared to be passed out at its table, sleeping off the contents of the empty glass dangling from its flickering hand. The shadow that had served them—if it was the same shadow—reappeared with bowls of a steaming white liquid that turned out to be hot honeyed milk, along with a plate of bread. Alif ate with a better appetite than he had had the day before.

"How do we pay this guy?" he asked Sakina as he tore into a piece of bread, realizing he had no currency of any kind, nor any knowledge of whether the djinn used currency to begin with.

"If you can't pay with things, you could pay with skills," said Sakina, motioning to the shadow.

"Well, wait a minute," said Alif, looking from the shadow to Sakina. "My skills are more or less limited to computers—I'm not sure how much help that is to an, ah, to a—"

Effrit, said the shadow, *I'm an effrit. And I've got a two-year-old Dell desktop in the back that's had some kind of virus for ages. The screen goes black five minutes after I turn the damn thing on. I have to do a hard reboot every time.*

Alif felt a new vista of serendipitous opportunity open before him.

"You've got Internet in the Empty Quarter?" he asked in an awed voice.

Cousin, said the shadow, *we've got WiFi.*

*   *   *

It took Alif no more than fifteen minutes to debug the *effrit's* machine. The problem was an old and very clunky spyware applet he had seen before, one that had slipped past a suite of antivirus software that was out of date. Alif removed the program and ran a few updates.

"I've deleted all your cookies just to be safe," he told the shadow. "So the sites you visit frequently may need to reinstall them. That'll happen automatically. Just make sure you keep your antivirus software up-to-date—there are new definitions almost every day, so you don't want to fall behind."

I've heard cookies are dangerous, said the shadow.

"They're not. You can't get a virus without executable content, which cookies don't have. But the spyware geeks like them because

327

they're a fast way to collect your information, so that's what a lot of phishing programs target first. Just keep your software current—including browser updates—and you should be fine."

Thanks. The shadow floated over the keyboard as Alif stood and began, as far as he could tell, to check its e-mail. Alif was pleased with himself. He turned to grin at NewQuarter and the sheikh, who lurked in the doorway of the back room to which the shadow had led them, looking dubious.

"Wow, *akhi*," said NewQuarter. "I'm impressed you just sat there and did that. I'm not sure I could string two coherent sentences together with a telepathic special effect hanging over my shoulder."

"It's still there," said Alif, hoping the shadow had not heard.

"Yes, I see that. Can we go now?"

Come back again soon, said the shadow, with a hint of what felt like sarcasm. Alif thanked it with more flourish than was probably necessary, attempting to make up for NewQuarter's rudeness, and hurried back out into the main room where Sakina was waiting.

"I think we should start by consulting someone whose job it is to know what goes on in Irem," she said. "I can only imagine that your friends are here in the city—Vikram would not have left them out in the wastelands. You've seen what it's like out there."

"I thought it was rather beautiful," said Sheikh Bilal.

"I think so, too," said Sakina, "but I wouldn't want to be out there alone for any length of time. There are older and stranger things than I prowling the dunes." She shouldered her bag and led them out the door into the street. The sky above was a brilliant rose color, like the most exquisite moment of sunrise stretched and spread from horizon to horizon. The moon sat heady and blue—nearly full, Alif noticed—just above the flat roofs of the buildings around them. Sakina followed a path known only to herself, ducking down alleys that ended in tiny squares overgrown with jasmine or dotted with pools of still water reflecting the moon; jewel-like places that Alif could only stare at for a moment before having to hurry to catch up. He heard Sheikh Bilal murmur in appreciation at the scenery as he walked along behind him.

"A marvel," the sheikh said. "Truly, the work of the Lord of Worlds surpasses all our puny understanding. You know, I read once that the human mind is incapable of imagining anything that does not exist somewhere, in some form. It seemed a paltry enough truth at the time—I thought, of course it must be so, since in a sense everything we will ever discover or invent has, in the eyes of God, already been discovered and invented, as God is above time. Seeing this, though, I begin to understand how much more profound that statement is. It does not simply mean that man's innovation is entirely known to God; it means there is no such thing as fiction."

Alif grinned, buoyant with the euphoria of the place.

"Puts a different spin on that conversation we had about the stupid fictional pork," he said.

"Have you changed your mind, then?"

"I'm not sure. I'm still hard-pressed to give a damn about World of Battlecraft."

"I'm not," said the sheikh in a more serious tone. "If a video game does more to fulfill a young person than the words of prophesy, it means people like me have failed in a rather spectacular fashion."

Alif slowed his steps to walk beside the sheikh.

"You're not a failure, Uncle," he said, the words awkward and insufficient in his mouth. "It's only that we don't feel safe. A game has a reset button. You have infinite chances for success. Real life is awfully permanent compared to that, and a lot of religious people make it seem even more permanent—one step the wrong way, one sin too many, and it's the fiery furnace for you. Beware. And then at the same time, you ask us to love the God who has this terrible sword hanging over our necks. It's very confusing."

"Ah," said Sheikh Bilal, looking melancholy, "but that's the point. What is more terrifying than love? How can one not be overwhelmed by the majesty of a creator who gives and destroys life in equal measure, with breathtaking swiftness? You look at all the swelling rose hips in the garden that will wither and die without ever germinating and it seems a miracle that you are alive at all. What would one not do to acknowledge that miracle in some way?"

"Enough," said NewQuarter, lagging behind and looking sulky. "I'm feeling overstimulated as it is. I need to conserve my brainpower."

As they rounded a corner, Sakina halted in front of a low wall with an arched wooden door built into it.

"When we go in," she said in a hushed voice, as though fearful of being overheard, "you must do your best not to scream or faint or do any of the other things you will be tempted to do. And the princeling must learn a little humility. Answer any questions he asks in as prompt and thorough a manner as you can. All right?"

"He?" Alif glanced back at NewQuarter, who made an unhappy face. "Who are we going to see?"

In response, Sakina pushed open the door. Beyond it was a tiled courtyard with a small fountain at the center, splashing merrily into a shallow basin; date palms ringed the perimeter, draping their fruit over the walls with generous dignity. At one end of the courtyard, a monster sat, or hovered, over a pile of cushions. It looked very similar to the giant apparition Alif had seen on the road at the edge of the city: an enormous torso topped by an improbable, toothy head, skin shining darkly in the half-light, its body fading into mist below the waist. He heard NewQuarter fall back with a muffled shriek. Sakina shot him a nasty look over her shoulder and went to kneel before the creature, ornaments shining in her braids as she bent her head.

"Noble sir," she said, "I've come with these three insignificant and unworthy *banu adam* to ask for information. I hope you will not refuse us."

The thing made a rumbling, displeased sound in its gullet.

"That all depends," it said, in a voice that reverberated in Alif's chest, "on what information you want."

Sakina looked back at Alif. He swallowed once, then twice; moisture seemed to have evaporated from his throat.

"My friends," he said in a dry wheeze. "Two girls—two women, I mean. They would have been brought here by a guy called Vikram the Vampire, if they were ever here at all. It's very important that I find them. I'm—I'm sort of responsible for the trouble they were in, you see."

"Vikram the Vampire," said the thing. "Vikram the Vampire has been dead these three months or more."

"I know," said Alif, attempting to keep impatience out of his voice. "But did he leave any such women behind when he died? Did he tell anyone where they were, or leave them with protection of any kind?"

"If he did, it was under the strictest confidence, and one does not break the confidences of the dead."

Alif looked at Sakina in despair.

"Noble sir," she said hastily, "no one can argue with your wisdom. But this boy also has a trust to discharge, and he cannot do so if he can't find the women to whom he owes that trust. We know that the mud-made cannot survive indefinitely in the Empty Quarter. Wouldn't it be better for us all if they were simply reunited and left this place?"

"You're assuming I know of these women and where they might be. I have made no such admission."

A dark shape was visible in the far wall beyond the misty outline below the creature's waist. Squinting at it, Alif realized it was a door. He was possessed by a wild idea.

"Forgive me, noble sir," said Sakina, "I merely assumed that a *marid* of your rank would know anything worth knowing in Irem."

The thing looked satisfied.

"That is not an unfair assumption," it said in a magnanimous voice. "Nevertheless, I can't help you. It may be that the situation is more complicated than you imagined."

"What in God's name does that mean?" NewQuarter broke out. Sakina hissed at him. He ignored her. "Do you know where these ladies are or not? Why is it so hard for you people to speak plainly?"

The *marid* drew itself up to its full height, towering over the courtyard like a stone idol. A low rumble issued from its throat and made the fronds of the palm trees quiver.

"Boy," it said, "you are in my house, and while you are in my house, I will tolerate no insult—especially from one as shriveled and weak-thighed as you."

Alif began to feel sick. Sakina put her face in her hands, saying nothing. Stiffening his back, NewQuarter glared up at the *marid*.

"God placed man above djinn, and *me* above most men you will ever meet. I think I'm entitled to a straight answer in response to a straight question."

Colors began to shift over the oil-slick surface of the *marid's* skin. It raised one massive fist above its head. NewQuarter did not move. A wild idea grew in Alif's mind until it became an imperative, bolstered by NewQuarter's deranged calm as the *marid's* fist descended toward his head. Preparing himself, Alif sucked air into his lungs until the sound of his breath was half-deafening. When he heard Sakina shriek, he bolted, running through the misty aperture of the *marid's* lower body—the scent of ozone again, and rain clouds—toward the door in the far wall. He was followed by a hail of raised voices. His feet pounded against the flagstones and set his teeth to rattling. Reaching the door, he yanked hard on the iron circlet bolted to it in lieu of a handle and was rewarded when the wooden arch budged slightly.

"Open, *open*," he screamed, feeling the damp aura of the *marid* closing in around him.

Bracing his foot on the lintel, Alif pulled until the sinews of his arms began to burn. The door swung toward him with a sudden gust of air. Alif stumbled backward, recovered himself, and rushed through into a large, domed room. Throwing his weight against the door, he slammed it shut on the *marid's* smoldering face with a howl of inarticulate triumph.

Inside there was silence. The room was pleasant and whitewashed, with latticed windows—which he had not noticed from outside—looking into the courtyard. Along one wall was an enormous sleeping platform lined with cushions as tall as a man. Songbirds twittered in an ornate silver cage atop a post. It was, Alif thought dazedly, like a film set from some old Bollywood movie, one that would inevitably feature dancing girls in candy-colored silk. It was only when he heard his given name that he realized he was not alone.

Dina was moving toward him from the sleeping platform. She said his name again, in a hushed and horrified voice, and he put one hand to his cheek, realizing how his gaunt unshaven face must look. She was wearing a black robe and veil but the material was finer than anything Alif had ever seen her wear and the garments seemed to have been tailored for her body, such that even in their looseness they highlighted the trim proportions of her shoulders and arms. He rushed toward her with a sob.

Chapter Thirteen

"Oh, God, oh, God—how did you get here? How did you find us?" She sank to her knees as he did, tears muddying the kohl that lined her grass-colored eyes. "I was afraid you were dead." Her voice broke on the last word. She fought to regain it through choked, unsteady breaths. "You're so thin! Please say something, you're frightening me out of my mind—"

Alif opened his mouth to tell her he was fine and promptly lost the power of speech. The tension that had been animating his body slackened and he swayed on his knees, feeling dirt and sweat and snot run from every opening in his skin. Forcing his lips to move, he managed to croak her name.

He was rewarded with a warm hand on his temple, smoothing the hair back from his face. He let his head fall to her knee and began to weep in earnest. There was a commotion in the doorway as New-Quarter burst in with Sheikh Bilal and Sakina close behind, followed by a tremor in the ground that could only have been the *marid* itself.

"Have you gone raving mad?" demanded Sakina, indignant with rage. Alif felt Dina put a protective hand on the back of his neck.

"It's all right," said Dina. "I know him. The convert knows him, too. He's safe."

There was another tremor. Alif looked up and saw the *marid* hovering just inside the door, arms crossed. Its head nearly brushed the underside of the domed ceiling.

"Very well," it said, thunderous and quiet all at once. "For your sake, I won't kill him, or the other puny rude one. But I don't want them around our patient—she shouldn't be upset or annoyed in her condition."

"What's going on? Who's going to be killed?"

The voice, nasal and American, was familiar. The convert, dressed in a hooded turquoise gown, rushed into the room through a smaller door in the wall perpendicular to the sleeping platform. Alif frowned. She seemed to have put on weight, particularly around the middle. It took him a moment to understand.

"How—are you—are you—?" His English escaped him.

She looked at him, embarrassment and pride at odds on her rounded face.

"Pregnant," she said.

* * *

Once they had convinced the *marid* that neither Alif nor the sheikh nor NewQuarter were any danger to the convert's health, he allowed them to sit on the floor while he hovered behind her, fetching cushions for her back by stretching one hand across the room to retrieve them. Dina kissed Sheikh Bilal's hand through her veil, murmuring tearfully that she was glad to see him well, and he touched her brow in blessing with a delighted smile.

"I would say that we have been searching hard for you," he said, "but really all credit is due to Alif. For a blundering fool he has proven very resourceful."

"What happened to you?" asked the convert. "What went down at the mosque after we left? You look *terrible*, no offense. Where have you been for the past three months?"

"You first," said Alif, trying not to stare at her belly.

Dina glanced at the convert with an unreadable expression. The convert flushed, and Alif thought her eyes looked damp.

"I almost don't know where to start," she said.

"Just go bit by bit," said Dina, surprising Alif by speaking stilted but understandable English. "Don't feel any shyness."

The convert narrowed her eyes, looking into the middle distance, avoiding Alif's curious gaze.

"Coming here felt—well, you'll know how it felt, since you got here yourselves. I didn't really believe what was happening. I was still resisting, resisting. Even when Vikram seemed not to look human anymore, I somehow made him look human in my head. I thought I was just going nuts because of the stress, you know. So, anyway. One minute we were walking down the hallway in the mosque, toward a solid wall, and the next minute we were standing on a dune in the Empty Quarter, looking down at this fairy-tale city. Naturally, I kind of went hysterical."

"Anybody sane would," muttered NewQuarter.

"At that point," the convert continued, "it was clear Vikram was not doing well."

Alif thought he heard her voice harden just a little, as though she found it difficult to say the dead man's name.

"He was bleeding and in obvious pain, though he kept up with his usual devil-may-care thing. He took us into the city—took us here, in fact, and had some kind of discussion with our generous landlord, the gist of which was that we would be allowed to stay for the night. I didn't realize how sick Dina was—her arm, I mean, needed to be treated."

Alif looked at Dina in alarm.

"It's fine now," she said, flexing it as proof. "Completely healed. There is only a small scar."

"So Vikram sent her out to have the wound cleaned and rebandaged and whatnot. And so then we were alone here. And he asked me to marry him. I brushed it off because this is something he did all the time to freak me out. I'd learned not to dignify it with a response. But something was different this time—he took my hand and looked me in the eye, really *looked*, like he was speaking to some other part of me, and said he was worried about leaving me and Dina here alone. We weren't safe without him. It was obvious that he was dying, you see."

The convert's face crumpled and turned bright red. Alif and NewQuarter stared at each other in dismay, unprepared to handle the tears of an unrelated woman. Dina cooed something reassuring, petting the convert's shoulder.

"He told me that if I married him we would have some kind of protection, some kind of immunity, even after he was gone," she went on in a steadier tone. "He said a bunch of other things, too, sweet things, trying to make me laugh because I was freaking out and all. He said he admired me and that he doesn't say so to very many people. But I told him I couldn't marry him even if I wanted to, because I can't marry an unbeliever. And he laughed and said he'd been a believer, 'for the better part of a thousand years,' I believe were the exact words."

"What?" said Alif. "Vikram? Vikram the madman who bites people?"

"He might be those things," said the convert hastily, "but did you ever know him to do or say anything really blasphemous?"

"I guess not." Alif subsided into bewildered silence.

"He told me if anybody had an issue with belief, it was me," the convert said. "Because I didn't believe in him. Because I had basically skipped a big chunk of my own religion, yet here I was lecturing him about the rules. And he was right. So I said *yes*. I didn't really know what else to do.

"Somehow, in a very short period of time two witnesses showed up, one of which looked like a horrible ball of fur with teeth, the other of which looked even worse, and we were signing a contract. And, you know, it entitled me to certain things in the event of his death, those things being favors he was calling in so Dina and I would be provided for as long as we needed to stay. So that was very clever on his part. And then it was done and we were alone again. And he touched my face—"

"We don't need to hear the details," NewQuarter interjected. The convert flushed again.

"I wasn't going to get into details. I was just trying to explain why I would—why any woman would willingly go along with a guy like Vikram. He was a much gentler version of himself, is what I'm trying to say. He made sure I felt safe with him. By the time I fell asleep that night, I was in love. Just like that."

Alif studied the plump, pale woman sitting in front of him, trying to imagine whether this depth of feeling had existed within her when they had first met. The few Americans he had encountered in his lifetime had all seemed flat to him, as if freedom weakened one's capacity for intense emotion by demanding too little of it. The convert had seemed, like the others, to be always performing: opinions brisk and pat, smiles rehearsed, identity packaged for consumption by an audience. To see her so candid, as she attempted and failed to preserve her self-assurance, was almost charming. Still, it was difficult to picture her in love, and in love with someone like Vikram.

"When I woke up in the morning I looked over and saw him for real for the first time. I mean every layer of what he was, which was something very old and very dangerous and made up of elements I had never seen before. And I wasn't afraid. Not of him, anyway—but I was afraid that he was going to die right there, in my arms. I could see the last bit of life bleeding out of him. I started to cry. He asked me why I was crying, thinking he had hurt me or something, and I told him, no, I was crying because I loved him and I didn't want him to die. So he petted my hair and told me he was leaving me with something I would love even more than I loved him, something that would ensure no djinn would ever hurt me. And then he asked me to go and get the *marid*.

"I jumped up and put on my clothes and ran out into the courtyard, looking, I'm sure, like a complete madwoman, and Dina was out here asleep on a cushion and the *marid* was sitting in a corner doing his thing, and they followed me when they saw I was so upset, and came back in here where Vikram was breathing his last. He told Dina to take care of Alif, and said something to the *marid* in a language I didn't understand, and then he called me over and kissed me and said 'Call her Layl.' Those were his last words. And that's when I knew."

Alif heard NewQuarter translating for Sheikh Bilal in a low voice. He himself could not decide how to respond: whether congratulations or condolences should come first.

"The world must feel much smaller to you," he said timidly, and then wondered what had prompted him to say so.

The convert considered this for a moment.

"No," she said. "Just the opposite. I feel like the horizon has been pushed back and there's infinitely more between it and me than I once thought. And yet I have less anxiety about everything. About what I'm supposed to do, what I'm supposed to think, how I can stay in control of my life. I've stopped trying. I just act, now, just respond to whatever the situation demands. I'm not so committed to the rational barrier between seen and unseen. It feels like—like passing straight from disbelief into certainty. Without stopping at belief in between. I'm not sure I ever had any of that, not really. You even pointed it out once."

"It was wrong of me to say so," said Alif, feeling ashamed. "I have no right to question anybody's beliefs."

"Well, you *were* right, in any case." She looked down and smoothed her gown across her spreading lap. It suited her, this state of fecundity, strange though it was. The smile that played across her face was sad in a way that was almost beatific, reminding Alif of an icon in the

Greek Orthodox church he had seen once on a middle school trip to a tiny Christian neighborhood in the Old Quarter. For an instant, the convert seemed not like a grim-eyed foreigner in borrowed clothes but an echo of her own civilization.

The *marid*, prompted by something unfathomable, rose and drifted toward the door, where Sakina was leaning silently with her arms crossed.

"He looks awful but he's actually the most fussy nursemaid you'll ever meet," whispered Dina. "Vikram made him promise to look after her until the baby is born, and you wouldn't believe how seriously he takes his responsibilities. Once she was craving this particular kind of American apple—"

"Braeburns," said the convert.

"—and he was gone for a whole day, and when he came back it was with two sacks of apples so large they had to be brought in by camel. I'm not joking."

Alif looked sideways at the titanic apparition in the doorway.

"I bet," he muttered.

"Well, I'm glad to see that you're in good health, regardless of the—unusual circumstances," said Sheikh Bilal, patting the convert's hand. "I wouldn't want to spend a season among the djinn, but I'd prefer it to what Alif and I have endured. If man's capacity for the fantastic took up as much of his imagination as his capacity for cruelty, the worlds, seen and unseen, might be very different. Which is why I would rather not speak of my own past three months in any more detail."

Alif felt a pang in his throat. Dina regarded the old man in wordless sympathy, brows rippling above the hem of her veil.

"And you?" Alif looked at her, attempting to project tenderness through every pore. "Have you been all right? Are you angry with me, like everybody else?"

Dina shook her head.

"I was too afraid you were dead to be angry with you," she said. "When you came through the door just now I swear I thought you were a ghost. You're so thin and so pale and you look so much older, I—" Her voice broke.

Alif laid his head on her knee again. She permitted him.

"Am I ugly?" he asked.

"No, no. But you're frightening."

"I thought about you every day. I mean, I couldn't tell the days apart, but I thought of you anyway. I sang those songs you used to sing on the roof—"

"You could hear me? God forgive me."

"Please don't say that." Alif stroked the silky material of her robe where it had pooled around her feet. "It was beautiful. At the time it meant nothing to me, your singing. It was just background noise. I was an idiot then."

"You were a boy."

"I was selfish."

"It doesn't matter now. You're alive and we have to make you well again or I'll die of grief."

"For God's sake," yowled NewQuarter, "I'm choking on all this sugar. Please, no more love stories today. No one else is to become pregnant or contract some kind of ill-fated marriage. I forbid it. Honestly, look at me, I'm turning green. You'll make me throw up."

Alif sat up, face hot with embarrassment.

"No one said you had to listen," he muttered.

"How can I not listen when you're *touching* each other? It's rather alarming."

"All right," said Dina, standing and shaking out her robe. "Two of you need to bathe and shave. The third can make himself useful, if he even knows how."

"I won't carry water like a menial," said NewQuarter indignantly.

"The young man is a member of the royal family," Sheikh Bilal explained to Dina.

"That's very nice for him. The djinn are not likely to care."

Alif looked up at her in admiration. He would not have suspected that Dina could be so unflinching. When he remembered her deft management of his smuggler friends in the souk, and the rapidity with which she had accepted what exactly Vikram and his sister were, he wondered why he should have had this impression of timidity; certainly she had never been timid. He had, perhaps, mistaken her modest silences for something they were not.

Within half an hour, during which Alif stood about feeling useless, tubs of hot water were arranged in the courtyard. He and Sheikh Bilal were sent out with towels and jars of soap as the sun, heady without being bright, floated above the swaying palms and brought out the scent of sap. Alif relaxed in his bath with a cloth over his face, murmuring responses to the sheikh's fervent praise of such luxuries as hot running water. The soap smelled of sandalwood and rose oil, emphasizing to Alif how profoundly he stank. When the water began to cool he emerged from the cloth and scrubbed every inch of skin he could reach, picking filth from under his slippery fingernails. The bath was murky with dirt when he stood

and wrapped himself in a towel. Fresh clothes had appeared while
he bathed: a loose linen tunic and pants folded neatly on the warm
stone behind the tub. He dressed, looking up when Dina slipped
through the doorway at the other end of the courtyard with a hand
mirror, scissors, and a razor.

"Where did you get this stuff?" Alif asked her. "I can't picture
the *marid* needing to shave."

"God only knows," she sighed. "Sometimes in this place you can
find what you're looking for simply by opening a drawer. I try not
to ask where it all comes from. Here, sit on the edge of the tub and
hold this. I'll cut your hair."

Alif took the mirror from her and held it up. For a moment he
was startled by his own reflection: the man in the glass did look
older. His black hair had thinned and lost its luster; his eyes appeared
slightly sunken. But the chin and jaw Alif had always thought too
soft had become prominent, decisive even, and were covered with a
beard of a few days' growth; the brows were thicker, with an arch
of concentration that reminded Alif of his father. He touched his
bloodless cheek.

"You're right, I look like a refugee," he said. "A middle-aged
refugee."

"You look much better now that you're clean," Dina replied.
"Though I'm sorry to say I think you may have had lice at some
point—there are bitten-up patches on your scalp."

"Don't touch me then, I'm hideous."

"No you aren't. This won't take long." She pulled a length of hair
between her fingers and snipped along the edge. He thought he heard
her catch her breath in a funny way, twice, and realized she was crying

silently. He tried to turn and look at her but she kept a firm grip on the crown of his head.

"Dina," he said. "Love, please—"

"Don't, don't say *love*. Not yet."

Alif opened and closed his hands, still wrinkled from the bath. It took all of his energy not to touch her.

"When can I see your face again?" he asked instead.

"When you and your father have come to see my father."

"Your father would throw me out in the street after everything I've put you through."

"He can do as he likes, but I won't marry anyone else, so in the end he has no choice."

It was half startling and half charming to hear her speak so frankly. Alif tried to turn again, but she pushed his head down with more force than was necessary and began trimming the hair along his neckline. He studied her feet as she shifted around his chair: they were unshod and coated in a layer of the fine iridescent dust of the Empty Quarter, making her seem a djinn herself. Tendons moved beneath her skin as she went on tiptoe to inspect her work. The sight made Alif ache. He let his hand drop and ran one finger along the arch of her foot, and heard her gasp; the foot danced away. She did not admonish him. Alif wondered how much she knew about men and women and felt an uneasy sense of responsibility, wishing Vikram was there to offer more of his crass but useful advice.

"When did I come to deserve such loyalty?" he asked, suddenly melancholy.

"You never did," she said, "but it was yours anyway."

"Why? I've been an ass to you for years."

She snipped at another segment of his hair with an exasperated laugh.

"Because even when I was annoyed with the boy you were, I liked the man I knew you would become. More than I liked any of the other men my parents were suggesting."

He was touched by the simple clarity of her answer, and wished he had a sentiment as durable to lay at her feet.

"For a while it was the only thing keeping me alive," he said. "The idea that your irritating principles wouldn't let you accept anybody else, and that if I didn't find a way to get back to you, you'd convince yourself you had to spend your whole life as a widow without ever having been married at all."

"Calling my principles irritating isn't a good idea when I'm holding a pair of scissors."

He laughed.

"You do—I mean—it isn't only that you feel obligated to me, is it? You do want—I know I'm not pretty, but—" There was real timidity in her voice now. This time he did turn, ducking her hands, and held her eyes with his.

"You told me not to say *love*," he said, "otherwise I would kill any anxiety about prettiness or wanting right now."

She looked down at him, wide-eyed, the scissors suspended in her right hand.

"Okay," she whispered.

"Okay I can say it?"

"Okay, I believe you."

He kissed her hand before she could pull away. She clucked her tongue, withdrawing, and steadied his head again, returning to her task. Alif watched her progress in the mirror, seeing shaggy tufts of hair fall away from over his ears and forehead until he began to look presentable. When she was done she brushed the trimmings from his shoulders and neck with a cloth.

"There," she said. "You could go out in public without disgracing yourself now. I'll leave you to shave."

"I may keep the beard," said Alif, rubbing his chin. "I feel like I've earned it."

"It looks distinguished. Or it would if you trimmed it properly."

He examined his neck and cheeks as she walked back across the courtyard toward the inner rooms of the house.

"We should decide our next move pretty soon if we want to get out of here," he called after her. "I've got to figure out what happened to the *Alf Yeom*, otherwise we'll go home to the same mess we left behind."

She looked back at him in surprise.

"There's nothing to figure out," she said. "I have it here. I've had it this entire time."

Chapter Fourteen

Back inside, Dina displayed her hidden wealth: she had taken not only the *Alf Yeom* but Alif's backpack, which contained his netbook and the flash drive onto which he'd downloaded Tin Sari.

"I went into Sheikh Bilal's office when I smelled burning plastic," she said. "You were in some kind of weird fit or trance. I wanted to clear out anything that might burn if the desk caught fire. Then I ran out and called for Vikram and the sheikh."

"I didn't even see you leave with this stuff," marveled Alif, holding up the flash drive. Apparently the blessing of the toothless dervish had stuck.

"I had it under my robe when Vikram took us away. You didn't seem like you were in a state to stay on top of things."

"I wasn't." Alif studied the green-flamed eyes above her veil with unfeigned adoration. "You're amazing. You're wonderful. I'm pathetic without you."

"You're pathetic with her," muttered NewQuarter, coming into the room from an interior chamber. "There is no hope for you whatsoever." He crouched next to Alif on the floor. "So, what do we do now?"

"Burn it," said Alif promptly. "We'll be rid of the whole mess. The Hand can do what he likes—the book will be out of his reach forever."

"No," said Dina. "We don't burn books."

"Who's *we?*"

"People with an ounce of brain."

"But you hate more books than almost anybody I know," said Alif, surprised. "How many times have you picked on me for reading my *kafir* fantasy novels?"

"When have I ever suggested you burn them? I am allowed to have opinions, aren't I? And I don't hate them—I don't give a fig about them. The only reason I cared is because you were so comfortable belittling me for believing things you only read about. I was afraid you'd turn into one of those literary types who say *books can change the world* when they're feeling good about themselves and *it's only a book* when anybody challenges them. It wasn't about the books themselves—it was about hypocrisy. You can speak casually about burning the *Alf Yeom* for the same reason you'd be horrified if I suggested burning *The Satanic Verses*—because you have reactions, not convictions."

Alif twitched as if slapped. He could tell this was an argument she had made many times in her head, before an absent shade of himself. He had simply given her an opportunity to voice it aloud. His blood ran hot and cold, unable to reconcile such a pointed critique with the depth of her loyalty to him.

NewQuarter had apparently elected to pretend he had not heard, and fiddled with the hem of his robe, brushing away some invisible pollutant.

"This damn dust," he said to no one.

"Why risk so much for me if you think I'm such a brainless hypocrite?" Alif asked.

Dina softened. Perhaps saying so to his face had not played out the way she had seen it in her mind.

"Because you're not. I shouldn't have said it that way. But there are some things that you haven't thought all the way through, and this is one of them."

Restless with conflicting instincts, he looked down at the manuscript sitting on the smooth stone floor between them. The convert slipped into the room, light-footed despite her condition, and knelt beside Dina with a silent, appraising glance.

"We could leave it here," said Dina. "The *marid* could keep it hidden. I'm sure he would if we asked."

"And if the Hand comes for it? Sakina seems to think he's got powerful friends. Whatever wounded Vikram back at the mosque did not come from our side of the visible light spectrum."

As if she had heard her name, Sakina appeared in the doorway leading in from the courtyard. Her leonine face was tense.

"What, what?" Alif did not bother to conceal either his frustration or his alarm.

"More trouble," she said. "The Immovable Alley has been sacked."

"Sacked?"

"Invaded. Raided. Shops overturned, mine included, merchandise looted and burned—all by the man you're running from and his recruits. They're looking for you, Alif, and for the *Alf Yeom,* and I'm afraid they're getting very close."

Sweat broke out on Alif's brow and beneath his beard. He rubbed his face with the back of one hand.

"What should I do?" he asked.

"I don't have any answers. But I doubt anyone here in the Empty Quarter will be willing to shelter you now, knowing what they'd be up against."

"If I say so, they might have to," said the convert, in much-improved Arabic. "A lot of people here owed Vikram favors, which means they now owe me favors."

"You would do that?" Alif felt a surge of desperate gratitude.

"Well, we can't have demons overrunning the place. I'm pregnant, you know. The nesting hormones are kicking in like crazy. If keeping you safe keeps me safe, you can have whatever I've got."

"And the book?" Dina picked it up and weighed it in her hands like a bag of produce. Alif thought quickly.

"What if we did ask the *marid* to hide it here? And I took a fake with me? Any old book would do—they just have to think I've got the *Alf Yeom* and I'm running away with it. That would at least keep the Hand and his creeps clear of you guys."

"I'll ask him right now." The convert rose and made for the door, holding the hem of her dress above her bare feet. She reappeared a few moments later, shadowed by her titanic nursemaid, who seemed to shrink in order to fit into the room.

"This thing you ask," it rumbled, "is no small favor. There is nothing lost but may be found, if sought. One of your own poets said so. If this book is wanted, it will not stay hidden forever."

"But you're good at hiding things," said the convert. The *marid* looked pleased.

"I'm very good at hiding things," it concurred.

"Maybe it doesn't need to stay hidden forever," said Alif. "Just long enough to get rid of the Hand. Who knows, it could be another couple hundred years before anybody gets wise enough to go looking for it again."

"A long time for you," said the *marid*. "A short time for me—and then I might have to go through this all over again!"

"But you'll do it?" The convert looked up at it with earnest eyes.

"If you wish," it replied in a voice like settling rubble.

"I do wish."

"Thank you," said Alif fervently. The convert gave him a smile of triumph. Alif took the book from Dina's hands, conscious of the way she let her fingers brush his in some inscrutable gesture of tenderness, and felt himself go hot and cold again, still bruised by her succinct appraisal of his failings. He felt the stiff folio of paper between his palms, inhaling its unsettling scent, now familiar enough to evoke a series of memories: the date palm grove in Baqara District, the lamplight in Vikram's tent, the otherworldly bustle of the Immovable Alley. Sheikh Bilal's computer, breathing out exhaust, the crucible for his failed masterpiece.

"You look like you don't want to let it go," the convert observed. Alif shook his head, dazed.

"I've resented this thing since the minute it became my responsibility," he said. "And yet—it's clear to me now that my life will be divided into what came before this book, and what came after it."

"Mine too," said the convert.

"And mine," said Dina.

Alif traced the flaking gold letters on the cover, running his finger over the first word of the title, the one that so resembled his name. The book warmed beneath his hands like a living thing, and seemed full of portent, hinting at layers of meaning he had not yet uncovered: stories within stories that had remained invisible to him even as he translated them into code. There was always something yet unseen. The ground itself was daily renewed, kicked up and muddled by passing travelers, such that it was impossible to repeat the same journey twice. Alif thought of all the times he had left the duplex in Baqara District bent on some mundane errand: the courtyard gate closing behind him with a rattle, rattling again when he returned the same way; to him, ordinary and frustrating, to the world, a process full of tiny variations, all existing, as Sheikh Bilal had said, simultaneously and without contradiction. He had been given eternity in modest increments, and had thought nothing of it.

"Alif."

Sakina was looking at him closely. He straightened his back and handed the book over to the *marid*, who pressed it between his hands. It vanished. The gesture was so natural that it took Alif a moment to find it strange.

"Where'd the book go?" he asked.

"Away," said the *marid*. "For now."

"But you can get it back?"

"Certainly."

Alif forced the air from his lungs in a sharp breath, then inhaled again more slowly.

"Do you happen to have another book that looks similar?" he asked the *marid*, avoiding its cloud-colored eyes. "Something that would convince an ordinary person at first glance? Something you wouldn't mind me borrowing for a few days?"

The marid made an indeterminate noise and disappeared into its house. It was gone for several minutes. Alif began to worry that he had offered it some unintended insult, and was on the verge of asking the convert as much when it reappeared. In its hands was a book bound in faded blue, looking no larger than a shred of confetti against the marid's thick fingers. It laid the manuscript in Alif's outstretched arms.

"Please be careful with this," it said solemnly. "It is the jewel of my library. You have many versions of this book in the sighted world but none I would call accurate, written as they were by the tribe of Adam. This one contains the only true and complete account of my cruel imprisonment by a young thief named Alla'eddin, many centuries ago."

Alif choked on an indrawn breath.

"The *Alf Layla*?" he rasped. "This is a copy of *The Thousand and One Nights*?"

"Just so."

"*Akhi*," squeaked NewQuarter, "we've been shooting the shit with the lamp genie."

"Shut up, shut *up*." Alif hugged the book to his chest and forced himself to meet the *marid's* gaze.

"Many thanks," he said, voice cracking. "I'll guard it with my eyes. I mean, it's not going to be safe, exactly, considering—"

The *marid* began to look displeased.

"—But I mean, it will keep *her* safe," Alif added in a rush, jerking his finger at the convert. "As long as the Hand thinks I still have the *Alf Yeom*, he'll leave the rest of you alone."

"Very well," said the *marid*, looking mollified. Alif blotted his brow.

"Okay." He turned to the convert. "How soon do you think we can meet with Vikram's—with the people who owe you favors?"

"Let's find out," she said.

✳   ✳   ✳

Within several hours, a strange collection of creatures had gathered in the *marid's* courtyard. A few were *effrit*, ambulatory shadows like the one whose computer Alif had debugged; a few more resembled Vikram or Sakina in their elusive, prismatic variance between human and animal and smokeless fire. Then there were some whose presence Alif could only sense, muffled invisible objects that announced themselves only by absorbing sound. The convert sat on a cushion at the edge of the fountain, back poker-straight, looking too nervous and too human to be administratrix of such a bizarre gathering. Alif hovered behind her, crossing and uncrossing his arms in an attempt to decide which pose looked more authoritative. The *marid* loomed over them like a banyan tree. Alif hoped its presence had the effect his own did not. He jumped when the convert cleared her throat.

"Thank you all for coming here to see me," she said. "I've called on you as a favor to a friend—Alif, standing back there—and as a result of what has happened in the Immovable Alley. Which is sort of his fault."

"Thanks," Alif hissed in her ear. "Now they're going to eat me."

356

"Basically, he needs protection," the convert continued, ignoring him. "Since the man who is hunting him has allies among the djinn."

Allies among the shayateen, said one of the *effrit*, its words reverberating uncomfortably in Alif's skull. *Not all of us are demons.*

"Yes, of course," said the convert. "I was just speaking generally. Anyway, you don't want these guys around, and neither do we."

"The solution to that is simple," said a tall yellow-eyed man. "We hand over this *beni adam*, and they go away."

Alif resisted the urge to bolt.

"That would be simple," said the convert, "but then they'd win, and you'd look weak. Why give them that satisfaction?"

"Because it would save us a lot of time and headache, frankly."

A ripple of laughter passed over the assembly. The convert pursed her lips.

"Okay, okay. Let's put it another way. You all owed Vikram favors, and as his widow, I am calling those favors in. Do this thing for me and the score is settled."

"I don't know about the rest of you," said a spare-looking woman with a pair of black, curving horns, "but I never owed Vikram a favor large enough to include my life."

Hear hear, said the *effrit. And why should the* beni adam *sit on his ass while we fight his battles for him? It hardly seems fair. We're not a bunch of mindless idiots enslaved in lamps, or milk cartons, or what have you, to be commanded by whatever third-born happens to come along.*

The convert looked back at Alif, biting her lip.

"I'm not planning to sit on my ass," he said indignantly.

Oh? And what do you plan to do instead? Kick and scream?

"I—"

Alif was interrupted by the appearance of NewQuarter, who came rushing into the courtyard from the street beyond it, holding in his hands a sleek Sony laptop the width of a thick envelope.

"Alif," he said in a gleeful voice, "look what I've got. This thing isn't even supposed to be out of development. No, wait, that's not the important part. I've been on that talking shadow's stupendous WiFi network, and I found—but you have to admire this machine with me for a minute. Some guy was literally hawking it from a blanket on the street, along with some very pretty wireless gaming mice. I'm starting to like this place." He sat on the ground a short distance from the convert and gave a curt nod to the collection of djinn beyond her. "But look, look at this."

Under the cool gaze of anthropomorphic shadows, Alif stuttered an apology and went to kneel next to NewQuarter.

"Can't this wait?" he muttered. "I already look like an ass."

"No, it can't. Here." NewQuarter swiveled the laptop toward Alif, displaying a pixelated blur, blocky horizontal chunks of image files and scrambled text.

"What is it?" Alif asked.

"That, my friend, is a screen grab from the City public utility Web site." NewQuarter clicked an arrow button. Another image appeared: more scrambled images and text. "This is the University of Al Basheera home page."

He clicked again.

"The transit authority." Another click. "The tourism board. There are dozens more like this. The whole City is digitally fucked. While we've been sitting here playing Aladdin our little modern-day Carthage has been sacked."

"Holy God." Alif pulled the screen closer. "Who? How?"

"At first I thought it was one of our people getting stupid," said NewQuarter. "You know, trying to foment revolution by shutting off the power or something. But everybody on the cloud is as confused as you are."

"The cloud's all right?"

"Of course it's all right. I set it up myself."

"But if the servers are in the City——"

"They aren't. They're sitting in my uncle's basement all the way in Qatar." NewQuarter grinned, making himself look even younger. "You see? It's good to have an upper-class snot on your side."

"Wow. Wow."

"So I was thinking," said NewQuarter, leaning forward, "what if it's not a black hat operation at all?"

Alif frowned. "What else could it be?"

"Something even more ominous. Who's got access codes and know-how and the stones to screw with all these different systems, all at once, without having to hack into anything at all?"

Alif looked back at the screen grab. "You don't think——?"

"That's exactly what I think. What if this wasn't meant to happen ——what if this is simply the byproduct of an enormous digital manhunt? Alif, what if this means the Hand has finally fucked up?"

A memory surfaced, carrying with it a feeling of grime and nakedness.

"He said he had people reverse-engineering the code I created out of the *Alf Yeom*——I warned him. I warned him something like this could happen if he tried to use it. He didn't believe me. He thought if he had enough processing power it would be different."

"If he's got access to your code, why does he still want that book so badly?"

"Well, look at where the code has gotten him—he probably thinks he can fix this mess if he can get his hands on the source material. He's obsessed with the idea that I'm just dense and can't comprehend the full magnitude of what the *Alf Yeom* could mean for computing."

"Do you suppose that's true?"

Alif thought of the thing in the dark and shuddered.

"No. That book is like getting gradually lost. You start out in a garden on a path, and it looks so easy—easier than a lot of the other paths you've traveled, which were hemmed in by all these if-then propositions and parameters and laws. So you walk, and the path gets rockier, and then there are gaps, and eventually you find you're not even in the garden anymore but out in some howling desert. And you can't retrace your steps because the path itself was all in your head."

Voices rose among the assembly of djinn. The convert gave Alif a chilly glare.

"I could use some help over here," she said.

Alif got to his feet, straightening the hem of his tunic, and hurried to stand beside her.

"I think we're screwed," she muttered without turning.

The woman with black horns crossed her arms over her sylphlike chest.

"We've decided," she said. "You're on your own. The risk is too great. We are each willing to fulfill our debts to Vikram, but not this way—if you wanted to procure something rare and precious, or needed escort to some unreachable place, that would be one thing. But we're not willing to lay down our lives for this boy."

The others murmured their assent.

"Wait," said Alif. "What if I did something for you?"

Like what? asked the *effrit*.

Alif made a few rapid calculations in his head.

"You know that for centuries there have been humans who tried to use *The Thousand Days* to gain power for themselves. They all failed. But the guy who's after me is very close to succeeding— close enough to make a huge mess, anyway. He won't stop with the *Alf Yeom*, or with the Immovable Alley. Soon enough he'll be here in the Empty Quarter. On a computer, he's as invisible to you as you are to the average, um, *beni adam*. But he isn't invisible to me. And he's started making mistakes. Which means I have a chance to stop him. You take care of his invisible friends, and I'll take care of him."

"How exactly do you plan on doing that?" whispered NewQuarter from behind his shoulder. Alif elbowed him in the ribs. The horned woman turned back to her brethren and began speaking in the same mutable language Alif had heard Vikram use with Azalel, and which Azalel had used in his dream. There were words he felt he should understand, but didn't, and he strained to catch anything familiar. Finally the woman turned back to look at him with measuring eyes.

"We're willing to consider your plan," she said.

Alif let out an explosive sigh.

"Thank God," he said. "Okay. Let's talk about how this would work."

✻　✻　✻

It was late—or at least it seemed late; the sky had turned from pink to violet, and Alif felt he could begin to detect subtle variations between night and day—when the conclave of djinn finally left the *marid's* courtyard. Alif watched them move silently through the gate, a column of uncanny foot soldiers, and prayed for the strength to carry out what he had promised to do.

"Use this," said the black-horned woman before she left, handing Alif a slim silver whistle. "Call us when it's time."

Alif looked at the whistle with skepticism.

"How does it work? Is it one of these things that emits a sound too high for humans to hear?"

"No." The woman's expression was not complimentary. "It doesn't emit any sound at all. You just blow on it, and we come to you."

Alif bit back a half dozen exasperated retorts.

"Oh," he said.

The woman nodded briskly. Turning, she trotted off to rejoin the column of hidden folk leaving the *marid's* courtyard, bowing to their ephemeral host on her way out. Alif took several deep breaths. The air tasted of night-blooming flowers. It made him unaccountably sad, and he wondered whether he had seen his last ordinary sunset the day he and Dina fled Baqara District.

"We may end up fairly dead trying to pull this off," said New-Quarter, echoing his thoughts.

"I may. You don't have to come if you don't want to. You've done a hell of a lot for me already."

NewQuarter shrugged. "I burned my bridges when I drove off the road and into the Empty Quarter. I doubt I could simply go back to being a comfy royal scion now even if I wanted to. There are probably State flunkies tossing my flat at this very moment. I just hope they don't break all my hand-painted Persian tableware."

"You're a good man, Prince Abu Talib Al Mukhtar ibn Hamza."

"My God, you remembered the whole thing."

They walked toward the far edge of the courtyard, where Dina was laying out a trio of sleeping mats.

"I hope you don't mind staying out here," she said. "We ladies sleep inside. It's usually quite warm at night, so you won't freeze."

"This is fine," said Alif. He watched her move, her bare feet slim and dusty against the stone, a gold anklet flashing just below the hem of her robe. He wanted to ask her about the accusation of hypocrisy that had so cut him, but lacked the courage to bring up the subject with NewQuarter lurking in the background.

"Where is Sheikh Bilal?" he asked instead.

"He went to the mosque earlier this afternoon," said Dina. "He said he planned to stay until the night prayer. Which means he should be back any minute."

"He went to a djinn mosque?"

"Yes, right down the street. You haven't heard the call to prayer?"

Alif recalled hearing a kind of high, keening song at several points throughout the day, but it did not resemble any call to prayer he had ever heard and he had not listened closely.

"I heard something—but it sounded more like—like *singing*. I think I even heard harmonies."

"That's their way. They use different scales. It's quite beautiful, once you get over the fact that it greatly resembles music."

The dry, Egyptian mirth in her voice made him chuckle. He relaxed a little. The courtyard gate opened again and revealed Sheikh Bilal, walking straighter than he had since their escape, his face brightened by inner repose.

"*As-salaamu alaykum*," he said.

Alif murmured the response. "How are you, Uncle?" he asked anxiously.

The sheikh sat down on one of the three sleeping mats with a sigh.

"Praise be to God. It will be a long while until I shall call myself well. I think perhaps too long—longer than I have left to live. But for now, I feel a great deal better than I did, and that is enough."

"How was the mosque?"

"Astonishing. It reminded me of a dream I had once as a young man studying in Cairo at Al-Azhar—I dreamed I went to worship at a deserted mosque in a low, green place, somewhere I had never seen, and while I was there I saw a congregation of djinn praying in just such a way as they do here. The imam was almost singing each verse he recited. Being young and pedantic, I interrupted him quite rudely and told him he was reciting the Quran in an inappropriate way. The congregation all turned and gave me a very dirty look. Then I woke.

"I felt quite ashamed of myself, thinking it had been a true vision, and I had offered terrible insult to my brothers in religion in the unseen worlds. One forgets, you know, that the urge to worship transcends our muddy understanding of the world we see. I always regretted that I was not invited back. And now I have been. You are young, so you may not understand what it feels like to be offered a second chance at my age, especially after so . . . so difficult a time, when one has seen his own death and accepted it."

"What do you mean by second chance?" asked Alif, conscious of an uncomfortable portent in the sheikh's words.

"I mean that they have kindly offered me a place here, to study and to teach. I am considering accepting that offer."

Alif and NewQuarter looked at one another in mute dismay.

"But you said you didn't want to spend time among the djinn, like the convert and Dina have," said Alif.

"I am exercising the prerogative of an old man and changing my mind."

"But why?" He could not stomach the thought of leaving Sheikh Bilal behind.

The sheikh looked up at the sky with a small smile, violet light reflecting in his milky eyes.

"Because I would be going back to the wreckage of a life," he said after a moment. "They will give custodianship of Al Basheera over to some State lackey trained at a de-Islamization school, and if I am not rearrested or killed, I will at least spend the rest of my days looking over one shoulder. As will you, unless you have some sort of plan."

"My plans are always ridiculous," Alif blurted in a sudden thrall of self-doubt. "Look where they've gotten us. I don't know why I can't just solve things the ordinary way like everyone else."

"Perhaps you don't have ordinary problems."

"I was a computer geek with girl issues. That sounds pretty ordinary to me."

NewQuarter snickered.

"Then perhaps we don't live in ordinary times," said the sheikh. "I know it's common for old people to complain about the modern moment, and lament the passing of a golden age when children were polite and you could buy a kilo of meat for pennies, but in our case, my boy, I think I am not mistaken when I say that something fundamental has changed about the world in which we live. We have reached a state of constant reinvention. Revolutions have moved off the battlefield and on to home computers. Nothing shocks one anymore. We are living in a post-fictional era. Fictional governments are accepted without comment, and we can sit in a mosque and have a debate about the fictional pork a fictional character consumes in a video game, with every gravity we would accord something quite real. You and I and the princeling can spend the night in the courtyard of a *marid* as calmly as we would in a hotel. It is all very strange indeed."

"I don't think what you're talking about is a modern issue," said NewQuarter. "I think we're going back to the way things used to be, before a bunch of European intellectuals in tights decided to draw a line between what's rational and what's not. I don't think our ancestors thought the distinction was necessary."

The sheikh considered this for a moment.

"Perhaps you're right," he said. "I suppose every innovation started out as a fantasy. Once upon a time, students of Islamic law were encouraged to give free rein to their imaginations. For example, in the medieval era there was a great discussion about the point at which one is obligated to enter a state of ritual purity while traveling on the hajj. If you were on foot, when? If you went by boat, when? If by camel, when? And then one student, having exhausted all earthly possibilities, posed this question: what if one were to fly? The proposition was taken as a serious exercise in the adaptability of the law. As a result, we had rules governing air travel during hajj five hundred years before the invention of the commercial jet."

Alif lay down on his sleeping mat.

"I'm not sure whether that makes me feel better or worse," he said. His limbs were heavy with sleep. "I wish you would come back with us, Uncle."

"I won't be alone. The convert will stay also, you know, until after her child is born."

"Wonder what that little prize will look like," said NewQuarter, pulling a face. He slid off his sandals and flopped down on the mat next to Alif's. "He'll probably have fur. Or fangs. Where will he live? How does one go about being half-hidden?"

"She," said Alif.

"Sorry?"

"She, not he. The baby."

"As you like." NewQuarter shut his eyes, pillowing his head on his arms. Alif did likewise, listening to Sheikh Bilal hum as he removed his head cloth and shoes.

The air was warm and tonic, carrying with it the scent of date sugar. Alif heard Dina's muffled laugh from inside the *marid's* house, echoed by the convert's voice, raised in some lighthearted protest. He thought of the City and what returning to it might mean, and about his mother, alone with the maid in their little duplex, fearing him dead. It seemed significant to him that during his time in prison he had only been able to look back at his life in Baqara District, and not forward to what it might be again. Even if he and NewQuarter succeeded, even if the djinn were able to stave off the Hand's demons, he might, like the sheikh, go back to the wreckage of a life.

"Alif," said NewQuarter, voice slurred with fatigue. "Is this going to work?"

"Doesn't matter," said Alif. "If we screw up, we won't live long enough to have to deal with the consequences."

"Good point," said NewQuarter.

A bird—if there were birds in the Empty Quarter—called from somewhere overhead: a trilling, edge-of-night song, like a sparrow's imitation of a nightingale. He felt his thoughts go soft and was soon overtaken by sleep. He had not been out for long when a dream settled on him: he saw the *marid's* courtyard, and Sheikh Bilal's sleeping figure, and NewQuarter, and himself, but the sky overhead was a dark, saturated, moonless blue, full of stars in constellations he had never seen. The sight arrested him and he hovered silently above his sleeping body, staring upward.

His reverie was interrupted by the sound of a woman crying. Unsettled, he looked around for its source and saw a shadow in the doorway of the *marid's* house: a golden, late-afternoon shadow, at odds with the blue darkness. It was Azalel. She came across the courtyard on velvet feet, covering her unveiled face with her hands. Her black-and-orange hair fell in disarray over her shoulders. The yellow robe she had worn the last time he had seen her was tattered and covered in dust, as though she had never removed it.

"Hello?" called Alif awkwardly, surprised by the sound of his own voice. Azalel looked up at him with eyes slitted like a cat's. The grief there was so wild and potent that Alif found himself afraid.

"Are you—why are you—" It was difficult to speak.

"I am here to see my brother's child," said Azalel in a low voice. "I like to watch her dream in her little womb." She hugged herself. "I can't tell whether she can see me or not. There are so few half-djinn children born now. Half mud, half fire . . . she's kept her mother and Dina and the old man from going mad, and that *is* something. So I like to think she sees."

Alif looked around helplessly.

"Am I awake or asleep?" he asked.

"Asleep." She padded toward him, rubbing the tears from her eyes.

"I miss Vikram, too," said Alif in a kinder voice. "I should ask you to forgive me. If it weren't for the trouble I'm in he might still be alive."

Azalel shook her head.

"No. He chose the moment of his death. It had little to do with you." She lay down and curled up on the warm stone, close to where Alif was sleeping. He noticed with regret that his mouth was hanging open in an unattractive fashion.

"You must have loved him very much," said Alif timidly. Azalel smiled and closed her eyes as though remembering something pleasurable.

"Sometimes," she said. "Sometimes I hated him. We were lovers once—or perhaps he was my father, or we were enemies who reconciled. We've known each other for so long that we've forgotten."

Alif hoped his dismay didn't show on whatever it was of him she could see. His sleeping face twitched faintly. Azalel stretched up her arms for him, waving her fingers entreatingly like a child reaching for a sweet. Alif backed away.

"I can't," he said. "I love someone else."

"You said that last time."

"This time I mean it."

Azalel curled onto her back and stared up at him with a face that was tired and needy and reminded him perversely of his mother. "It's all right. I just want to smell your hair. The smell of your hair hasn't changed since you were a child."

Charmed and unwilling to hurt her, Alif lay down. He felt himself inhabit his body, waking for a brief moment as the black-and-orange cat nosed his temple, purring.

"Dina always said you were a djinn," he muttered, halfway between sleeping and waking. "I thought she was kidding."

"So did she. My pretty mud-children, playing on the roof . . ." The cat settled with her back to his chest. With bewildered guilt, Alif thought of the time when, as a small boy, he had attempted to trim her whiskers with a pair of scissors; he also remembered pulling her tail. It had never occurred to him to think it odd that she neither bit nor scratched him for it. As he slipped deeper into sleep, he heard her begin to sing: a soft, wordless cat-song of love gone and children grown, trilling and sad.

"I'm scared I won't be able to fix things," his dreaming mind confessed.

"Don't worry," came Azalel's voice, sounding far away. "I'll help you."

Chapter Fifteen

"Are you sure you'll be all right?"

The convert rested one hand on the gentle swell of her belly, still just barely noticeable beneath the generous cut of her robe. She smiled at Alif.

"God willing. I'll have the *marid*, and now Sheikh Bilal, as well—and I have a feeling we'll see each other again, one way or another."

Alif hoped that if this was true, it would be elsewhere, under a brighter and more comprehensible sky.

"I'll come back to see your daughter," he promised. Vikram's daughter, he added in his head, still baffled by the idea.

"Good. I'd like that." She reached out and pressed his shoulder. "Be careful."

"I'll try." Alif turned to Sheikh Bilal and kissed his hand. "Goodbye, Uncle. It's been a great privilege to know you."

"God save us, you talk as if I'm about to die." The sheikh winked. "Knowing *you* has been a great test. However, it has brought me to this undreamed-of juncture, and for that, I thank you. Vikram was right—you will need every one of your wits in the days and years ahead. Use them well."

NewQuarter handed Alif his backpack. He shouldered it, and turned to see Dina coming out of the house shod incongruously in a pair of sneakers, a messenger bag slung over one shoulder.

"*Yallah bina?*"

"What's in the bag?" asked NewQuarter, eyeing it.

"Things we might need."

Alif glanced anxiously at the slender ankles visible beneath the hem of her robe, so fragile-looking, and remembered the grim sound of the shot that had penetrated her arm as they ran from the State security agent.

"Maybe you should stay here until this has blown over," he said. "It's going to be dangerous."

"I know. That's why I wore sneakers." She moved to stand beside him, eyes crinkling in a smile. Alif suppressed the urge to take her hand. Sakina came through the garden gate with the *marid* billowing like a thundercloud behind her, arms crossed over its muscled chest.

"Ready?" Sakina asked.

A surge of adrenaline rose in Alif's chest, rushing outward into his limbs in a bloom of heat.

"Ready," he said.

Sakina ushered them toward the gate. Alif turned one last time: the convert, the *marid*, and Sheikh Bilal stood at the center of the courtyard like a tableau, watching silently. The water that splashed in the fountain seemed to speak for them. Alif raised one hand in an awkward farewell.

"Peace be upon you," called the sheikh.

"And upon you," said Alif. The gate closed behind him.

Sakina led them along the street outside the *marid's* house at a rapid pace, dodging around the murky assortment of street vendors and passersby that clogged the thoroughfare. The mosque that had so taken Sheikh Bilal appeared on their left: an airy, graceful structure of white stone, open on all sides, crowned by a dome that let in the rosy light of the sky. Alif glimpsed a number of pale figures inside, keening to themselves the words he had learned in infancy—Say: He is God the One, God the Absolute; He begets not, nor is He begotten; and there is none like unto Him.

He tripped over the thong of one of his sandals, and wished for his own clothes; the robes NewQuarter had given him were beginning to feel affected, the garb of an elite to which he did not belong. Hobbling a few steps, he caught up with Sakina, following her braided head around a corner and down a flight of stone steps into a kind of subterranean market. The scent of oud wood and and animal must filtered out from behind stalls crammed with bottles and boxes, cages of creatures with increasingly exotic plumage, gadgetry Alif recognized and much he didn't. NewQuarter's head bobbed in front of him, a flashing white cloth among living shadows. He quickened his pace.

The market wound around itself for several blocks, stopping at a kind of arched grate, through which Alif could see the desert. It was slippery against his vision: one moment he saw the pinkish sky and luminous dust of the Empty Quarter belonging to the djinn; the next he saw a more familiar landscape of yellow dunes and scalding blue above them.

"Through here," said Sakina, hoisting the grate upward with a powerful swing. "It will feel a little weird."

Alif looked back at Dina. Her eyes were clear and unafraid above her black veil.

"Let's go," he said.

They stepped through one by one, disappearing into a confluence of light. Alif tasted ozone again, and something metallic, as though he had clamped down on a strip of tin foil with his teeth. He gasped, emerging into bright sand, and floundered to find his footing. He heard NewQuarter retching nearby.

"Fuck," the younger man said weakly, "I never want to do that again."

Dina sat down on the sand and fanned the lower half of her face with the loose edge of her veil. Sakina alone seemed unfazed, standing impatiently over them with her arms crossed.

"Pull yourselves together," she said. "We're still many kilometers outside the City."

"You're not saying we have to *walk*?" NewQuarter looked up at her in horror.

"You don't. But I do. And three mud-mades are a lot to carry."

"Carry—" Before NewQuarter had time to get the question out, they were pulled off their feet. Alif flailed in the air, encountering sand beneath one foot but not the other. A sudden jerk leveled his body above the flying earth. He closed his eyes against the tears dragged from them by the wind as it rushed past his face. He could hear Dina gasping for breath and reached for her; his hand encountered only the hem of her robe. Their speed increased. Alif felt alarming pressure on his bowels and

374

bladder and fought the probable outcome; the concentration this involved distracted him and, in what seemed like another moment, he was tumbling down along a concrete sidewalk.

Breathing deeply through his nose, he pressed his cheek against the ground. There was a sound behind him like claws grinding into asphalt, as from the land-bound steps of some giant bird of prey. He heard NewQuarter's cry of surprise and looked up: in front of them was a smashed storefront, its innards charred and looted. Alif got to his knees and then to his feet, ignoring, by instinct, the amorphous shape that was Sakina.

As far as he could tell, they were in one of the ambivalent residential neighborhoods between the Old and New Quarters, not far from Baqara District. Yet the landscape was unrecognizable. Windows were black with smoke, open cafés deserted, the gates of duplexes and apartment buildings barred and locked. Along the wall of one building, the word ENOUGH was hastily spray painted in Arabic and Urdu, dripping red chemical streaks toward the sidewalk.

"What's going on?" Dina's voice was high with fear. "What's happened?"

"The Hand crashed the Internet," said Alif grimly. "And possibly the utility grids along with it."

"Looks like people got upset," said NewQuarter, sounding very young.

There was a scrambling noise in a nearby alley: Alif looked around the corner to see a cadre of teenage boys hurrying past with a flat-screen TV balanced between them. They resembled the dock boys who had harassed Dina as they sat on the water to eat lunch in another lifetime. A sensation that was neither fear nor excitement rose up from Alif's extremities.

"NewQuarter," said Alif, "is this it? Is this our revolution?"

"If it is, it's already scaring the shit out of me," said NewQuarter. "Where is everybody? Why are they stealing things? Is this really what happens when people can't get into their Facebook accounts? Where is our glorious coup?"

"You've got bigger problems," said Sakina, condensing into a human shape. "I smell sulfur. There are dark things loose, and close by."

"He's pulled out all the stops," said Alif. "What is he so afraid of?"

"You, presumably," said NewQuarter.

"No way. He hates me, but not enough to go this nuts. Not enough to let a bunch of demons off the leash over the entire City."

"Them, then," said Sakina. She pointed down the street. A low roar issued from around the corner. Alif's eyes widened. A mass of protesters appeared, marching dozens deep across the breadth of the boulevard, holding signs and placards in Arabic, Urdu, English, Malay; there were women bareheaded and veiled, old men in the red armbands of the Communist Party, men with beards and robes.

"I suggest we clear the road," said Sakina mildly. Alif bolted into the safety of an alley, with Dina and NewQuarter close behind. The mob moved past, chanting, "The people want justice," and, "Down with fear, down with State security," in something less than unison.

"I can't believe it," said NewQuarter. "Are you seeing this?"

"They're marching together," said Alif, half to himself. "All the disaffected scum at once. I probably know a lot of these people."

"We did this, *akh*. Computer geeks did this. We told these ruffians they could all have a voice, but they had to share the same virtual platform. And now that the virtual platform is gone—"

"They have to share the real world."

"IRL."

"In real life."

"Holy shit."

Their reverie was interrupted by the sound of gunfire, and then by a low hiss. A canister of white gas rolled down the street toward the protesters. Alif glimpsed State security police in body armor a block away, wielding batons. At a distance they looked like a phalanx of black beetles, their eyes and mouths obscured by reflective face shields of tempered plastic. Alif thought of his captors at Al Basheera and felt a cramp in his midsection where their kicks had landed.

"We need to get out of here," quavered Dina.

"Alif needs a working uplink," said NewQuarter. "The plan was to get to my apartment."

"Is that still possible?" Sakina raised an eyebrow.

Alif looked at her doubtfully.

"Can you, um—carry us, again?"

She sighed.

"Please," said NewQuarter. "It's not far. It's a penthouse in the big white building off of Victory Square, on Boulevard 25 January. In the New Quarter. Obviously."

"Very well." There was another jerk, and Alif was aloft again, stomach lurching toward his throat. The City coalesced below him into a matrix of dust-colored dots. Alif began to gasp as the air grew thin and was on the verge of asking Sakina to set them down when she did just that, tumbling them one by one onto the roof of a large white condominium. Alif dropped to his knees and held his pounding head, distantly aware of some indelicate noises coming from NewQuarter's direction.

"I think I'm done with that particular mode of transportation," quavered NewQuarter, rubbing one sleeve across his mouth. Sakina sniffed, looking insulted.

"You asked me to carry you," she said.

"I know, I know. Many thanks." NewQuarter gave her a weak salute. She turned away and seemed to gather herself, like a great tawny bird preparing to launch itself skyward.

"Where are you going?" Alif called in alarm.

"With the dark things around, it's even less safe for me here than it is for you," she said, beating her arms against the wind. "I'm not coming back without an army."

Alif thought he could actually see feathers along her slender limbs. He pinched the bridge of his nose.

"About that," he said. "They are coming, right? The convert's djinn friends?"

"They've said so."

"What's the word of a djinn worth, theoretically speaking?"

Sakina laughed. With a tremendous lurch, she disappeared into the indifferently white sky. Alif stared after her, attempting to pick her out among the gulls wheeling overhead, but saw nothing.

"Don't just stand there, for God's sake. We have zero time to waste." NewQuarter led the way toward a stairwell at the corner of the roof, fumbling with a ring of keys. Dina swayed on her feet as she followed him, as though drunk; when Alif took her hand to steady her she made an inarticulate sound of complaint.

"Are you all right?"

"Too much flying around. Trying not to be sick inside my veil. It's the worst thing. When I was thirteen and had dysentery I threw up at school and had to spend an hour in the girls' washroom rinsing and drying everything."

He remembered her at thirteen: slight, silent, and stubborn, and always hovering nearby.

"You should have asked for help," he said, not quite caressing her hand.

She shrugged. "It was a matter of pride. I was the only girl in the whole school who wore *niqab*, and everybody was waiting for me to take it off."

"You're either brave or silly."

"Funny, I think the same thing about you."

"Please, please shut up," called NewQuarter, jiggling a key in the lock of the stairwell door. "This is not the time for sweet nothings." He wrenched the door open and clattered down a set of cement stairs leading into the building. Alif followed, leading Dina. The stairs were dim; bulbs sputtered in frosted glass sconces that had been smashed with a blunt object. A streak of liquid that ran along one elegantly frescoed wall was almost certainly urine.

"God, they've tossed the whole building!" NewQuarter picked up a shard of glass and let it drop, despondent.

"Which they?" Alif looked around in dismay at the carnage.

"The Hand's people, the protesters—perhaps we're not meant to know which."

"But you're on their side! Why would the protesters—"

NewQuarter turned on him with an impatient glare.

"They don't know I live here, you dolt. And even if they did— that's a revolution we nearly walked into out there. A revolution, Alif. I could hand out leaflets listing all the ways I've risked my skin and betrayed the emir and the State, but I'd still be a royal, and they'd still come for my head."

"Why would they do that?" Alif heard a series of loud pops from somewhere down the street, followed by a chorus of shouts.

"Because they can't help themselves. It's all coming out in torrents now. Revolutions are ninety percent social diarrhea."

"Spoken like a true aristocrat," muttered Dina.

"How can we be sure it's really a revolution?" asked Alif, hoping despite himself that it was not; he could talk of freedom but would readily have settled for familiarity.

"Of course it's a revolution. Did you see the number of women in the streets? Last week it would have taken a forklift to get those same ladies out of their houses. The emir is doomed."

They emerged into a parquet-floored hall made wretched by the domestic debris of the flats that lined it. Alif stumbled past the carcasses of inlaid tables, Tiffany lamps, Turkish carpets, and statuary of various kinds, his mind growing steadily number. He started when he heard NewQuarter wail.

"They smashed the plates after all," he said. "Those things are hand-painted. They cost me a hundred dirhams apiece."

Alif looked over NewQuarter's shoulder at a shattered door leading into what had once been a well-appointed bachelor flat. A dozen blue-and-white china plates lay on the floor in pieces, creating a harried mosaic that NewQuarter scattered with his foot and an angry howl. More popping sounds echoed through a broken window overlooking the square. Alif thought he heard screams.

"I think they're firing at the demonstrators," said Dina in a low voice, flinching as another volley of shots rang out. Alif inched away from the window. A thin wail rose up from the square below, along with the smell of burning rubber. The tinny voice of a man on a megaphone called upon the crowd to stand firm and form a line in front of the police.

"This place isn't secure," fretted NewQuarter, pacing back and forth across his marble-floored living room, righting upended furniture as he went. He stopped beside a gutted antique clock topped with a golden elephant and was freshly overcome with grief. "I was hoping we could stay here while you coded," he continued a moment later in a calmer voice, moving about the floor again, "but all my computers are gone . . . door broken, lock smashed—basically we're fucked."

A loud crash and a series of scuffling noises from the floor below punctuated his remark. Alif froze, locking eyes with Dina, who trembled silently. NewQuarter paused his restless circuit of the room, sucking in his breath and holding it until he turned red. The noise below ceased.

"Even the damned flying woman has deserted us," NewQuarter squeaked. "We have no way out of the City now."

"You're the one who said you'd never let a djinn carry you around again," hissed Dina. "She was insulted."

"Well, aren't you the voice of fucking reason."

"Shut up," said Alif. The noise had started up again. It sounded like the scuttling of a trapped animal but there was a dry quality to it, a chitinous quality, like the sound of rough cloth sliding past itself. It set Alif's guts working. He began breathing very hard.

"I know what that is," he whispered. "Oh, God. Don't let it come up here, don't let it—Dina, please—" A cursory part of him felt unmanned by calling out to her so piteously but he didn't care; he was alone in the dark again. He imagined the room around him growing dimmer and colder, and the riot in the square dying away. From outside came the sound of bare feet padding up the stairs.

"What's happening to the light?" whimpered NewQuarter. Alif felt another stab of panic.

"You see it, too?"

"What do you mean, *too*? What the hell is going on?"

Breathing in frightened little gasps, Dina stepped toward the shattered door.

"Dina!" Alif hissed, regretting his moment of weakness. "Stay here!"

She ignored him. In a small voice, she began to recite the final words of the Quran.

"Say: I seek refuge in the Lord of Daybreak," said Dina. "From the evil of that which He created, from the evil of the rising darkness, and from the evil of spellcraft, and from the evil of the envious when he envies."

The footsteps paused, then continued in a burst of preternatural swiftness.

"What is that thing?" shrieked NewQuarter.

The air seemed to go out of the room. Alif dropped to his knees, rocking back and forth, all thought driven from his mind.

"Say: I seek refuge in the Lord of mankind," Dina continued. "The King of mankind, the God of mankind, from the evil of the creeping whisperer, who murmurs in the hearts of mankind, of the djinn and mankind."

A low cackle wafted through the remains of the door.

"Yes, the right words," came a voice. "The right words, yes."

Alif curled into a fetal position. Somewhere behind him, NewQuarter let out a high, awful sound, like a child waking from a night terror. Dina remained where she was, a lovely black void against the gathering murk, her narrow back the only thing between Alif and the creature dragging its slow thighs through the doorway. It looked at him without eyes. A moment of recognition passed between them. Alif moaned, hands pressed over his ears, assaulted by the memory of his cell and the shrinking circle of footsteps that padded about him in the dark.

"I seek refuge in God from the outcast Satan," said Dina. "Say the words with me, please."

Alif realized she was speaking to him and obediently tried to move his lips, but no sound emerged.

"Please," said Dina again, a tremor in her voice.

"I seek—I seek refuge—" He struggled to speak, pulling himself onto his hands and knees. As he lifted his head, Dina stepped backward into the light coming in through a smashed window. For a moment she was not black but gold, shedding rich afternoon sun from the folds of her robe.

The creature hesitated.

"I seek refuge in God from the outcast Satan," said Alif. The fear that had seized him bled away, replaced by something furious and bright. The dark thing crept forward. The sunlight fell on it and on Dina alike, seeming to say with its terrible indifference that beyond the unseen were forces yet more invisible.

"I seek refuge in God from God," said Dina.

The dark thing shuddered, recollected itself, and flung its rubbery body at her, a tooth-filled hole opening in its blank face. NewQuarter's screaming rose several octaves. Alif struggled to his feet and struck out at the creature's wriggling limbs, pulling it away from Dina, who stumbled backward with a gasp. Alif wrenched the dark thing's long arms away from its body, struggling to maintain a grip on the slick surface of its skin. It let out a shriek and turned on him, opening the hole in its face until the ring of teeth extended beyond the black perimeter of its flesh. It went for his neck.

Dina's composure broke. She began screaming Alif's given name with a blind terror that threatened to override his bravado. The creature's onslaught knocked him to the floor, slamming the back of his head into the marble tiles. Light sheared through the tender tissue behind his eyes and he gasped, blinking, struggling to bring his attacker back into focus. His eyelids were suddenly leaden, his body slack.

When he blinked again, he was surprised to see Vikram leaning over him.

"What a fine mess this is, younger brother."

He was veiled in shadow, a premonition of twilight against the searing brightness in Alif's head.

"I thought you were dead," Alif muttered.

"Then you're not entirely an idiot, because I am dead."

Alif began to panic.

"Then I'm dead, too," he said. "Oh, God——"

"What a tremendous baby it is," scoffed Vikram. "You're not dead. And even if you were, it would be no excuse to snivel so wretchedly."

"It doesn't matter. I'm screwed anyway. State is shooting at people in the streets, the Hand's got black eyeless things looking for me, and I don't actually think I'm good enough at what I do to stop him——"

"Suddenly it discovers humility. I thought you were supposed to be some kind of undersized genius."

"I'm not, I'm nothing. I'm pathetic."

"My sister didn't think so."

"How would she know? It was only the one time——"

"For God's sake, that's not what I *meant*. She says she sat on your windowsill many nights and watched you work for hours without pause. Surely you must have produced something of value."

It took Alif a moment to realize what he was talking about.

"Tin Sari? How is that supposed to help?"

"How should I know? Wave your skinny little fingers and say some magic words or whatever it is you usually do."

Alif thought for a moment, bewildered.

"If I could get Tin Sari to recognize the Hand," he said, "theoretically I could bomb him with all kinds of things remotely, without having to track down every one of his digital fingers. But it would take weeks to gather enough data to develop a profile."

"Hmm," said Vikram. "If you've been hiding from this man for so long, presumably you already know *what* you were hiding from."

Alif sighed in frustration, at a loss to explain to Vikram why his logic was unsound. He opened his mouth to retort but stopped himself: unbidden, the dead man's words turned over in his mind, revealing something he had not considered.

"You're right," he said incredulously. "The data's already there —or rather, it could be inferred from past attacks on our systems. We've got years of diagnostics in the cloud, all of us —NewQuarter01, and Abdullah from Radio Sheikh, and Gurkhaboss, and everybody. It might work. It could work."

"Very tidy, for an unconscious twit." Vikram reached down and ruffled Alif's hair with a clawed hand. There was something disappointing in the weightlessness of his fingers. Alif discovered he had regained feeling in his arms and legs. The world began to right itself.

"I'm hallucinating," he observed.

"I will say that you are, and leave you to ponder the implications," said Vikram. He turned to go, loping back into the hazy light. "By the way," he said, "when you wake up, duck."

Alif ducked. There was a tremendous crash overhead, a symphonic overture of escaping cogs and chimes. With a croak, the eyeless creature rolled off his body. Alif looked up to see NewQuarter standing over him with the remains of the antique clock in his hands.

"You found your courage," Alif wheezed.

"I also pissed myself," said NewQuarter.

Alif tried to sit but found himself jerked back down and dragged across the floor by the straps of his backpack. Dina began screaming again.

"Give it us," the creature hissed.

Alif rolled onto his side, struggling free of his pack. The creature pounced on it like a cat, ripping open the nylon lining. It seized on the fragile binding of the *Alf Layla* with a cackle. Alif dove for the book, catching the opposite end before the dark padded fingers had a chance to wrestle it free. The creature yanked the book toward itself with a snarl. Alif felt his shoulder joints pop in a way that would have been pleasant at the hands of a masseuse in a hammam but in present circumstances made him yelp; he scrambled backward, relinquishing his hold on the manuscript.

"Fuck you!" he shrieked. "And tell the Hand to fuck himself, too!"

The hideous mouth gaped wide and a fetid howl blasted Alif's face. The creature clutched the book to its chest. Bounding across the floor in an erratic pattern, it leaped out the shattered window facing the square and disappeared.

For a moment all Alif could hear was terrified panting. He pulled himself up, winced, and lay back down. Pleading incoherently, Dina sank to the floor beside him, parting the hair on the back of his scalp with fingers that shook.

"You should have just let him take it," she said. "I don't know why you fought like that."

"I promised the *marid* I'd keep an eye on that thing," Alif muttered. "Anyway, it's just a bump."

"Like hell," said NewQuarter, bundling his robe up around his waist. "I'm surprised you've still got a skull. That was a real crack. You were completely unconscious for a few seconds."

"I thought it was going to kill you," quailed Dina.

"I thought it was going to kill *you*," said Alif, attempting a smile. "You walked toward it like it was a stray cat you were going to shoo out of the garden."

"You were really brave," said NewQuarter. He looked down at the robe bunched between his hands and made a face. Sighing, he let it drop, revealing a wet stain. "Ironically enough," he said in a feeble voice, "that went more or less perfectly to plan. Hopefully we've bought ourselves a little time."

"Only as much time as it takes for that thing to get back to the Hand and the Hand to realize we've duped him and then get really, really mad." Alif propped himself up on his hands. "I've got to code. We still need a working uplink."

"That's the only thing I believe I can still manage," said NewQuarter, walking stiff-legged toward a bedroom off the main hall. "Boot up your netbook and look for a wireless network called CityState. I will presently recite the access code."

Dina handed Alif his shredded backpack. He lifted out his netbook, shaking his head several times to clear the last of the spots dancing in front of his eyes.

"Are you sure this network is still up?" he called to NewQuarter. "It looked like the Hand managed to screw up every IP in the City."

"It's up." NewQuarter's soiled robe flew out the door of the bedroom and landed in a heap in the hall. "He can't touch this one. Satellite."

"He can if he has access to the land-based routing facility."

"He can't if I own the satellite."

Alif gaped at NewQuarter as he came out of the bedroom wearing a fresh robe.

"You're too young to own a flat as nice as this one," said Alif, "much less a satellite."

"How wrong you are. I could have bought a gold-plated Mercedes like that fat idiot Suleiman, number fourteen in line for the throne. You should be happy—the reason this City is so rotten is because the other twenty-five princes have more money than they know what to do with. I, on the other hand, have exactly as much money as I know what to do with. In the information age, he wins who has a clean and reliable Internet uplink. Censors be damned."

"Your own *satellite*."

"My own satellite. Now shut up and start typing."

Alif ran his fingers up and down the home keys on his netbook. He tried to picture in his mind what he had to do. The memory of the great tower he had built on Sheikh Bilal's computer distracted him; he wondered if he would ever again create something so beautiful, flawed though it had been. The drudge work of ordinary coding seemed banal now. Without the *Alf Yeom,* he was another gray hat toiling away line by line behind a bright screen, unwatched and unregarded.

"Out of curiosity," said NewQuarter, "what do you plan to do?"

Alif pulled his flash drive out of the shredded backpack and held it up. It was undamaged; the blessing of the blind dervish had stuck.

"Give the Hand a tail," he said. "One he can't shake off."

He worked with furious energy. As NewQuarter had promised, the cloud was intact. It contained chat logs full of hypotheses about his methods and techniques, diagnostics and analyses, and entire file chains dedicated to records of the Hand's attacks on their digital outposts. Alif cleaned the data and fed it to the Tin Sari botnet, muttering *bismillahs* every time he struck the *enter* key.

"Do you have a cold pack, or ice we could put into something dry?" he asked NewQuarter at one point. "The netbook is starting to run very hot."

"How many motherboards do you melt on a weekly basis?" asked NewQuarter with a sigh. He picked his way across the room from the door, where he had been standing guard with a piece of splintered wood.

"Not as many as you might think," said Alif without taking his eyes from the screen. He put out his hand; Dina touched it with hers.

"How are you?" he whispered.

"I'll be better when this is over," she said. The pressure from her hand increased. Unwilling to draw away, Alif typed one-handed for several minutes, plugging in lines of code one by one, creating a payload of malicious software that was, he hoped, primitive and toxic enough to turn any operating system into pixelated soup.

"I don't get it," said NewQuarter, swinging his stick at the air. "What's so special about this profiler botnet of yours? The Hand isn't some bucktoothed thirteen-year-old running DOS attacks. He's already got revolving IP addresses—you know how this goes, he's so good that sometimes there's never an origin IP at all. The man is as close to untraceable as it gets."

"Not to Tin Sari," said Alif. "In order to avoid this, he'd have to become someone else."

"I don't follow."

"There's nothing to follow. I wrote this application and I have no idea what makes it work. But it does. That's all."

NewQuarter plunked down on the marble floor with his stick over one shoulder, looking impressed.

"That's called mastery," he said.

Alif sighed, finger hovering over the *enter* key.

"No. A master is someone who understands what he creates. I'm so stupid that I've overlooked something very simple," he said. "Everyone say a prayer. I'm going to execute this thing. And then we need to pray some more because it may simply shut down before it can profile the Hand, or after it profiles him and before it starts launching bombs."

NewQuarter dutifully raised his hands to his face.

"I'm not sure I can pray for a computer program," said Dina.

"Do it for me," said Alif. She acquiesced, breathing into her palms. Alif cast his eyes down and made something between a prayer and a wish, aware of how close he was to ruin, how many and various had been the unintended consequences of his actions. The noise in the square below grew louder.

"We need to keep moving," said NewQuarter. "It looks like things are getting nastier down there."

Alif nodded briskly.

"Can you put this in your pack?" he asked Dina, handing her the netbook. "Mine is pretty much kicked." He dangled the shredded nylon husk from one finger.

"Sure." She zippered the netbook into the messenger bag she'd brought from the *marid's* house and hefted it over one shoulder. "Let's go."

They hurried across the living room. NewQuarter braced himself against the remains of the door and shoved; it came off its hinges and crashed into the outer hallway.

"There," he said. "Now the revolutionaries can properly loot the place. They've left a lot behind."

He led them down the hall toward the main stairwell, cutting a path through the glittering debris of his neighbors' flats. They passed a bank of silent elevators, their doors jammed open to reveal mirror-lined interiors. Alif was startled by a glimpse of his reflection and muffled a cry.

"Quiet," hissed NewQuarter. "We have no idea what else might be lurking around this place."

"What's happened to the people who live here?" whispered Dina. "Where has everyone gone?"

NewQuarter glanced around with a blank expression.

"Dead or fled," he said. "Most of my neighbors were foreign corporate types working for the oil companies. Their embassies have probably evacuated them."

"I never thought it would come to this," muttered Alif, kicking at the electronic guts of a flat-screen TV lying on the ground.

"Really?" said NewQuarter. "I thought this was what we wanted."

Chastened, Alif fell silent. They left the hall through a glass door and crossed a rooftop courtyard lined with smashed pots of tuberose and hibiscus. From here, the riot in the square was a muted, homogenous roar: a human sea at high tide. Alif did not stop to listen closely. They reentered the building at the far side of the courtyard, arriving at a lounge area furnished with oversized leather armchairs and what had formerly been a wet bar, reduced now to an empty cabinet, its contents long since carried off.

"By process of elimination, we now know your place was not looted by Islamists," Alif joked weakly.

"We don't know that," said NewQuarter. "They could have taken the bottles away to smash them, or to turn them into Molotov cocktails. We've come into this uprising in the middle. It's like watching a half-melted ice cube—impossible to infer its original shape, or that of the puddle it will eventually become."

"You're so negative," scolded Dina.

"No I'm not, I'm a student of history. Revolutions only get names after it's clear who won." NewQuarter hurried them along, pushing open a set of large, brocade-paneled double doors that looked to Alif like they belonged in the lobby of an expensive hotel. On the other side, a grand marble staircase twisted down away from them toward the ground floor.

It was covered in tarry black matter. At first, Alif thought the staircase had been befouled with the contents of several restrooms, but, to his horror, the dark things began to move and shift, reaching out with froglike arms, turning eyeless faces toward the gallery at the top of the stairs where he stood with Dina and NewQuarter. There were too many to count.

"God save us," whispered Dina. Alif struggled against the urge to hyperventilate. He stepped in front of her, reaching across her body with one protective arm.

"Run," said NewQuarter hoarsely.

"What? No—"

"Run, you fools, run."

A wriggling instinct overcame Alif's self-control. He scrambled after the retreating white blotch of NewQuarter's robe, towing Dina behind him. Hideous flapping noises pursued them, curiously dry—the sounds of padded feet galloping up the stairs. They bolted back across the courtyard. Alif heard Dina cry out and turned to look: she had stumbled over a flower pot and lay sprawled among hibiscus blossoms.

"Wait!" he called to NewQuarter. The dark things were pelting toward them on all fours, silent but for their uncanny footfall. Alif grabbed Dina's arm and hauled her to her feet. She took a step and cried out, favoring one leg. Alif cursed.

"Put your arm over my shoulder," he told her.

"I'm too heavy!"

She was right. Alif tottered toward the glass door on the far side of the courtyard with Dina clinging awkwardly to his back, watching with a sinking sensation as NewQuarter's face grew paler and more frantic.

"Hurry!" he squealed, yanking open the door. Alif dragged himself through. Dina kicked the door closed behind them with her good foot. The glass shuddered as a dozen dark shapes hit it at once, their spastic bodies struggling against the invisible barrier. They drew back as one, paused, and charged the door again. A crack snaked its way through the glass.

"Son of a dog!" NewQuarter scrambled away from the door on his hands and knees. Alif stared at the crack in the glass, suddenly unable to move.

"My bag." Dina tugged at his sleeve. "In my bag."

"What?"

"Tear gas."

Alif fumbled with the zipper on her messenger bag. Inside, along with his netbook, were a length of thin rope, a pair of pliers, a lighter, and a half dozen other items, along with a small black canister emblazoned with various health warnings in English.

"Things we might need?" said Alif, incredulous.

"Yes, yes, from the *marid's* house. Don't ask. Just get the gas."

Alif pulled out the black canister. The dark things threw themselves against the cracked glass in a litany of thumps, creating an ever-wider radius of damage. The door began to bulge outward. NewQuarter was screaming in earnest now, hands bunched around his face. Alif fumbled with the pull tab on the black canister, hands slippery with sweat. It slid out of his grasp and rolled on the floor.

"For God's sake!" Dina darted toward the tear gas and snatched it up as the glass finally splintered. Instinct made Alif double over to protect his face. There was a loud hiss; an acrid white smoke filled the hall and burned through Alif's sinuses. He stumbled away, choking. A chorus of amphibian pain and outrage was audible through the fog. Hands propelled Alif forward, into the door-lined corridor where NewQuarter's flat stood. His eyes smarted.

"Keep going," came Dina's voice behind him. He obeyed, weaving erratically on his feet, grinding the heels of his hands against his eyes. There was a cough and a moan to his right: he fumbled blindly, caught NewQuarter's collar, and pulled him along without a word. The barren door frame of NewQuarter's flat appeared in front of him. He blundered through it into the remains of the opulent living room, sucking fresh air into his lungs. Hacking vigorously, NewQuarter pulled free of his grasp and slumped to the floor. Alif looked around for Dina. She limped through the door frame behind him.

"Thanks," he rasped. "I sort of screwed that up."

She shook her head and coughed, then gave a hiccupy, hysterical laugh.

"Well," she said, "at least we're back where we started, instead of somewhere worse."

"Oh, not quite."

Alif jumped, blinking, searching through the watery haze of his vision for the origin of the voice. It was familiar. So, too, was the smell of sulfur that permeated the room, which seemed too dim for midday, and too stifling for winter. He was seized by dread.

"Hello again, Alif," said the Hand. He was seated with his back to the window, dressed in a white robe; to Alif's smarting eyes the sun behind him seemed to throw a perverse halo around his figure. "And Abu Talib—who would have guessed that beneath such a puny, underdeveloped exterior there lurked a dangerous provocateur. You've caused me quite a bit of unexpected trouble and expense. Does your mother know what you've been up to?"

NewQuarter merely whimpered in response. The Hand was seated in a desk chair rescued from a corner of the room, as calmly as if he were taking a meeting at his own office. He was flanked by two twin voids, fissures of nothing that pulled the warmth from the air around them and moved like living beings. Alif glimpsed obscene hints of tooth, nail, and tongue in the writhing darkness, which, though silent, spoke of carnage for which there were no words.

"Alif," quavered NewQuarter, "I owe you an apology. I could never have believed—"

"Oh, for God's sake, be a man," said the Hand, lip curled in disdain. "I don't like the idea of killing someone barely old enough to shave, any more than you like the idea of dying. NewQuarter01 my ass cheek. I've been hunting you for years. You must have started up with this hooliganism at fourteen."

"Thirteen," said NewQuarter.

The dark things that had pursued them through the building began creeping into the room on dry toadish feet. Dina shrieked as one of them brushed past her leg.

"You think these are disgusting? You should see their larger cousins. These might as well be a litter of kittens," said the Hand. He reached out: the creature nearest him stretched up its distended neck and caressed his fingers with its cheek.

Alif began to laugh silently.

"Something funny?" The Hand's voice was sharp.

"No," said Alif, "it's not funny at all. It's just that the Islamists have been saying for years that State is propped up by demonic powers. I never imagined they might be right."

The Hand made a disgusted noise in the back of his throat and stood, pacing.

"A pack of crazed, bearded homosexuals, the lot of them. What do they know of demonology? What you see in this room is not dangerous, Alif. I'll tell you what is. The spirits that lurk in your bloodstream, poisoning your mind day after day, eroding your will. They breed in the marketplace, sapping you with goods you don't need and of money you don't have. God was right: those are the demons a wise man fears most. And they were well in evidence in this City long before I came along. This place is festering with *shayateen*, yet you despise me for conjuring up a few helpers as one would call a dog."

Alif noticed the Hand was perspiring.

"What about those people?" he said, pointing out the window at the turmoil in the square below. "They don't look possessed to me."

The Hand gave a short, barking laugh.

"They suffer from another malady, just as you do—the delusion of freedom."

"Are you going to hurt them?" whispered Dina, speaking up for the first time. The Hand smiled restlessly.

"I don't have to hurt them. I will set my little friends upon the crowd, and they will hurt themselves. Suspicions will grow, factions will arise, secularist and Islamist will discover they cannot cooperate, men will decide women are not their comrades. Someone will get bold and pull a knife. And that will be the end."

Alif swallowed hard, staring out the window at the square below. The crowd had swelled to an astonishing size. There seemed to be more people than street; the broad intersecting avenues of the *maidan* were invisible beneath a crush of human movement. He wondered how many of the demonstrators he knew—how many he had aided, unseen, disguising their digital origins from the man who sat in front of him. He thought of Egypt and the anonymous friends he had allowed to suffer out of fear for his own skin.

"Never again," he murmured.

"What's that?" The Hand narrowed his depthless eyes.

Alif forced himself to look the man steadily in the face.

"Go to hell."

Flushing red, the Hand took several steps toward Alif. Alif shook, but stood his ground. Fumbling in his pocket, he took out the whistle the goat-horned woman had given him and clenched it in his fist.

"I beg your pardon?" The Hand's voice was deadly.

"I said I'd live to see you fed to the dogs," said Alif, "and I'm still alive." He raised the whistle to his lips and blew.

He waited. Nothing happened.

The Hand began to laugh. It was a terrible sound, a mad sound, rising out of his chest like the mindless howl of a jackal.

"Alif, Alif," he choked out, "put that idiotic thing away. Your friends are not coming."

Sweat slid between Alif's arms and legs and down his back.

"What do you mean?" he asked, suddenly timid.

The Hand only laughed harder. He sat back down in NewQuarter's desk chair, muscles straining in his reddened face.

"What did I tell you back in that filth hole of a cell? I've won." He reached out. One of the twin voids beside him began to twist like a flame in a strong wind. It grew a vaporous limb and, reaching inside itself, drew out a dusty manuscript bound in blue.

"You've lost your bargaining chip. My little friends lifted this today." The Hand took the book and ran his fingers along its spine.

"Take a closer look," said Alif, emboldened. "It's not what you think it is. You're holding an old but ordinary copy of the *Alf Layla.*"

The Hand tossed the book at Alif's feet, saying nothing. Alif wiped his palms on his trousers and trembled as he bent to pick it up. The scent hit him before he touched the binding. He closed his eyes.

It was the *Alf Yeom.*

Chapter Sixteen

"Is he dead?" Alif asked in a leaden voice. "The *marid*. Did you kill him for it?"

"Oh, no," said the Hand, resuming his seat. "I simply bottled him up again. He could be useful at some future juncture. Magnificent creatures, the *marideen*, but stupid as a bag of bricks. It wasn't hard. He's over there in the corner."

Alif looked: an unassuming two-liter bottle of Mecca Cola sat on the floor next to one of the Hand's formless sentries. Storm-colored mist curled upon itself inside, sluggish and sullen.

"And the convert?"

"You mean the pregnant girl? Do you take me for an idiot? If she'd let me I would have delivered her to her embassy in a private car. No one wants unhappy Americans on their hands. As it was, I left her in the Empty Quarter for the djinn to do with what they will. Though she was rather upset by this turn of events, I have to say. It was she who told me you were expecting company. Once your little band of heroes saw what I'd done to the *marid*, they wisely decided to stay home."

"Cowards," murmured Dina.

"I disagree. The djinn are rarely cowards—it's just that they are, as a rule, practical rather than honorable."

Alif thought of Vikram in his final hours, bleeding to death in the convert's arms.

"That's not true," he said.

The Hand looked annoyed.

"Whether you agree or not is immaterial. What incentive does someone who is unseen have to keep his word? None. We are only honest because we must live in the light of day."

Alif heard Dina say his given name in a soft voice. For reasons he did not immediately understand, he felt shaken by it, and by the motives she might have had for pronouncing it at that moment. He glanced back at her, unseen as she herself was behind her black veil, and met her eyes and felt the threads of his life pull taut, revealing at last the modest image he had woven into the tapestry of the world. He turned back to face the Hand.

"'You're full of shit," he said calmly. Behind him, NewQuarter made a strangled noise. He ignored it.

"It's because of people like you that we have to go unseen in order to be honest. You've made the truth impossible anywhere but in the dark, behind false names. The only thing that ever sees the light of day in this City is bullshit. Your bullshit, the emir's bullshit, State's bullshit. But that's over now. All the people you've chosen not to see are out there calling for your blood. And I, and NewQuarter, and all our friends, all the ones you've been hunting and kidnapping and shutting up in prison all these years—we're going to give it to them."

The sweat on the Hand's brow grew more pronounced. He tore off his head cloth with a restless jerk and tossed in on the floor; bareheaded, he looked smaller, his hair an untidy thatch threaded with gray.

"I thought we were talking about djinn," he said in a cool voice.

"A djinn is not the only way to be invisible," said Alif. "There are other ways, equally involuntary."

"You're a very cheap philosopher," sneered the Hand. "Much good may it do you. I have the *Alf Yeom*. I've got your *marid* in an empty soda bottle. I have a battalion of servants no earthly army can touch."

Alif realized what was missing from the room.

"Where are your guards?" he asked. The Hand gave another barking laugh.

"Are you blind?" He motioned to the voids that stood beside him, the seething mass of dark bodies moving about the room.

"No, your *human* guards. Your State security people. The ones who bashed in my ribs at Al Basheera and starved me in prison."

The Hand licked his lips.

"I have no need of human guards," he said.

"The emir's cut you loose, hasn't he," said NewQuarter incredulously. "You screwed up, and he's decided it's safer to feed you to the angry crowds than to defend you."

Rising again, the Hand pulled at the collar of his robe, which clung gray and damp to his neck. "The emir is an old fool, and his foolishness will cost him his throne. He's under the illusion that his people love him and that if he purges his government of a few corrupt officials, everyone will calm down. He doesn't realize that the people in that square are not going home."

He leaned against the windowsill, heedless of the ragged fringe of glass that ringed the empty frame. A red spot blossomed on his shoulder. Alif stared at it in dismay. He had been unprepared for this, for a Hand unshackled from the regime. Alif knew the bitter, boundless energy that came of having no dignity left to lose—it was what had made the difference between the idle boy with a computer he had been at fifteen, and the threat he had become a few years later. It was what had made him, in his own way, dangerous. He recognized the rage in the Hand's opaque eyes, and was seized with fear.

"What are you going to do," he asked.

The Hand's lips parted in a smile.

"Exactly what I planned to do," he said. "Restore the natural order of things. I built the State's digital infrastructure—they can't keep me out. And the people in that square must be made to know the poison that lies at the heart of all false hopes. They can oust the emir if they like, but they must learn to make do with me. And thanks to that"—he pointed to the *Alf Yeom*—"this City will be under a metafirewall that will make China's Golden Shield look like a leaky bucket. The Alifs of this world will either crawl home or die in a prison cell, as you were intended to do. As you *will* do, in very short order."

"You're sick," whispered NewQuarter. "You're crazy."

"And you are a dead man flapping his gums. The people out there want to see princes strung up by their feet. I may start with you."

The eyeless things grew restive, boiling around the floor and walls on their swollen feet. Alif gnashed his teeth.

"You're bluffing. You can't build any firewall. The book will betray you like it betrays everybody. Look at the damage you managed to do to every ISP in the whole damn City."

A dark, blank face snapped at his ankle. He bit back a yelp, hoping the Hand had not seen him start.

"That was your sloppy coding," the Hand said stiffly. "Now that I have the *Alf Yeom*, I will correct your mistakes."

Alif's eyes strayed to the manuscript lying on the floor between them. The eyeless creatures avoided it as if by instinct, leaving a circular perimeter around the book as they orbited their master. The noise from the square had redoubled and seemed now to come from all directions at once, including the floors below. There was the sound of a window shattering, close by.

Alif was possessed by the same impulse that had overtaken him in the *marid's* courtyard, when he had bolted for the door that led him to Dina: the certain knowledge that most problems had very simple solutions, if one was willing to make sufficient sacrifice.

"Prove it," he said. Behind him, Dina took a sharp breath. The Hand looked anxious, as though Alif had erred from the script he was meant to follow.

"What do you mean?" he asked cautiously.

"Pick up the book, open it, and tell me how you would outcode me," said Alif. He was startled by the evenness of his own voice. NewQuarter grabbed his sleeve. He jerked away irritably. The Hand raised one eyebrow, glanced down at the book, looked back up at Alif, and licked his lips.

405

"Very well," he said, and picked up the *Alf Yeom* between careful fingers. Alif watched as he thumbed through the flaking pages, scanning the text. His face changed, growing eager, almost manic.

"Yes," he said. "The frame story, you see—Farukhuaz and the nurse, and this theme of marriage. You noticed, of course, that marriage plays a very small role in the subsequent stories. Naturally, this is because it refers not to literal marriage but to the union between analog—that's Farukhuaz—and digital—that's the nurse. The necessary blending of rational and irrational, of discrete and algebraic functions. The frame story is the platform, the subsequent stories are individual programs . . ." He dragged the heel of one hand across his glistening forehead. Wiping it on his robe, he returned to his task, flipping pages three and four at a time, the greed in his eyes a terrible dead light.

"Have you read it through all the way to the end?" he asked.

"No," Alif admitted. "I jumped around. I stopped after I came across a story that was—it was about someone I knew. I couldn't go on after that."

"Your own weakness," said the Hand with contempt. The twin voids shimmered behind his shoulders like great dark wings. His fingers trembled. The room was silent but for the crisp sound of paper and the thrum of dissent below. Alif looked nervously over his shoulder, hoping for some unspoken vote of confidence from Dina or NewQuarter. But NewQuarter had bitten his lips raw and stared at Alif in wordless accusation; Dina was unknowable, her eyes cast down. Alif tasted bile.

He jumped when he heard the Hand cry out.

"Is this some kind of joke?" The book dangled from the Hand's fingers, open to a chapter heading Alif couldn't see.

"Joke?" Alif's fraying nerves made him smile like an idiot. He fought for control of his face. The Hand was pale, jabbing with one finger at a page near the end of the book.

"'*The Fall of the Hand, or A Sad Case of Early Retirement,*'" he read. "The final story. Is this your work, you ass-coveting little shit? Is this elaborate hoax your attempt to drive me mad?"

Alif looked from the book to the Hand and back again.

"My *what?*"

"Read it," the Hand shrieked, hurling the book at Alif. He caught it awkwardly, crumpling the fragile pages against his chest. Looking down at the title page of the last story, he read his own name.

The Tale of Alif the Unseen.

A muffled cacophony of feet and shouts drifted up from the flat directly beneath them. Alif read the title over and over, attempting to make sense of what had occurred. A buoyant, illicit feeling stole over him and he felt drunk on something much headier than wine.

"That's not what it says when I read it," he murmured at last, at a loss for anything more eloquent.

"What the hell do you mean that's not what it says? Are you illiterate?" One of the eyeless things jumped for the Hand's sleeve with a congested snarl, tearing off a length of white cotton between its teeth. The Hand seemed not to notice, staring instead at Alif with an expression that frightened him.

"I warned you," said Alif, his voice cracking. "I told you this book is tricky."

"Tricky?" The Hand spat on the floor, suddenly vulgar. "So it's a trick, is it? Shall we see how it ends?"

Alif read the title once more. He discovered he did not need to know.

"I think it's too late for that," he said, handing back the book. "You can read it if you want. I won't."

The Hand snatched the manuscript, scanning its final pages at a frantic pace. His face drained of blood.

"'If he had left the room that instant, he might have lived,'" he read. "'But he lingered to read the last chapter of the book, which was full of sly silences and half-truths, revealing nothing.'"

An alarm chimed out from the innards of Dina's messenger bag. The fan inside the netbook began to whir gently. It was echoed, several seconds later, by the hum of electricity in the walls of the building. The lightbulbs in an unmolested chandelier hanging from the ceiling flickered on, filling the room with sudden luminescence.

"The utility grid is coming back online," whispered NewQuarter. "Whatever you did—"

"Shh." Alif cast a furtive glance at the Hand, hoping he had not heard. But the man's eyes were vacant. He stood very still, staring at the broken door and the hall beyond. He made no movement when one of the eyeless things nipped at his fingers and drew blood.

The hum of electricity increased, becoming an almost palpable vibration. Alif imagined he could hear the physical transfer of information as the City's ISPs booted up: the packets of ones and zeroes traveling outward from data hubs, crossing oceans, recruiting allies for the revolution across a thousand social networks, from a million LCD screens, behind which, though unseen, were people who were ferociously alive. The hum in the walls was answered by a roar from the square below as demonstrators discovered their smartphones and tablets were online once more. The Hand's digital grip on the City had slackened. The world would look into the square through the eyes of a thousand news feeds and posts and uploaded videos, and witness the cost of change. For a moment Alif was no longer afraid, savoring the mingled uproar of man and machine.

"What is that sound?" howled the Hand. Shaken from his reverie, he clapped his palms over his ears.

Alif smiled.

"The delusion of freedom," he said.

Voices echoed from the hall outside. The shadows of the ascending crowd dappled the walls, spoiling the pristine expanse of white before NewQuarter's threshold. A vanguard of boys armed with sticks burst into the room, shouting in three languages.

"You're dead!" screamed the Hand. "You are all dead men!" He turned on Alif, mouth twisted into a grimace from which sanity was absent, and made an arcane gesture with his left hand. The eyeless things turned as one. Alif backed toward the window as they scuttled after him. He was half-aware of Dina struggling toward him through the crowd and of NewQuarter cursing, his pale robe swallowed in the dusty press of flesh.

The mob that filled the room did not seem to see the dozens of fanged mouths that howled at Alif as he stumbled over broken glass and slammed into a metal guard rail outside NewQuarter's window. The square reeled a hundred feet below, one unified wall of noise and jostling bodies. It rose up at him in a rush of vertigo. He pressed his back against the guard rail, steadied by the unyielding warmth of the metal. The Hand was bellowing in some awful language. He raised his left arm, fingers snapping shut into a fist. The eyeless things jerked, squealed, and leaped at Alif's throat.

Alif dodged. Momentum carried the two creatures nearest him through the window, howling as they vanished into the overheated air. The others fell back and warily pressed their bellies to the floor. The crush of human protesters did not alarm them. Somehow they avoided being trampled underfoot, bending and twisting like shadows on water. No one looked at them.

With a cry of frustration, the Hand shouldered his way across the room, toppling a fat man armed with a cooking skewer in his haste. Alif tensed, preparing himself. He had never thrown a punch—not a real one—but he made a fist anyway, then made it anew when he realized his thumb was on the inside. As the Hand reached out, Alif raised his arm to swing. But the Hand did not reach for Alif.

He reached for Dina.

She had made her way through the crowd toward Alif, calling something he could not hear over the din. The Hand grabbed her robe at the neck and yanked her head back. One edge of her veil slid away, revealing dark curls damp with sweat. Her eyes went wide and round. Alif screamed at the top of his voice but the sound was lost amid the shouts and chanting of the mob, and a wall of flesh and cloth and pasteboard signs closed in and cut off his view. He struck the person nearest him—a woman, a middle-aged woman, wearing a beige plaid head scarf—feeling only momentary remorse as she screamed and stumbled back. Alif rushed through the opening she had created, searching for the Hand's white robe or Dina's black one. The eyeless things peered at him from between the legs and elbows of the crowd, silent and obscene.

Finally he saw familiar slim brown fingers reaching out, and caught them. They closed on his. Over some anonymous shoulder, Alif saw the Hand grit his teeth and twist the fabric of Dina's veil behind her head, pulling the material flat against her nose and mouth. Her fingers jerked out of his grasp to claw at her face as she fought for air. Alif threw himself at the Hand, knocking the taller man backward into a group of teenage boys. The Hand cried out in surprise. Releasing Dina, he pinwheeled his arms, but it was no use: he slid inelegantly between two pimpled, roaring youths, one of whom gave him a look of half-interested disgust before elbowing him in the throat. With a sputter, the Hand went down, disappearing beneath the throng.

"Are you all right?" Alif could barely hear himself speak. Dina's chest heaved beneath her robe; there was a red smear in her left eye where a blood vessel had burst. She leaned against Alif without answering. He lifted her in his arms, pushing sideways through a circle of men shouting recriminations at one another: one wore the red armband of the City Communist Bloc, the other the woolly beard of an Islamist. The room was choked with the rank butchery smell of perspiration and blood. Alif made his way toward the broken window, following a whisper of hot but breathable air, shielding Dina's head from flailing fists and banners. When he reached the window he set Dina down on her feet and leaned against the adjoining wall with a gasp.

"Your eye," he said. "Did he hurt you?"

"Not much." Her voice was hoarse and barely audible. She straightened her veil with hands that shook. "We have to get out of here before the crowd blows up. Where is Abu Talib?"

Alif stood on his toes and craned his neck, scanning the room. He thought he saw NewQuarter's white head cloth bobbing in the midst of the crowd, but it was eclipsed by the looming face of a man with gelled hair, reeking of cigarette smoke and punching his smartphone in the air like a weapon.

"The Internet is back!" he bellowed. "Mobile service is up! Electricity is online! Get everyone into the square!"

Bluish light vied with the declining sun as half a hundred phones and tablets emerged from pockets and bags. The dark things skittered around the room, suddenly agitated, snapping as they blundered into one another.

"Is this you?" Dina tugged at the sleeve of Alif's shirt. "Is this because of what you did?"

"Yes," said Alif in a faint voice. The messenger bag where his netbook lay churning out algorithms was invisible beneath the crush of bodies that filled the room, yet his work was a tangible presence. If he closed his eyes, he could see his commands scrolling up the screen and imagine every step of the silent mathematical siege that had taken place as Tin Sari exposed what digital hiding places remained to the Hand. Alif felt no triumph, merely a physical sense of relief. It was only when Dina touched his fingers that he realized they were trembling.

"Are you going to tell them it was you?" Dina cupped her left eye with one hand and regarded him solemnly with the right. "Everyone knows what happened at Basheera. You'll be a hero."

Alif flexed his shaking hands. The energy of the crowd was shifting as people babbled into cell phones and punched out text messages, rallying unseen others for the final push. Alif heard one man say the emir was in hiding; another claimed State security forces had been authorized to shoot to kill.

"Being a hero was never the point," said Alif, and realized it was true. "The point was what's happening right now. The point was to win."

Dina's good eye regarded him with admiration. High on the energy of the crowd, Alif was struck by an urge to kiss her, right there in the sweaty miasma of revolution, like the hero of an American film. He might have forgotten himself and tried had he not heard a terrified scream—male, but only just—issue from across the room. Jostling ensued, and a chorus of raised voices began calling for rope.

"What's going on?" Alif asked the man with the gelled hair, who was shouting orders over the crowd. He turned and smiled, revealing tobacco-stained teeth.

"Looks like we've caught a prince," he said. "The little bastard who owns this flat."

Alif felt the blood drain from his face.

"Abu Talib," said Dina in a horrified voice.

Alif did not respond. He began shoving people out of the way, forcing himself toward the center of the room. Answering fists and elbows pushed against his ribs but he ignored them, intent on the white head cloth that flashed between the unfamiliar dark heads of the protesters. He had not gotten far when someone seized his wrist and curled blunt nails into his flesh. Alif yelped, wriggling, and found himself being hauled back toward the window.

"You clever little shit." The Hand's face was bruised. A thin line of blood ran from one side of his mouth. "You've kicked me off the grid. Clearly you got farther with the *Alf Yeom* than I thought."

"I didn't use the *Alf Yeom*," gasped Alif. "I used my own software. I used Tin Sari."

"Don't lie to me. That amateurish key-logger? I field-tested it on your friends. Thirty-two percent success rate. That's worse than guessing." The Hand's grip tightened on Alif's arm.

"You were impatient." Alif dug in his heels but the Hand's strength was surprising for a slender man, and he prevailed. "You have to give it time to collect enough data. It takes weeks."

"You're still lying. No botnet could learn to identify an individual personality, even if you gave it years."

Alif's feet slid and crunched on broken glass. The noise from the riot below boomed through the empty window. With alarm, Alif realized the Hand meant to push him out. The eyeless things slunk toward him from beneath and between the jostling limbs of the crowd, their blank faces oddly curious. Alif kicked, howled, and twisted, sending fragments of glass sliding across the tile floor, now slick with a mud of congealed spit and sweat and dust. The Hand seemed not to notice his frenzied attempts to free himself and kept his grip on Alif's arm almost idly, as though imbued with a strength he did not know he possessed.

"It shouldn't work," he persisted. "Your botnet. No program can probe what is unseen in human hearts."

"It doesn't." With supreme effort, Alif wrenched his arm free. He leaned against the metal beam that framed the window, panting. "It doesn't have anything to do with the unseen. It works because it exposes the apparent. The words you use, how you use them, how you type them, when you send them. You can't hide those things behind a new name. The unseen is unseen. The apparent is inescapable."

The crowd surged, pressing the Hand against Alif and Alif against the window frame. Dina was invisible among the fists that beat the air. The physical contact sent a spasm of panic and disgust through Alif, so intense that he could feel his hands shake. Though sun poured through the window, he was assaulted by memories of the dark and the man who had put him there. Flailing, he closed his hand around a jagged tooth of glass sticking up out of the windowsill, relieved, in a way that frightened him, by the pain that sliced through his palm.

"Little worm." The Hand wrested one arm free and seized Alif by the throat. "Little worm, gnawing and gnawing until you pulled everything down. Who are you? Who *are* you?"

Struggling to breathe, Alif waved the shard of glass in a wild arc, slicing across the Hand's shoulder and neck. The man howled as a red line bloomed on his white robe. His left arm slackened, his hand releasing Alif's neck to dangle uselessly at his side. He tried to rally, pushing himself up to gesture clumsily at the eyeless things, closing the fingers of his good arm into a fist. Nothing happened. The creatures stared up at the Hand with their membranous faces, mild and interested and unmoved. They were practical rather than loyal, just as he had said.

The Hand stumbled backward into the crowd. The last thing Alif saw in his fading eyes was disappointment.

✳   ✳   ✳

From just out of reach, Dina was pushing toward him. She was heedless of her veil as it caught on someone's backpack and pulled away, revealing, for a precious instant, the lower half of her face. Her mouth, the mouth Alif had not kissed, was taut with fear. In another instant she had vanished, hidden behind the bodies of men who were shoving each other and shouting. The crowd heaved in panic as one of the men threw a punch that sent another reeling. Alif found himself shoved hard against the windowsill, his feet scrambling for purchase on the floor. He saw Dina's green eyes framed in black cloth, very close. Someone made a grab for his collar. It was too late: Alif tumbled over the window ledge. Reaching out, he touched nothing but air.

Chapter Seventeen

Dina's cry, terrified and low and too old for her, reminded him to panic. Alif wheeled his arms in wild circles, fending off the roar of the crowd as he hurtled toward it. In the split second left to him he found much to regret, and prayed the end would be quick.

He was rewarded with a sharp jolt. Talons closed around his ankles. Momentum reversed itself and he was jerked upward, carried aloft by incremental wing beats.

"Suicidal?" Sakina glared down at him, her face a hawkish blur of woman and animal.

Alif went limp with relief. Blood rushed to his head as he craned to look up at her.

"I don't know," he said. "Maybe."

Sakina careened around the building, gaining altitude. The air was full of half-visible figures. Alif recognized the black-horned woman who had given him the silver whistle, and the shadow whose computer he had fixed, and a hundred other faces too strange and fleeting for memory; many more than the little assembly the convert had gathered in the *marid's* courtyard.

"I thought you weren't coming," said Alif.

"We weren't," said Sakina. "But you didn't tell us you were under the protection of a *sila*. No one wants to risk offending one of those, no matter what the cost. When she told us to go, we went."

"I don't know any *sila*," said Alif, baffled.

"Well, one knows you. She calls herself Azalel."

Alif let his head hang back, unaccountably happy. Then he remembered.

"Dina," he said, struggling. "NewQuarter—"

"If you keep squirming, I'll drop you."

Alif made himself still. Sakina banked left, dropping like a stone from the colorless sky, and deposited Alif on the roof of a cigarette-and-newspaper stand at the edge of the square. His legs collapsed beneath him. He lay on his back against the corrugated metal roof, exhaling long breaths through his mouth. The thrum of the crowd was growing feverish; they were tiring, the black line of State police had thinned, and the moment of decision was near.

"Will you be all right?" Sakina hovered in front of him. Alif could see the demonstrators through her back, as though she were a curtain of gauze between him and the rest of the world.

"No," he said weakly. "Yes. You go. I'll manage."

"As you say." She lofted upward, veering toward the strange constellation of djinn streaming through the sky.

Alif slid off the roof, jumping several steps to catch his balance. Wading into the crowd, he was assailed by the tart smell of sweat. He closed his eyes, overwhelmed, swaying with the pressure of overheated bodies and the drum of feet on the cracked pavement. He had not believed, not truly. To choose a new name, to sit behind a screen and harry a few elites; the Hand was right, it had felt like a game, a fiction. Yet it had been enough.

"Up there! Look!" A teenaged girl to his right, sweating in a thick head scarf, pointed toward the white facade of NewQuarter's building across the square. There was a commotion in one of the windows on the top floor. Alif realized with a shock that it was the very window from which he had fallen. Agitated, he pushed his way through the crowd.

"Goddamn it, goddamn you, let me through!" He shouldered a large mustachioed man out of the way. The man turned on him with an indignant flare of his nostrils.

"You think we're out here for our health, boy? If you're not committed, you should have stayed home."

Alif opened and shut his mouth, at a loss as to how to respond. A few feet ahead of him, several women had begun screaming, whether from fear or elation he could not tell. Following their upturned faces, he saw a figure in a white robe bundled out the window by a score of hands. It spun in the air, dropped two stories, and halted with sickening finality as a noose snapped taut around its neck.

"It's a prince!" crowed a man with a thick gray mustache who stood nearby. "They're hanging princes! God is great!"

"No," breathed Alif. "No, no, no, please, no." He began to shiver in the sticky human heat. His triumph fled, replaced by an awful heaviness that seemed to siphon all the warmth from his limbs. In an instant, the demonstrators to his right and left had become howling savages stripped of any noble purpose. He could conceive of no freedom worth such an irrational sacrifice.

The mob began to cheer.

"What the hell is wrong with you?" cried Alif, shoving an exultant teenager who stepped on his foot. The boy gave him an astonished look.

"What's wrong with *you*, man? That's a prince up there! We're lining the bastards up one by one!"

"He was my friend, you shit pile! He was on your side, you stupid sisterfucker!" Alif shoved the boy again. The boy smashed his fist into Alif's cheek in an almost perfunctory way and slipped back into the crowd. Alif reeled, one hand pressed to his smarting jaw. A gap opened in the throng, revealing an empty patch of sidewalk: he stumbled toward it, collapsing on the filthy ground, racked with sobs that seemed to recruit every muscle in his body. The waning sun colored the square pink and the twilight wind, immune to revolution, carried the scent of tar and seawater over the crowd. Alif pulled it in by the lungful. Its salt tang made him imagine he was drowning. NewQuarter had been no more than a boy, yet they had strung him from his own window, these people for whom Alif had sacrificed so much. The thought of his friend meeting such a useless end, the undignified victim of his own ideals, was too much to bear.

Alif stared sightlessly at the flushed and roiling sky. It was the scene of another battle, as though Heaven thought to reflect the upheaval below: in wave after wave, the djinn of the Empty Quarter crashed against the inky horde spilling out of NewQuarter's window. The front line between the two armies looked like a struggle between dawn and evening, and shivered as Alif watched, at once too bright and too indistinct to stare at for longer than a few seconds. At certain points, the conflict appeared like nothing more than a ripple of dark cloud vying with the setting sun and Alif was seized with panic, convinced the past few days were the product of his own exhausted mind. In these moments he feared he was asleep and would presently wake up to the darkness of his cell.

Then his sight would bloom with the shapes of the hidden people, foggy and winged and goat-headed, serpentine and feline, spilling through the air like the birth of creation. They used no weapons that Alif could name, yet there were distinct signs of war: a combatant would flare up suddenly in a burst of smokeless fire and tumble out of the sky like a meteorite, reduced to nothing by the time it reached the ground. It seemed to Alif as though the hive of dark things was shrinking. Its outline became erratic, falling back toward NewQuarter's window and snaking down the wall of the building. Far below, the dark line of State police had broken at last and the insurgency spilled out of the square into the streets.

Alif's perimeter of sidewalk was quickly overrun. He did not move as the parade of feet raced past him. Women were ululating at top volume, as though for a wedding or a birth. Alif watched them, transported and yet unmoved. The sight of NewQuarter's corpse dangling from the window had killed his awe. Perhaps this was all freedom was—a moment in which all things were possible, overtaken too soon by man's fearsome instinct to punish and divide. State had fallen. What would replace it might be better or worse. The only certain thing was that it would be theirs.

"There he is! Thank God, thank God!"

Alif looked up reflexively at the familiar voice. Dark and wide-eyed, her robe smeared with grime, Dina was struggling toward him. Behind her, rumpled but alive, was NewQuarter, holding an empty bottle of Mecca Cola over his head with both hands.

"Look!" he cried jubilantly. "I pinched the *marid!*"

Alif struggled to his feet. Lurching forward, he flung his arms around the astonished prince.

"I thought you were dead," he blubbered. "Up there. When they said it was a prince—I thought it was you."

"Oh balls, *akhi*, you cry more than my sister. Stop it, stop it." NewQuarter struggled free, tucking the swirling bottle under one arm. "That's not me, you skinny moron, that's wretched Abbas. When I told them who he was, they thought I was much less interesting, and decided lynching him was a better use of their time."

Alif looked up at the hanged man with fresh eyes. He hadn't noticed the blood staining the left side of the white robe. The body swung a little in the evening breeze, already stiff. The remnants of the Hand's blind swarm scattered around him, scuttling down the side of the building without seeming to register his presence. Alif felt nothing. That the corpse was the Hand did not quell the horror he had felt when he believed otherwise. The Hand was right: there were demons that trooped silently in the bloodstream of man, and they were foul.

"So it's over," said Alif. His voice was dull and uncomprehending even in his own ears.

"Over my ass hairs. It's just begun. You're a hero, *akhi*, a hero twice over—once for getting arrested and becoming a national symbol, once for cleaning up the Hand's mess and restoring the City grid.

The people don't know that second part yet, of course, but once they do, you'll probably be elected president or something. President Alif. I'd vote for you. But wait—are we even having a democracy? I've got no idea what's going on."

"They'll probably nationalize all your money," Dina muttered.

"Good luck," said NewQuarter cheerfully. "I've already spent it." He bounced on the toes of his sandals, shaking the Mecca Cola bottle.

"Don't do that," fretted Dina. "You'll hurt him. You should just let him out."

"Fuck that, I want my three wishes."

Alif stopped listening. The incongruous sight of a bare head above a black robe had caught his eye: a woman had lost her veil and a group of armed boys had gathered around her, jeering and clutching. The spill of the woman's silky dark hair was familiar, as was the set of her shoulders and the jet beads woven into the hem and cuff of her dress. Alif sprinted toward her.

"Get back," he shouted at the boys. "Or get out your mother's religion, you sons of dogs!"

The tallest boy eyed the blood on Alif's shirt warily, then backed away. The others followed. Alif shouldered his way toward the woman, trembling in every limb. Intisar looked up at him with a blank, exhausted face, searching his eyes as though he had answers to questions she had not yet asked.

"What are you doing here?" questioned Alif. "Are you all right? Are you hurt? Or—" He glanced up at the gang of boys retreating toward the square. "God, something worse?"

She shook her head.

"I was looking for you," she said, her voice barely audible above the crowd. "I knew you would be here. They raided my father's villa. I'm supposed to go straight to my aunt's house, but——"

A knot of dancing women jostled them; Alif drew her away. Intisar looked up at the body dangling from NewQuarter's apartment block.

"Abbas," she said, without emotion.

Alif swallowed.

"Did you love him?"

Her eyes widened, incredulous, and the mouth he had so idolized dropped open.

"No," she said. "No, never. How could I? He was *old* and terrible —and I loved you."

"You *left* me."

She shook her head, pulling a lock of night-colored hair across her face in an unconscious imitation of the veil she had lost.

"I wanted you. But I didn't want Baqara District, and sneaking around, and not having nice things—I know what that makes you think of me, but I couldn't help it. I only know how to live one way." She tucked the lock of hair behind one ear. "It doesn't matter now. My family is ruined. What I was means nothing."

Her tone was full of meaning. Over the scent of sweat and the watery breeze, Alif could smell her perfume: a moneyed admixture of flower and wood. He remembered the way it had lingered on his pillow after she had slept in his bed.

"Mohammad."

He turned at the sound of his name. Dina was standing behind him on the sidewalk, her phosphorescent eyes flickering between his face and Intisar's. The bottle of Mecca Cola hung from her hand, uncapped and emptied of its stormy inmate, and in combination with the dirt on her robe it rendered her slightly ridiculous. Alif looked around for the *marid*, but saw nothing.

"I made Abu Talib—I mean NewQuarter—give him up," she said. "He's going back to the Empty Quarter with the others. He says you owe him for that copy of the *Alf Layla* you lost."

"I—"

"I'm going home now."

Even at a distance he could see the rapid rise and fall of her chest. He looked at her, looked at the ground, and looked at Intisar. Intisar's face had grown hostile. Beyond her, barely visible through the canyon of steel and glass, the Old Quarter wall caught the fading sun and blazed up.

"Mohammad," Dina repeated. At some point she had lost her gloves. Her red-brown hands were visible, the nails trimmed short, toying restlessly with the empty cola bottle and cap. Without the backdrop of the Empty Quarter, she looked like such an ordinary girl: a quiet, veiled, eternally irritated daughter of Baqara District. It was as if the events of the past several months had made no impression on her. Yet Alif could now recognize this as a defect of his own sight and knew that Dina, by some unfathomable mystery, was herself occult, and had waited in her silent way for him to reach the door of understanding that had always been open to her.

"Wait," he said. "I'm coming with you."

Intisar stared at him incredulously.

"Do you need money?" he asked her, feeling several years younger and twice as awkward. "Do you have a way to get to your aunt's place? You shouldn't stay out here, it isn't safe."

Intisar shrugged. She looked haughty, like an imperious child who had been denied a treat. Alif wondered how he had failed to notice her tendency to pout.

"Please don't worry about me," she said. "Go home."

Alif felt Dina's fingers brush tentatively along the heel of his wrist. He closed his hand around hers.

"Peace be upon you," he said to Intisar.

"And you." She turned away, slipping through the exultant mob toward the heart of the square. Alif looked at Dina and smiled. Her eyes crinkled above the seam of her veil.

"I wonder if it's possible to get a cab in this mess," he said, glancing around. The only vehicle he could see was the burned, overturned skeleton of a police van.

"I wouldn't count on it," said Dina. "Let's just walk."

"It's a long way to Baqara District on foot."

"That's all right. We have lots to talk about."

They made their way toward the nearest side street, weaving around a pack of boys lighting canisters of insect repellent on fire in celebration. Someone had unfurled a flag from the lowest story of an apartment building, and children had emerged to play at jumping up to touch the trailing edge. The atmosphere was manic, resembling, in a way that disappointed Alif, the chaos that followed a football match. Bits of paper had begun to fall from the air: fragments of the huge portrait of the emir that had once graced the northern face of the square. They filled Alif with dread that took him a moment to place.

"The book!" he said, stopping in his tracks. "My God, what happened to the book?"

Dina shook her head.

"I lost track of it when you fell out of the window," she said. "In that mess, I wouldn't be surprised if it was trampled into muck. Or maybe one of those awful things took it. Or one of the demonstrators who raided the building. Who knows."

Alif plucked a curl of paper from his hair, feeling guilty.

"Mohammad—what was in that last story?" Dina looked up at him with a searching expression. Alif took a long breath. They had gotten clear of the crowd and walked along a commercial street past a row of shuttered shops. Alif realized they were not far from the storefront where Dina had been shot, and where Vikram had saved them from the State security agent. Here he had begun to be transformed by the story of himself.

"Nothing we couldn't have written together," he said to Dina. Her eyes crinkled again. They were silent for a time. Night birds had begun to sing in the stunted, dusty trees, and the breeze from the harbor carried with it the sound of cheers and shouts and horns.

Acknowledgments

Corresponding as it did with the birth of my first child, the completion of this book would not have been possible without the help and support of the following people: my tireless agent, Warren Frazier; my digital assistant, Mohammed Abbas; cybermullah and blogfather Aziz Poonawalla; tech philosopher Saurav Mohapatra; my wonderful editors at Grove/Atlantic—Amy Hundley in New York and Ravi Mirchandani and Mathilda Imlah in London; and most of all my mother, who flew out for the delivery of the baby and stayed on for the delivery of the book. Lastly, thanks to all of my Twitter followers, who have provided me with everything from research references to scones and coffee. Bless you all.

Note on the Author

G. Willow Wilson was born in New Jersey in 1982. After graduating with a degree in History and coursework in Arabic language and literature, she moved to Cairo, where she became a contributor to the Egyptian opposition weekly *Cairo Magazine* until it closed in 2005. She has written for politics and culture blogs across the political spectrum, and has previously written a graphic novel, *Cairo*, illustrated by M. K. Perker, and a series of comics based on her own experiences, for DC Comics.